PRAISE FOR PATERNUS

Best Mythology/Folklore Book of 2016
Reality Bites Magazine

Best Debut Novel Finalist
Reddit Fantasy Best of 2016

Top 10 Debut Novels of 2016
Fantasy Book Critic

Finalist
Mark Lawrence's #SPFBO 2016

Amazon #1 Bestseller
U.S., U.K. & Canada

"Epic, innovative urban fantasy. A great read!"
–**Mark Lawrence**, Gemmell Award winner and international bestselling author of
Prince of Thorns and *Red Sister*.

"An imaginative, exhilarating ride – highly recommended."
–**Anthony Ryan**, New York Times bestselling author of *Blood Song* and *The Legion of Flame*.

"A crucible in which myths are melted and remade to thrilling effect."
–**M. R. (Mike) Carey**, author of *The Girl with All the Gifts* and the *Felix Castor* series.

"A really unique novel."
–**Anna Stephens**, author of *Godblind*.

"Intelligent, intricate, suspenseful, and epic."
–**Nicholas Eames**, author of *Kings of the Wyld*.

"Expansive, ambitious, and engrossing."
–**Josiah Bancroft**, author of *Senlin Ascends*.

"A mighty debut."
–**Jonathan French**, author of *The Grey Bastards*.

"Fast-paced, gloriously intricate"
–***Kirkus Reviews***.

. . .

THE PATERNUS TRILOGY
BOOK ONE

Paternus Books Media, DBA
P.O. Box 1027
Perrysburg, OH 43551
www.paternusbooks.com

Paternus: Rise of Gods / Dyrk Ashton. — 1st ed.
KDP HB3
ISBN: 978-0-9971737-8-9

Cover Illustration: John Anthony Di Giovanni
Front Cover Typography: STK-Kreations
PBM Logo: Brie Rapp
Author's Photograph: Lee Fearnside

"I seem to remember someone very close to me,
and wise, or so I thought, once telling me—"
"—anything is possible."

CONTENTS

Prologue   I

PART I

1. Kabir   5
2. Flowers & Figs   11
3. Obsidian   20
4. Mendip Hills   27
5. Order of The Bull   31
6. Flowers & Figs 2   36
7. Order of The Bull 2   42
8. Flowers & Figs 3   47
9. Order of The Bull 3   57
10. Flowers & Figs 4   67
11. Order of The Bull 4   75
12. Flowers & Figs 5   81
13. Order of The Bull 5   91
14. Flowers & Figs 6   99
15. Order of The Bull 6   119

PART II

16. Il Capro   123
17. Flower & Figs 7   125
18. Mendip Hills 2   131
19. Flowers & Figs 8   133
20. Mendip Hills 3   141
21. Flowers & Figs 9   145
22. Mendip Hills 4   153
23. Flowers & Figs 10   158
24. Mendip Hills 5   163

PART III

25. Flowers & Figs 11   171
26. Flowers & Figs 12   182
27. Flowers & Figs 13   210

28. Flowers & Figs 14   232

29. Flowers & Figs 15   244

30. Flowers & Figs 16   252

31. Flowers & Figs 17   265

32. Mendip Hills 6   281

33. Flowers & Figs 18   282

Epilogues   286

The Story Continues   289

1. Wake   291

Also by Dyrk Ashton   303

Acknowledgments   305

About the Author   307

What Is Paternus?   309

PATERNUS: RISE OF GODS

PROLOGUE

"Humankind has had its groundbreaking discoveries, mighty wars, great nations and saviors' births by which you mark your timelines of history. We Firstborn have also seen events that might seem resounding and important, and they were. Earthquakes that tore continents apart, volcanic eruptions and meteor strikes that shook the world and turned day into everlasting night. We have endured bitter glacial periods, mass extinctions and wars countable only by Father himself. Grand civilizations have risen, prospered for millennia then crumbled to dust. And yet, even the eldest among us gauge our lives in relation to four major occurrences: The Cataclysm, The First and Second Holocausts, as well as, of course, The Deluge.

"Now, if any of us survive, there will be this."

* * *

The stories told here all begin today, at the same time on the same day in late September. Odd as it may seem, the eastern-to-middle portion of the United States and the Amazon jungle of western Brazil are in the same time zone. England is five hours ahead, and the eastern Anatolia region of Turkey is seven hours ahead.

* * *

Parvulus: *n.* human [negative; derogatory]. *pl.* parvuli.
Mtoto: *n.* human [neutral; affectionate]. *pl.* watoto.

PART I

KABIR

F rom the roof of a sold out concert hall, tinted beams of searchlight wave at the full moon, a gray smudge in the murky Detroit sky. The heavy *thump* of bass can be felt for a quarter mile around.

Inside the auditorium, Kabir stands with his arms crossed near the roped-off hall that leads backstage. Six feet two inches tall with a thick mane of gray hair combed straight back and sideburns speckled black, Kabir is built like a linebacker in spite of his age, all shoulders, pecs, and biceps tucked into a finely tailored gray Armani suit, with a silk heliotrope tie.

Kabir is a bodyguard. It's what he does. Always has. They call him a legend in the business of rock and roll security, despite his best efforts to keep a low profile. In the thirty-six years he's been doing this, no one he's been assigned to has ever been touched.

Thirty-six years, already? A blink, really, but in practical terms, plenty long enough. He'll miss it when he moves on. The music, the noise, the crowds.

Over his shoulder, the half-naked teen pop diva under his care for the evening prances on stage in glitter and lights, belting out one of her latest chart-toppers. It's her last song of the main set and people with backstage passes are already lining up along the wall. The crowd roars as she builds to the song's climax, something about brushing your teeth with whiskey, threesomes, and other youthful naughtiness.

Kabir isn't listening to the words. He's busy doing what he does best. Being vigilant. Protecting. He surveys the mass of ecstatic fans with sharp copper eyes that seem to x-ray rather than simply see. Searching for signs of malice, seeking out bad intent, looking for trouble.

And here it comes.

"Hey, that's Stag Larsen," one of the bouncers from behind the rope near Kabir shouts above the pounding music.

Kabir's seen him already. How could he not? Six feet five inches in height, 290 pounds, wearing a two-sizes-too-small t-shirt tugged over his thick sculpted chest and a satin jacket thrown over one shoulder, Stag is Detroit's latest and greatest hope for a mixed martial arts heavyweight title. He high-fives fans, winks at girls despite the gorgeous swimsuit model draped on one arm, and grins back at his entourage. The crowd parts before him like a shoal of herring in the path of a shark.

"Did you see Stag fight Dinky Suarez last night?" Kabir hears the bouncer continue, speaking to another security guard next to him. "Stag's better, but Dinky got fucked on that call..."

Kabir's already moving. He smelled the other man before he saw him. Being able to pluck the stink of rage out of the air and pinpoint its source, even in a sweat-filled, beer-soaked, disinfectant layered auditorium full of people – well, for Kabir, it's a gift. Dinky Suarez, who lost to Stag in the cage just last night, is stalking through the crowd. All 340 pounds of him. Sweat glistens on his tattooed face and there's murder in his eyes. Dinky's an inch shorter than Stag but a big heavy bastard. A lot of it's fat, but he can dish out some serious punishment, and take it too. They say he hits like a wrecking ball.

This isn't Kabir's purview. He's personal security, not a bouncer, but innocent people, not to mention Kabir's fellow security personnel, could get hurt. He's acting on instinct. The instinct to shelter, shield, defend.

The singer finishes her song in high crescendo. Unaware of the impending brawl, she heads backstage, throwing kisses to an audience that screams for more.

Dinky reaches Stag well before Kabir does. "Hey Larsen, you faggot!" A couple members of Stag's entourage, two smaller and less established fighters themselves, happen to be in the way. Dinky takes them out with a single punch each. Each one falling topples three of the crowd. People scream and jump back, pressing the surrounding mob into a tightly packed ring. Stag shoves his jacket at his girlfriend, pushes her out of the way and starts bouncing on the balls of his feet, fists raised, a twisted smile on his craggy face.

"Punk-ass bitch," Dinky taunts, "no ref to save you now!"

"Bring it, pussy," Stag shouts, and Dinky brings it all right – long black hair, denim biker vest, skull tattoos on swinging fists, and wrath. They go at it hard, blow after blow sounding like baseball bats on sides of beef.

The crowd is thick in a circle around them, and Kabir won't just toss people out of the way. "Excuse me folks," he growls, "pardon me."

Three good-sized bouncers break through before Kabir. Two leap on Dinky, the third grabs Stag from behind.

Bad idea, guys, Kabir thinks. And he's right.

Dinky jerks away, throws a jab and a round house and the bouncers who jumped him are both out cold before they hit the floor. Stag ducks out of his man's grasp, lifts him by arm and groin and sends him flying into a couple of Dinky's biker buddies who've shown up at just the wrong time. They take down another half-dozen bystanders.

Kabir's going to have to hit these guys hard. Not so hard as to do permanent damage, but enough to get their attention. Show them they're not really at the top of the food chain. Not quite.

Stag and Dinky square off again but Kabir breaks through and pushes them apart.

Stag bellows, "Outta the way old man."

"Take it easy, fellas." Kabir doesn't shout, but his deep crunchy voice is easily heard over the racket of those in the crowd who haven't noticed the fight and are chanting for an encore. "We don't want anybody to get hurt."

"Stupid fucker." Dinky dips, rolls his shoulders and delivers a perfectly executed uppercut to Kabir's heavy square jaw, giving him all he's got. And what he's got is a lot.

Onlookers wince and groan as they see and hear the punch land.

Kabir doesn't budge.

Dinky's eyes go wide. His hand goes numb.

Kabir turns his copper eyes upon him and aims a quick jab at his ribs. Dinky's whole fatbody quivers. He drops to his knees like a slaughtered bull.

Stag grabs Kabir's shoulder. "Hey, fucker!"

Nice vocabulary these guys have. Kabir spins and open-hand slaps Stag right across the face.

The crowd gasps. Stag's ears ring. He sees stars. His legs noodle. He's never been hit so hard, so fast. He takes a sharp blow to the solar plexus and his breath rushes out. He goes to his knees. Kabir turns his attention back to Dinky.

"No no!" Dinky shouts, clutching his injured hand to his chest and holding up the other in an attempt to fend off Kabir. Kabir snatches his outstretched hand, twists, and Dinky flops to his back.

The onlookers can't believe what they're seeing. Kabir, crouched between the two men, holding them close in a huddle as if the three of them are best friends having an intimate conversation.

What they aren't close enough to discern is the agony in Stag's eyes, the veins popping beneath the 'roid rash on his forehead, the cords of muscle standing out from his neck, the back of which Kabir has in a grip so tight Stag doesn't dare move due to the icy pain and popping sounds of his vertebrae. The crowd can't smell the full weight of Stag's tangy cheesy B.O., or that Dinky reeks of a massive over-application of Axe cologne. They also can't see Dinky's hand turning purple, the tears in his eyes from Kabir wrenching his wrist to the brink of snapping, or hear Kabir's softly spoken question, "We done?"

What the crowd *can* see is both men frantically tapping out in surrender on Kabir's broad back. And very soon, thanks to a multitude of smartphones, so will a lot of other people.

* * *

Kabir marches Stag and Dinky into the outer lobby. They're surrounded by a boisterous mob snapping pictures and shooting video with their phones – and there are more in the lobby.

Who needs paparazzi these days?, Kabir groans to himself. He considers the aftermath of his actions appearing on social media everywhere. He can already visualize the tagline: "Stag Larsen Bitch-Slapped by Aging Bouncer." *What was I thinking?*

He hands Stag and Dinky over to a half dozen of Detroit's finest then ducks into a "No Access" hallway that leads backstage. The cops can talk to him later if they need to. He's got work to do. His earpiece chirps.

"Hey Kabir." It's Rosen, head of security.

"Yeah."

"Nice job out there. Impressive, as usual. Thanks."

Kabir doesn't respond.

"Anyway," Rosen continues, "the boys out back say some homeless guy made his way into the car port. They don't know how he got there. Could've been sleeping in the trash all day, I guess. Will you check it out?"

"Why not just bounce him?"

"Well, they say he asked for you by name."

Kabir scowls. *Must be some mistake.* "I'll be right there."

* * *

Kabir continues along the hall toward the back of the building. Through the walls he hears the cheering of the crowd and the music kick in as the encore begins.

Maybe it is time to do something else, he considers. It's been on his mind of late. He's known too well in this business, by too many people. *They'll begin to wonder, if they haven't already.*

Kabir pushes through the heavy double doors to the private section of the parking garage reserved for talent. In the car port near the exit to the alley, two personal security guards in suit and tie, and a driver, lean against a stretch limo.

The taller bodyguard, Hansen, sees him first. "Hey Kabir. Sorry, man. We were just gonna haul his ass out until he said he knew ya."

Kabir grunts in reply. Hansen's young and not real competent but nice enough.

"We asked him to wait in the alley," the shorter bodyguard, Spelling, adds. Kabir's worked with Spelling for years. He's an ass but good at his job. "Just a little bitty dude. Fucking weird, though. Creeps me out."

"Wearing like three coats," says Hansen.

"And sunglasses."

"Definitely has a thing for sunglasses."

"And smells like shit."

"Nasty."

"Real nasty."

Kabir rounds the limo and heads to the exit.

The limo driver watches him go. "Strong silent type, huh?"

"I think he invented it," says Spelling with a grin. "Did I tell ya the guy's a legend?"

Kabir squeezes past the gate arm into the alley and takes a deep breath of the cool wet air, inhaling the familiar scent of dirty water and diesel fuel. *Ah, Detroit.* He checks the sky, a flat gray haze dimly infused with the light of the city, and the position of the blurry blot of a moon. *Just after midnight.* Colored beams of searchlights slice the thick atmosphere. The vibratory beat of the music can still be heard from inside.

The alley where Kabir stands runs between buildings alongside the concert hall. Access to the main street is a block up to the right where a key card is required to open the ten feet high gate topped with razor wire. Not the kind of climb the homeless usually tackle. Like Rosen said, the bum could have been sleeping in the trash. Right now there's no sign of him. To Kabir's left the drive ends at an adjoining building and turns right into a blind alley. Kabir heads that way. This guy was probably a roady some time ago or an alcoholic door man, maybe a washed up junky musician. Or it could be Kabir doesn't know him at all. Anyway, he'll get this straightened out and get back to work in short order.

Kabir's mind wanders back to his previous line of thought. Maybe he *could* take some time off. He'll find another job eventually. Always does. Have to change his identity, give up his most recent name. The one he took in honor of his mother's side of the family. No big deal. It's not like he hasn't done it before. Maybe he'll go someplace remote and just relax. He used to travel for work. That got too risky, increasing the chance of running into people he once knew too soon. Unlike some of the others of his kind, he can only alter his appearance so much. But a chance to see the world again would be nice.

A genuine smile spreads across his ordinarily stony face. *That's what I'll do. See some old friends, visit family. Hell, I might even see if I can track down Father.*

He rounds the corner to the blind alley, lost in thought, then slows as he hears a male voice singing a nursery rhyme, high, soft and angelic:

"Oh, the Incy, Wincy Spider,
Climbed up the water spout.
Down came the rain,
And washed the spider out.
Out came the sun,
And dried up all the rain,
And the Incy Wincy Spider,
Climbed up the spout again."

A foul odor reaches Kabir. The voice becomes creaky and discordant.

"Here, *kitty kitty.*"

Kabir balks. His mind grapples with the vaguely familiar scent and voice. Ahead of him to the right are two dumpsters against the wall. Beyond them the alley is blocked by a chain-link fence topped with coiled razor wire like the gate out front. There are usually plenty of lights back here, high on the walls. All are now broken but one back in the main alley, striking inky shadows. There's no sign of anyone.

Kabir stalks forward cautiously, makes out the shape of a figure crouched in the darkness between the dumpsters. It stands slowly to no more than five and a half feet tall, but Kabir's skin prickles and the hair on the back of his neck and all down his back bristles straight.

This is the "homeless man" who knew Kabir's name – or at least what Hansen and Spelling *saw* as a homeless man. In that form it wouldn't be the least bit menacing. What Kabir sees is no vagrant, however, but the creature's true form, its Trueface. And it sees Kabir's.

Kabir reproaches himself harshly. How could he have let his guard down? His *guard.* It's been so very long. He's gotten soft.

"*Max...*" the name passes Kabir's lips as an exclamation of deepest loathing.

Max hunches low to the ground. "Hello, Zadkiel." He chortles. "My apologies. I mean, *Kabir.*"

Kabir has never fled from anything only to save himself. Now, faced with this little homeless man, he considers it for the first time in his very long life. But he knows, running will not save him. Not from Maskim Xul. And it's always better to go down fighting. Always.

It leaps.

* * *

In the garage by the limo, Hansen, Spelling and the driver are jolted by a roar so inhuman and ghastly they question whether they heard it at all. Spelling tries his radio, calling for Kabir. No response. Hansen and the limo driver stand frozen in place, but Spelling heads straight for the back of the car. "Open the trunk!"

It takes a moment for the command to register before the driver fumbles the keys out of his pocket and hits the button to pop the trunk.

Spelling snatches two shotguns from a case inside and shoves one in Hansen's hands. "Come on." He calls on the radio for Rosen to send police as he and Hansen approach the back of the alley, then pulls a small flashlight from his belt.

Hansen's having difficulty differentiating between the muffled pulse of the music from the concert and his own pounding heartbeat.

They round the corner with shotguns raised.

No sign of Kabir or struggle. Just scattered rubbish. They move carefully to the front of the dumpsters, shotguns at the ready. The space between them is clear. Spelling checks inside. Empty. He tries Kabir on the radio again and hears a tinny squeak at his feet. He nudges a moldy piece of newspaper with his shoe, uncovering a coiled, shiny object. He trains his light on it and crouches.

"Shit."

It's Kabir's earpiece. The squeaking sound they heard was Spelling's own voice. He pulls the paper away and sees something else. He hands the flashlight to Hansen, reaches into his breast pocket, retrieves a pair of latex gloves, the kind security employees carry in case they need to search someone.

"Is that a bone?" Hansen asks.

Spelling picks the thing up, hefts it, finding it surprisingly heavy. Six inches long, ivory white, serrated along one edge and tapered to a deadly point. He tips it up in the light. Bits of meat and tendrils of nerve hang from the wider end, dripping blood.

"Dude, I think it's a *tooth*."

2

FLOWERS & FIGS

Sixty miles south of Detroit, blue-silver moonlight bathes slate rooftops of aging Victorian and Edwardian homes in the Old West End, a neighborhood near downtown Toledo, Ohio. Neglected maples and oaks line streets of cracked asphalt like weary crooked sentinels, nudging up worn flagstone sidewalks with their roots – which doesn't help Fiona Megan Patterson because she's clumsy, and tonight she's mad as hell.

It's just after midnight and Fi is walking home. The walk of shame. Or at least it would be if she'd actually *had* sex tonight. Fi will be eighteen in a month and after countless nights of wistful yearning she thought tonight would be the night – her first time.

It started out well enough, an impromptu date after work with the quiet yet affable, disheveled but incredibly handsome Zeke Prisco, a guy who works at St. Augustine's Hospital where she has an internship. They had a pleasant dinner, then retired to his small but cozy (in a bohemian sort of way) attic apartment. A couple glasses of wine helped her relax. They made out on the couch, and when she thought the moment was right, buzzing with anticipation at the heat and tingling thrill of his closeness, she took off her shirt. Half naked and vulnerable, she leaned in for another kiss – but he pulled away and started mumbling about the time, that it was late and they both had to work tomorrow. She was too embarrassed to argue. She tugged her shirt back on (backwards, so she had to awkwardly spin it around). He offered to walk her home, insisted when she declined, but she insisted right back.

Possible explanations whirl through her mind. Maybe Zeke was even more nervous than she was. *But he's been with a zillion girls, has to have been. Why not me?* Maybe he was worried because he's older, 22, and she's legally underage. Maybe the bottle and a half of wine he put away all by himself rendered him incapable of doing the deed. It could be he just doesn't like her *that* way. *Or,* Fi groans inwardly, *I'm not pretty enough...*

She tucks her thumbs in the straps of her backpack and scowls at the sidewalk.

What am I so upset about, anyway?, she scolds herself. She and Zeke have only been out a couple of times, and it isn't like she's looking for a serious relationship. *Who has time for that?!*

Sure, Zeke's ridiculously good looking. And talented. When he plays the guitar, *everybody* melts. That's what he does at the hospital for extra money while he's in college, play for the old folks. He actually went to Julliard on a scholarship right out of high school, though he dropped out halfway through first year to take care of his foster mother when she was diagnosed with cancer (*he is definitely sweet*), and never went back after she passed away.

An uncanny feeling she's being watched suddenly creeps over her. She halts, glances behind her, scrutinizes shadows of trees and shrubs, between parked cars and homes on both sides of the street, listens to the sounds of distant traffic, leaves shuffling in the breeze, the yowl of cats brawling down the block. Then she looks up and catches sight of the brightest full moon she's ever seen. It stalks her from beyond the trees as she proceeds along the sidewalk, peeking around maple branches, sneaking behind curtains of red-brown oak leaves. *Like a bright white donut hole stuck splat in black pudding*, she muses in momentary distraction, *with a corona of powdered sugar*. The shadows it casts are jet black with edges crisp as the late September air and fallen leaves that crunch underfoot. She breathes in the clean leafy scent of autumn. It smells wonderful, but does nothing to improve her mood. She almost trips over the crappy sidewalk – again. *Dammit!*

So here she is, frustrated, bewildered, ashamed, more than a little pissed off, and now she has to go home and face her Uncle Edgar. He expected her shortly after 8 PM when she got off work, but she couldn't bring herself to call and let him know she'd be late and hear the disappointment in his voice, thinly veiled by his ever-present and infuriating stoicism, so she sent him a text. He didn't respond, but that's no surprise. She doesn't think he knows how to read a text, let alone send one, though she's shown him how at least a dozen times. She guesses he's somewhere in his sixties or seventies (he'll never tell), but it isn't his age that makes him technologically averse – it's his inability to accept change – his steadfast, quintessential Englishness.

Normally Edgar goes to bed at precisely 9 PM, but tonight he'll be waiting up, sitting in the living room (the "parlor," as he calls it), reading by candlelight like he always does, no matter how many times she's told him it'll ruin his eyes. And he'll be reading the Bible, in Latin or Greek, no less.

She approaches the dilapidated building that slouches at the back of her uncle's corner property. It was once a carriage house, back when the house was built in the early 1900s, then used as a garage. Now it's collapsed in the middle and leaning in on itself from both ends. It has a melancholic feel of abandonment, but that's precisely why it was one of her favorite places to hide away in, read, and indulge childhood fantasies when she was younger, having been more than a little melancholic herself much of the time after her mother died.

She's just past the building and angling off the sidewalk to the back yard when the sound of footsteps running up behind her causes her to whip around in alarm.

"Fi!"

She recognizes the voice, and in the light of the moon and a nearby streetlamp, the handsome features and slim figure of a young man dressed in jeans and button down shirt under a denim jacket. "Zeke?"

"Fi. Yeah, hey!" He doubles over, breathing hard and clutching at a stitch in his side. "What are you doing here?"

"Phew, I need to get more exercise," he gasps. "Ugh... and not drink so much wine." He swallows hard and his eyes go wide. Clapping a hand over his mouth, he points in an indication for her to wait, then bolts to the corner of the carriage house and pukes.

Fi looks on in disbelief. "Zeke, are you all right?"

"Oh yeah, no worries," he gulps, wiping his mouth on his sleeve. "Much better now. Sorry about that."

He combs his fingers through his hair – dark brown, wavy and full, long enough to flow down over his collar. Once. Twice. A habit that never fails to make Fi catch her breath. Even now, it's almost enough to make her forget he totally rejected her less than an hour ago and just barfed on her uncle's garage.

"I'm glad I caught you before you got home," he says, then nods over her shoulder. "Is that your house?"

Fi turns to view the narrow yard with its withering lilac bushes, untrimmed forsythia hedge along the sidewalk, and uneven stone walkway that leads from the carriage house to the back of the hulking three-story Edwardian home with flaking blue paint.

"Yeah," she answers. "My uncle's house."

"I guess I caught you just in time." He offers a small smile. "I thought I was going to have to knock on every door in the neighborhood."

Fi grimaces. This is awkward enough, but Zeke showing up at the door would have been worse. She hasn't told Edgar about him, and hadn't planned to anytime soon.

"Why are you here?" she asks.

Again with the fingers through the hair. "I just couldn't leave things the way we left it. The way *I* left it."

When Fi finds herself in tense situations, she goes into default mode – hide her true feelings, smooth things over. This definitely qualifies. "It's fine, Zeke, really."

"No, Fi, it's not." He takes a step closer – and freezes at the sound of a low menacing growl.

An enormous dog stalks from the shadows of the hedge, hackles up, head held low, teeth bared in a vicious snarl, eyes gleaming with predatory intent. Zeke's skin goes tight and clammy.

"Mol!" The dog halts. Fi has one hand on her hip while pointing at the beast with the other. "What are you doing out here?"

Warm relief floods over Zeke, but he remains very still. *"That's* your dog?"

"My uncle's dog," Fi corrects.

"You told me he was big, but, *Jesus...*"

"Some of the largest breeds can reach 250 pounds." Fi winces, feeling like she's just channeled her uncle. Edgar's always quick with a random fact – especially when you don't ask for it – drawn from his seemingly unlimited supply of eccentric knowledge. She finishes the statement as if in apology. "He's only two-ten."

"*Only...*" Zeke responds. He studies the dog. Thick and incredibly muscular, with longish golden-brown hair and a giant pit-bullish head. *"Maul.* That's appropriate. I'll bet he can do some 'mauling.'"

"It's M.o.l., not M.a.u.l."

"Oh, like *Molossus,* the ancient Greek war dogs? Cool!"

Mol tilts his massive head inquisitively.

Fi smirks. Of course Zeke knows that sort of thing. In addition to being good-looking, talented and sweet, he's smart, too. After his foster mother died he spent three months in South America doing volunteer work, just to get away and clear his head, then another three in Africa (so he's handsome, talented, sweet, smart, *and* a humanitarian). When he returned he went back to school and has almost completed a general studies degree with concentrations in history, literature and philosophy already. He'll graduate after Spring semester and has a chance at an assistantship for grad school at Harvard, of all places. He'd wanted to go for their Folklore and Mythology undergrad but he couldn't afford it, just like he never could have gone to Julliard without a scholarship, but now there's a competition he's been taking part in and the winner will have their tuition and fees paid for. As a finalist, he has to deliver a paper at a conference in Atlanta on Tuesday. Some kind of comparative analysis of Korean and Norse mythologies. He told her "the similarities are striking for such distant and disparate cultures, so I'm proposing they share certain mythemes that go back much further than anyone previously considered" – and at that point he quit explaining because Fi's eyes had glazed over. Whether it was because of the subject matter or that she was mesmerized by his pretty face, she wasn't sure. Probably both. His goal is a PhD in Philology, *whatever that is.* He'd be taking classes in classical archaeology, classical philosophy, and ancient history. And mythology, of course. Mythology is Zeke's *thing.* He and Edgar would probably get along great, Fi thinks, considering their shared interest in all things old and irrelevant. Another reason *not* to introduce them.

"The Molossus are extinct, though," Zeke continues, still watching Mol. "He looks kind of like a Great Pyrenees, but... some kind of Mastiff mix?"

"He's a mutt."

Now Mol tilts at *her.*

"Am I safe?" Zeke asks. "I mean, is he dangerous?"

Fi snorts, "Mol?" She pats her thigh. "Here Mol. Come on boy." The dog grunts and sits in the grass. Fi shrugs. "He isn't overly friendly, but he's a big baby." Mol groans and lies down with his head on his paws. "I think he's still mad at me for riding him around like a pony when I was little." Fi snaps her fingers and points at the house. "Mol, you get home, right now." He pays no attention, rolling his big brown eyes to gaze at Zeke instead. Fi huffs, "Like I said, he's my uncle's dog."

Keeping an eye out for any reaction from Mol, Zeke takes a tentative step toward Fi. Once fairly certain he isn't going to be eaten, he says, "Fi, I—"

"Zeke," she interrupts, "it's *okay.*" Of course it isn't, but she *really* doesn't like uncomfortable conversations of any kind. *Especially* heart-to-hearts. Or – gulp – breakups. Her mind races recklessly, as it often does. Even if she *did* want a relationship with Zeke – which she doesn't – she wouldn't know what to do in one anyway. She hasn't had the best of role models. Her father left her mom before Fi was born and her Uncle Edgar has never been married, and he certainly doesn't *date.* The only woman Fi's had in her life since her mother died is Mrs. Mirskaya, the brusque

Russian immigrant widow who babysat Fi for much of her youth, and whom Fi worked for at her Russian store through most of junior high and high school. Not the kind of person Fi can talk to about boys. Besides, relationship-equals-vulnerability-equals-heartbreak. Fi's had enough of that in her life, *thank you very much.*

But who am I kidding? I've got nothing to worry about. Zeke can have any girl he wants. Any *woman* he wants. He's brilliant, talented, focused, driven – everything Fi's damn sure she *isn't.* All they really have in common is they're both busy all the time, they're both "only children," having no brothers or sisters, and they both lost their parents when they were young. His died in a fire when he was a baby, Fi's mom in a plane crash when Fi was seven. That could be why they bonded in the first place. The shared tragedies, that they're both orphans. Well, at least she *thought* they'd bonded.

Zeke wishes Fi would listen, and look at him with those beautiful green eyes of hers. He watches her hand go anxiously to her lips. Full, wide lips, great for kissing, and smiling. A smile that beams sunshine. But she's far from smiling now, and he knows it's his fault. She presses her fingernails to her teeth as if she's going to bite them, but instead pushes a wayward strand of red hair that's escaped from her ponytail back over her ear. He loves it when she does that...

He takes a deep breath, gathering his resolve. "Look, Fi, I don't know why I shut down like that tonight. I wasn't thinking. Or maybe I was thinking too much. *Shit.* I like you Fi."

Great, he "likes" me, Fi groans to herself. *Here it comes, "we still have to work together, so let's be friends."* Fine with her, that's definitely for the best.

Zeke squirms. "I mean, I *really* like you."

Fi frowns. *Oh, that's much better. Just get it over with, will ya?*

He takes another deep breath. "I think I just didn't want to, you know, get too hot and heavy when I'm leaving Monday night for the conference. I'll be gone for a week. And honestly, I didn't say anything before because I'm not sure how you feel about me... other than for, you know..."

This just keeps getting better. Now he thinks I'm a slut.

Zeke hushes another pending protest from her with a gesture of his hand. "And, I'm a coward, all right? I admit it. But you've got this wall up – and I get it, I do. It's a self-preservation thing. Not letting anyone get too close."

You've got that right!

"I do it too, but I'm trying not to. I don't want to be that way anymore, be *that guy* anymore. We've both lost people we love and we don't want to get hurt like that ever again."

All the while he steps closer, his voice genuine, soft brown eyes sincere – but Fi's so incredibly nervous and worked up all she can think about is his breath's going to smell like vomit and, God help her, she's going to laugh, an uncontrollable, crazy person's laugh – *wait* – did he say *"love?"* Her insides turn oily and cold.

Zeke marshals on, "This is totally insane, what I'm about to say, but... Fi?"

She's begun to shake.

"Are you all right?"

Her eyes roll back in her head and she goes limp.

Zeke lunges and catches her gracelessly, jamming one knee painfully into the side-walk just before her head hits the ground. *"Fi!"*

She's quaking all over and unconscious – obviously having a seizure – but Zeke has absolutely no idea what to do. If she suffers from some sort of condition she never told him about it. Should he put a spoon in her mouth? *They don't do that anymore, moron.* And it's not like he just happens to have a spoon in his back pocket. Call nine-one-one. Run and get her uncle. Scream for help!

Then he feels hot steaming breath on the side of his face, accompanied by a deep rumble in his ear. The hair prickles on the back of his neck. *Mol.*

Zeke turns very slowly, tries to keep his voice calm and even. "Mol?... Good dog?"

The monster hound is only inches away, glaring at him, unblinking, *pensive* even. Gazing into those clear brown eyes, a bizarre thought pops into Zeke's head – *this is no ordinary dog.* Then he imagines powerful jaws snapping closed on his face, fangs stabbing his skin, crunching into his skull, and Mol shaking him like a rag doll until his neck snaps.

But the tension sags from Mol's big hairy face. He heaves a heavy dog's sigh, looks to Fi, and whimpers.

* * *

Fi has no sense of Zeke's trembling arms holding her tight, or the spasms that wrack her body. All is calm and darkness. And she dreams. A dream that she's an *old man dreaming...*

Soft light on open water, pulsing, alive. It flares brightly –

An infant floats on his back, sputtering, giggling, rocking on a broad ocean of reddish waves. Naked, chubby and pink, sky blue eyes beaming. His baby face, round tummy and little pee-pee bob on the surface while his pudgy hands splish-splash in the water.

The baby gurgles, spits, blinks at the full moon, impossibly close, looming in a break between storm clouds that throb with heat lightning, pink, purple and green. Soft sultry rainfall tickles his face. His eyes are stormy gray. He coos at fireworks blasted aloft by a nearby volcano, ahhs at the hiss and steam of flaming orange lava flowing into the sea. His eyes are golden brown.

Shooting stars whiz through the hazy atmosphere, red, blue, and yellow. One keeps coming, hurtling hot and fast. It strikes, sending a plume of vaporous sea-water shooting into the air. A torrent, a rushing wave, and the baby tumbles into the red depths. Then he's paddling upward, emerald green eyes wide open. He pops to the surface, burbles water, and shrieks with delight...

* * *

"Fi! Oh God. Fi, please."

Warmth and wetness on her cheeks, up her nose, in her ear, across her lips. Slimy wetness and dog breath. The vague memory of a dream, slipping away. Then it's gone.

Her eyes flutter open.

"Oh my God. Fi, are you okay?"

A fuzzy image of someone hovering over her, then Zeke snaps into sharp focus. *Night air. Moonlight. Mol.*

"Shit!" she cries. She shoves Mol and Zeke away and scrambles to her feet. "Oh no. No-no-no."

"Are you all right?"

She frantically wipes dog slobber with her sleeve. She already knows the answer and is mortified, but she has to ask, "Did I have a seizure?"

"Yes!" he shouts, then steadies himself for her sake. "Yes, you did."

Fi breathes deliberately, trying to alleviate the humiliation, stave off the panic. It doesn't work. "I have to go." She spins and hurries toward the house. Mol trots after her.

Zeke stands there, stunned. "Fi..."

She makes herself stop and face him. "I'm fine." He starts toward her, opens his mouth to speak, but she holds up a hand to cut him off. "Zeke. *Please.*"

Her voice is so desperate and pleading that Zeke stays where he is, stricken but resigned.

Fi can't bear to see him look at her that way. She knows it's little consolation but offers anyway, "I'll talk to you tomorrow," then turns away.

Her mind's a maelstrom, whirling at hurricane speed. On top of everything else, *a seizure?* She'd cry if she could, but she never cries. Not since her mother died.

This is not how Zeke imagined this evening going *at all* – but he knows Fi has to feel the same way. Even worse. He watches her approach the back of the house, her head hanging low, then sighs deeply and begins the lonely walk home.

Fi curses as she stumbles up the sinking crooked steps to the screened in lattice porch, then realizes – at least Edgar didn't come outside. This old house has thick walls, and Fi's convinced that her uncle is a little hard of hearing, even though he won't admit it. She can be thankful for that.

The screen door creaks at her pull and the impression she's being watched returns with a sudden tingling chill up her spine, so ominous it halts her in her tracks. She quickly surveys the back yard. Nothing there. The place where Zeke stood is empty, but he wouldn't make her feel this way. Humiliated, remorseful, yeah, but not scared. And Mol's right here. She has absolutely nothing to fear. Nothing *rational*.

You're crazy, that's all, she tells herself, only half joking. Her attention is drawn once again to the gleaming full moon. It gazes back at her like a blind but omniscient cosmic eye.

* * *

Upon entering the outdated but sizable kitchen, Mol heads further into the house and Fi recognizes the tantalizing aroma of Beef Bourguignon. Edgar prepared her favorite dinner. Having missed it adds further regret and guilt to the tumult of emotions she's experiencing already.

Behind what looks like a closet door next to the pantry is a narrow set of what once functioned as servant's stairs that lead up to the hall outside her bedroom on the second floor. She's used them to sneak in and out of the house before, but she can't bring herself to do it when she knows her uncle's waiting up.

She passes into the open stairwell, sees candlelight and the warm glow of the fireplace through the open double-wide living room doorway just down the hall. Good old Uncle Edgar, predictable as always. Last chance. She can head straight upstairs right now. Instead, she straightens herself, shoves a rebellious lock of hair back over her ear and enters the living room.

Edgar is on the couch, scratching Mol behind the ears, an open Bible in his lap. In Latin, this time.

"I'm home, Uncle," she announces meekly.

Edgar looks up as if just realizing she's there, his impassive narrow face framed by bushy gray sideburns that travel down to his deeply cleft chin. The firelight glints in his flint-colored eyes. "Miss Fiona," he greets her with his polite English accent. He presses a thumb and forefinger into his eyes, squeezes the curved bridge of his proud hooked nose with long calloused fingers, then tucks a stained silk ribbon he uses as a bookmark into the crease of the Bible.

"Sorry Uncle. I..."

He stands, tightening the sash of his wool tartan robe (his "sleep coat"), which half-conceals striped pajama pants. "Are you well?" he asks, as if she hasn't spoken.

She won't tell him about her night with Zeke, *absolutely not*. And as for the seizure – that can wait. "I'm fine, thanks."

He pauses only a moment before responding. "Excellent." He steps to the hearth and closes the folding glass doors. Edgar would probably be about five feet ten inches tall, but his shoulders are hunched and he walks with a stoop, which makes him appear shorter. His hair is mostly silver, streaked with black, pulled back and knotted in a tight braid that goes to the middle of his back. Fi asked him once why he had long hair. He said it was the "in thing" when he was coming into his prime, which she took to be the 1960s or 70s, when the style was more fashionable.

Fi's eyes lift to her uncle's heirlooms mounted above the fireplace, thick with dust. An antique medieval shield with a smeared red cross, the color degraded to rust, over a background of cracked white paint. Hanging down behind it is a long two-handed greatsword in a tarnished steel sheath. He says they've been in his family for centuries. They remind her of him. Old, outdated, inflexible.

He retrieves a brass candle holder from the arm of the sofa, pinches out the flame of another perched on a stand. "Good night, then," he says, and shuffles around her in his worn fur-lined moccasins, keeping a personal space of at least three feet between them like he always does. He stops at the doorway. "There's a bit of beef in the cooler, if you're feeling peckish."

"Thank you," she calls over her shoulder. *Cooler.*

Mol gives her a lingering look then follows her uncle. Standing alone in the flickering firelight, Fi listens to them ascend the creaking staircase.

He never hugs her, her Uncle Edgar. In fact, he never touches her at all, not since he insisted she take over the task of raking the tangles from her own wildly unmanageable red hair when she turned thirteen. Luckily the curls have relaxed as she's grown and her hair now has only a slight wave.

She shrugs her backpack, hugs it to her chest, and stares into the fire.

* * *

Moonlight beams through paisley lace curtains, projecting dappled patterns across the otherwise unlit room. Tucked tight in her antique brass bed, Fi dreams that she's an old man dreaming. A soft pulsing light and a baby boy, floating on an ocean of reddish waves.

Remember this time, she commands herself with that part of her mind that's still her own, *remember...*

* * *

In a tiny room, sterile white, a withered old man gasps awake on a hard twin bed, wide-eyed and bewildered. A simple thought sparks in the darkness, struggles for space amongst the brambles and fog that infest his addled brain, forcing a tiny gap in which to breathe. *I don't dream!* He clutches at thin sheets and stiff foam pillow. The thought trips over itself, *I don't dream*, stumbles, *I don't...* and falls, *I...* The old man's sky blue eyes swirl to golden brown, then stormy gray, and emerald green, then fade, becoming dull, colorless, vapid. Brambles close in and the smothering fog of dementia billows, once again pervading every corner of his mind.

3

OBSIDIAN

The cavern pool is dark and still, the only movement the flickering reflection of amber torchlight and feathery mist that crawls on its surface. With barely a ripple, Ao Guang's bald head and long angular face rise until his nose is just above the water. Breath escapes in a slow huff, dissipating the mist, and he sniffs the humid air. His lime-green eyes scan a domed chamber of glassy purple obsidian. Wide chiseled steps lead up and out of the pool. In the middle of the straw-strewn floor above squats a roughly hewn altar of stone. Torches jut from the walls, held by crude sconces of pounded gold. Ao cuts through the water and trudges up the steps, a lumbering giant, long-limbed and intimidating.

Baphomet emerges next. Short white hair and goatee, noble features, light complexion, with eyes of the faintest pink. He comports himself proudly to the floor of the chamber.

Dimmi follows, dark of skin, eyes and hair, sputtering as he stalks up to Baphomet's side. All three wear the same military-style khaki shirts, pants and boots, drenched and dripping.

"No need for cloaking here, I'd imagine," says Baphomet in Olde English. Ao Guang clacks his crooked angling teeth together once, loud and unnerving.

The men's images shudder like reflections in a shaken mirror – and become no longer the images of men.

Dimmi has peaked furry ears, black marble eyes beneath a jutting brow of golden fuzz, spotted black, and a mouth like a smiling gash. He shakes vigorously, spraying water from his coarse coat of hair the color of sand, with jagged black stripes. Baphomet glares at him.

"Sorry," Dimmi apologizes in a language known to linguists today as Akkadian. "I've never liked the water, ever, never ever."

Of course not, it might make you clean, Baphomet remarks to himself, folding his arms to his chest. Tall horns climb from his forehead, sweeping in a backward curve to end in dagger-sharp points. White fur covers his goat-shaped head and his waist down to his cloven hooves, but he refuses to shake himself, preferring to drip dry in a civilized manner.

"Anything?" he asks. Dimmi bounces softly on his stubby legs, digging at one ear with a black claw. *Can't he ever be still?*, Baphomet wonders.

But then he is. Dimmi closes his eyes, his ears twitching. He snuffs deeply with his wet black nose. "Something. But..." He shakes his head. "I do still hope it's female, business *and* pleasure, fun fun fun!" He chitters and yips at the possibility.

"Ssshhh," Baphomet cautions.

Dimmi forces a yawn in an effort to stifle himself, his face becoming a ring of jagged fangs around a fat pink tongue. He boasts he can fit an entire parvulus's head in that mouth, and has been known to rip the face from the skull with a single twisting bite – one of his favorite tricks – especially when he manages to remove all the flesh in one piece, leaving the eyes intact so he can see his victim's shock before the pain takes hold.

Baphomet turns his attention to Ao Guang, "Ao?"

He's just feigning regard, Ao Guang is convinced. *He doesn't care what I think.* He straightens to his full eight feet of height. Torchlight slithers across smooth gray scales that cover his chest and stomach like armor plates. His algae-colored back is even more heavily armored, ridged to the tip of his tapered tail which still hangs in the water. His head is crocodilian but his snout exceptionally long and thin. He cracks his mouth, droplets of water forming at the ends of needle-sharp teeth that edge the length of his jaws, and snaps it shut with a *clack*.

It frustrates Ao Guang deeply that their master retains Baphomet as his most trusted adviser and made him the leader of this little sortie. Ao is five times his age – and the years make him strong, even more than his size and the species of his gharial mother. Baphomet may be an accomplished leader with a compelling personality second only to the Master, but Ao Guang is not without legend or glory.

Few Firstborn who have lived in the age of the parvuli have not become legend. Their histories are rich and very long, and their names virtually countless. The history of human civilization is far lengthier than any parvulus knows today, having begun well before the Second Magnificent Holocaust, even before the First. High societies and literate, artistic cultures have come and gone, risen from primitivity, been knocked back into stone ages or wiped from the face of the earth by natural disaster and war, then built and again destroyed. But the memories remain, handed down generation to generation. And before the humans, there were Firstborn. There have always been Firstborn. Almost always. There has always been Father.

Most of the Firstborn are now dead and forgotten. Even the knowledge of those still living endures only in myths and hushed fables told to frighten troublesome parvulus children. For the most part, today's humans not only don't realize Firstborn exist, they don't believe they ever have. Except for a precious few, the most primitive and faithful among them, they've completely forsaken the gods and monsters of their forefathers. Ao grins as much as the structure of his gharial mouth will allow. *That's all about to change.*

He snaps his jaws again, the interlocking teeth clearly visible even with his mouth closed, and takes a deep rumbling breath, concentrating on the task at hand. Clear nictitating membranes open downward over vertical black pupils. He eyes the altar then peers at the openings of two crevices, one in either corner at the back of the chamber.

"Looks like the right kind of hole for a Firstborn." He speaks in pre-Sino-Tibetan, from before the last Ice. His voice is deep and grating, the sound of shoveling gravel. The lips at the bulbous end of his snout move like a human's might, but spiky teeth protrude every which way, forcing him to enunciate deliberately.

"I've stayed in a few like this myself," Baphomet replies. He's smaller in stature than Ao Guang, less than six feet tall, but his horns rise as high as the top of Ao's massive head. They call him The Goat, though his mother was more like a mountain Ibex. Still, his knees bend backward like his mother's did, and the pink irises of his eyes are cut across by horizontal pupils. Unlike his bovid mother, however, he has humanlike teeth with sharp incisors – gifts from Father, like his roughly humanoid physique – and a taste for flesh.

Baphomet is fully aware that Ao Guang resents him, considers him a shameless seeker of status and attention, but he couldn't care less. Besides, it's true. He's always garnered worship from Firstborn and parvuli alike. He likes the company. He's had to operate in the shadows since the Second Holocaust, careful to avoid the prying eyes of Father and his loyal Deva, but he's been manipulating humankind through dark cults and secret societies for millennia. At one time he had hundreds of thousands of followers all over the world. There are still quite a few. Some hold positions in the highest echelons of government and industry.

Recently, he and the Master combined their significant resources to seek out and assemble the remaining Asura, the Firstborn who opposed Father in the First and Second Holocausts, as well as locate their enemies, the Deva, Father's Firstborn warriors.

It hasn't been an easy task. The Asura lost both great wars, and those who survived have been hiding or sleeping for much of the last two myria. Until only a few years ago the mighty Ao Guang, once worshipped as the Dragon King of the Eastern Sea by clans who later became the Chinese, was lolling in the mangrove eco-regions of West Africa where the natives whisper warnings of a terrible beast they call Ninki Nanka. Dimmi had been less reticent. Maintaining his human cloak, he'd been hiring himself out as a mercenary to whomever would pay the most in diamonds, gold and flesh. He was prowling Sub-Saharan Africa, taking advantage of the strife there to fuel his fiendish proclivities for torture and rape, when the Master and Baphomet approached him.

Now after centuries of preparation, they've recruited enough of the surviving Asura and learned the whereabouts of a sufficient number of Deva to proceed with the master's plan.

At the last minute, their networks submitted a report of a mysterious swamp beast in one of the most inaccessible regions of South America. The Master's scheme was already in motion, but he doesn't like loose ends. Three days ago Baphomet, Ao Guang and Dimmi were air-dropped by helicopter into the muddy Brazilian Amazon River, just over the border from Peru. They are tasked with finding out if the rumors of the creature are true, and if so, if it is Firstborn. They are to recruit it to the Master's cause if possible. If not, they'll just have to kill it.

It rained the first two days they slogged through sucking mire and clinging jungle in search of the unidentified swamp beast. Eventually they followed a tiny tributary because Dimmi smelled smoke, and came across a tribe of native parvuli, naked and brown, who'd been entirely undaunted by the sight of the strange adventurers, even when they revealed themselves in Trueface.

The natives proved remarkably stolid. One by one they were questioned while the others forced to watch. Ao Guang hung them upside down over a fire pit, reveling in their screams, the odor of burning hair and roasting flesh. Other than the wails of agony of the tortured, none of them uttered a word. Only the last surviving among them, a female child, finally spoke of a powerful bruja, a witch who appeared out of the jungle to heal them when they were sick. But only after Dimmi painstakingly chewed off her soft grubby hands and gnawed one of her arms up to the elbow did she confess her people made offerings near a hidden lake located to the north. Dimmi had taken this as good news, particularly liking the idea their quarry was female. The Goat himself was encouraged, though it gave him pause. There have never been many female Firstborn, and they are strong.

The moans of the dying girl followed them into the undergrowth, her last words prophesying agonizing deaths for what they had done to her people. Ao Guang has spoken little since. In silence he dove through the reflection of the full moon into the black water of the lake and discovered the flooded tunnel that brought them here.

Baphomet studies the cave. *This place is old*, he thinks, the cavern cleft from fissures in dark purple volcanic glass, born in a rhyolitic eruption when this earth was young. The temple within it is not so very old, however, he considers as he eyes the torches and altar. He has been in this area of the world before, most recently along the coast of what is now Peru, "vacationing" with the Master amongst the Moche culture, sharing with them the joys of hematophagy. The glyphs carved in the edges of the altar are from a society older than the Moche, pre-Olmec even, but are still of parvulus origin and hold no power over him. They represent utterances of protection and healing. *Pathetic*. They'll protect no one today. There are three of them, and they have The Gharial. Ao Guang may not be a True Ancient, but he is one of the oldest surviving Firstborn, reared in the age immediately following the Cataclysm on what is now the land mass of East Asia – though when he was young, tectonic drift had not yet brought that part of the world to precisely where it lies today.

Dimmi sniffs the air.

"What is it?" Baphomet asks.

Dimmi moves cautiously to peer into the darkness of the crevice to the right, but something else catches his attention. He yips and jabs a clawed finger at the area behind the altar.

Dimmi's Truename, the name bestowed upon him by Father at birth, is Idimmu Mulla, words the Sumerians later incorporated into their language to mean "demon" and "devil." His mother had been one of what parvulus paleontologists have dubbed *Pachycrocuta brevirostris*, an extinct species of hyaena. Heavyset creatures that weighed over 400 pounds. He has many of his mother's physical traits, but the shape of his head is more humanoid, more so than either Baphomet's or Ao Guang's, which makes him even more terrifying to parvuli for some reason. His sloped shoulders are positioned low on his body, supporting a long thick neck, and his hands almost touch the ground. He's as tall as Baphomet (sans the horns), and rippling muscle bulges beneath his furry hide. He's far younger than Ao Guang and less than half the age of Baphomet, but Baphomet has seen him defeat older Firstborn and would not relish coming to blows with him – though he'd never let Dimmi know that.

Baphomet runs his hand along the slab atop the altar as he edges around it. Each of his five fingers ends in its own small cloven hoof, shiny and black. On the floor behind the altar he sees a familiar sight, a five pointed star, rendered with a smudge stick of burnt ash. He isn't old enough to have invented it, but he knows the sign of the pentagram all too well. He prefers his pentagrams inverted, however, and this one is not. He was the first to turn it on its head, though it was against his wishes one of his abecedarians, Stanislas de Guaita, incorporated the face and horns of The Goat within the symbol when Baphomet revived one of his ancient cults as The Cabalistic Order of the Rosicrucian in France.

The pentagram isn't all there is to the figure on the floor. It's drawn within an octogram, an even older symbol, and both are placed on a tightly wound spiral of lighter ash, laid down before the octogram and pentagram were etched over it.

Baphomet raises a hand to his chin and strokes his tuft of beard in contemplation. The other hand he holds loosely in front of him, rhythmically clicking the little hooves together. *Click, click, click.*

That's not a good sign, Dimmi worries to himself, wringing his hands. *He only does that when he's anxious about something, or confused. And Baphomet is very rarely anxious or confused.*

Ao Guang concentrates on the two crevices that lead from the chamber, trying to ignore Baphomet's annoying clicks and Dimmi's incessant fidgeting.

Baphomet crouches and runs the twin hooves of a pinky finger through the charcoal lines at the edge of the octogram. On the far side of the symbol is a ring of river rock around a burnt-out fire, near it a heavy copper kettle of no special construction or origin and a number of chalices of various composition, including one of ruby glass. Around the upper curve of the symbol various articles are arranged. A tortoise shell, a mortar and pestle of basalt, a weaved cingulum coiled up, a pile of twigs from an almond sapling. Leaning against the wall is a besom (a witch's broom), and a stang – it's not unusual such a staff would have two prongs at the top made of antler, such as this one has, but these come from an animal that's been extinct for at least six epochs.

Baphomet turns his attention to crude palm-leaf shelves erected along the back of the altar's base. Each is lined with blown glass bottles of herbs and attars, many of which he recognizes by sight or smell. Balm of Gilead, Hyssop, Linden Flower, Tamarisk, Yerba, and Yew. There are many others he can identify, and more that he cannot.

Hanging on leather cords from spurs of rock at the back edge of the slab are three talisman pendants. Baphomet fingers the first, made of precious green Jadeite, then the second, black Serendibite, and the last... Baphomet lifts it gingerly by its cord, careful not to touch the pendant itself, which is metallic but bright red, the color of fresh blood. The first two are made of some of the scarcest stones in all the worlds. The only rarer are found infrequently in the fragments of meteorites, the only source he can imagine the material of this third pendant coming from.

He replaces it and rises, crossing his arms. These are all standard wares of parvulus witches, wiccans, warlocks, shaman, sorcerers and wizards alike, all who claim to have special powers. Charlatans, for the most part. Nevertheless, they are from all over the world, and some are very, very old. The name of The Madman comes to mind, but Baphomet knows exactly where he is, buried in England, and another team of Asura are on their way to him this very day. Baphomet has also noticed that some customary objects used by human magi are missing. No wing bone of an eagle, foreleg of wild boar, human foot or tail of cow, and not one eye of newt. What perplexes him more, however, is a single rune inscribed into each of the three pendants, all of them different, and he does not recognize the symbols. They look something like the Enochian glyphs conjured up by two of his lesser pupils, the 16th century whelps Billy Dee and Edward Kelley, but these are different. Simpler, in a way. Primal. Beautiful, really.

Baphomet strokes his goat-beard pensively, commences once more to clicking the finger-hooves of his other hand.

Dimmi resists the urge to flee. Baphomet's behavior is very peculiar and it has him rattled. *I am not a coward*, he tells himself. *I just have a strong inclination for survival.* A yip and chitter rise in his throat, but he swallows them down. He knows Baphomet trusts him, or at least trusts him to fear their master enough to do his bidding. *I cannot fail!* There's also the Master's psychotic sidekick to consider. Dimmi shudders at the thought of Max, resumes bouncing softly where he stands and scratches the backs of his hands nervously. Next to the predilections of Max, Truename Maskim Xul, Dimmi's own diabolic tendencies pale.

Dimmi begins to laugh, a harsh giggle-shriek/cackle-bark. He does it when he's nervous, a habit he acquired from his mother he's never been able to break. He sees Ao Guang glaring at him with his slitty green eyes. *Stop it.* Dimmi rebukes himself. *You're better than this!* But he can't help it, and he's getting louder.

Baphomet is about to reprimand him, as well as suggest they do *not* split up to search the cavern, when they hear a faint scraping from deep within the crevice nearest Dimmi.

Dimmi leaps back to the top of the steps at the edge of the pool and crouches on all fours. Baphomet backs around the altar to stand next to him. Ao Guang looms over them both. All three peer intently into the darkness.

The scraping continues, and deep in the fissure they see light. A dim, purplish glow. Slowly, the light moves closer, spreading from the depths, and they realize it's the obsidian walls themselves that emit the soft luminescence.

Baphomet squints and thinks he can make out a hand – thin, dark, clawed – sliding along the wall of the tunnel, at the leading edge of the advancing radiance. Then they hear something else. A low murmur interspersed with clicks and grunts.

"What is it?" Ao whispers above Baphomet's ear.

Baphomet does not take his eyes off the light.

All Firstborn have an innate sense of language due to the common Phrygian grammar inherited genetically from their father, but Baphomet has also devoted a significant portion of his life to the study of languages. A wielder of words is a wielder of power. And the older the words, and the older the being plying them, the more power they have. Whatever is proceeding up the tunnel is chanting in a tongue he does not know.

"I believe," he answers Ao Guang, "*it...* is time to leave."

Light blazes from the crevice and the entire cavern emits a blinding flash like violet lightning.

* * *

When his eyes recover, purple spots dancing in his vision, Baphomet can make out the dark form of a creature squatting on top of the altar, silhouetted by the glowing wall behind it. Vertical pupils in eyes of burnished gold gleam in judgment over them. The beast lets out a whisper of a *hisssss*, and there's the fragrance of lilacs, eucalyptus, frankincense resin and musk.

Ao Guang doesn't so much kneel as buckle to his weakening knees. With a sputtering *plop* and *squish*, Dimmi loses control of his bowels and bladder. His whimpers sound for all the world like a sobbing parvulus child.

The landscape irises of Baphomet's eyes grow wide as he recognizes the creature before them, one who hasn't been seen or heard from since the bloody Second Holocaust, which ended almost twenty thousand years ago.

"*Ama Kashshaptu...*" he whispers in Sumerian. *Mother Witch.*

4

MENDIP HILLS

The White Watcher watches.

It's one of those nights with a flawless sky of the deepest black, the stars tiny pin-pricks of light, the full moon a pure white circle hole-punched in the ceiling of the world.

Circling high above what the watoto call Somerset County, in the South West of England, The White Watcher sees for miles in every direction, and his sight is good, perhaps the best in all this world for distance, in both the light of day and dark of night.

The land below is a map in relief, darkened shades of green, brown and blue, blotted with sparkling lakes, and woods of ash and maple, still garbed in their autumn leaves. Scribed with dead-straight canals, a few back roads and fewer freeways, rambling rivers and streams, intersecting dry-stone walls that divide pasture from field and dry land from bog. The White Watcher can make out the flat void of the Bristol Channel to the west. To the south he can't quite see to the sea.

Directly beneath him the moors of the Somerset Levels shimmer through bristling black grass and a silken layer of mist. Just to the north, the dales of the Mendip Hills cup silvery fog, luminescent from the light of the moon. Beyond the hills the Avon Valley is a basin of cottony gray.

Ireland, Scotland, Shetland, Wales, England, the Isle of Man, the Bailiwicks of Jersey and Guernsey, all are The White Watcher's domain, his self-appointed ward. Every night he flies over these isles, making his rounds. He does not interfere, just watches. Alone. Unseen.

It was once the craggy peaks of Carrauntoohil, the tallest mountain in Ireland, that The White Watcher called home. Then the watoto began climbing it for sport in greater and greater numbers, so he relocated to Ben Nevis in Scotland, the highest peak in all the British Isles. More mountaineers came, and then the flying machines. He now spends the daylight hours in a cave along the northern coast of Ireland only accessible by diving past stony cliffs into the cold ocean waters, down to the hidden entrance well below the surface. The same cave he was dragged into when the Deluge drowned the world.

Something peculiar catches The White Watcher's eye. Placing his arms against his body, he dives for a closer look, careful not to pass before the moon. He extends his wings to level out, keeping below the ridgeline and downwind, and alights on a wooded hilltop. Peering through the branches of an aged maple tree, he spies it, moving east along a path in the rolling forest half a mile away, keeping to the shadows. A dark shape of the kind he hasn't seen in a very long time. Something not human. Something big.

* * *

Bödvar Bjarki trudges through the undergrowth, parallel to the dirt trail, picking his way over rocks and rotting tree trunks, ducking beneath branches, steering clear of the sharp light of the moon. An oversized canvas rucksack on a sturdy frame is slung on his back. From inside comes the muffled sound of sloshing water and a high gurgling voice humming a happy tune. He reaches over his hairy shoulder and raps on the top of the sack, which makes the sound of knocking on wood. "Shhhh!" he admonishes. The humming stops.

To one side of the rucksack, slipped through a loop, is what looks like a ridiculously large replica of a sword, the blade alone six feet long and twelve inches wide – but this is no replica. Forged by Arges himself, it has had many names, but the one that stuck and by which it is still known today in Russian fables, is Kladenets. Bödvar has hidden and retrieved it many times over the millennia, never lost it to Father's Deva searchers when they were sent out to gather the great weapons. It is good to sense its weight on his back. He feels like a knight errant once again, a bogatyr of old.

In his right hand he carries a hammer, equally ridiculous in size. The handle is a smooth hickory fence post, the head a rectangular block of steel, two feet long with a short conical spike on each end. It was crafted by no master metalsmith. There's nothing special about it. Except it weighs nearly 1,000 pounds. Bödvar hardly notices.

Bödvar Bjarki, The Bear, is over ten feet tall, built like a man who's built like a bear, with arms longer and legs shorter than a natural man's would be. A pink tongue the size of a hand towel extends from a thick-lipped mouth that runs the width of his big round head, laps over his sharp bear's teeth and fangs, and licks the flaring nostrils of his broad pug nose.

Bödvar has been told these paths are seldom traveled at night, but if any parvuli do come along, donning his human cloak will do him no good in this day and age. He's just too big.

There was a time, not long ago in the greater scheme of things, when the sight of an enormous human warrior inspired awe and respect. Especially an ugly one. Not today, Baphomet, the Master's second in command, has warned him, so he has to sneak to circumvent campsites and commercial quarries and avoid rural roads. He growls to himself, *Who ever thought The Bear would be sneaking?!* He could cloak as his mother's kind, but he's pretty sure the sight of a ten foot bear in today's England, especially one of a species long extinct, would raise just as much of a ruckus. His only other choice is to press against a cliff and cloak as shadow, or curl up and appear as a rock or fallen hunk of tree. *Hiding from parvuli is even worse than sneaking.*

He isn't built for stealth, obviously, but his hearing and sense of smell are keen and his vision well suited to darkness. He has observed no one so far, but even though Baphomet made it clear he is to avoid confrontation with the parvuli if at all possible, he kind of hopes he will. He could use a snack. He isn't much better at following orders than he is at sneaking. Never has been.

Do what you're told on this job, he reprimands himself. *Show them you can follow instructions, for once.*

He suppresses the urge to uproot a tree that stands in his way. Suddenly he's in a foul mood. Then again, he's *always* in a foul mood, and pretty much always has been. Violent, angry and mean, a tortured and terrible beast, he has driven away anyone who has ever been close to him. Unless he got them killed first, or murdered them himself. He blames his father, who is most certainly bipolar (Bödvar learned that term recently through this new science called the "internet"), prone to periods of exuberant glee but also fits of manic, violent behavior, as well as the deepest of depressions. If there's such a thing as "tri-polar," Father is it.

Most Firstborn have found some way to relax, some contented perspective with which to endure the millennia as they passed. Not Bödvar. *But today is a good day,* he affirms to himself, taking a deep breath. *Today I have something to do.*

He was relaxing in the boreal forests of Siberia when the Master and Baphomet found him just three months ago, having recently awakened from what would be considered a very long nap by human standards. They were quite enthusiastic about what the parvuli had achieved in the fields of science and technology while he slept, and proceeded to tell Bödvar all about it. He yawned the entire time.

"Who do you want me to kill, and when?", was all he said when they were done prattling on. They told him. He accepted. Gladly.

In the days before Bödvar boarded the ship to England, Baphomet tortured him with more tedious gibberish. Apparently, the United States (*who?*) had "satellites" with "hyperspectral imaging" capabilities that they tasked to find underground bunkers where their enemies could be hiding. The Master and Baphomet had "pulled some strings" (*these satellites have strings, apparently*) utilizing their contacts in the "military-industrial complex," and believed they had succeeded where all others had failed. They'd found the cave, here in the Mendip Hills, where Myrddin Wyllt, The Madman, had been imprisoned by his lover over 1,500 years ago. Baphomet explained in excruciating detail how they could probably arrange for a "bunker buster missile" strike, but he had convinced the Master that it would draw unwanted attention, they weren't sure it would work on a Firstborn, and they'd have no proof The Madman was dead even if it did. An Asura Firstborn team would be much cleaner and more effective. In and out, no fuss, no muss, and they'd have confirmation of the kill.

Bödvar knows about the disappearance of The Madman, of course, and that no one had been able to find him after his imprisonment. Some of the rest of what Baphomet said makes sense now, too. Bödvar spent most of the time waiting for his mission watching "television" and "surfing the net," absorbing what he felt was important (and wishing he could forget the rest). He can even hold his own with the modern English now. Firstborn learn fast. Much has changed in this world, he has to admit, over an astonishingly short amount of time. One thing hasn't, he's glad to see. There are still wars.

The rucksack hums again, lilting and reedy, oddly amplified by the vessel in which Bödvar's "partner" on this mission is contained. He can't place the tune, but whatever it is, it's extremely annoying.

"Hush," he shouts. It doesn't stop. He raises his hand to rap the top of the pack again but decides against it. He'll have to let it out soon. He'd rather it not be too angry with him.

He turns his attention to the bright glowing screen of a device that looks tiny in his enormous paw. Baphomet gave him this little box of "electronics," which he called a "GPS," and insisted that Bödvar use it to find the cave. It's pretty simple, really. Green dot pinpoints where he's located on the digital map, red dot marks where he wants to go. The two dots are right on top of each other.

He's here.

He eyes two large ash trees that stand against the face of a bare limestone cliff, then checks his surroundings. Fairly secluded. More trees provide cover, and he can't see the path a hundred yards back down the hill. That won't help when he starts pounding on rock, though. The sound may be heard for a mile. Once he begins, he'll need to keep his hearing and sense of smell keen to approaching parvuli.

But right now there's another problem. The night is retreating, pursued by the faintest hint of daylight to the east. The sun will soon be revealed in all its glory by the unstoppable spin of the earth. Birds are already chirping.

Fucking birds.

Bödvar growls and chucks his hammer to the dirt. Here he stands, right where he needs to be, and he's forced to find someplace to hide and while away the day, then return when night comes again to complete his task. That was a most adamant command of Baphomet. "Do not open the cave in the light of day, under any circumstances." All part of the Master's "master" plan, Bödvar figures. Or maybe it's for the benefit of his partner in the rucksack. From what he's heard, it's not a fan of daylight.

Well, there's nothing for it, he's going to do what he's told. He groans, picks up his hammer and stomps off to find someplace to wait out the sun. The rucksack sloshes and hums as he shoves through the brush.

"Hush!"

5

ORDER OF THE BULL

How does she move her tongue so fast?, ponders the little round fellow in the long fur coat. No matter how many times he hears the trilling wail of zaghruta singing, Tanuki is always amazed. The scantily clad performer of the oryantal dansi approaches the fruit stand where Tanuki clutches half a dozen small crates of dates, undulating her body in seemingly impossible ways beneath her bedleh costume of shining gold and turquoise.

An ensemble of musicians huddle against the stone cliff in an empty space between vendors, fervently playing reed flute, drum, fiddle and lute. The shapely mtoto female circles Tanuki, whose ample cheeks could be seen to blush if he didn't have a dense, close-cropped beard of the same peppered tan as his fur coat and the Russian ushanka-style hat he wears with the ear flaps up.

The dancer's braceleted arms move serpentine above her shoulders. She lightly brushes the fur of his hat and his beard with her fingers then backs away, her pelvis gyrating so quickly the belt of sewn coins at her waist is a blur. She smiles at him, lets loose another shrill zaghruta wail. Between her staccato hip movements and vibrating tongue, Tanuki is captivated.

"Master Tanuki?"

Tanuki snaps out of his musing as a distinguished looking, elderly mtoto woman approaches. "May I take that for you?" she asks in modern Turkish. She is the High Abbottess of their sect, the Order of The Bull, in charge of day-to-day management of the monastery, as well as an Apis High Priestess.

"Yes. Thank you," Tanuki replies in the same language. He hands her the wooden boxes of dates, nodding with regard.

The Abbottess passes them to a young man, a Cellarer Novice, who looks up at a wagon mounded high with goods, calculating how to make them fit most efficiently for the long trek home.

Tanuki's cohort of monks consists of six men and six women, all dressed alike in tagiyah prayer caps, white shirts with billowed sleeves beneath cepkens (a type of Turkish vest), drab baggy pants, and a sash. Each carries a wooden staff with a woven strap attached.

Tanuki and this group from the monastery camped nearby last evening, then rose well before daybreak and arrived at the bazaar early this morning when many of the merchants were still setting up their booths along the rock walls on both sides of the narrow canyon. They've been haggling and packing since. Space is running short. The two wagons they brought with them, each pulled by four small but sturdy Anadolu horses, and the six mules and another dozen individual Anadolu are all laden with wares from the day's procurement. Each man and woman of the group wears a canvas backpack, all loaded with goods as well. This is the last autumn bazaar in this remote area of Anatolia, in the north-east of Turkey, and they are stocking up for the long winter in the Kaçkar Mountains where their monastery is located.

They have many hours of travel ahead of them. Tanuki squints at the sun. *Just after 7 AM, time to go if we're going to make it back by nightfall.* He digs into his purse and drops a generous helping of Turkish liras into the porcelain bowl on the ground near the musicians, at which they marvel.

He smiles at the Abbottess, who nods their readiness. Two young monks hurry to Tanuki, toting a hefty backpack between them. They strain to lift its weight to his shoulders, but he slips his arms through the straps, receiving it with ease. He bows lightly to the young men, placing his palms together in the Buddhist añjali-kamma gesture. The caravan makes its way through the crowd.

This is a rural market, very unlike the lavish Grand Bazaar of Istanbul. There are no soccer shirts, cowboy boots, or bootleg movies here. They pass tables of oils, spices, nuts, dried beans and durum wheat. Neat piles of fruit and carts mounded with vegetables. They have purchased plenty of all of these but nothing from the many stands of meat and fish, not even the Turkish staples of sardines and anchovies. All of them in the Order are vegetarian by choice – though Tanuki has snuck some etli yaprak sarma today, vine leaves stuffed with flavored meat and rice, while the rest were otherwise engaged.

They pass vendors dishing out spicy sucuk sausage and kebabs. To drink, there's tea, Turkish coffee, thick and sweet, and cacik, a thin yoghurt beverage with minced cucumber. Others ply a staggering variety of cheeses, soups, breads and sweet pastries. Tanuki has sampled much of it, far more than he needs, but the savory aromas still taunt him. He expresses a visible sigh of relief when they are past the food stands to the dry goods. Booth after booth of traditional clothing of bright and colorful design, vibrant vases, finger bowls and plates of every imaginable hue, some decorated with intricate Iznik floral designs, others with luxuriant painted grapevines. Tanuki browses past tiers of embroidered kapalicarsi, handmade Turkish shoes. He always wanted a pair, though they'd never fit his fat furry feet. He considered commissioning a custom made pair but was convinced by his Brothers his toe claws would probably shred them in short order.

Then there are the sellers of the world famous Turkish carpets and rugs. Tanuki brushes his hands lightly across them, feeling the differences in texture and weave. The cheerful merchant doesn't mind the fingering of his merchandise. Tanuki acquired the finest and most expensive rug at the bazaar from him earlier this morning, a gift for Big Brother Arges.

They hear the music before they reach the gathering crowd. Besides offering the prospect to buy and sell goods, this bazaar also provides the locals with an opportunity to celebrate the fall harvest. Tanuki grins. *And the Turks never shirk their celebrational duties.*

In an open circle where the canyon widens, six men in black caps with vests over white shirts and pants tucked into high black boots are lined up, hands on shoulders, moving deliberately and dramatically to the accompaniment of traditional folk music. The crowd around the circle claps in time as the dancers swing their legs, sway, and stomp in unison.

Tanuki applauds with delight. He'd dearly love to join the dance or snatch up one of the musician's shepherd's pipes, fifes or baglamas and play along with them. He could easily catch up with the monks if he were to send them on ahead, but it wouldn't be good etiquette. He nods to the Abbottess and they continue on their way.

Abruptly, it seems, they're passing out of the east mouth of the canyon into the clear autumn air, the stony rolling countryside laid out before them, the sounds and smells of the bazaar fading away behind.

Tanuki drops back to confirm with the Cellarer Novice that all the dates have been packed securely. He has taken pains to purchase plenty of dates today, his Brothers back home will be happy to see, and would be mightily sore at him if he hadn't. Asterion The Bull and Arges The Rhinoceros do love their dates.

* * *

The cavalcade of monks travel east over the undulating, rocky terrain, the mountains to their left and the Çoruh River valley to their right, the only sounds the muffled clopping of the animal's hooves and the soft conversation of the monks. Humps of spiny thorn cushion and milk-vetch spread sporadically as far as the eye can see, the multiplicity of tints of summer having given way to the gray and brown of coming winter, soon to be covered in white. The formerly colorful Asteraceae now reduced to swaying thistles, and all that's left of the glorious flowering mulleins are bare stalks rising from rosettes of velvety leaves lying flat on the ground.

Eventually they angle north toward the mountains. Not far to the south and east are the trickling waters that form the beginnings of both the Euphrates and Tigris rivers. Some call the Euphrates-Tigris Basin the "cradle of civilization," others claim the Nile River Valley deserves that designation, still others the Yellow River Valley of China or Mexico's Yucatan Peninsula. *They are all deserving, and not*, Tanuki muses. These areas were all home to early "advances" in mtoto culture, but there are plenty of other places in this world where civilizations have waxed and waned. Not all of them were mtoto, or particularly "civilized."

In ages past lions and tigers roamed these steppes, but they're long gone. Tanuki still hopes to catch a glimpse of a rare Anatolia Leopard, though. He fondly recalls venturing out with Arges in bygone days, surreptitiously destroying pitfall traps the Romans set to capture leopards for gladiatorial spectacles. On one occasion they spied a half dozen Roman centurions approaching so Arges hid in one of the pits. When the centurions peered in to see what they'd caught, he sprang out with a mighty roar. Three of them shit themselves, one fainted. Tanuki has never seen watoto run so fast.

Chuckling to himself, Tanuki sees he's outpaced the group. There's a pond near the path, so he calls back to ask if they'd like to rest. The monks are extremely fit, but they don't protest and are happy to tend to the horses and mules.

Tanuki removes his backpack and wades into the clear shallows of the pond to enjoy the refreshing coolness on his bare feet. He looks down into the mirror surface of the water. To his own eyes, the mtoto cloak he wears outside the monastery is gone.

Thanks to the unique physicality of their father, all Firstborn have the ability to alter their form to some extent. A combination of an actual reorganization of matter and a psychological projection, in varying degrees. Tanuki usually doesn't bother with a physical change because he isn't enormous, very oddly shaped, or four-legged, and he doesn't have pesky horns or antlers to get in the way. For Tanuki, simply impressing upon the acuity of watoto is enough.

Mtoto perception is very practical and became more so as they evolved, governed by their sensory-motor schema of stimulus-response, action-reaction and habitual recognition – essentially, the need to immediately make sense of what their senses bring to them and determine its use value or whether it is friend or foe. This also, however, limits them. They have a very hard time seeing what they don't understand or have never seen before.

Since the watoto are naturally inclined not to perceive Firstborn as they truly are, with very little effort Tanuki can "project" a familiar appearance, much like a human can project an air of confidence, strength, or sexuality. Without saying a word, even watoto can appear to be confident, strong, or sexual to those around them, even if they are timid, weak, and terrible in bed. Thus, in the presence of watoto, Tanuki can simply consider himself a jolly bearded fellow in fur coat and hat, and *voilà*, that's how the watoto perceive him. It doesn't work on animals, or some small children, but the grown-ups don't pay much attention to them anyway.

Since Firstborn are fully aware of their own existence, they can usually see through the cloak of others with ease. Whether they wear real clothing, the illusion of clothing, or none at all, it matters not. Some are better at cloaking than others and can take all manner of forms, particularly the elders. Most, like Tanuki, always retain characteristics of their Trueface, just morphed to human understanding. Like all of them, however, Tanuki can easily appear as the species of his mother, as a lump of earth or stone if he lies still, even a shadow in dim light.

It is kind of sad that the watoto are so easily duped, but this simplistic perception of theirs is also the primary reason they've survived as a species. There are advantages to going though life with blinders on. If at any time throughout their existence they had full comprehension of how truly vulnerable they were, any real inkling of the odds against their survival, they may have just lain down to die. Thanks to their unlikely combination of qualities, however, being at once brilliant and ignorant, adaptable yet naïve, and most of all tenacious, they've now reached the highest rung of the evolutionary ladder. Well, almost.

Tanuki contemplates his reflection. He's little more than 5' 8" tall but more or less humanoid in shape. A bit on the chunky side, though he likes to tell Arges that it's because of the fur. His arms and legs are as hairy as the rest of him, with short black claws on his stubby little fingers and toes. He has a wet black dog's nose, deep brown eyes and sharp little canine teeth top and bottom, with fuzzy peaked ears high on his head. There are dark circles around his eyes, but they aren't from fatigue. Tanuki may be young for a Firstborn, but all have endurance and constitutions far beyond that of any mtoto. He could carry his pack at the pace they've been keeping today for weeks on end, without food, drink or repose. He wouldn't like it, but he could do it. No, he isn't tired. He has circles around his eyes because he's Tanuki. *The* Tanuki, in fact. The only one left. It's just the color of the hair there. He gets it from his mother, a natural Tanuki, *Nyctereutes procyonoides viverrinus*, a canine species native to Japan that survives to this day. They're also called "raccoon dogs" because of their surprising resemblance to the nimble-handed creatures, right down to their short pointy snouts, bushy tails, and black bandit masks.

Tanuki has all those traits, including the bushy tail, though he can't see it in his reflection because it's behind his butt where tails are supposed to be. He can see his big fuzzy balls, though. It's difficult not to, considering the angle of the water below and the fact that they *are* pretty big. But they're covered with short dense hair, the same color as the rest of his fur, so he doesn't consider them obscene or even all that obvious.

He's stirred from contemplation of his fuzzy nutsack by a high whistle, the sound of the Abbottess signaling the monks to prepare to move on. Tanuki ascends from the pond and stoops to his backpack. In a blink he's cast in shadow and out of the corner of his eye he sees a dark patch flit across the sun's reflection on the water. He jerks his head up and scans the sky, but there is nothing there. He looks back at the monks, who are busying themselves with a final tightening of straps on the wagons. There's no indication they've noticed anything out of the ordinary.

Just a wisp of cloud, or maybe a bird, he rationalizes. *But there are no clouds, and it would've had to be a damn big bird. Must have been a jet. A very fast, high-flying jet.*

Gullible as ever, he scolds himself. Still, he has a hard time shaking the inexplicable chill that's come over him.

6

FLOWERS & FIGS 2

Fiona Megan Patterson wakes. *I'm supposed to remember something,* is her first sleepy thought. *Aren't I? A dream, maybe?* She knows she dreams, but she doesn't remember many. That's very common. She's read about it.

Fi stretches under the covers, groans and looks out her bedroom window. The bright morning sunlight has turned the paisley design of her lace curtains into a soft white frieze.

The memory of last night floods back. Not only did she *not* finally have sex, she was totally humiliated as well. *And* had a seizure. Right in front of Zeke! She moans, mortified, pressing her forearm over her eyes. It's not just the humiliation or the "relationship" problems, either. She hasn't had an episode in ages. What if they're back, for good? She decides to keep it to herself for now. Meanwhile, she'll just have to live with the nagging fear that it could happen again, any place, any time. She remembers that feeling. It *sucks*.

She squirms, watching patterns of light and shadow from the window play across her colorful star-patterned quilt. Mrs. Mirskaya, her old babysitter and one-time employer, made it for her using patches of fabric and intricate needlework to craft Russian folk designs of swirling fairy tale birds, minarets and gray thrushes, colorful onion domed bird houses, matryoshka dolls, and pomegranates with blooms.

Her eyes roam over her little bedroom. It's one of the smallest rooms in this enormous house, but Uncle Edgar let her pick any room she wanted when she moved in. She chose this one because it's intimate and cozy. She loves its worn wood floor, the uneven horse-hair plaster and lathe walls and ceiling, and the window of wavy dimpled green glass set in an original wood frame with weights on cords that rumble in the walls when you open it. There's just the one window, but it's always been her portal to imagining what life might be like in the wide world outside Toledo. The collection of travel posters and cheap paintings tacked to the walls attest to her wandering spirit. London, Paris, Venice, Berlin, Prague, Norway, Greece, Egypt, India,

Africa, and many more. Edgar has been to every one of these places. Fi's been to none of them, but she's promised herself she will. Some day. There's also a poster of Albert Einstein sticking his tongue out, which she just thinks is funny, and a graphic chart of human anatomy, a sign of her chosen area of study. *Lame*, she thinks. *It's all lame.* She manages a self-deprecating smile. *Just like me.*

Her eye catches the only two pictures she has of her mother, standing in frames on her dresser opposite the foot of the bed. In one of the photos a smiling woman with shining red hair sits holding a silver flute, a publicity photo for the symphony. In the other, five year old Fi leans her head on her mom's shoulder in the park, both of them grinning. Fi has no pictures of her father. She never knew him. He left before she was born and they've had no contact, not a single letter or even a card on birthdays. She used to fantasize he had a good reason for leaving, that he lived a secret life doing something really important, but now he's just dead to her. As far as she knows he might really be dead, but she's learned the less she thinks about him the better.

When Fi was seven her mother was killed in a plane crash on the way back from a concert in Vancouver. Fi was staying with Old Lady Muskrat. That's what she calls Mrs. Mirskaya when she's not around, much to her uncle's chagrin, (but she does have a mustache and buck teeth). When the police and an airline representative showed up at the door with the news, Uncle Edgar was right behind them.

From what Fi understands, her mother met Edgar shortly after Fi was born. He had recently moved to Toledo from London, but some months before then he'd received a letter from Fi's father, whom he claimed was his cousin, telling him about the new love of his life and their unborn child in America. Apparently Edgar had seemed quite saddened to hear that Fi's father had abandoned them.

Fi's mother had no living relatives, so the day after her death Edgar took Fi to Children's Services to begin the custody process. The courts wanted proof they were related. DNA tests confirmed they were, and not too distantly. He also had paperwork that linked him to her father's family. The courts were satisfied, she was given into his care and he took her into his home. This home. That was ten years ago. Edgar could have left the country, Fi reminds herself, just not shown up for her, or downright denied custody. But he didn't.

She's very fond of her uncle, though he frustrates her at times, embarrasses her at others. Still, sometimes she feels bad that she doesn't spend more time with him. Sometimes she feels like she doesn't know him at all. He doesn't talk about himself or his past. She doesn't even know his favorite color. When he is in a talkative mood he just goes on about ancient history, the foibles of science and "jolly old England." She feels bad when she gives him a hard time, too. It has to have been difficult for him. He never had any children of his own, then suddenly took it upon himself to take care of a sad little girl he hardly knew.

She was worse than just sad, though. After her mother's death she turned into a brat. Hyperactive, bored at school, depressed, unable to concentrate. So she took it out on Edgar, and Mol. She acted out, talked back, threw snit fits. Not violent or vicious, she was just such a grouchy little *turd*.

She never had many friends, not close ones, anyway. The mean kids in grade school called her an orphan. Technically that's true, but she told them they were stupid, that orphans have no family and she lived with her uncle. They'd laugh and call him "Uncle

Hippie Mutton-chops." When she played soccer (not very well) he'd pick her up from practice in his old beat-up Bentley. They'd call out, in bad English accents, "Oh Fee-oh-nah, it's your but-lah, come to fetch you home!"

Her "episodes" didn't help, either. It only happened once at school, in third grade, but that was enough. Most kids just stayed away. Others teased. She'd wet herself that time, too. It didn't always happen, but often enough. For many of her old classmates she'll always be remembered as "pee-pee Fi."

Thank God it didn't happen last night with Zeke! Which reminds her, she's going to have to talk to him today. Definitely *not* looking forward to that.

She got terrible grades in middle school, detentions. Never dyed her hair pink, pierced her nose or got tattoos. But she thought about it. Her experimentation with cigarettes, pot and alcohol didn't last long. Except for the occasional glass of wine she never liked it, no matter how cool it was. She just isn't cool. That's all there is to it.

She finally got her shit together a few years ago. Mostly a matter of focusing her OCD tendencies on school and staving off the ADD. She's never been officially diagnosed, but she swears she's both. She's always dived into things intensely, whatever caught her fancy, whether it be fantasy books, drawing and painting, playing the flute or jigsaw puzzles, and would stay up all night for weeks on end, completely devoting herself to her flighty focus. Then she'd suddenly lose interest and something else would take its place. She can do schoolwork regularly now, she just considers it a job, never misses a class and way over-studies. She aced all her classes sophomore and junior year and actually got to graduate early. She's always wondered, though, if the school just wanted to be rid of her.

Now she's enrolled in pre-med in college. Straight A's, so far. Edgar encouraged her to study whatever she wanted, said that he'd manage to scrape up the money and cover the rest with loans. But that's the problem. She just doesn't know *what* she wants to do. *What do you want to be when you grow up, Fi? Huh? Grow up?* Hell, most of the time she doesn't know what she wants at all, period. She thought about international business for awhile, then journalism, so she could travel, but settled on health care. For now. It *is* the *practical* thing to do. And honorable, her uncle says.

For all the trouble she's caused him, Edgar has never grounded her or punished her in any way. He has never even given her a talking to about responsibility, mutual respect or common courtesy. In one of her more maudlin moments in her younger years, when feeling guilty about having a tantrum over not being allowed to have chocolate cake (in spite of the fact that they didn't *have* any chocolate cake and she already had ice cream for dessert), she asked her uncle why he put up with her. He looked genuinely taken aback and said, "Why, this is what family does, dear." Then he made her a chocolate cake.

As crazy as Edgar makes her sometimes, he's the only father she's ever known, and she truly believes he's done the best he can. She'll be grateful to him forever. She just has to learn how to show it.

Fi hears a soft *tick tick* and muffled *hiss* coming from the old radiator in the corner of the room. Edgar must have turned on the heat last night. Not because it's all that chilly yet but to test the boiler before the real cold comes. He does the same thing about this time every year. Her uncle is nothing if not a creature of habit – *Oh shit.*

Speaking of habit, every Sunday morning since she first came to live with him,

Edgar brings her breakfast in bed before going to church. At 8:00 AM, on the dot. And it's Sunday morning. Over the years she's tried everything she could think of to dissuade him from it, but it's become a tradition, and her uncle is *all about* tradition.

She checks the clock. 7:59 AM. She needs to get some clothes on, *right now*. She tosses the covers back and hears Edgar coming up the stairs, whistling "Swing Low, Sweet Chariot," his favorite song. Maybe the only song he knows. Well, that, "Amazing Grace," and "The Battle Hymn of the Republic."

He'll knock, he always does. She leaps to her dresser, grabs a pair of boy short underwear from the overflowing, half-open drawer and tugs them on. She catches her own bright green eyes in the dresser mirror. "Irish eyes," Edgar calls them. Her hair is somewhere between light auburn and soft copper in color and tumbles down over her pale shoulders. Even when in a ponytail or bun there are strands that escape across her brow and cut down the edge of her left eye, threatening to obscure her vision, so she pushes them back over her ear often, as she does now. She's been asked a dozen times if she dyes her hair that particular shade, but it's entirely natural. She gets it from her mom.

At 5' 4" tall, Fi considers herself medium height. There have always been shorter girls in her classes and some much taller. "I don't know what they're feeding people these days," Edgar has commented. "It's a known fact that human beings have been consistently increasing in height as a species for a very long time—but today! You would have been considered an Amazon in my time, dear. I was thought to have quite an impressive stature in my younger days, now I am average height at best. My father was considered a veritable giant among men, and he was just six feet tall."

There's a firm rap on the door and Edgar's voice comes from the other side. "Miss Fiona? Breakfast!"

"One second!" She flings clothes from a pile on the floor until she finds a tank top that doesn't look too dirty and pulls it on. She runs to the closet, throws a jacket off the door hook and snatches her bathrobe from underneath, slips into it and jumps back in bed.

"Come in," she shouts, dragging the quilt over her legs.

Edgar opens the door and peers in to make sure it's safe. Fi fears he's never gotten over the time when she was 14 and feeling ornery and hid in nothing but underpants and bra to jump out in front of him as he headed up the hall to the bathroom. "Flabber-gasted" is a good word to describe his reaction. He ran away faster than she's ever seen him move. He never mentioned it afterward, but since then he's been cautious when coming anywhere near this part of the house.

Assured that all is clear, he enters, wearing the only suit he owns, maybe has ever owned, a three piece navy blue pinstripe with a golden silk necktie, and carrying a silver tray with a plate under a dome cover. "Good morning, Miss Fi. Happy Sunday to you."

"Good morning, Uncle Edgar." Mol trots in and throws himself down with a loud *thu-whump*, hard enough to shake the room. "Good morning, *Mol*." The big dog grunts, rolling onto his back and wriggling to scratch himself.

"And what are we busying ourselves with this morning?" Edgar asks, eyeing the unfolded clothes on the bed, open dresser drawers, laundry on the floor, desk strewn with papers and open books. "Ah, tidying up, I see."

"Funny, ha ha."

"It's your sanctuary dear, do with it what you will." From the look on his face, however, the condition of her room is not what he'd prefer.

He steps up bedside, pulls a folding stand from under his arm and sets it up. On it he places the tray, which also contains a glass of orange juice, a steaming cup of coffee, a bowl of cut fruit and buttered English muffins – real ones, not the spongy American knock-offs – with a dollop of orange marmalade on the side. He lifts the lid and steam rolls out. "*Voilà!* Eggs Hussarde with heirloom tomatoes" (of course he says 'toe-mah-toes,' like a good Englishman should). "I even made that foul black substance you like to drink," he adds. "What is the word for it?"

"C-o-f-f-e-e," she plays along.

"Oh yes," he grimaces.

Fi pulls the tray to her lap and digs in. At least she knows he won't bring up the fact she missed dinner and came in late last night, and never will. He isn't one to dwell on things. "What's done is done," she's heard him say on more than a few occasions. Usually after she's done something rotten or broken something.

"You know, Uncle," she says, taking half an English muffin in one bite, "you really don't have to do this anymore."

"You don't like the Hussarde? It's the Marchand de Vin, isn't it? Too much thyme?"

"It's delicious, as always, thank you." Whatever else Fi might say about her Uncle Edgar, he's a damn good cook. More like a chef. "You know exactly what I mean. Breakfast in bed, every Sunday. I'll be 18 in a month."

"So a woman of legal age is not allowed breakfast in bed? I've been in America all this time and I still learn something new about this queer country every day."

He's in a particularly good mood. That hasn't happened much lately. He's always polite, but he has been more and more despondent of late. She doesn't know why for certain, but he works for some rich guy Fi has never met and the man became ill a few years ago, a slow but progressive condition of some sort. That was about the time Edgar began to seem down.

Fi isn't sure what her uncle's title is, some kind of property manager for his employer's homes – plural – the guy has houses all over the world. Edgar arranges to have them cleaned and maintained and pays the household bills. The reason he moved to Toledo was to oversee the restoration of the man's most recent acquisition, one of those huge old stone mansions along the river south of the city.

Edgar lifts a rumpled bath towel from its perch on a chair, holds it between fore-finger and thumb as if it's disgusting. Fi gives him a look and he folds it.

"I know very well that you have been indulging me and my brekky routine all these years because you think I like it," he says. "The truth is, I do, and that's exactly why I do it. This may come as a surprise, but what you prefer has never been my greatest concern."

"Obviously!" She makes as if to throw an English muffin at him. She doesn't, of course. She'd never mess up his only suit before church, even if it does look like it was made in the 1920s. Which actually makes it kind of cool. "It's good to hear you finally admit it," she says.

He settles into the chair. "I know you're growing up, dear, as you have made so very clear on every possible occasion since you were ten. Very soon you'll move away to attend medical school, then have a residency, a job, meet a man (a good man or not, probably not), become married, relocate to someplace exciting and exotic, or more likely terribly mundane, and have thirty-seven horrible children."

"Oh God!" Fi exclaims, then covers her mouth, having taken the Lord's name in vain in front of the only person she knows who might actually care.

"I doubt you've done *Him* any harm," says Edgar, glancing at the ceiling. "I will, however, say an extra prayer for *you* this morning, young lady."

"Sorry Uncle."

Edgar shrugs. He's religious, but other than saying grace before meals he never speaks of it. He gave up asking if she'd go to church with him years ago. She always said she had to study.

"So, how are you faring with classes?" he asks. "And work?"

This is more like the conversation she's used to having with her uncle. Simple, impersonal, to the point. "Classes are good, work is fine."

"Good, good. And your boyfriend?"

She chokes on a piece of egg. *How could he possibly know about Zeke? And he is not my boyfriend!* All she can manage in reply is a muffled, "Huh?"

"*Peter*, dear," Edgar clarifies, "the elderly gentleman you're always taking flowers to. And dates, is it?"

She relaxes. "Figs. He loves figs. He's okay, I guess. He smiled again last week."

Peter is very old, a patient at the hospital where Fi works for her internship. He's "taken a shine to her," as her uncle puts it. He really has, actually, as much as he can, and because of that the hospital has assigned her to him full-time. Well, part-time, since Fi only works three or four days a week. The fact is, she's the only person Peter responds to, as limited as it is. She's "taken a shine" to him, too. He seems so lost and alone. On the rare occasion when she can get him to look at her, her heart leaps. When he smiles, which is rarer still, it brightens her whole week.

"Kindness is the best medicine, dear, and I know you're giving him that." He notices the digital clock on her bed stand. "Goodness me, is that the time?" He pulls out his pocket watch. "No, actually it's one minute behind." He stands, stuffing the watch away. "I must be off. You can leave the dishes," then he adds with emphasis, "in the kitchen sink, Miss Fi. I'll do them upon my return."

"I'll do the dishes, Uncle."

Edgar grabs his chest. "The Lord be praised, miracles do happen."

Fi points her fork at him. "Get. Out with you. Begone!"

"Well, if that's the thanks I get," he snorts. He pats his thigh and Mol rises with a groan, heads into the hall. Edgar pauses, hand on the doorknob. "If it truly be your heart's desire, dear," he says kindly, "after your 18th birthday I will trouble you with breakfast in bed no more." He places his hand on his heart, "I solemnly swear," and pulls the door shut softly.

Now that she hears it, Fi isn't sure she likes the sound of that after all.

7

ORDER OF THE BULL 2

Tanuki and his caravan of monks, pack animals and wagons pass through a gate in a wall of white stone. Ten feet high and three feet thick, it was originally built by The Bull himself. The monks maintain it fastidiously to this day.

The wall circumnavigates the entire prefecture owned and controlled by the monastery, known locally as Taurus Minor. It is officially termed protected land and a nature preserve where hunting and trespassing are strictly forbidden by Turkish law. When the flying machines became prevalent, the Order made claims they scared the wild leopards and the area was declared a no fly zone. To this day it's monitored by radar operated by the government but funded by the monastery.

One doesn't live as long as most Firstborn without obtaining significant wealth and pervasive tendrils of influence. It happens almost naturally. Aside from the Order's longstanding sway in Turkey, Tanuki himself has powerful contacts in Japan, having financed through anonymous holding companies much of the key technological growth that has made that country an industrial power since what the watoto refer to as World War II. His personal fortune is significant, but the Order of The Bull, easily the oldest of its kind in this world, has a net worth equal to the Vatican. The only reason they don't have more is they don't *need* more, and decided long ago that to seek affluence for the sake of affluence is counter to the Ways of The Bull.

The Turkish people and authorities never venture into Taurus Minor without permission, out of a mixture of obedience to the law, respect, and superstition. There are rumors of the place, fables and old wives tales claiming an ageless power dwells in these mountains – and they're right. The monks don't proliferate such stories, but they don't quell them either.

Recent technological advances are proving particularly troublesome, however. Anyone can access satellite photos of anyplace from anywhere. Reality TV of the cryptid and supernatural-investigation persuasion is ubiquitous – and a thorn in the side of anyone who might have ancient secrets they'd like to keep.

Tanuki and his troop climb higher into the steppes, marching through pastures, meadows, and harvested fields, waving to shepherds tending their flocks along the way. Squat stone homes crop up here and there, with youngsters playing near streams or feeding chickens that scratch about in stony yards. At the edge of a serene lake a group of young men wrestle, all wearing bright green pants with cuffs rolled up below their knees. They break from their grappling and hail merrily. All the while the land continues to rise toward the base of the mighty *Kaçkar Dağları*, the Kaçkar Mountains, sometimes called the Turkish or Pontic Alps, severely contoured with peaks and crags of jagged limestone. The highest, at almost 13,000 feet, are frosted in snow year round. *How that mtoto general from Athens, Xenophon, or any of his 10,000 soldiers, survived their forced retreat from Mesopotamia over these mountains is still a mystery to me*, Tanuki reflects, even though he'd seen them do it, and even helped in a small way by pointing out the safest paths.

The outskirts of the village proper appears and the muffled thuds of the animal's hooves become clip-clops on cobblestone. There are none of the shining painted domes and spires of Byzantine, Seljuk, or Ottoman influence here, like those seen on the Mediterranean side of the country. Simple homes and shops jut along inclines to right and left like crooked teeth, squares and rectangles of white stone with flat roofs, arched windows and doors, though a few of the public buildings are roofed in red tile.

The sun is setting across the plains to the west, the last of the diffused daylight receding as a thin cloud cover moves in. Light snow begins to fall, white confetti floating gently from the sky, celebrating the return of Tanuki and his company of monks. Villagers grin and wave as they scurry about preparing for night. These are the Oblates, faithful watoto affiliated with the Order of The Bull, as their families have been for generations, but not monks themselves.

One last steep rise to a final plateau at the base of the mountain and they reach the monastery walls. Thirty feet high, ten feet thick, the stones each the size of a delivery truck. Tall gates of hardwood timber from far away forests open without so much as a creak, and are parted completely by the time they reach the entrance.

Inside the monastery they're greeted by joyful monks who hasten to help with the ponies and mules. As the doors of the gate swing closed, Tanuki's mtoto cloak, including his fur coat and hat, fade away. He's now simply Tanuki, in Trueface.

Here, the disorder of the village layout is left behind. The monastery grounds were designed by The Bull, an architect, stone mason and master builder himself, according to a strict and logical plan, and are perfectly kept. The paths are paved with white stone, lined with lamps fueled by natural gas piped from wells on the monastery property, the buildings an eclectic mix of exotic architectural designs: circular structures with flat roofs, Nagara-style buildings shaped like beehives, mound-like stupas, stepped ziggurats, tall towers with spires, high-windowed halls with columns and domes, an open ampitheatrum, even a modest pyramid. The Bull constructed these buildings in part to honor the various heritages of the monks, but also because he likes to try his hand at all manner of stone-craft.

The monks with the wagons and pack animals head for the Cellarium, the monastery storehouse. Tanuki follows. He isn't expected to help, but they're always delighted when he lends a hand. Besides, he has items he wants to make sure get repacked for direct delivery to The Bull and The Rhino, and a couple of very special gifts he'd rather handle personally.

* * *

Tanuki adjusts his backpack and purse as he steps from the Cellarium walkway to the wide central path leading straight through the monastery grounds. Snowflakes melt on smooth paving stones lit golden by the lamps. Tanuki looks up to let the flakes tickle his furry face. Dark narrow clouds scoot across the backdrop of night. A break reveals a clear moon, still nearly full, its craters sharply defined. The snow glitters in its silver light. Another cloud bank draws over it like a curtain and it's gone.

On his way up the path, Tanuki strides past the Armory. All that is kept there are wooden staffs, with which the monks train vigorously and are quite adept, and some light armor from ages past. On the roof of the armory stands the Gong Pagoda, a two story open structure housing a round bronze gong, eight feet in diameter, and a twenty-foot long tubular gong made of steel that hangs vertically from the rafters of the second floor, down through a hole to the first.

The path dead-ends into the largest and most impressive building in the monastery – the Temple of The Bull. Rectangular, the far end flush with the sheer rock face of the mountain, it's built in the Greek Doric peripteral style and looks much like the Parthenon of Athens did before it fell into ruin. There are no windows, and unlike Grecian and Roman temples, no decorative friezes depicting mythological battles on its exterior. Those are displayed inside the temple, and there's nothing mythical about them.

An iron portcullis rises with a clinking of chains and the massive doors swing inward. Two Sentinel Brothers hasten to opposite sides of the entrance and take their places, facing each other. They tap long staffs on the floor and bow in unison as Tanuki enters, snow swirling around him.

The youngest of the two monks greets him with cheer, speaking in Japanese, "Master Tanuki-san, welcome home."

Tanuki takes the monk's hand in both of his. "Greetings, Ebo. I hear congratulations are in order." He speaks in English with a Japanese accent. "You have a new young one, I understand. A boy, and a namesake. Is he well?"

"Little Ebo is very well," replies Ebo appreciatively. "Thank you for asking, Master. We are truly blessed by Apis."

Tanuki is suddenly serious. "He doesn't have..." he pulls the man close, "you know... horns?" The older monk laughs.

Ebo blushes and gawps, "Oh, no Master, no horns."

"Hooves? A tail, perhaps?"

Ebo shakes his head, embarrassed.

Tanuki pats Ebo's hand. "That's good to hear. You just never know." He grins and bows to each of them, then continues into the expanse of the hall.

The older monk delivers a teasing punch to Ebo's shoulder. Ebo blushes again. They close the doors and push linen towels over the snow-wet floor with their feet.

Inside the hall, rows of columns march along the length of the room on the right and left. Attached to each is a glowing gas lamp. This is the naos, the main hall where assemblies and prayers take place, large enough for all the ordained monks to gather. The only furnishings are a few stone benches along the outer walls, but in the center stands a larger than life bronze casting of Asterion, 20 feet in height, smooth and shining in the lamplight, seated on an unpretentious, squarish throne of white marble. Tanuki grins every time he sees it. Asterion has always been skeptical of idols or monuments. On the rare occasions that he allowed representations of him to be displayed, he insisted they not depict him in his true form, only as a natural bull, such as in the Hindu representation of Nandi, or as the head of a bull, as in the ancient Egyptian depictions of Apis. The monks were very persistent, however. Year after year, generation after generation, they petitioned him, respectfully, to allow just one. Something modest, perhaps, but *something*. Finally, Asterion acquiesced – and they commissioned *this*. When it was unveiled with great ceremony and rejoicing, Asterion just shook his big head and retreated to his lair.

So, there he sits, the big Bull, staring down at me with his ears forward beneath gilded horns, his eyes seeming to follow my every move. Tanuki walks toward the statue in a zigzag, as he's done a thousand times, just to see if the eyes really do follow him. Of course they don't, but still...

After they freshen up and don their best monkly garb, three of the monks will be bringing goods from the bazaar to be taken up to Tanuki's Brothers. To pass the time, he peruses the frieze relief sculptures on the walls that would normally be seen on the outside of such a temple. Asterion sculpted them millennia ago, with a little help from monk apprentices. Arges and Tanuki worked on a couple of them. The Bull put those in the darkest corner in the back. Tanuki can't blame him. They aren't very good. Though Arges still likes to grumble about it.

Tanuki wanders in the gaslight and shadows to the shuffle of his bare feet, click of his toenail claws on slick stone, soft hiss of burning lamps and huffing flicker of flame. The friezes are wrought in the Greek style, but if an outsider were to consider them to be based on myth, they would observe there are figures represented from stories around the world. There is Zeus of the Greeks, but also the Roman god Jupiter. Then Romulus and Remus, but Abel and Cain as well. Odin and Thor, Shiva and Ganesh, Anubis and Sekhmet, captured forever in all their immortal glory. Titans, Giants, Aesir, Vanir, angels, demons, Deva, Asura, bhutas and ganas. A veritable who's who of the panoply of gods and demigods, and hundreds of lesser creatures of lore. Thunderbirds, spiders, snakes, bears, bats, dragons, centaurs and ape-men, in addition to trolls and dwarves, gremlins, goblins, ghouls, flying fiends of the sky and monsters of the deep blue sea reflect in Tanuki's gaze. Most prevalent are half-men/half-beasts of a staggering variety, including a dozen configurations of human/canine and human/feline.

But these images aren't taken from ancient mtoto imaginings or far-stretched truths. They are genuine reminders of the First and Second Holocausts, the loss of friends and family, the cost paid by the Deva Firstborn for mtoto survival and their triumph over the Asura – the "unfriendly" Firstborn who twice attempted to exterminate or enslave all watoto on this earth.

The friezes depict natural human men and women as well, the watoto, from the primitive to the modern, *homo habilis* to *homo sapiens*, and all those in between, fighting alongside some of the Firstborn and against others. Fighting for their very existence.

"Watoto." Tanuki rolls the word around on his tongue. It's the term the Deva First-born have used for the humans, for all the homo species, since they first came into being. It still exists in Swahili and means the same thing it's always meant: "babies." The singular form is *mtoto*, for "baby." When Tanuki was young, he asked his father why they called the humans watoto. Father told him it's because the *homo* genus evolved so recently, they live such short lives, and are so very fragile. Then he added with a wry smile, "And because it's fun to say."

The Asura Firstborn call the humans *parvuli* (plural) and *parvulus* (singular), which are words that remain in Latin. Most of the meanings aren't nearly as nice as "babies." "Young," "small," "slight" and "child" aren't so bad, but as an adjective, parvulus has the connotations of "tiny," "mean" "petty," "cheap," "brief, "unimportant," "trivial," "less than," "insignificant," and "unequal." Ugly and cruel, like the hurtful names many watoto call each other today. Tanuki sighs. *If they'd only realize they're all the same – and just how lucky any of them are to be alive.*

Tanuki comes to the friezes he and Arges crafted of themselves. He shakes his head, making little "tsk tsk" sounds with his tongue. *Nope, not very good at all.* Then, in the farthest corner of the hall, are the two that always affect him the most. The first is one of the few representations of Asterion seen in the monastery other than the statue. It is of him grappling with his arch enemy (other than Baphomet, The Goat), The White Giant, Mithras, whom The Bull slew in hand-to-hand combat during the Second Holocaust. The next portrays a fearsome horned "dragon" on its knees, reaching up with a clawed hand, trying to dislodge what looks like a natural mtoto male clinging to its back with his arms locked around its neck. A breeze wafts through the hall. The lamps flicker, causing shadows to dance across the dragon and man, making them quiver, pulse, come alive...

"Master Tanuki?" Ebo doesn't shout, the acoustics of the hall carry his voice clearly enough to Tanuki's dark corner of the temple. Tanuki tugs his eyes from the frieze and strides toward the door, where three young monks with snow melting on shoulders and hair are waiting. A young woman, an Infirmarer Novice who assists in the monastery's medical facilities, stands behind a pushcart stacked with wooden boxes and bagged goods. The other are a Lay Brother who tends the monastery gardens, and the Cellarer Novice who had been at the bazaar this morning. Each wields a hand truck piled high with goods.

"Shall we?," Tanuki asks. They've all been in the naos, but these three have never seen the Lair of The Bull, high in the mountain where Asterion, Arges and Tanuki reside. Tanuki grins. *This should be most interesting.*

8

FLOWERS & FIGS 3

Fi's ponytail slaps at her backpack as she speeds down the stairs (heedless of the countless times she's tripped on them and fallen), wearing black stretch pants and a white quilted jacket over a long-sleeve blouse with tank top underneath. She ignores the taped-up "artwork" covering the walls. She isn't a bad artist, maybe even talented, and though she hasn't spent much time painting or drawing in the last couple years, her uncle has made the stairway walls a makeshift exhibit of her work since she was seven. She liked it when she was a kid. Now it's just embarrassing.

She makes her way down the wide, wainscoted hall, breathing in the ever-present scents of hearth, old varnish and candle wax, then stops short, realizing she didn't do the dishes, didn't even bring them down from her room. But it's already almost 10 AM. She has to be at work at eleven and she needs to make a stop on the way. The dishes will have to wait. One more thing she'll have to make amends to her uncle for.

She comes through the oversized front door onto the porch to quite a surprise. It's warm out, and bright and sunny. She checks the thermometer on the window. 72 degrees. Rare for late September in northwest Ohio, but it happens. Good, it'll make for a nice walk to work. She removes her jacket, skips down the front steps and strides up the patchy gravel driveway.

Adjusting the straps on her backpack, she glances back at the old house. A smile blooms on her face. Even with its peeling paint and sagging shutters, right now the sun is shining and it feels like home.

* * *

As she approaches the sidewalk at the end of the drive, Zeke steps out from behind a large oak tree. Fi's initial reaction is that her heart jumps, though not from fear. Then she hides a frown. Here comes the "talk." She *does* have to ask him a favor, though... and she might as well get this whole "relationship" thing settled.

"Good morning!" Zeke grins.

How can he do that? What about the little fact that he jilted her last night, and she had a freakin' fit right in his arms? "Hey," she replies.

"Sorry about just showing up. I tried to call."

She pulls her phone from her pocket. *Oops.* "I forgot to turn it on." She wonders if she left it off subconsciously because she was afraid he'd call, and wanted to avoid the inevitable. She holds the button until it powers up. "So, that's twice in two days. You stalking me now?"

"Yup. You look like you could use a little stalking."

Fi raises an eyebrow, "I look that desperate?"

"No. Maybe just a little sad."

"So much for my poker face."

"Look, I'm sorry about last night, really."

"Yeah? Me too. Did I flop around like a fish?"

"What? No! Look, don't worry about that, okay?"

"Oh, I'll worry about it all right."

"Hey Mol!"

Fi looks over her shoulder to see Mol sitting casually at the corner of the porch, tongue flopping out of his mouth. "Mol, dammit!"

"He isn't supposed to be out?"

"Not really. I mean, he's got a doggie door."

"Must be big enough for a horse."

"It's in the back, an old cellar door behind some bushes." She shrugs her backpack and hands it to Zeke. "Do you mind? I don't want him to follow us."

"Sure."

"I'll be right back."

Zeke tries not to grin as he watches Fi wrestle the big dog into the house. It looks like Mol has every intention of going in, he just doesn't want to make it easy on her.

A few minutes later Fi retrieves her backpack. "Sorry about that."

"No problem."

"I even hooked his doggie door. Edgar'll be home in a couple hours, anyway."

They proceed up the sidewalk, neither of them knowing what to say first.

Zeke finally eases into it. "Beautiful day, huh?"

To which Fi abruptly announces, "The doctors don't know why I have the seizures." She waits for a response, but Zeke just looks on attentively. "There were a lot of tests when I was younger. It's some form of epilepsy, but we don't know where it came from."

"That's idiopathic."

"What?"

"Idiopathic. It means 'of unknown cause.'"

"Oh." Fi does know that. "Yeah." And of course Zeke does, *the freakin' walking encyclopedia.* She thought he was saying something else. "I had the first one at my mom's funeral."

"Wow, sorry." What else can he say to *that?*

"The doctors finally figured out the right dosage and combination of meds. I used to have to wear a medical bracelet and everything, but I haven't had an episode since I was 12. We thought they were gone for good, that maybe it was just a phase or I was cured or something. Until last night."

Zeke cringes with guilt. If the seizures are brought on by stress, he can only blame himself. "Fi, I—"

She cuts him off, "You won't tell anybody, will you?"

"No, not if you don't want me to—"

"Please?"

"I won't. I promise."

"Thanks. I mean, I know I should tell my uncle and inform the hospital, but they'd never let someone like that take care of the patients. And they'd be right to let me go, I know that, but it could've just been a one time thing, right? I'd get Edgar all worried and lose my job for nothing."

"Fi, you don't have to explain—"

"I doubled up on my medication, and if it happens again I'll tell everybody, I promise."

"Fi, I already said I wouldn't say anything and I meant it, okay?"

"Okay." Now she feels like a terrible-imposing-rambling ass. "Thank you."

"Of course."

Zeke is being so incredibly nice and understanding, so ingratiatingly *Zeke*-like, Fi hates to bring up the other issue, but he looks like he's working up the courage to say something so she blurts it out anyway.

"I think maybe we should take some time off, not see each other for awhile." She winces, hardly believing she actually said it out loud. She won't look him in the eye, but she glimpses the shock on his face.

This is, again, not at all how Zeke expected this to go. Fi definitely has a way of keeping him on his toes. Maybe it's part of the reason he's so attracted to her. He can't say he blames her. He wants to ask why, but he's pretty sure he knows, and making her explain herself, to relive the rejection and embarrassment, would just be selfish and mean.

The silence gets really long, and really uncomfortable. Fi knows what's coming, the inevitable blow up, or the pleading. Either way, she braces herself.

"Okay," he finally says.

Well that was easy, she thinks. *I guess I made the right decision!*

"I want you to know, though, that I don't feel the same way."

Oh...

"I'm leaving for the conference tomorrow night, anyway, I guess—"

"Yeah. We're both really busy and all."

"But, can we talk when I get back?"

Now Fi's very confused. Part of her wants to say "no" and be done with it. The other wants to take it all back and throw herself on him. What happens is she mumbles a noncommittal, "Sure."

They come to a corner and Fi realizes where they are. "Um. I have to go that way," she points, "and make a stop."

"Mrs. Mirskaya's?" Fi has told him about "Old Lady Muskrat" and her store. He'd like to meet her. She sounds like quite a character. Normally he would offer to go with Fi, but under the circumstances... "See you at the hospital?"

"Yeah." She makes only brief eye contact. "See ya there."

He forces a smile. "Okay." She smiles sheepishly back. He has the walk signal, so he continues across the street.

Fi watches him stride away, his shoulders hunched. Her smile fades. *What have I done* now?

* * *

The bell hasn't stopped tinkling above the door to Matryoshka, Russian Market and Café, before Fi is attacked.

"Fiona! *Golubushka!* (little dove!). *Kak pozhivaesh?!* (how are you living?!)."

Having grown up with Mrs. Mirskaya as a babysitter and then worked in her store for several years, Fi picked up quite a bit of Russian, but she can't respond because her face is smashed between breasts that are each bigger than her head.

Mrs. Mirskaya releases her and kisses her three times, big wet smacks, alternating between cheeks. "*Zdravstvu!* (hello!)," she exclaims, "*skol'ko let, skol'ko zim?!* (How many years, how many winters?!)."

"It's been two days," Fi replies with a roll of her eyes. Mrs. Mirskaya always greets her this way. Ever since Fi no longer required a babysitter and then stopped working at the store, even though she comes in at least three times a week on her way to the hospital. It's kind of a ritual between them.

"Too long, *lapochka.* (little paw.)," Mrs. Mirskaya reproaches in her wonderful old world accent, propping her fists on the broad waistband of her ankle length skirt. Old Lady Muskrat looks to be in her early sixties, a heavy-set woman with bristling black hair streaked in gray, more than a little dark hair on her creased upper lip, and prominent front teeth. She wears a vest she couldn't button if she wanted to, because her enormous boobs shove out her blouse like intercontinental ballistic missiles preparing for launch.

She points at Fi with a knowing smile. "Today, I have just the thing for your Peter." Fi wants to say she doesn't have a peter, she's a girl, but just grins to herself for thinking it and follows Mrs. Mirskaya, who's already scurrying back to the counter.

Acoustic Russian romance music issues from tinny speakers, and the aroma of baking bread is heavy on the air. Not just any bread, but rich and black, made with molasses and dark rye. There's also the cabbagy-oniony-beety smell of simmering borscht and a strong undertone of fish. Mrs. Mirskaya is always making borscht, but she's either recently opened the chest refrigerator to scoop salty pickled herring from a barrel for one of her customers, or she's been nibbling on *vobla* again and has fish-breath. Maybe both, but almost certainly the latter. Vobla are little fish from the Caspian Sea and the rivers that feed it, salted and dried. A lot of Russians eat them like potato chips, leaving only bones and skin, insisting they're especially good with beer. Fi can't even sniff one without retching. Mrs. Mirskaya munches on them all day long.

While Old Lady Muskrat busies herself behind the counter, Fi steps into a narrow aisle to wipe the warm dampness of the sloppy kisses from her cheeks. She's very fond of the old Russian, but, *Yuck!*

Banks of fluorescent tubes cast uniform blue-green illumination over the tight space, with three rows of shelves piled to the tipping point. The walls are covered with hooks and racks bristling with goods. Not a square centimeter of space is wasted.

Fi eyes the shelves, shaking her head. When Mrs. Mirskaya restocks, she just fills up empty space with new stuff, taking very little care for organization. You might find the orange marmalade on one shelf and the lemon marmalade in a completely different aisle. Nobody complains. It's part of the charm of the place. And if they can't find what they want, they just ask. She angles her ample bulk and big pointed boobs down the tiny aisles and goes straight to it.

The shelves were far more orderly when Fi worked here. She resists the urge to reorganize the scattered colors of natural hair dyes and instead wanders to the back of the store where café tables snuggle against walls covered with deep red wallpaper embossed in gold. Throughout the day, Mrs. Mirskaya offers simple Russian fare, tea, and vodka. Lots of vodka. This is where she taught Fi how to do a shot then sniff a piece of the black bread to clear her nose of the alcohol vapor and bite a pickle to kill the sting. Even in her early teens, more than a few times she left work with a warm buzz from a shot or two, or three. She was hoping to see a few regulars and say "hello," but the place is empty.

Mrs. Mirskaya's clear contralto voice floats song-like through the store. "Oh Fee-o-na! Vaht are you doo-eenk?" Fi squeezes back up an aisle to the counter.

"Hey," she says, picking up a fuzzy Cheburashka doll from a basket on the counter and hugging its big round ears to her face.

"*Ei'—zovut loshady!*" replies Mrs. Mirskaya, who's facing the other way, working on something that makes the sounds of crinkling paper and squeaking ribbon. The phrase means "'hey' is for horses," and Mrs. Mirskaya never misses a chance to say it, especially to Fi.

Alla Pugacheva sings a melodious love song on the sound system. Mrs. Mirskaya hums along. Fi suddenly feels mischievous, taken by the impulse to sing "Cheburashka's Song," from the Russian animated series. Cheburashka is kind of the Russian version of Mickey Mouse, and Fi knows every word of the song by heart. Her caretaker used to play episodes on old VHS tapes for her over and over again. Fi makes the doll do a manic little dance on the counter while she sings double-time, and loudly:

> *"Ya bil kogda-to strannoy*
> *Igrushkoy bezimyannoy,*
> *K kotoroy v magazine*
> *Nikto ne podoydot.*
> *Teper' ya Cheburashka!*
> *Mne kazhdaya dvornyazhka,*
> *Pri vstreche srazu lapu podayot!"*

In English, it means something like:

> *"I was a strange*
> *And nameless toy,*
> *Who at the shop*
> *They would avoid.*

But now I'm Cheburashka!
And to me every stray,
Offers up their paw, when we meet, right away!"

"Stop torture poor Cheburashka," scolds Mrs. Mirskaya as she turns to the counter. In her hands are delicate violet flowers in a cone of green paper tied with white ribbon.

"Orchids," Fi exclaims, dumping Cheburashka back in his basket and taking the flowers.

"Your Peter will like," Mrs. Mirskaya states confidently, plucking a crispy strip of vobla out of a bowl on the counter and popping it in her mouth.

Fi breathes in the subtle bright scent of the flowers, which almost cuts the stink of fish. "Yes he will, they're beautiful."

Mrs. Mirskaya transfers half a dozen fresh Adriatic figs from a wood-strip carton to a small paper bag. "How is the *starik?* (old man?)," she queries.

"You mean Peter or Edgar?"

"Pssh! *Chertik moy* (you my lil' demon). Your uncle is not old. And he was just here yesterday for shopping."

"Did you help him find his special mustard?" Fi asks with a sly smile. Mrs. Mirskaya eyes her suspiciously. Her husband died over twenty years ago, before she came to the U.S., and Fi has long suspected she has a crush on her uncle, so Fi drops hints or tries little digs to see if she can get a rise out of her. The old lady always dodges with talk of the worthlessness of men or just ignores her. Sometimes Fi teases her uncle about it, too. Edgar poo-poos the idea, saying "One woman in the house is quite enough, what on earth would I do with two?"

The last time she brought it up she asked him, "You know what they say about a woman like that?"

"I do not, and I don't think—"

"Shade in the summer and warmth in the winter."

Edgar blushed, said "Oh my..." and scuttled back into the kitchen.

"Peter's doing fine, I guess," Fi responds, unshouldering her backpack. "Not much change, for better or worse."

"Not for worse is good, no?"

"Not for worse is good, yes," Fi answers. "Thank you for asking." She stuffs the figs into the bottom of her backpack and carefully slides the flowers in along the side. Her demeanor turns serious. "But today, you're letting me pay," she asserts, pulling money from a side pocket.

"Keep your dirty American money," says Mrs. Mirskaya, crossing her arms defiantly. "Is no good at Matryoshka."

"Come on," Fi pleads, offering the cash. "You can't—"

"I do not see what I am seeing!" she interrupts.

"But those are orchids! How much—"

"I do not hear what I am hearing!" she shouts, or sings, more like, steamrolling Fi's words.

"You can't keep giving...!" but the sturdy Russian is already turning the music up and singing along with Alla Pugacheva, her voice vibrant and obstreperous. "Mrs.

Mirskaya," Fi cries, "you've got to let me pay sometimes!" The shopkeeper pulls her Russian bayan accordion from beneath the counter and plays it as well as sings, completely drowning Fi out.

Fi shoves the cash in her pocket, exasperated. This is how it goes every time since Fi stopped working here – they annoy each other, on purpose, then Fi tries to give her money and Old Lady Muskrat refuses – though usually it isn't quite so dramatic. Fi doesn't dare buy the flowers and figs anywhere else, though. Mrs. Mirskaya would take it as a terrible insult, and Fi realizes deep down that doing this for her makes the old woman happy.

Fi slings her backpack on, stomps to the door, but when she turns back she can't help but smile at the sight of Mrs. Mirskaya singing, playing and swaying away behind the counter. Fi waves. "*Spasibo!* (Thank you)! See you in a few days!"

The woman who played nurse-maid, mentor and practically mother to Fi over the not-so-many years nods and does a theatrical little turn.

Halfway up the block, Fi can still hear her sonorous voice and the piping chords of the bayan.

* * *

The sun continues to hold its own, pressing a gap of flawless blue sky between cottony clouds. Fi steps along the sidewalk, enjoying its warmth and light. The lovely weather does little to smarten the stark city streets in this area of town, with their cracked concrete, heaving asphalt, abandoned brick buildings and chain link fences embedded with soiled white litter. The passing of an occasional car, a few ratty-looking sparrows flitting by, and stalks of sickly weeds are the only signs of life on this quiet Sunday morning.

A few blocks ahead is St. Augustine's, the hospital where Fi works. The six-story building of caramel-colored brick was once a YMCA, shuttered in the 1980s. A few years ago it was renovated by a corporation that operates several hospitals in the area with a considerable grant from an enigmatic philanthropic group called The October Foundation. The grant, which amounted to hundreds of millions of dollars, came with the stipulation that it be used to create a long term care facility for elderly patients who are both indigent and suffering mental illness. Peter, the old man Fi spends most of her time with, meets both criteria.

She began working at the hospital three months ago, thanks to an internship program between St. Augustine's and the university's medical campus. Peter was discovered on the front steps her very first day, his only identification a torn slip of paper that read *Peter*, pinned to his shabby baby-blue bathrobe. Fi had gone outside to help bring him in, and though he was practically catatonic, lying there in his old-fashioned night-cap and matted pink slippers, for one brief moment he looked right at her. A smile crept across his gaunt wrinkled face and he inexplicably said, "There you are!" He hasn't spoken anything quite so coherent since.

The doctors chalked Peter's condition up to "severely impaired global cognitive faculty." Dementia, in other words. He was relegated to the north hall of the fifth floor where untreatable patients are sent to wait out the end of their days.

Fi hadn't given up on him, though. Zeke has been a great help too, and Big Billy, an orderly at the hospital. It was Zeke who found out that Peter had an affinity for the song "Greensleeves," and Billy discovered his infatuation with the stars. But it's Fi whom Peter relates to the most, if you could call it that, and she who brings him flowers and figs.

In her first week, she was making rounds with one of the doctors and they checked on Peter in his room. Amidst his usual incoherent mumblings she thought she heard him say "flowers and figs," over and over. She figured, *what the hell, I'll give it a shot*, and brought him daisies and the sweet little fruit from Mrs. Mirskaya's market the next time she came to work. The response was extraordinary. Even the doctors took notice. Peter actually clapped his withered hands – quite an accomplishment for him – and held the daisies under his nose all day. Which is kind of funny, since daisies smell like ass. Since then, Fi's been assigned to Peter every time she works. Every once in awhile he smiles when she arrives. Those are the best days.

Most of the time she just walks him through his various therapy sessions, makes sure he eats something and sits with him while he watches TV (though what's happening on the screen doesn't seem to register). She reads to him too. Anything will do, even medical journals, which she borrows from the doctor's lounge. Sometimes she'll sit next to him and just flip through the pages while he stares at them. The faster she turns them the more he seems to like it. Something about the repetitious movement appeals to him, she guesses, because he certainly can't be getting anything else out of it. The patients have no computer access, but she occasionally sneaks him into an empty office and clicks through screens for him, surfing the web. If he perks up, she'll follow certain threads. Some of it's important stuff, news, world events, science, but mostly they watch music videos and stupid human tricks on YouTube. A lot of the time, when they're alone, she just talks to him, telling him random stuff about her day, school, even boys, and Uncle Edgar. She senses he might be most interested then, as much as he is capable.

Fi waits for a TARTA bus to pass and crosses the street. Her thoughts return to Zeke, like restless fingers to a fresh bruise. She's been attracted to him since she first laid eyes on him, playing his guitar in the hospital rec room. She'd catch him watching her sometimes, too, but for a long time she was unable to form words when he was near. She's convinced all the women want him. *Of course they do. He's hot!*

But he's more than that. The kind of guy who listens to you. Really listens. And with him, she gets the feeling that what you see is what you get. No bullshit. There's still a mysterious air about him, though. And a sadness, she thinks, though he handles it well. *Unlike I do mine.*

Only in the last couple of weeks have the two of them had any semblance of a real conversation – about music, his six months overseas as a volunteer relief worker, the paper he's working on for the conference, sometimes Peter, but mostly about a whole lot of nothing important – which is nice, actually. Last week she finally bit the bullet and hinted they ought to go to dinner. Zeke looked stunned, then smiled and she felt like her feet would leave the ground. Last night after dinner it was she who suggested they get some wine and go to his place. He's old enough to buy it, even if she isn't. Third date, right?

I was too pushy, she suddenly blames herself – *It's all my fault* – then she counters – *Stop torturing yourself. This is for the best, really – Really? – Really!*

There is something special about Zeke, though. She just can't put her finger on it. It's like an invisible string connects them, tied to something inside her – but that something is numb. She feels the tug, but what it's tugging at she doesn't know. She's convinced, as cliché as it sounds, that when her mother died, something died in her as well. Her heart just doesn't work like it should. It would make her sad if she allowed herself to dwell on it. Hell, she might be perfectly normal. Everybody might feel the way she does, all the time. But somehow she doubts it.

A voice comes to her, a pleasing lyrical tenor singing on the warm breeze. She looks up from the sidewalk and slows. The hospital is just ahead on her right, but a homeless man she's never seen before sits hunched against the building between the corner and the entrance, the unlikely source of the sweet melody. If she crosses the street to avoid him she'll just have to come right back, swipe her card at the door and make sure security sees her through the camera before they buzz her in. All the while he'll glare at her, beg, say rude things or try to break her heart with some sad story. If he's a decent guy, she'd make him feel ashamed. She resolves to continue on her present course and hand him some change.

As she comes closer, she hears the words of the song:

"There was an old lady who swallowed a fly,
I dunno why, she swallowed that fly,
Perhaps she'll die!"

This guy looks bad even for a vagrant, and weird, in striking contrast to his beautiful singing voice. He's small and stout, sitting with his back against the wall, knees drawn up to his chest, in gray trousers and black boots. He wears a tattered vest under a gray woolen jacket but he has two more coats, one black, the other gray like the first, with the arms tied around his waist. His clothes are sullied with ground-in dirt and God knows what else. The strangest thing, though, are his sunglasses – not just one pair, but four – each placed above the other from the bridge of his flat snotty nose on up over the brim of his grimy stocking cap. Each pair is a different size and style but all have reflective yellow lenses. He holds a torn cardboard sign with the nonsense *Will Eat For Food* scratched in what looks like dried blood.

The little hobo grins at her. His face is crusted in filth. Slaver froths on his lips, drips from his moldy teeth, runs down the forked and twisted beard that juts from his chin.

"There was an old lady who swallowed a spider,
It wiggled and jiggled and tickled inside her..."

Then the smell hits her. Working with the elderly and indigent in the hospital, she knows the sour odor people can have when they're really bad off. Rot and infection, shit and death. But this guy is rank in a different way, like a corpse or rotting fish, or a corpse in a pile of rotting fish. Fighting the urge to retch, she tries not to breathe as she digs in her pocket for change.

"Here ya go," she says hurriedly as she holds out the money, trying not to open her mouth any more than she has to in a futile effort to keep out the stench.

Still grinning, the homeless man completes the verse.

"She swallowed the spider to catch the fly,
But I dunno why, she swallowed that fly..."

He reaches with his wretched right hand. It's caked in black crud, and the last two fingers are missing.

"Perhaps she'll die!"

At that moment a chill wind buffets Fi, and it occurs to her that the sun is gone. That fast. Just gone. She glances skyward to see black storm clouds tumbling in. She drops the coins into the man's palm.

"Thankee, missy, thankee," his voice creaks. "What be your name?"

Fi feels fixed by his gaze, even though she can't see his eyes through his sunglasses. Disturbing, profane, violating her, body and soul. She doesn't answer.

"Some folks," he says with a leer, "they call me *Max*."

And the rain hits, icy cold, which comes as a shock in itself, but then thunder cracks, startling the hell out of her. She turns to run to the hospital door and the portico that promises cover – but the man's three-fingered hand clamps onto her wrist.

The coins he's dropped bounce, tinkle and spin on the freshly wetted concrete.

9

ORDER OF THE BULL 3

The gate to the secret elevator rises. A slab of stone slides aside, revealing a wide lamplit hallway running to the right and left. The three young monks remove their shoes while Tanuki exits, but stay timidly where they are until Tanuki bows and invites them in. "Welcome to our humble abode."

Down the hall to the right are Tanuki's, The Rhino's, and The Bull's personal chambers, as well as The Bull's private library, and a vault – their personal armory – but Tanuki leads the monks to the left. They hear low voices ahead. Tanuki motions for them to wait. He sets his backpack down, pads quietly to the end of the hall and listens.

The voices coming from the next room are the calm clear baritone of Asterion, and the agitated, rough bass of Arges. This is a conversation Tanuki has heard before. Arges can be quite single-minded and the subject is close to his heart, one that has made him prone to periods of depression of late.

They aren't speaking in Turkish, but Minoan, the language of ancient Crete. They tend to use it when in private conversation, even when they're entirely alone. Tanuki understands the words with ease.

"Only two hundred and seventy-five remain," Arges grumbles. "Just two hundred and seventy-five, of an entire species."

"It is unfortunate, of course," Asterion replies, "but we've seen it countless times. Species come and go."

"But these are Sumatran Rhinoceros," Arges retorts, "direct descendants of my mother's kind. They are my brothers and sisters."

"Tanuki and I are your brothers as well, and this is a journey from which you could possibly never return. What will you do, wait in the woods for poachers, then jump out with a roar and scare them away?"

"I will smash them. Pop their skulls like grapes!"

"Then what? Do you believe for a moment you would fool anyone by cloaking yourself in human form? An enormous hulk of a man with one eye, wearing a horned helmet? Would you hide behind a tree? Cloak as a boulder in the tall grass? Run away? The watoto have eyes in orbit, surveillance equipment of types we have not encountered in all our lives. They would acquire your image on digital cameras and share them with the world. They would hunt you down, and they would capture you."

"Let them try," Arges snaps back. "At least I would cause a ruckus, bring much needed attention to this travesty."

Asterion tries a different approach. "If your existence were to become publicly known, the last thing any mtoto would be thinking about are a few wild rhinoceros."

Arges harrumphs.

"They may not be able to kill you," Asterion asserts, "but it's possible, with the technology they have today. Worse, perhaps, they might *not* kill you. They have cages, bunkers, that perhaps even you cannot escape. What then? Experiments? Maybe you would be put on display. I can see the headlines now, 'The Cyclops Lives.' Only not in the *Enquirer* this time, but on the covers of *Time Magazine*, *National Geographic*, scientific journals. You would undoubtedly be questioned by some diabolical method that may be impossible to resist. Have you considered what trouble this could cause for the rest of us remaining Firstborn?"

Arges's voice loses its emphatic tone. "It's our fault, you know."

"Yes. In a way, it is."

Tanuki wonders, *what* would *the watoto think of Arges if they caught him? What would they really do to him?* Tanuki isn't overly concerned, however. Asterion's level-headed logic will prevail, as always. It never stops Arges from arguing, though. He likes it, and Asterion humors him. These two have been friends for a very long time and lived through much together. They know exactly how to deal with each other, to placate – and how to push each other's buttons.

Tanuki also has something in his purse he hopes will help, paperwork formalizing the creation of a non-profit organization for the preservation of wild rhinoceros, funded by Tanuki and Asterion to the tune of three hundred million U.S. dollars. A contact from Istanbul surreptitiously passed it to him at the bazaar this morning. Tanuki will present it to Arges today. He can hardly wait.

From around the corner comes the defeated voice of Arges. "What have rhinos ever done to anyone?"

"Nothing, brother, nothing," is Asterion's simple but sympathetic reply.

Tanuki hears Arges shuffle across the floor. He takes his cue and waves the monks to him.

Tanuki enters the main chamber, the young monks in tow. This is the area of the Lair of the Bull where Tanuki, Asterion and Arges spend most of their time during the day. "Chamber" is hardly the right word for it, though. It's a cavernous hall, 60 feet wide and 300 feet long, with a forty foot high barrel vault ceiling, carved into the living limestone of the mountain, polished smooth. Doric columns line the walls. Between each is mounted a lit gas lantern.

Tanuki steers the monks to the right, where a stone counter partially separates the hall from the kitchen where Tanuki prepares their one meal each day. He bids them to place their parcels in front of the counter and enters the kitchen.

Arges has been cooking, he notices, setting down his backpack. *Fumbling my fine cookware with his big fat finger-stumps.* Asterion also prepares meals on occasion, but he never leaves paprika spilled on the counter, a tipped salt shaker, containers askew on the shelves and open on the counter, or burnt rice stuck to the bottom of a pan on the gas stove. Asterion would never burn rice in the first place. At least Arges turned off the stove this time.

The monks have everything neatly piled and stacked when Tanuki steps back around the counter and are anxiously adjusting their robes and straightening their sashes. Tanuki looks them over. They gaze back expectantly, show visible relief when he smiles and nods. Tanuki retrieves a rolled carpet from a stack and they follow him into the main hall, straight and proper, bare feet padding on the polished floor.

The hall is sparsely decorated, the scant furniture made of the same stone as the hall itself, including the sets of free-standing shelves of books and pottery arranged in a sensible manner to "break up" the vast expanse of floor. There are only a few chairs, but here and there are low stone tables of various sizes with cushions lining each side, and Turkish carpets piled with pillows.

Asterion sculpted all of the furniture, as well as the hall itself, which he cut from a mere crack of a cave when he first came to this place so long ago. It isn't austere, but there aren't a lot of frills, either. It's clean, organized, practical, solid, strong, and balanced, just like Asterion himself. The open layout was chosen for more than aesthetic reasons. Having to move around indoors with horns on one's head was also taken into consideration.

A third of the way to the end of the hall, on the right-hand side, is a large hearth with an arched mantle. Another third of the way down, on the opposite side, is an identical hearth. Natural gas fires blaze in both. Heat and cold have little effect on Firstborn, but Asterion likes the ambience.

Opposite the furthest hearth, a hulking black figure crouches over something on the floor near the right hand wall. Tanuki makes straight for it. He can sense the nervous excitement of the monks behind him. Even the High Priests and Abbottess see Asterion very rarely, and the rest only once a year, in early May, when he comes down and addresses all of them for about fifteen minutes, then disappears back into his Lair. Very few are ever admitted into the Lair itself. A week ago a lottery had been drawn so that those who would accompany Tanuki to The Bull's chambers after the bazaar would be chosen fairly. The high priests and house staff didn't enter the drawing, leaving it open only to those who might otherwise never see Asterion's quarters. The monks trailing Tanuki are the three who won. They can barely contain themselves. It wouldn't surprise Tanuki if they peed their robes.

They hear a scraping sound as they approach, like stone being drawn along stone in long even strokes. It's accompanied by humming, in tempo with the scraping, slow and low. The sound of contentment.

Tanuki stops ten feet from Asterion, who's facing the opposite direction, crouched over a long column of marble. The monks silently line up next to each other behind Tanuki, each holding their hands folded before them. Now they see the source of the scraping sound. Asterion is carving flutes into a new column, using nothing but the thumb-hoof of one enormous hand.

"Aster, I'm hoooome," Tanuki says in English.

Asterion ceases humming, but they hear his breathing. Deep, extended breaths, the sound of air passing through a mountain fjord or wind making its way between the trees of an open forest.

Tanuki clears his throat. "I mean... *Your Majesty*, I have arrived." Asterion hates to be called "majesty," "highness," or any other kingly term, but Tanuki can't help himself. "And we have guests. *Scheduled* guests."

Still facing away from them, Asterion rises and claps dust off his hands, which sends a sound like cinder blocks being banged together booming through the hall.

"The Little Brother returns," he welcomes Tanuki in proper British English. He turns around – and there he is, The Bull, in the flesh.

Tanuki hears stifled gasps from the monks, who remain meekly behind him. He can't blame them. *Even after all the years I have known him, Asterion still has to be one of the most impressive beasts on this earth.*

At just over eight feet tall, The Bull towers above Tanuki and the three monks, a monument of muscle, hoof and horn. His face and broad head are those of a natural bull, his horns creamy white with swirls of silver-gray, a full five feet long apiece, ending in fine points that face straight ahead. The lobe of his furry left ear is pierced, where a faceted blue garnet held by a sturdy golden stud glitters in the lamplight. He surveys them with his great brown eyes. Tanuki always feels transfixed by that gaze, framed in those horns, like Asterion is pointing at him or reaching to corral him – and The Bull rarely blinks.

From the waist up he's built like a competitive mtoto weightlifter – but not the fat kind – with a V-shaped torso far more massive than any human's could ever be, and a neck so thick it's practically no neck at all. Short black hair that shines deep red in early morning and late evening sunlight covers his body. His legs are like those of a man, though much bigger, and his feet end in cloven hooves where his toes would be. A single hand could easily wrap around Tanuki's whole head. Each of the fingers end in a single pointed hoof, like half of a cloven hoof. When Tanuki and the monks had approached through the hall, they had seen a dorsal stripe, sometimes called finching, running down the middle of his back, the same creamy white color as his horns.

The Bull has been known by many names over the epochs, and inspired myths and religious practices throughout the world. He was Apis in the Nile River delta of pre-history, Nandi to the earliest peoples of the Indus Valley, and in the Levant he was worshipped as Moloch (a name later besmirched by Baphomet The Goat, when he turned The Bull's followers to human sacrifice beneath Mt. Olive), to name a few. Most of the monks of the Order are descendants of disciples of The Bull from all three regions. He is also the fabled Minotaur, falsely vilified by wretched King Minos. Constellations have been named after him, as well as a sign in the western Zodiac. It's no coincidence the vast mountain ranges that cross eastern Turkey, of which the Kaçkar Mountains where Asterion, Tanuki, and Arges now reside are a part, are called the Taurus and Toros Mountains. The name The Bull prefers, however, his Truename, by which he was known to the ancient citizens of Crete and has always been recognized by his fellow Firstborn, is Asterion.

The monks of the Order of The Bull know every name by which he has ever been identified and the story behind each of them. *It's with this knowledge and the blood of generations of followers of The Bull in their veins these young monks now face their "god."* Tanuki turns to them. *Well, maybe not "face."*

All three monks have hit the floor and assumed the pachanga-vandana, the prostrate position of five-point-rest, bent forward on their knees with forehead, elbows and palms touching the floor. Tanuki looks back to Asterion, who rolls his brown softball eyes and heaves a deep sigh. The Bull is not particularly fond of the more submissive practices of the monks. He tolerates them only because the priests insist it's necessary. Tanuki shrugs his furry shoulders.

"You have returned from your foraging, Little Brother," says Asterion. "With friends." He sees what Tanuki has tucked under his arm. "And a rug."

"A gift for Big Brother," Tanuki responds.

Asterion tilts his head to point across the hall with one horn. In front of the hearth, Arges lies on his side facing the fire, snoring softly. The young monks are so enamored with The Bull they haven't even noticed.

Tanuki steps to the side, setting his carpet on end. Asterion approaches the prostrate monks.

"Young partisans," he addresses them.

All three of the monks speak at the same time, in English, taking their cue from the language being used by The Bull, "Your Majesty."

Tanuki holds his tongue and maintains a straight face as Asterion shoots him a look. Asterion tried, centuries ago, to dissuade his followers from all such subservient terminology and conduct, but it was a disaster. They moped, believing they'd somehow displeased him, that he didn't love or need them anymore. Asterion finally gave in. "Sometimes I wonder who's truly in charge around here," Tanuki heard him say.

Asterion continues, "My friends, good citizens and faithful servants. Please rise."

The monks stand apprehensively, careful to avert their eyes. The Bull looms over them, only a few feet away.

"See me. Look into my eyes," he bids them, reaching to place his enormous hands on the shoulders of the two outermost monks. They crane their necks to do as he says.

Well, look at one eye, anyway, Tanuki suggests in silence, *they* are *pretty far apart.*

Asterion shifts his gaze to each of them as he speaks. "May you live with good health, discipline and love, with time and plenty, but none to spare. Reach and be reached, aid and be aided, learn and be learned. So it is spoken, so it will be done."

The monks repeat together, their voices quaking, "So it is spoken, so it will be done."

Asterion leans close and exhales onto each of them in turn. They breathe in deeply as he does so. When he's finished, their cheeks are flushed, eyes gleaming, faces radiant with moisture.

It's an ancient belief, beginning with the Apis monks of Egyptian Memphis, that the breath of The Bull bestows vigor, long life and fertility. Maybe it's true. Even if it isn't, Tanuki can't help but feel happy for the youngsters. To all in the Order it's the highest of honors, and Tanuki is surprised that Asterion has done it for these mtoto whelps on this informal occasion. *Maybe the old Bull's softening,* Tanuki wonders.

Asterion steps back, places the palms of his hands together in añjali-kamma and bows to them. They return the gesture.

Tanuki addresses the star-struck youths, "There is one more thing." He beckons them to follow and leads them to the far end of the Lair where columns line the wall just like those along the length of the hall, but these are just twelve feet tall and their tops support an upper wall, well below the ceiling. Tanuki pulls lightly on a thick rope of woven hemp. A crack forms in the center of the wall beyond the columns – which isn't a wall at all but a heavy weighted curtain made to look like the stone of the hall inside, the surface of the mountain outside. The curtain opens all the way to the sides. Beyond the columns a broad terrace is revealed, open to the sky. Tanuki leads the monks out onto it, beyond the ceiling that extends part way over the terrace. Snow still flutters down from thin clouds, the full moon a light misty ball above. The floor of the terrace extends another thirty feet beyond where the ceiling ends. The monks approach the edge tentatively since there is no banister or handrail. They look down and catch their breath. Though it is night, the lamplit monastery can be seen a thousand feet below, and beyond the wall, the lights of the village.

"On a clear day," Tanuki tells them, "you can see to the ends of Taurus Minor and beyond." The monks grin, wordless at the thrill of their good fortune.

Asterion crafted the terrace and opening in such a way that, from the outside, one would have to be at the same elevation as the hall to see the columns, let alone into the hall itself. A hundred years ago this was all they needed for privacy. The hall stood open to the elements for millennia. Now a helicopter could approach easily. A small one could actually land on the terrace. Even though the vast estate of the Order is a no fly zone, Asterion had a few decades ago erected the camouflage curtains. "A brilliant idea, Aster, and practical," Tanuki remembers telling him. Arges had grunted and groused, his usual response.

Tanuki takes a deep breath of the fresh mountain air and looks out into the night. His eyes are much better than the watoto's, especially his night vision. He can see far into the valley, and it is sublime.

Shortly after The Deluge, Asterion and Arges had left their respective islands in the Aegean and Adriatic Seas with The Bull's most loyal followers. They explored throughout Anatolia, moving progressively north and eastward before choosing this location to make their new home. The monastery was nearly completed when Tanuki joined them. A group of shepherd monks found him wandering the cold steppes, forlorn and alone. Recognizing him for what he was, a Firstborn, they brought him to The Bull, who knew him as a friend and ally from the Holocausts and welcomed him with open arms. Arges grumbled, of course, but Tanuki has been with them ever since.

From this terrace they've seen the history of Turkey unfold. The rise and fall of the Hittites, the Trojan War, the Hellenic migration, the birth of the Phrygian kingdom of Mithridates, the Mysian invasion, the long period of Hellenic civilization of Aegean Anatolia, the reign of Croesus, the ascent and decline of the kingdoms of Ionia, Lycia, Lydia, Caria, Pamphylia, and the Assyrian empire of Urartu. Then came the Persian invasion, the retaking of the region for Greece by Alexander, the incursion of the Celtic Gauls and their establishment of the kingdom of Galatia, the founding of the Kingdom of Pergamum, the coming of the Romans, the rise and fall of the Byzantines and Seljuk Turks, the Mongol invasion under Ghengis Khan's son Ogedei, the supremacy of the Ottoman Empire, the Russo-Turkish rivalry, and the Crimean War. Except for a few instances they simply watched them come and go like the tides. The recent mtoto wars they call World War I and World War II didn't affect them in any way.

Leaving the curtains open, Tanuki ushers the monks back through the main hall and down the hallway to the elevator. They bow silently, but as soon as the door closes he hears a muffled whoop of joy. Tanuki smiles and heads for the main hall. *They can be a delight, the little watoto.*

* * *

Tanuki returns to find Asterion lifting the column he was working on when they arrived, as if it's nothing more than a cardboard tube.

"Well, how did I do?" Asterion asks, standing it against the wall and wiping stone dust from his hands with a Turkish cotton towel. He isn't accustomed to visitors, and Tanuki is pretty sure he forgot about the visit today. Well, not *forgot*, Firstborn have nearly flawless memories. More like he let it slip his mind.

"Majestically," Tanuki replies. "A little out of character, don't you think?"

"Too stoic? Too stern?"

Tanuki just looks at him.

"I was caught a bit off guard," Asterion confesses. "I'm not sure what came over me."

"Feelings, perhaps?"

"Bah," Asterion waves him off. "Perish the thought." Then he approaches and stoops close, hands on knees, and whispers as much as he can with his ponderous voice, "Is it accomplished?"

Tanuki smiles and pats his purse, "It is," then reaches inside. "But first, I have something for you." He pulls out a small package, wrapped in plain paper, tied with string.

"You remembered," says Asterion, taking it.

"Of course."

"Thank you, Tanuki," then more formally, in Japanese, with a bow of his impressive head, "*Dōmo arigatōgozaimashita.*"

"*Anata wa hijō ni kangei sa rete iru* (You are very welcome)," Tanuki replies.

"So," Asterion's voice returns to a whisper, "it is all prepared, as we hoped?"

"Oh yes."

"And you have the papers?"

"Are you actually excited, Aster?"

"Noooooo." Asterion stands straight. "We can give it to him later, or tomorrow. He's sleeping now, anyway."

"Like that matters." A mischievous grin spreads across Tanuki's face. "You know *me*."

Asterion crosses his great black arms and smiles. "I do indeed."

Tanuki raises his voice to well above a conversational level. "Why Aster, you've made us a new couch. I have just the thing!" He snatches up the rug. Whistling obnoxiously, he carries it across the hall to where Arges lies on his side in front of the lit hearth, facing away from them.

Asterion moves to a hand-carved cello stand near the wall twenty feet away. His stride covers the distance in a few steps. He lifts the instrument, which is about twice the size of a regular cello, specially made for him by Matteo Gorfriller himself in the early 1700s – also a gift from Tanuki. The Bull knows that Tanuki had to special order the strings as well. That's what is in the paper-wrapped package.

"I just bought this today," Tanuki continues, still overly loud, as he stops near the sleeping Rhino, "at the bazaar." He cuts the twine that binds the rug with one short claw.

Asterion strolls over with his cello as Tanuki unrolls the rug along Arges's massive body. He eyes the carpet. "It is very nice."

"Don't tell him yet," Tanuki says, "it's a gift for Arges."

"Oh yes?"

"For his cat-naps. I mean, rhinoceros-naps. His old rug is getting pretty ratty. Between you and me, fairly ripe as well."

Tanuki stands with hands on hips, inspecting Arges. Lying down, the top of The Rhino's side is level with Tanuki's eyes. His thick hide is light reddish-gray, wrinkled, rough, creased and plated, with patches of course red hair on his shoulders and back. Lying there, he looks like a long mossy boulder.

"Is this new sofa a work in progress?," Tanuki asks The Bull.

Asterion is content to play the straight man. "Why do you ask, Tanuki?" He eases himself into a stone chair that faces the hearth, leans the cello against his knee and unwraps the new strings.

"Well..." Tanuki rubs Arges's back, pats it, pushes on his shoulder a couple of times. Arges grunts but doesn't move. "It's a little lumpy." Tanuki tugs on a tuft of Arges's back hair. "I'm not sure about your choice of upholstery, either."

Using both hands to help himself, Tanuki hops up, scrabbling to get his belly atop Arges's side. "Er... ugh." He pushes himself to a sitting position, turning to face The Bull, who is replacing the snapped and curling D-string on his cello. Tanuki kicks his short legs like a child in a grown-up's chair, his heels swinging into Arges's back. *Thump-thump. Thump-thump.* "And it's kind of high. For me, anyway."

A deep voice grumbles from the "sofa." "Get your hairy ass off me, fuzz-nuts."

"Ahh!" Tanuki bounds from his perch. He hits the carpet and spins, raising his hands toward Arges in a defensive karate stance. "Aster, you've made a talking couch!"

"Looks that way, doesn't it?" Asterion replies.

Arges stirs. "Ha, ha. Ha, ha, ha." He pushes up on his hands, turns to glare at Tanuki with his one big eye, fringed by long reddish lashes above and below.

Tanuki shrieks, "Ack! It's alive!"

Arges pulls his legs under him, looking much like a natural rhinoceros, then stands upright on two legs.

Tanuki recoils. "Eeeek!"

Hunched and yawning, Arges scratches his butt, the sound of rock on sandpaper. He keeps his eye on Tanuki. "Asshole."

Asterion grins. "You're on your own, Tanuki-san."

Arges looks to Asterion. "You encourage him."

The Bull makes a face of complete innocence, feigning shock at Arges's wild accusation. Tanuki crosses his arms, looking up at the hulking beast before him.

Arges, The Rhinoceros, has none of Asterion's athletic definition. At just over seven feet tall, he's shorter than The Bull but stockier all the way around, bigger boned, thicker skinned and heavier, the same thickness from sloping shoulders to hips, with short fat arms and squat columns for legs. His hide is wrinkled and pebbled, tougher than steel and rougher than unpolished stone. Tussocks of coarse red hair, like the fur on his back, sprout from his upper arms and chest. His head is long and broad, kind of like a human's, mostly like a natural rhino's, with his mouth low on his face, thick square lips and a broad flat nose with flaring nostrils. A short fat horn projects from his forehead, with another shorter one above it squatting forward on top of his hairless pate. His ears, much like a natural rhino's, rest high on his head, bristling with hair. They have a wide rotational range and he can move them individually, which Tanuki finds disconcerting, mostly because his own ears are nowhere near as articulate, nor as keen.

The Rhino's eyes, if he had two, would be quite close together. His one remaining eye, lustrous brown like varnished walnut, is much larger than a natural rhino's would be. His other eye had been lost to an evil Asura Firstborn, plucked out in battle when Arges was sorely wounded during the Second Holocaust. The preternatural healing capacity of even an older Firstborn does not extend to the complete regeneration of lost organs or limbs. A thick heavy lid hangs over where the missing eye had been. It doesn't weep, twitch or blink. In fact, it almost appears as if he never had an eye there at all.

His fingers are even thicker than The Bull's, but shorter. It's a wonder he was able to assemble the delicate jewelry he used to make, but no surprise he can wield a hammer for days on end, pounding metal into magnificent weapons, or pull them glowing hot from the fires with his bare hands. His feet are practically round, flat on bottom, with three thick toes on the front of his right foot. His left foot has no toes. Long ago, The Rhino had been instructing some of his own kind in the art of metal-smithing in a forge built in a live volcanic cavern beneath a high mountain. There was an earthquake and he slipped into the molten lava while trying to save the others. It would have killed any natural being, or at least taken the foot off completely, perhaps the entire leg. For The Rhino it charred his three heavy toes and left his foot blackened and scarred. Walking upright he has a limp, so he often chooses to move about on all fours. The Rhino was lucky, however. The earthquake turned into a full blown volcanic eruption, one of the most destructive this world has ever seen (what remains of it is now known as Mt. Toba). It was the opening strike of the First Holocaust. Many perished that day, including The Rhino's two Firstborn rhinoceros brothers, three nephews, and two of his own sons. It was Asterion who pulled Arges from the collapsing cavern, saving his life.

"Do you like your new rug?" Tanuki asks.

"It is..." Arges stops there, looks at Tanuki askance.

Tanuki sits, pats the rug for The Rhino to join him. "Take a load off, Big Brother. Aster and I have something to show you."

Another cleverly orchestrated jest at my expense, Arges assures himself. *The fur-ball looks like a little kid wanting daddy to sit and play.* But The Rhino doesn't play, and he sure as hell is not Tanuki's daddy.

Arges's mother was a precursor to the entire *Dicerorhinini* rhinoceros tribe, which once included the now extinct Woolly Rhinoceros and the Merck's or Narrow-nosed Rhinoceros. The only surviving species of the tribe is the *Decerorhinus*, the Sumatran Rhinoceros, creatures that have barely changed in over seventeen million years, and are now the rarest of rhinos on this earth.

Truename Arges, The Rhino spent much of his early life with his mother's kind, wandering the plains of the continent now referred to as Eurasia, perfectly content with grazing, mating, fending off predators, the usual. He had many families and lost them, endured climatological and geological upheavals, saw a few small Firstborn civilizations come and go, and traveled the world, but he always returned to the rhinoceros, to rest and to live.

Then Father came to visit. With him was another Firstborn, one whom Arges had only heard stories about, and everything changed. Even legends have legends. None had spawned more than The Prathamaja Nandana. The First Daughter.

10

FLOWERS & FIGS 4

"I gave you money, please let go!" Fi cries. She pulls with all her might but the little hobo's grip is unbreakable, his three-fingered hand unnaturally rough, hard, and cold.

The rain comes harder, pounding them both. The man's stench grows even worse as he gets wet. Brown-black water runs off of him. Fi gags. Lightning flashes. Thunder booms. Fi jerks harder, trying to extricate herself from the horrible man's clutches.

"Don't be afraid of a little weather, missy," he croons. "There's worser things in this world." He pulls her closer, his carious mouth spreading in a wide wicked grin. "*Much worser.*"

"Let me go!" she pleads. *If only the camera near the door to the hospital could see this wide, the security guards would be out here in a second.* "I gave you money!"

"So you did, missy," and just like that, the homeless man releases her. "So you did."

Fi stumbles back, spins on her heel and bolts. In moments she's up the stairs, beneath the portico at the door and reaching into her backpack for her employee ID.

She glances back to see the man watching her through his yellow glasses, leering in a way that makes her shiver from more than just the chill of the rain. Thunder rumbles again, a gust of wind splashes drops in her face.

She wipes her eyes – and the little hobo is gone. And so are the wind and rain. As quickly as they came, the clouds are breaking up, revealing blue sky above.

Fi glances around to see where the man might have disappeared to. If she sees him again she should tell admissions here at the hospital. This guy is definitely a candidate. She reconsiders – then he would be inside, with her. The thought makes her shiver harder. *If I see him again, I'm calling the police!*

She hits the buzzer, slides her photo badge through the card swipe then holds it up to the security camera above the door and says, "Fiona Patterson." The door buzzes and clicks. She yanks it open and rushes inside, breathing a sigh of relief as the door locks shut behind her.

Fi makes her way down the entrance hall to the door to the lobby. That door buzzes and clicks and she enters a spacious room with couches along the wall to the right. To the left is a wide glass window, the wall of a good-sized security booth. A pleasant-looking young man in a dark blue uniform and wearing a headset (the kind with one earpiece and a microphone on a stem), presses a button and his voice comes through a speaker. "Hi Fi."

"Hey Stan," she replies.

The door to the booth opens and another guard comes out holding a clipboard. He's a burly fellow with a crew-cut, the short sleeves of his uniform rolled up over his biceps.

Fi greets him, "Hi Shane."

"Good morning, Fi. Just need your John Hancock, as usual." He hands her the clipboard, and Fi is entirely unaware of his eyes moving involuntarily from her wet hair and face to the rivulet of water dripping down her neck to her chest – which is barely concealed beneath her soaked white blouse and tank top. He can even see goose bumps. "Uh," he looks back up quickly, "Is it raining out there?"

"Came and went," Fi replies, heedless of her practical nudity or Shane's distraction. "Just my luck I got caught in it." She finishes her signature, writes in her time of arrival and hands the clipboard back to Shane. She pushes her hair back behind her ear and takes a deep juddering breath.

With supreme concentration on keeping his eyes off her breasts, Shane asks, "You okay?"

"Oh, yeah. I'm fine. But... there was this homeless guy..."

She tells them about the smelly little hobo grabbing her. "It isn't a big deal," she finishes, playing down her fear, "just thought you might want to know."

"Definitely," Shane says seriously. "I'll do a sweep outside, see if he's still around."

"I'll tell the rest of security to keep an eye out, too," adds Stan.

"Thanks guys. Have a good day."

Stan says, "You too," and Fi walks to the security door at the far end of the room. Stan presses a button and the lock opens, allowing Fi to pass into an alcove with a stainless elevator door and stairs up to reception. Fi takes the stairs.

* * *

Stan watches the image of Fi striding up the steps on a flat screen security monitor while Shane heads outside to look for the homeless man. The monitor has a color touchscreen divided into sixteen sections, each showing the video feed from a different camera in and around the building, complete with tiny digital lettering that states their location – and this is only one of several monitors in the booth. There are cameras on each corner of the building outside, and in all the public areas inside. He can also see Sarah, the reception nurse, and Bob, the guard who sits behind her, in the reception booth of the waiting room on the second floor. And there are Joe, the Head of Security, and Lisa, another security guard, in the main security booth that's built into the corner of the recreation room on the third floor.

A hell of a lot of security for a hospital, Stan has always thought. Then again, this isn't a great neighborhood, and they do keep a lot of drugs here.

Fi stumbles on one of the steps, catches herself on the handrail, and continues on. Stan shakes his head. *That's our Fi.* He scans all three monitors. Nothing exciting, as usual. He returns to his Sudoku numbers puzzle.

* * *

In the spacious waiting room on the second floor, Fi greets Sarah, the reception nurse, a middle-aged woman who always wears a cardigan over her scrubs, and says "Hi" to Bob, the security guard who sits behind her, dozing in front of another bank of surveillance monitors. Sarah rolls her eyes at Bob's half-conscious snort of a reply and Fi hurries on her way to the locker room. She needs to change into her scrubs, but what she's really looking forward to is getting out of these wet clothes and washing the nasty hobo slime off her arm.

* * *

Already unbuttoning her blouse, Fi bursts through the door of the unisex locker room and runs right into Zeke.

They both shout in surprise as he stumbles backward and falls onto a bench with Fi right on top of him. His guitar case clatters to the floor.

"Shit. Sorry!" she exclaims, reaching for his fallen guitar, pressing herself harder against him in the process. He reaches for the case at the same time, and for a moment they're stuck there, one atop the other, her hand on the handle of the case, his on hers, their faces only inches apart.

Fi's reminded just how terribly handsome he is, with his deep brown eyes, those long lashes, and his dark brown hair combed back, waving down over the collar of a blue oxford shirt. He doesn't wear scrubs like everyone else in the hospital, just jeans, with the sleeves of his shirt rolled up to his elbows.

"Hi," is all Zeke can think of to say.

Fi pushes herself up, flustered and embarrassed. "I am so sorry."

"No no, my fault," he says, sitting upright. And he smiles – -a genuine, reassuring, comfortable smile.

"I... need to get dressed." She hesitates, pushing her hair back over her ear, then musters her resolve and steps past him to her locker.

"Are you all right?" he asks as she dumps her backpack on the bench. "You're soaked."

"Yeah, it's just a freak rain. Hit out of the blue. And a creepy homeless guy grabbed me outside."

"What?" Zeke stands, his expression changing from curiosity to concern. "You got grabbed?"

"It's nothing, really. If anybody can handle crazy old people it's me, right?"

Zeke's not entirely convinced. That sounded more like a question than a statement. "Yeah, sure," he answers, following it up with an awkward pause.

"I've got to change quick or I'm going to be late for rounds." She resumes unbuttoning her blouse.

"Okay," he replies, but he still stands there.

"Zeke?"

"Oh," he gushes, "yeah," and there's that smile again, this time accompanied by the fingers through the hair and a reddening of the cheeks. "I'm going." He retrieves his guitar and goes to the door, but stops, wanting to say more—

"See you on the floor," says Fi.

He nods and exits, regretting his cowardice once again.

* * *

Out in the hall, Zeke slumps against the wall. He'll let her have the week, he decides. Then, when he gets back from the conference, he'll sit her down. *Make* her listen. Tell her how he *really* feels about her. That he's loved her since the moment he saw her. That somehow he knows he'll always love her, and always has. Then at least he'll know he's done everything he could. What happens after that is up to the fates.

* * *

Fi groans, places her palms against the locker. It would have been nice, being with Zeke. Better than nice. But it's just not meant to be. Why should she expect anything different? Still, she wonders for the hundredth time if she's made the right decision, and resolves again, for the hundredth time, that she has. She doesn't need that kind of drama in her life, and now she can be free of it. As long as she can get him out of her head, that is.

She pulls off her shirt and sniffs the sleeve, then crumples it and jams it into her locker with an "ugh" of disgust.

* * *

Fi hurries down the hall in turquoise scrubs, the short-sleeve top over a long-sleeve white T-shirt, her hair pulled back in a newly re-done ponytail. She has a few minutes before her shift starts, so she slips into the break room, sets the flowers and bag of figs on the counter and pours herself a cup of "that foul substance," coffee. Taking a sip, she can't resist a smile. *My uncle is such a dork.* She retrieves a paper grocery bag from the cupboard, places the figs inside and begins to put the orchids in as well, but peels back some of the green paper and lifts them to her nose.

The door bursts open and in sweeps Big Billy, startling Fi enough that she almost drops the flowers.

"Fabulous Fiona!," he calls in a high tuneful voice, sidling up to pour himself a cup of coffee. "I may have the very best gossip ever in the history of the whole wide world, girlfriend," he says, keeping his voice down, checking the door.

Everything about Billy is big – his build, personality, penchant for hyperbole, flair for the dramatic, appetite for salacious gossip – and his cock, too, if he's to be believed.

Billy is an orderly and Fi's only real friend at the hospital. Maybe the best friend she has, period, though they never hang out outside of work. He's in his mid 20s, built like a football player, though a little softer and rounder, with a flattop buzz cut of bright orange hair and a round baby-face. He says he actually did play football in college, somewhere in the South, in what he calls his "previous life," when he "pretended to be a breeder. I had sex with girls. *Eww!*"

Billy is easily the biggest guy in the facility, 6' 5" tall, 260 pounds, but so light on his feet he swishes, on purpose, because Big Billy has enough gay for the whole city, maybe the whole state, and he lets everybody know it. Most everyone at the hospital likes him. He's been heard to say within earshot of the few die-hard homophobes who don't, "The only thing I like better than suckin' cock, is kickin' ass." They pretty much stay out of his way.

He takes Fi by the elbow and leads her to a chair at the break table. He sits next to her, overflowing with excitement.

"Your Peter has been a very naughty boy," he spills. "God love him."

"Oh no, is he okay?"

"Fi, he's better than okay. He got his weenie wet."

"Wait... *What?*"

"Salazar – you know Salazar, the night janitor?"

Fi shakes her head.

Billy waves it off. "Doesn't matter. Anyway, he and I are buddies. Sometimes, if you know what I mean. I helped him get his job—"

"Billy!" Fi knows he'll prattle on forever if she doesn't keep him on point.

"Okay, so I got here real early this morning, about five, and Salazar was just leaving. He grabs me in the parking lot and tells me that he was on his way out after his shift and realized he forgot his phone in the closet on the fifth floor. So, he's heading down the hall and he hears something in Peter's room, and sees the door is open a little. He peeks in, and guess what he saw?"

"Billy," Fi protests. "Come on, what?"

Billy is barely able to contain himself. "Peter, on his back, with the biggest grin you've ever seen, because..." he pauses for dramatic effect, "Dr. Williams was on top of him, riding him like a bucking bronco. Yee-haa!"

Fi's hands go to her mouth. "Oh my God."

"Isn't that awesome?"

"Billy, that's terrible!"

"You've got to be kidding. You should be thrilled for the old fart. *And* Dr. Williams. I don't think that woman's gotten laid in, like, *forever.*"

"I don't believe it."

"You're just jealous that somebody besides you made Peter smile. *And* that everybody's getting laid but you."

"What? I am not!"

"Uh-huh," Billy nods knowingly. "Anyway, Salazar wouldn't lie, that man does not have the imagination to make something up like that. Believe me."

Fi is quiet while what Billy's told her sinks in. "What should we do?"

"What? Like tell anybody? Hell no. Anyway, who could blame her? He is smokin' hot, for an old guy."

"Billy! He's a helpless old man!"

"Oh please. Everybody knows he's hot. And he's not that helpless." He holds his fingers up to put quotation marks around "helpless," then leans closer. "There's nothing wrong with Peter's peter, you know. Get that warm sponge out for his bath and, 'hello!' He's uncircumcised too."

Fi buries her face in her hands. It's just not funny – or at least it shouldn't be – but there's something about the way Billy talks. He's got absolutely no filter and nothing is sacred, but somehow he makes even the most insane things sound reasonable. She watches him, sitting there with his arms crossed, one hand fiddling with his necklace. The pendant is kind of a triangle, but convex at the base and concave on the sides, more so on one side than the other, made of copper with funny little markings, and strung on a cord. Says his dad gave it to him and he just *adores* it. He looks so flippant and self-assured that she can't help but laugh.

"See?" Billy becomes more serious. "I promise, if it gets out of hand I'll file a report. Meanwhile, I'll spread the word to keep an eye on them."

Fi gives him an admonishing look.

"Only the staff I trust," he adds. "No doctors or admin. We wouldn't want Dr. Williams to get fired. She's cool, right? Or they could move Peter to another facility. We don't want that, do we?"

Fi shakes her head, "No."

"It just happened this once, as far as we know, so we'll leave 'em be for now, okay?"

Fi acquiesces, "Okay."

Billy checks his watch, then tucks his necklace back into the collar of his scrubs and pulls his chair right in front of her. "Now, dish."

Fi acts like she doesn't have any idea what he's talking about.

"You're not getting off that easy, Fi-fi."

Fi wants to scratch the eyes out of anybody else who calls her "Fi-fi," but somehow, when Billy says it, it's kind of endearing.

"Your date last night? With Mr. Sexy-pants?"

Fi doesn't have anybody she can talk to about things like this. No close friends. And Edgar? Absolutely not. Mrs. Mirskaya? No way. It would feel good to share with someone, so she tells Billy about her failed evening with Zeke – except for the whole having-a-seizure-on-the-sidewalk part.

Billy listens to the story, then says, "Fi, okay, he's hot. *Really* hot. But you know you could have any guy you want."

Fi snorts, "Yeah right."

"That's what I love about you. So humble." He pats her on the knee. "And clueless."

"What*ever*."

"Everybody wants you."

"No they don't."

"Even the girls. And you know those two tight-bodies downstairs, Stan and Shane?"

"No way."

"Uh huh."

"Guys will sleep with anything," she scoffs. "I'm nothing special."

"True."

She smacks his arm.

"No, dork. I mean the 'guys will sleep with anything' part. You're gorgeous, girl. Socially awkward, clumsy as shit, obviously, and a nerd, but an irresistible, scrump-dilly-icious one."

Fi crosses her arms. "You don't want me."

Billy flashes his signature sly, ornery smile. "Well... that depends. Do you have a *dick?*"

Fi changes the subject. "I think it might be my fault, what happened with Zeke. I was too pushy."

Billy shakes his head. "Honey, there's no such thing as 'too pushy' when it comes to men. Did you pull his cock out and put it in your mouth?"

Fi goggles in disbelief.

"Well, did you?"

"No!" Then she blushes, says sheepishly, "I took my shirt off."

"Eew!"

"Billy!"

"Okay, okay, I'm sure they're very nice, but I think we have our proof." Now he's getting smug. "I was right all along."

"Oh no..."

Billy expels an exasperated breath. "G-a-a-a-y! I keep telling you. He just doesn't know it yet."

"You think everybody's gay."

Billy flashes his smile again. "Just the sexy ones."

As if on cue, Zeke walks in. He sees Fi and Billy and gets a deer-in-the-headlights look.

Billy winks at Fi. "Speak of the devil."

Zeke's mortified.

"Gotta go!" Fi jumps up, leaving her cup on the table. She retrieves the bag of flowers and figs from the counter, but when she turns, Billy has already positioned himself between Zeke and the door.

Fi shakes her head frantically at Billy, hoping to keep him from doing anything... *Billy-ish.*

"Z-e-e-ke," Billy coos, "I've got a proposition for you."

Too late.

"Um..." is all Zeke has in reply. He and Billy have kind of a running thing. Billy hits on him, he politely refuses. *This can't be any different from that,* Zeke thinks. He hopes. It's just that seeing Billy here talking to Fi, after last night...

Billy steps a little closer. At six feet tall, Zeke isn't a small man, but facing Billy he feels like a skinny kid.

"I'll tell you what," Billy proposes, "I'll get down here on my knees and you close your eyes. If you're not smiling in two minutes, I'll believe you're not gay and I won't bother you any more."

"Billy, you are *so* funny," Fi exclaims, squeezing between them. She grabs Zeke by the arm and pulls him to the door. "Zeke and I have to work." She shoots Billy a look, *"We'll talk later."*

Billy smiles his sly, ornery smile once more. "O-k-a-a-y."

She drags Zeke out the door, but then he stops her. "It's all right, Fi." Holding the door open, he calmly faces Billy. "I'm flattered, Billy, as always, but it's just not going to happen."

Billy smiles down at him. "Whatever you say, Zekey. The offer still stands. You have a sparkly day, now."

"You too," Zeke replies, then wonders what he just said. The door shuts on silent pneumatic hinges.

"I really do need to get to my rounds," Fi blurts out before he can speak. "See you at music therapy!" She hurries down the hall, muttering under her breath, *"Maybe."*

11

ORDER OF THE BULL 4

When Father brought The Prathamaja Nandana to Arges's homeland she was seeking a meteorite she'd seen falling through the sky the week before. Arges had seen it too, and knew where it struck. He led her there, eager and speechless in her presence. She even enlisted his help in extracting ore from the celestial rock. Arges was fascinated. He begged her to show him more, to teach him. She refused and left him standing on the savannah, alone and rejected.

A year later she returned and agreed to mentor him. He never knew why she changed her mind, and only much later did he realize what a tremendous honor it was.

The Pratha had always been hermetic, especially since the Cataclysm, preferring to be alone with her meditations and experiments. She'd only taken one apprentice before and it hadn't turned out well. Still, she accepted Arges under her tutelage and introduced him to what would become his lifelong passion – Metalsmithing. He had a natural inclination for it. Incredible strength, patience, practical intelligence, an artistic yet pragmatic eye (no pun intended, he had two eyes at the time), and his thick hide made him even more resistant to heat than most other Firstborn.

Training began with manual labor. Mining ore, crushing rock, building forges, carrying wood for the fires, working the bellows, making charcoal, building wagons and pulling them. She taught him how to use the basic tools of the trade, to work the materials of the earth with fire, the subtleties of quenching with sand, saltwater, oils, even blood. They found crude oil oozing to the surface of the ground and refined it for use as fuel, lubricants and protective coatings, harnessed gasses from bubbling bogs and swamps. She showed him the uses of coal and explained how all these natural resources had formed over the aeons of the life of the world. From her he learned how to examine chemicals and minerals through touch, taste, smell, and sound – and The Rhino has exceptional olfactory senses and hearing.

Pratha was a hard master. Many times Arges felt she was trying to make him quit, but he never did. She'd go long periods, sometimes years, without speaking to him, and refusing to allow him to speak. Just watch and do. At other times she displayed great tolerance and profound kindness.

After many years of study, when Pratha felt he'd become proficient in what she called the "material" skills of smithing, she told him to put down his tongs and step away from the fires. He was ready for the next level.

It began with meditation and solitude. He was resistant at first, as resistant as a stubborn rhino can be, which is very, but she insisted, and The Pratha could be quite persuasive. They would sit in silence or mantra for days at a time, then months, then years. Over this time she showed him how to put himself into an alternative state of mind, to overturn his normal, habitual, analytical, relative way of seeing things. With intense concentration and by clearing his mind his perception became absolute, where the distinctions between inside and outside, subject and object, simply ceased to exist. Normal vision and thought were replaced by empathy and intuition. By focusing on the metals in this way, when he was smelting, casting, hammering, or treating them, he could sense when their crystalline structures were just right, which materials could be alloyed with others and when, as well as what the outcome would be. He could "see" and "hear" the materials on a molecular, even atomic level, perceive the tones and notes of their minute particle vibrations and move the notes about, ever so slightly, with thoughts, ancient words and phrases Pratha taught him, orchestrate them to create rhythms, melodies, and make them sing. Myrddin Wyllt later referred to the process as "transcendental transmogrification" after Pratha relayed some of these skills to him. Myrddin mostly took what he learned in different directions, though, such as alchemy, and did silly things like turn lead into gold.

Making truly special objects, however, took truly special materials, the kind that don't naturally occur on this earth. They come from rocks that fall from the sky. So Arges and Pratha traveled the world chasing falling stars, building rafts to travel the seas when necessary, diving deep beneath them when they must. Due to the properties some of these extraterrestrial ores possessed, Pratha and Arges could make things that were, for all intents and purposes, indestructible. They couldn't be broken or melted down except by methods known only to them. More importantly, and frighteningly, they could be used against Firstborn with deadly force.

The very rarest of these materials gave the objects they crafted other qualities as well. Some could draw energy from their surroundings, or expend it. They could heat, cool, expand, contract, even move of their own accord. Some, through a higher level of transcendental transmogrification, could be imprinted, imbued, infused, "programmed," with recognition, intention, memory, and discernment. This was Pratha's final lesson to him.

Upon introducing this concept, she retrieved an unassuming wooden box from her private belongings. From inside, she had him lift a disk-like object, a flat ring open in the center, about ten inches in diameter. She told him to grasp it from the center only, never to allow any part of his body near its outer edge because it was sharper than anything he had ever seen or would ever see again. The disk was light as air and the hue of a powder blue sky.

She took it from him, laid it on her palm, then whispered a mantra he'd never heard her speak. The disk began to emanate a soft hum. A rainbow of colors shimmered on its surface. It rose slowly from her hand, humming louder, and began to spin at tremendous speed. She raised her other hand, straight up, palm out, the first two fingers extended. The disk floated to suspend itself over her fingertips. Then she told Arges she made this thing. It belonged to Father, but he wanted her to show it to Arges so he'd understand what could be accomplished – and impress upon him the devastation an instrument such as this could bring about.

Only much later, toward the end of the First Holocaust, did Arges witness what the disk could do in the hands of Father. It laid waste to an entire army of Asura Firstborn and other wretched beasts in a matter of minutes. That was the day it was named Shudarshana, Vishnu's Chakra.

It could take many years to fabricate one of these very special objects. The making of the Chakra took Pratha 50 years. Even after epochs of experience, the forging of the Trishula trident took Arges 75. The fighting staff Ruyi Jingo Bang and the hammer Mjölnir occupied all his time for 100 years apiece. He spent almost a millennium collecting the materials for Father's exceptional spear, Gungnir, then another century and a half forging it.

When the watoto were still new and few, Father and Pratha forbade him from giving them weapons of any kind, as well as from teaching them metalsmithing. Long after Arges completed his apprenticeship with Pratha, all of that changed.

During the First Holocaust, when the watoto were in danger of complete annihilation, Father decided they should be permitted to protect themselves against their Firstborn aggressors, the Asura, and their armies of fiendish followers. At his behest, the manufacture of weapons and armor became not only Arges's assigned duty but also his *raison d'être*. He made swords, spears, axes, hatchets, pikes, hammers, clubs and other weapons of more exotic and mysterious natures. He crafted helmets, shields, gauntlets, breastplates, tassets and grieves of every manner known to man today, and many a manner more.

"Mortal" weapons, those capable of slaying enemy watoto, Arges made and distributed in abundance. "Mighty" weapons, practically indestructible and capable of wounding Firstborn, he made fewer of, and was more judicious in choosing to whom they were given. The truly special weapons, those of the highest power and quality, they called the "Astra." These went only to the most trusted of Firstborn and watoto alike.

Most everything Arges ever made is gone now. A precious few are in Asterion's private vault here in the Lair of the Bull, and a number of others remain in the hands of other Firstborn. Arges also heard Father hid some in secret places long ago. He knows of only a few Mortal weapons and limited articles of jewelry still in the hands of watoto, in private collections or on display in museums. They may think they have some idea of their origin, but they really haven't a clue.

Arges has always been grateful for his time with Pratha. She taught him much more than smithing, having shared some of her epochs upon epochs of accumulated wisdom and experience. She taught him about life, the world, Father, and a few things a male of any origin would be happy to know.

He is well aware she didn't teach him everything she knew. She had secrets and esoteric knowledge she would never share, interests that went far beyond the working of metals, and there were things she could intuit and understand that he never will. Her command of language was far greater than any living being, and her metaphysical understanding of the world and connection to it were unsurpassed by any but Father himself.

The depths of the sciences known to Arges and Pratha are still unfamiliar to watoto to this day – and that's probably for the best. They would not understand. What watoto believe they comprehend and can explain they call "science," or more specifically, "physics." What they can't prove or fully grasp but might be possible they call "theoretical physics," or "metaphysics." What they believe to be impossible, absurd, or can't fathom in the slightest, they call "magic."

When Arges and Pratha finally parted ways he returned to his family and showed his Firstborn rhino brothers, Brontes and Steropes, what he could do. They were as captivated as he'd been, so he taught them everything he'd learned. Almost everything. Together the three of them became known as the greatest smiths who ever lived. It was only much later, after his brothers were long dead and Arges lost his eye, that they came to be known as the "cyclops." Due to the short lives, feeble memories and grand imaginations of the watoto, all of his kind have since been described in legend, fable and myth as having only one eye.

Though the name given to The Rhino by his father is Arges, one early clan of watoto took to calling him Hephaestus, a name later appropriated by one of the insolent *petit* gods he'd trained as a smith. The peoples of Asgard called him Völundr, then Dvalinn for a time, and their descendants on this world, Weyland the Smith. The Romans knew him from stories passed down for generations as Vulcan. To the proto-Hungarians he was Hadúr, god of the fires and war, and in cosmologies of Africa he is remembered as Gu, Vodun of iron.

Arges doesn't feel much like those personas these days, nor any of the many other monikers tied to his legendary skills. He rarely descends the elevator down past the level of the Temple of The Bull to his forges in the root of the mountain anymore, and then it's only to repair some household item, make a new cog or shaft for one of The Bull's inventions, or just run a rough hand over a silent anvil, dusty die, or door of a cold furnace.

* * *

"Arges, Big Brother. Come, sit down," Tanuki insists from his seat on the carpet. "Seriously. We have something to show you."

"Something more exciting than a new rug?" Arges grumbles. "Is that possible?"

"Okay, be that way," Tanuki retorts, mock disappointment in his voice. He makes to get up.

"All right," Arges reluctantly agrees, "all right." He plunks down next to Tanuki, facing the chair where Asterion is fidgeting. *Fidgeting?* Arges thinks, *The Bull doesn't fidget. What nonsense is this?*

Tanuki pulls a sheaf of rolled up papers from his shoulder-bag. His voice takes on an officious air. "Through no small effort on my part, with considerable and generous contributions from our brother Asterion and myself, and after meticulous, painstaking due diligence—"

"Oh, just give it to him, Tanuki," Asterion interrupts, setting his cello aside.

"You take all the fun out of it," Tanuki replies. He unrolls the papers and turns them toward Arges. "May I present to you The Hephaestus Fund for the Preservation of Wild Rhinoceros, the most significantly financed and legitimate of its kind on this earth."

Arges squints at the first sheet without taking the papers, reads headings like *Articles of Incorporation* and *By-laws*, terms that mean nothing to him. He opens his mouth to ask what the hell this is all about when they hear it – rising from the monastery below, floating through the softly falling snow, spilling over the edge of the terrace and into the cavernous hall. Arges stiffens, his ears jerking to attention. The hair on Tanuki's back bristles straight.

The gongs are ringing...

* * *

Pang! Bong! Pang! Bong!

There are many combinations in which the round and tubular gongs of the monastery are rung, each for a different purpose. This is the simplest, round gong first, then tube, in alternating succession. It's also of the highest order. Though built not long after The Deluge, the monastery of the Order of The Bull has remained untouched by countless conquests and wars. They've never heard the sounding of this particular alarm before – but they all know what it means. *The walls are breached. Enemy within.*

Tanuki looks to Arges, who's staring at Asterion. The Bull sits stock still with his hands clenching the arms of his chair, eyes closed, ears cocked, alert and listening.

They hear other sounds. Cries of villagers outside the monastery wall. Shouts of monks within. All the while the alarm continues,

Pang! Bong!

Tanuki drops the papers for the rhinoceros charity, their significance forgotten, leaps to his feet and darts for the terrace.

"Tanuki!" Arges grabs for him but only brushes the fur on his bushy tail.

Tanuki reaches the terrace at a sprint, speeding between the center columns, and skids to a stop at the edge. One thousand feet below, the monastery is lit with lamps, as always, but there are also torches scurrying hither and thither.

Tanuki can see well by the moon's cold glow, even though its light is diminished behind a thin veil of cloud and obfuscated by meager snowfall. He can even see his shadow on the light gray stone of the terrace floor – which is obliterated briefly as something flashes before the moon. The chill Tanuki felt when the sun was mysteriously blocked earlier in the day returns tenfold. It's one thing to be cast in shadow in daylight. At night, it's another matter entirely.

He frantically searches the sky as Arges arrives next to him. "Tanuki, what is it? What do you see?" Unfortunately for Arges, he inherited the notoriously poor eyesight of his rhinoceros mother. His sense of smell, however, has no equal. He takes a deep draught of the air, exhales slowly. "Gods," is all he says. Not an identification per se, but a curse, and a prayer.

Tanuki fears, however, The Rhino is not wrong.

"There!" Tanuki points below.

An expansive black shadow slithers fast over the roofs of the monastery buildings.

The Gong Pagoda goes dark beneath it – and explodes. From this distance they see it before they hear the sound. The shadow is gone as quickly as it appeared, leaving projectile fragments of stone, metal, and flesh scattering the grounds. Then comes the stone-shattering *crunch*, twisted ringing whine of metal, screams cut short, and more screaming.

From high on the air comes another sound, much louder than the gongs had ever been. The mountain vibrates with its onslaught. The booming horn of a ship, an air raid siren, the air-horn of a fast-approaching train, a klaxon of doom…

Tanuki, Arges and Asterion have heard it before, but not since the final battle of the Second Holocaust – the war cry of Ziz, The Quetzalcoatlus, primordial terror of the sky.

* * *

Ziz pumps his magnificent wings, driving himself up into the ashen sky above the monastery. His natural pterodactyl mother had been an excellent glider, but he is First-born. He can *fly*, fast and forever.

Ziz had not planned to announce himself. He'd flown hard, even in daylight, cloaked in shadow, though the Master ordered him to travel only by night, and approached the monastery from the opposite side of the mountain. There he concealed himself and waited for darkness to come before descending cautiously. As careful as he was, the parvulus maggots somehow spied his approach and commenced to banging their metal toys. *They are ruing it now.* The Quetzalcoatlus isn't overly concerned. At least it allowed him to express with his cry the blood-boiling exhilaration of impending combat.

Ziz spins, dives, banks to glide along the face of the mountain. The bloodlust of aggression inherent to all higher creatures has taken hold. It exists in the parvuli, primitive as they are, but even more so in Firstborn. The sheer thrill that comes only from fighting for one's life and meting out death. He revels in it. And he knows, deep within his cave, The Bull feels it too.

Patience, Asterion. I'm coming…

12

FLOWERS & FIGS 5

Fi's life is not what she would call exciting. Last night with Zeke and today with Billy, then the two of them together, it's all been a little too much. She looks forward to getting on with her simple routine.

She enters the spacious recreation room on the third floor. Sunshine streams through arched windows that go practically floor to ceiling, all signs of rain she experienced upon her arrival gone from the sky outside. Patients lounge at tables and on couches, mesmerized by flat screen TVs. Some shuffle in circles while others sit quietly in wheelchairs, staring into space. There's a full-size shuffle board that's rarely used, and shelves of books and games line the walls. Half a dozen staff are scattered about, chatting amongst themselves.

Billy must have headed this way while Fi was in the staff office checking her schedule. He's at a table speaking closely to a young nurse. From the look on her face he's telling her about Peter and Dr. Williams. Fi isn't sure she's happy about that. Billy wiggles his fingers at her in "hello," then points surreptitiously past her to the other side of the room.

Fi turns to where there's a glass-walled security booth. Another one. Joe, the Head of Security, sits at a counter inside eating pretzels, watching more surveillance screens. He wears the same kind of headset with microphone the guards have downstairs.

Another guard, Lisa, stands at the open door at the end of the booth, having a conversation with Dr. Williams, the Chief of Medical Staff – and the woman who has supposedly been boinking Peter. She must be what Billy was pointing at. Dr. Williams is probably in her mid-fifties, shoulder-length black hair with a wisp of white over each ear. She was probably gorgeous in her youth but never married, as far as anyone knows. She's one of those brilliant but driven women who gives her whole life to her work, Fi figures. *Honorable, but kind of sad. Will that be me, someday?*

Dr. Williams spots her, "Miss Patterson!" and strides over, waving a file folder.

Fi freezes, stricken by the thought they've found out about her seizure. *Zeke promised! He wouldn't tell, would he? Stay calm. Breathe. Speak.*

"Dr. Williams, good morning."

Dr. Williams reads from the file in her hand, "Fiona Megan Patterson," then looks up at her, "is everything all right here at the hospital?"

Fi isn't sure what to say. Truth is, they treat her extremely well, the patients have the best care she can imagine and she loves working here – so she tells Dr. Williams that.

"Good!" Dr. Williams exclaims, appearing to be relieved – and even more on edge than Fi. "I mean, good. Excellent. Because I have your peer evaluation here, and you have rave reviews. The staff, and the patients who have the wherewithal to respond, simply love you."

"Oh," Fi says tentatively. "Thank you. That's... great."

Dr. Williams glances around and steps a little closer, lowering her voice. "And you are working wonders with Peter. He's a very interesting case, as you know. Does he seem all right to you? Any change in his behavior?"

"Um... No. Not to speak of."

Dr. Williams breathes with obvious relief. "Okay. Well, keep me apprised, will you please?"

"Sure, absolutely."

"Thank you, Fi. For everything you do here."

"You're very welcome. Thank you for the job."

Dr. Williams seems confused. "No... thank *you*, again. You know, this evaluation means a pretty significant increase in your internship stipend."

"Wow, that's great."

Dr. Williams smiles nervously, then straightens and strides out of the room.

Fi watches her go. *That was weird.* A relief, ultimately, but weird. Dr. Williams rarely talks to her, let alone gives her praise. *Maybe Billy's friend Salazar* was *telling the truth.*

Fi surveys the room, then smiles as her eyes settle on a particularly withered old man sitting hunched in a wheelchair in a soft block of light from the windows. A heavy-set woman in brightly flower-patterned scrubs is kneeling in front of him, spooning something to his mouth from a bowl on a standing tray.

The woman sees her approach. "Fi, darlin', thank God." She wipes dribbled oatmeal from the old man's chin, then stands with some effort.

"Hi Mary," Fi greets her. "Is he giving you any trouble?"

"Trouble?" Mary scoffs. "You a comedian now? If he only would. It'd be better than doing absolutely nothin', which is absolutely what he's always doin'. He hasn't eaten since yesterday morning, though. Dr. Williams has had me trying to get him to eat something all day."

"Dr. Williams?"

Mary nods. "Mm-hmm. She seems to have taken a special interest in his welfare lately. But now he's all yours. I'm goin' home to my bathtub." She hands Fi the towel and spoon. "Work your magic." She pulls a napkin out of a pocket in her scrubs and wipes beads of sweat from her brow. "Phew!"

"Hot flashes again?" Fi asks.

Mary fans her face with her hands. "Every time. I don't know if it's the getting up and down or if it's just him. The man gets me positively rosy."

Fi grins. "I think he has that effect on a lot of people."

Mary sees the bag in Fi's hand. "I see you brought the good stuff. You know I tried to give him figs last week. Wouldn't touch 'em. I had three different nurses try 'em on him. Kind of an experiment. Nothin' doin'."

"Really? He wouldn't eat any?" Fi sets the spoon on the tray and moves it out of the way.

"Not a bite. It's you girl. You got the Peter touch."

Fi raises an eyebrow. Mary realizes what she's said and chuckles. "'Peter touch.' Oh my. Well, have fun honey."

"Thanks, Mary. Enjoy the rest of your Sunday."

Mary murmurs "Mm-hmm" and walks away, chuckling and shaking her head. "'Peter touch'... my my..."

Fi kneels in front of Peter's wheelchair. He isn't wearing the standard hospital gown or approved white bathrobe like the rest of the patients. He won't have it. He doesn't fight if you dress him that way, but if you leave him alone for even a minute you'll come back and find him naked. The only clothes he'll keep on are the same ratty nightcap, mangy pink slippers and threadbare baby-blue robe he was found in. Fi studies his face. There's apparently nothing wrong with his sight but his eyes are cloudy and dull, so much so that the color is impossible to discern.

"Peter?" she asks softly. No response. He reacts to things sometimes but doesn't actually *interact*, and never really communicates. Other than flowers and figs, the one thing that usually gets a rise out of him, if you could call it that, is a clear night sky. Billy stopped in to check on him one night a couple of months ago. Peter was lying in his bed, staring out the window and mumbling what Billy thought was gibberish. It took him awhile to realize that Peter might be looking at the stars.

Billy told Fi about it, and when she had her next night shift, which is only one day every other week, she asked for permission to take Peter to the roof. Dr. Williams was hesitant but told her to go for it as long as she put a blanket on him to keep him warm. Fi took a book and a little reading light to keep herself occupied. Peter stared into the sky for hours, mumbling to himself. The words made no sense to her, but every once in awhile she thought she heard something she recognized as an actual name of a star or constellation. Dr. Williams took this as a good sign, so she and the other doctors decided that Fi should take him out whenever she had a night shift and the weather was amenable. Each time, Peter reacts the same way. He becomes tranquil, motionless except for the slow turn of his head and the movement of his lips. After their stints on the roof he's especially calm the rest of the night and the whole next day.

Uncle Edgar has a passing interest in Peter since Fi talks about him a lot, so she told him about the stars. Edgar thought about it for a minute, then said, "Maybe he was once a scientist, an astronomer or astrophysicist."

"That would be cool," she mused.

"Or, perhaps he was a seafaring explorer who navigated by sextant, or a wise king in an ivory tower who gazed at the heavens through a telescope of crystal and gold.

Fi smirked, "Now you're just making fun."

"Am I?" It's hard to tell with Edgar, even after all her years with him, when he's joking and when he's deadly serious. "I'm not so young myself, you know."

"Oh, I know."

Edgar ignored the jab. "What I'm trying to say is, at Peter's advanced age, the night skies might represent for him something that remains constant. While his life has whirled by, everything changing around him at breakneck speed, perhaps the stars are his connection to eternity, timeless and forever. Maybe the heavens are all he has left."

"He's got flowers and figs," Fi added.

"Yes he does, dear," Edgar said with a smile, "and he's got you."

Edgar sometimes surprises her by saying things like that, out of the blue. Profound things. Profound to her, anyway. He has a way of making her feel like she matters. And the truth is, she doesn't feel that way very often.

"Peter, it's Fi," she tries again.

A furrow flits across his brow, but it looks like that's all she's going to get out of him. She was really hoping to see that rare smile today. She studies him for any sign of recognition. His full head of white hair is plastered to his scalp under his cap, as always, and hangs below his shoulders. He's got wide-set eyes beneath a broad brow, high cheekbones and a strong jawline – Fi can tell, even though his chin is mostly hidden by a white beard that scraggles down to the middle of his chest. He has an intelligent face, she thinks, and something about his features makes her believe he had to be quite handsome in his day. Now, he just looks old. Old, sad, and lost.

He can't weigh more than a hundred pounds, though his measurements say he's six feet tall. His shoulders may once have been broad, but now they're drooped and emaciated. His legs and arms are skin and bone, the flesh mottled purple and yellow. His joints are swollen, as is common among the aged, accentuated by his thinness, making his knuckles, knees and elbows especially knobby. His fingernails are yellowed, but not ragged, and of a length that reminds Fi of the nails on Zeke's right hand, which he keeps overly long for playing his guitar, except that Peter's are like that on both hands. He gets terribly irritated if anyone tries to cut them, or his hair, but neither seem to get any longer. He doesn't scratch, pinch or claw like some patients do, and his hair isn't matted, greasy or smelly, so the staff just leaves him be.

The oddest thing about Peter is the way he smells. All the staff who work with him agree that he doesn't smell like an old man. That musty sour odor the elderly often have. All the other patients in the facility smell like that, some more than others, but not Peter. He doesn't even have bad breath. He never perspires visibly, which isn't uncommon for old folks, but he does have a faint scent of sweat, though not the bad kind. Other than that, what else he smells like is where everybody disagrees. Mary says its cucumbers, Clary sage and baby powder. Billy swears it's pumpkin pie and doughnuts. Zeke claims it's patchouli, ylang-ylang and myrrh. Fi has no idea what ylang-ylang and myrrh smell like, but she is not a fan of patchouli. Makes her think of old hippies.

Fi and the others are well aware these scents are all known aphrodisiacs. This information is even in Peter's file, though the doctors (except for Dr. Williams, for some reason), scoff when they read it. To Fi, Peter smells of flowers. Rose, jasmine, lavender – but she also gets a hint of licorice. The truth is, she gets a little flushed herself when Peter's close, sometimes. If she's brutally honest with herself, she can *kind of* understand why Dr. Williams had succumbed – but just kind of. She'd never do anything about it, that's just freaky. Still, she can't help imagining how attractive he must have been in his prime.

"Peter, I brought you something," she says, retrieving the orchids from the bag. She pulls the green paper down from around them, reaches to place them in his hand – and Peter suddenly grabs her by the wrist. The orchids go flying.

Fi gasps, "Peter!" *He's never done anything like this before.*

Slowly, he pulls her forearm to his face. Fi is amazed at the firmness of his grip. For a second she worries that he might bite her. His teeth may be yellowed and stained but he has all of them, and according to the staff dentist they're perfectly healthy. But instead of chomping on her arm, he *sniffs* it.

His cloudy eyes narrow as he inhales deeply. Then he begins to shake. His temples throb, veins pop out on his forehead – and he's gripping her harder.

"Peter, please." As shocked as she is, she tries to keep her voice down so as not to draw attention. She glances around, sees Billy watching them with concern. She shakes her head and holds her free hand out to indicate that everything's okay. Billy rises from his chair and walks toward them anyway.

Now Fi's hand is turning purple. *His eyes*, she notices. *They look almost... red.* "Peter, please," she whispers forcefully. "You're hurting me."

He inhales sharply and releases her. She jerks her arm back, rubs her wrist, but doesn't move away. He mumbles something. It actually sounds like "sorry."

"Peter?"

He rarely looks at anyone. His eyes just kind of wander in your general direction, if you can get his attention at all. But they settle on her now – and there are tears. He speaks below a whisper, but this time there's no mistaking the words. "S-s-sorry. S-so, sorry..."

Fi is astounded. He begins to sob. "No, Peter, it's okay. It's all right." Tears stream down his cheeks.

Billy arrives, the young nurse he was conversing with right behind him. Even a few of the other employees and some patients are looking their way.

"It's okay everybody," Fi reassures, waving them off. Billy doesn't go, but he doesn't come any closer. She collects the spilled flowers into Peter's lap. "Peter, look, I brought figs." She takes his shaking hand, sets a fig on his palm. His sobbing subsides. Without looking at it he lifts it to his face, smells it, and slowly pushes the whole thing in his mouth.

"There, see?" she comforts. "Everything's all right."

Billy touches her on the shoulder. "What the hell? Are you all right?"

"I'm fine. He's fine." She stands, shakes off the shock. "Did you hear that? He spoke. To me. He said he was sorry."

"No he didn't," Billy says, incredulously. Then he sees the look on her face. "Really?"

"Yes, really."

"Wow. Maybe his little tryst last night with Dr. Williams is bringing him out of his shell." Billy thinks for a moment, keeping his eyes on Peter, then says, "Better put it in your notes for the day, I guess."

Fi's distracted, gazing at Peter. "I will, believe me," she answers, then looks to Billy. "The talking part, not the grabbing. Okay?"

Billy grins. He does love secrets. "Okay. I'll be right over here if you need me, Fi-fi." He walks away, taking the young nurse with him.

Fi watches Peter eat another fig. *What could have possibly made him do that? What was he thinking?* She looks at her arm and it occurs to her – this isn't the first time someone's grabbed her today. She smells her wrist, but there's only the trace of soap she used to wash it earlier.

Peter's now calm as can be, holding the orchids against his cheek, fig seeds spilling into his chin whiskers as he chews away.

* * *

In reclaiming the old YMCA, the hospital completely renovated the Olympic-size pool in the basement. Now it's only chest deep, sectioned off with buoyed ropes and stainless steel rails. At one end, a lifeguard-slash-medic watches over a small group of the more ambulatory patients who walk in circles in the water, guided by a therapist.

Fi tries not to make too big of a splash as she jumps in at the opposite end. She fingers the controls on the hydraulic lift at the edge. Peter, in swimsuit and life vest, sits strapped in a cushioned chair, which swivels gently out over the water then lowers until he's in up to his belly. Fi unstraps him and gently slides him into her arms. Some of the patients hate the chair and need to be carried in, but Peter doesn't mind. Or he hates it. There's really no way to tell.

She places his arms over a foam floating device then walks him back and forth across the pool a dozen times, encouraging him to use his legs as much as possible. Any of the other patients would be moaning and exhausted but Fi is breathing harder than he is.

She urges him back to the lift. Keeping one hand on his arm, she adjusts the seat straps then turns to find him with his head tilted back, looking up. She follows his eyes. All she sees are banks of bright, low-glare luminaires attached to the concrete ceiling.

"What do you see up there?" she asks.

Peter stands straight up, supporting himself with his hands on the floaty.

"Peter?"

He suddenly stiffens, slipping out of her grasp, and topples backward with a splash.

"Shit," Fi exclaims, shoving the floaty out of the way and scrambling to him.

Thanks to his life vest he only goes under for a second before she grabs him up and holds him in her arms. He sputters but seems unharmed. Fi glances at the lifeguard, who hasn't noticed. *Thank God.*

"Peter, what has gotten into you today?"

He starts to giggle.

"What the...?"

He splashes in the water, still gazing at the ceiling. Then the light that falls on him dims, a night shroud rippling with pink, purple and green. Fi looks up again and blinks forcibly at what she sees.

A stormy night sky with pulsing auroras of color. Shooting stars streak by. Lava flows from a volcano erupting in the distance, throwing up steam as it pours into the sea. Fi clenches with fear – she's having a seizure. Right here in the pool, with Peter. *I should never have come to work today. I should have stayed home. Peter!* Stricken with fear, she looks back down.

In her arms, on his back in reddish waves, is a frolicking baby boy. His eyes twinkle and swirl from sky blue to stormy gray, then golden brown and emerald green. He looks at her and smiles.

Fi squeezes her eyes shut, shakes her head vigorously.

When she opens them she's still standing in the pool, and lying in her arms is just Peter, the old man, his eyes only cloudy gray.

Everything is fine. No seizure. No convulsions. She's incredibly relieved. *But how is this possible?*

Peter ceases to splash and giggle, though he still stares at the ceiling, as if he can see right through it.

* * *

The whole incident at the pool felt more like déjà vu than a hallucination. Fi *knows* she's seen that baby before, those shooting stars, that red ocean. She just can't place it.

Then it hits her. *It's from a dream. A recurring one.* She had it during her seizure last night, then dreamed it again later. She grabs her head, rubs her temples. *But it's just a dream!* She's got this inexplicable feeling, though, that it's not *her* dream. And what just happened at the pool, with Peter? That was no dream, and she definitely didn't have an episode.

I am going crazy. She's always considered herself a neurotic mess, on the edge of losing it altogether most of the time. A "basket case," she used to say, but her uncle corrected her in his Edgarian way. According to him – and she's never been able to prove him wrong – the term doesn't come from asylums having inmates weave baskets for therapy, as many people believe. It originated with World War II military jargon for a soldier so badly wounded that he had to be carried around in a basket. That didn't make her feel any better, of course.

"Ahh," she shouts, jumping up from the toilet in one of the stalls in the women's restroom. She wasn't relieving herself, but after what happened in the pool with Peter she really didn't want to run into Billy or Zeke or anyone else, so she spent her break hiding here.

She lurches out of the stall, hunches over the sink – and notices a woman janitor near the door with a mop, giving her a curious look.

"Uh..." Fi says. "Hi."

The woman backs out without a word.

Fi splashes water on her face and rubs her eyes. She's tired and she remembered a dream about a baby, that's all. It's been a stressful couple of days. She's almost 18, dreaming about babies, even daydreaming, can't be *that* out of the ordinary. She has absolutely no interest in actually *having* a baby, not *now*, but dreams are dreams and you've got no control over them. Still, that's all they are. *It's why they call them "dreams" and not "realities."*

She aggressively dries her hands with a paper towel, whips it into the trash. Time for music hour. With Zeke. *Great.*

* * *

Peter's wheelchair squeaks softly as Fi pushes him down the third floor residence hall toward the recreation room. She'd put him down for a nap after their adventure in the pool. He didn't sleep, she doesn't think. Rarely does, apparently. Billy says he closes his eyes on occasion but not for very long. But Peter hasn't made any further trouble, either. *Thank God.*

They enter the rec room at the opposite end from the security booth. There are fewer patients than earlier and the light from the high windows is more diffuse due to clouds rolling in again. She aims Peter toward a dozen or so chairs arranged in an arc in the center of the room where staff members are getting other patients into place.

Seated at the open end of the arc, Zeke plucks strings and adjusts tuning keys on his guitar. He looks up at Fi as she pushes Peter's wheelchair to a stop nearest his right. They exchange uncomfortable "hellos" and she takes an empty seat next to Peter.

When it looks like everyone's ready, Zeke says "Hello everybody. What would we like to start with?"

Fi shoots him a look. He knows very well that none of them can answer.

"Apple pie!" shouts an old man with an I.V. in his arm and an oxygen breather in his nose. Zeke glances at Fi as if to say, *See?*

Fi frowns. *They can't answer in a way that makes any sense, that is.*

"Okay, by popular demand," Zeke announces, "we'll begin with a little ditty called the 'Opus 15 Sonata' by Mauro Giuliani, also known, apparently, as 'Apple Pie.'" He launches into the bright, quick tune.

Fi can feel the immediate positive affect on the patients, and the staff as well, including herself. Though she's heard him perform this song before, she is always moved and impressed. It's got to be a particularly difficult piece to play, not only by the sound of it, but also because of the way Zeke concentrates, eyes closed, head down and bobbing with the tempo.

Lisa props open the security booth door and leans against the frame, listening to the music. The old man with the I.V. hoots and smacks his knees in what he thinks is in time with the music. It isn't. An old woman with silver hair that falls almost to the floor behind her chair pets the flowered throw pillow she never lets go of and sways her head from side to side.

Fi notices that Peter, however, is frowning uncharacteristically, tight and exaggerated, and his eyes are blinking erratically. Zeke sees it too and looks questioningly at Fi, who shrugs. Zeke plays more slowly, finds a good place to end the song. Mr. Apple Pie claps, as do the staff.

"For Peter," says Zeke, and begins a soothing familiar tune.

Peter's expression relaxes and he closes his eyes. This song calms him better than any other, every time. Fi smiles, then catches Zeke watching her, smiling as well.

"Merry Christmas!" Apple Pie shouts.

The song Zeke plays is "Greensleeves." Uncle Edgar's voice pops into Fi's head. "That was not originally a Christmas ballad, you know. The *historians*," (Edgar always refers to experts of any sort with an air of disdain) "cannot definitively identify who wrote the original tune." He went on, as he does, to explain that it was registered in England by as many as half a dozen different composers in the years 1580 and 1581, each with slightly different lyrics about a salacious lady who wore a gown with green sleeves, and it is sometimes attributed to King Henry the VIII. Edgar scoffed when he told her that, spouting, "Preposterous. Henry couldn't carry a tune in a bucket," as if he actually knew him. "And the song is much older than *that*. Henry wasn't born until the year of our Lord 1491, for crying out loud." As Edgar tells it, the melody was originally used by traveling minstrels to aid in the memorization of news from across the lands, first in Italy, then in Great Britain. It didn't become associated with Christmas and New Years until the late 1600s, and the "What Child is This?" version wasn't composed until 1865, by William Chatterton Dix.

Fi shared this information with Zeke, who found it far more interesting than she did. She doesn't know why she remembers some of the stuff Edgar tells her. Sometimes she wishes she didn't.

Peter sits completely still in his wheelchair – except his eyes suddenly pop open.

* * *

A buzzing sound lifts Stan's gaze from his latest Sudoku. On the monitor in front of him a group of men can be seen standing on the front steps. Stan taps the screen, enlarging the image.

In the center of the group, closest to the wide angle lens of the camera, a man with dark combed back hair looks up at him with deep black eyes, the tall collar of his black leather trench coat turned up well above his ears.

Stan touches a speaker icon on the screen. "May I help you?"

"It is visiting hours," the man queries, "is it not?"

"Yes it is, sir," Stan replies.

Shane leans over Stan's shoulder for a closer look at the group. On either side of the high-collared man are pale young men in designer shirts and jeans, each of them holding an umbrella, though it isn't raining. Behind them are two big guys with identical spiky black hair, long black fur coats, and sunglasses. Farther back are a couple of fellows with beards, glancing around anxiously.

Shane nods to Stan, taps the nightstick and mace on his belt. Stan says, "Come on in, sir," and presses a button to release the front door lock.

* * *

In the recreation room on the third floor, Peter gasps quietly, unnoticed by Fi, and his eyes go even wider.

Zeke continues to play "Greensleeves," picking up the pace and adding some additional flair.

Fi smirks, watching his fingers move deftly over the frets. *Now he's just showing off.*

* * *

The group of men file down the entry hall that leads from the front door. When the outside door has closed completely, Stan hits the release for the door to the lobby.

* * *

Sarah sits at her counter in the combined reception area/waiting room on the second floor, filling out paperwork. Behind her, Bob watches his surveillance screens, headset hanging around his neck, feet up on the control panel counter, fingers intertwined over his ample belly. He can see the lobby downstairs and Stan in the security booth, but his attention is on the group of men in the entry hall.

"Look at this bunch," he says to Sarah.

An ample woman herself, Sarah groans as she leans back to check out the screen. "Well, well. We have visitors." She looks more closely. "Who on earth dressed *them* this morning?"

Bob chuckles. "Somebody oughtta smack their mamas."

* * *

In the security booth in the recreation room, Joe catches the activity in the lobby on one of his monitors. He adjusts his headset and enlarges the view.

* * *

The men enter the lobby, the guard booth to their left. Shane stands at the far end of the room, near the security door that leads to the rest of the hospital. He crosses his arms and nods to the high-collared man, who smiles back. A friendly smile, but one that does not reach his eyes.

Stan hits a switch for two-way communication as the high-collared man steps to the window. "Welcome to St. Augustine's, sir. Name, please?"

"Pardon?," the high-collared man replies. "My name, or the name of the person I'm here to see?"

"Yours, sir."

"You can call me Kleron."

"Thank you, Mr. Kleron."

There's a snigger from the group, which remains clustered at the door. Kleron shoots a look that knocks the grin off one of the pale young men. He turns back to Stan, his mirthless smile returning. "Just Kleron, thank you."

"Yes sir, whatever you like. And who are you here to see?"

Kleron's black eyes glint with his insincere grin. "I believe he's calling himself *Peter*."

13

ORDER OF THE BULL 5

Tanuki and Arges leap back from the edge, buffeted by wind as the monstrous form of Ziz swoops past the terrace.

Arges spins. "Asterion!"

The Bull remains in his chair, eyes closed, appearing for all the world to be asleep. Sitting there, fingers curled over the ends of the square arms of the chair, he looks just like the statue in the temple below. A quake runs through his body. The arms of the chair crack, stone crushing in his hands. His eyes snap open, the chestnut-brown now burning red.

He bolts to his feet. "To arms, brothers!" He strides toward the back hall, heading for their private armory.

Arges places a hand firmly on Tanuki's shoulder and ushers him inside. "Come, Tanuki. You must go. Now."

"Arges—" Tanuki's reply is cut short by a booming concussion that shakes the hall. Arges doesn't stop, but angles to the right, toward the nearest hearth.

Another *boom*, accompanied by a loud *crack*. The chamber shakes. Arges spins into a crouch, shielding Tanuki from the debris that plumes from the collapsing back hall.

How could he know?, Asterion asks himself as he eyes the tumbled stone. Access to the elevator, their private chambers and the armory is gone. He and The Rhino could dig it out, but there isn't time. They will have none of the formidable weapons crafted by Arges. *So be it*, The Bull resolves. *Hoof and horn have always served me well.*

Arges looks Tanuki over for injuries. He's unharmed but shaken, as much by the atypical attentiveness of The Rhino as the collapse of the hall.

"Arges, I'm fine," he insists.

Arges grunts and drags him to the hearth, pounds once on the keystone of its arch. The keystone recedes and the back of the hearth slides upward. Tanuki knows about this secret passage, one of many, but—

"Go to the safe room," Arges tells him, "but do not stay. Retrieve your pack. Take the—"

A loud *whoosh* and heavy *thump*. A gust of wind pummels them, smelling of snake – heavy musk and cat piss. Tanuki turns slowly, not wanting to look but compelled to.

Ziz's wings flap deliberately as he settles on the lip of the terrace, stirring the air throughout the hall. His fifty foot wingspan nearly blocks the opening. He stoops, folding his wings in half where three-fingered talons protrude from the upper wing bones, the outer length folding up along the back of each arm. He curves his snakelike neck, positioning himself to see in. Tanuki estimates the length of his head at eight feet, not including the crimson crest bone on top of his skull, and over six feet of it is beak – a pointed, pile-driving spear, his most fearsome weapon.

Ziz peers between the columns with a dinner-plate-sized yellow eye, opens his beak but a crack, his mouth lined above and below with curved piercing teeth. Though he has no lips and his mouth does not move, he emits a single word, his voice the sound of gas escaping a bog.

"A-s-s-s-t-e-e-e-r-r-r-i-i-i-o-o-o-n-n-n-n..."

The Bull snorts, glaring. "Ziz! Foul dragon. What is your purpose here?"

Ziz doesn't blink, but the round pupil slowly contracts. "D-e-e-e-a-a-a-th-th-th-th-th-th."

"Then you shall have it." Asterion replies.

Turning his eye on Arges, Ziz utters another name, "X-e-c-o-t-c-o-v-a-ch."

Something leaps from his back, strides to just inside the pillars. Tanuki's nose wrinkles at the vulgar odor of wet fowl. The creature's orange eyes scan the hall, lingering only a moment on Asterion before locking on Arges.

The Rhino's whole body tenses. He spits the loathsome name from his lips. "*Xeco.*"

Tanuki inhales sharply. *The Terror Bird.*

Xeco was born in a South American region now called Chile. His mother was a giant predatory flightless bird, one of what the watoto have named *Kelenken guillermoi* of the *Phorusrhacidae* family. He stands over nine feet tall, with a long craning neck, legs of an ostrich but stouter, and clawed gripping feet. His wings are little more than stunted arms, like those of a Tyrannosaurus or Velociraptor, but with five clawed fingers on each hand instead of three. His head and beak together are a massive hatchet-hammer designed for one purpose, chopping and rending the bodies of his prey. Unlike the eyes of Ziz, which are on the sides of his head, The Terror Bird's face forward, peering over the anvil of a beak that's almost two feet long, with a wicked hook like that of an eagle. Except for his arms and legs he's covered in filthy yellow feathers with a crest of orange on the crown of his head.

From the Yucatan peninsula down through Patagonia in South America, early watoto knew and feared him as Xecotcovach, but also Tecumbalam, the "Face-Gouger," a bird-beast who, according to Mayan mythology, tore out the eyes of the Tsabol, the Mayan name for the "first men." The myth is not entirely inaccurate, and in a battle during the Second Holocaust, it had been Xeco who plucked the right eye from Arges.

That Ziz and Xeco are here together is a terrible thing, but not a great surprise. They've been partners in crime for epochs. What has Tanuki more disturbed is that there has been no news of either of them for thousands of years. All good Firstborn, and many not so good, had hoped they were dead and gone forever.

Xeco shakes his head and flaps his arms to shed the wet of the snow. He leers at Arges, orange eyes gleaming, and opens his beak. In broken English, the words come croaking, as if from a monstrous parrot, "Hel-lo He-phae-stus. Pol-ly want... an *eyeball.*"

Arges snorts, shaking with rage – but even though the battle fury is upon him and he's faced with his arch nemesis, he turns his attention back to Tanuki. Taking him by the shoulders, he says, "Follow the tunnel. *Down*, not up. Go to the northern sea. Get away. Tell others."

Tanuki searches his mind, comes up blank. "Tell who?" They haven't spoken to any other Firstborn in centuries.

Asterion huffs with force and crouches forward, one hand on the ground like a football player readying for the snap. He swings his head and horns in broad swipes, paws the ground with his free hand, finger-hooves gouging the stone floor.

Arges shouts, "Asterion. Are you insane?"

"Aster, no," Tanuki cries.

Asterion knows his chances of defeating Ziz are slim. The beast's advantages are many. Size, obviously, and strength, which comes with his great age. His reach of wing and neck, and that pike of a beak. *But I am The Bull*, he reassures himself. *Ziz is a stupid, vicious monster. The limited space of the hall can work to my advantage. If I can draw him in. If I can get close, inside his striking range, and stay there...* He turns the strategy over in his mind. Without an Astra weapon, the best he can hope for is to injure Ziz enough to make him go away. He has to try. *And if it happens that I am vanquished, I will be remembered well. Ziz will recall the pain of this day for the rest of his miserable life, and when he passes, when that day finally comes, all will rejoice.*

Asterion heaves back, then thrusts his massive head forward, releasing a mighty bull's bellow.

In reply, Ziz plunges his elongated head and neck between the pillars, slamming his shoulders into them. They crack and groan, chunks split off near the ceiling and crash to the floor. The horrible cry heard from the sky shreds the air of the hall.

Arges shouts to Tanuki, "Find him, if you can. Tell him what has happened here. I love you, Little Brother."

Tanuki can't believe this is happening, and certainly not the last words of his Big Brother. "I..."

Xeco, The Terror Bird, postures, arms out. Lowering his head, he opens his monstrous beak and lets out a deafening *Screeeeeeeeeeeee!*

Arges shouts louder, "Go brother, go. The fate of us all lies with you."

With a shove from Arges, Tanuki springs through the fire. He turns for one last look, then runs off down the tunnel as fast as his stubby legs can carry him.

For a moment Arges stares at the flames, thinking of all his magnificent furnaces, in this world, in Asgard. Beautiful forges, scorching and steaming with molten metals and quenching pools, where he wrought stunning and deadly things. He remembers his mentor, The Prathamaja Nandana, and the songs of his beloved sea-nymph, Galatea. He recalls all the families he has had, and lost.

He pounds the keystone again. The back wall of the hearth moves downward. *My family is here now. All the family I have.* The passageway door *thumps* to a close. He smashes his fist down on the keystone, crumbling the top of the hearth.

The Rhino turns toward his enemies, drops to a crouch, his single eye burning red. *If it is within my power, I will not let them come to harm.*

The Terror Bird bears down upon him, coming fast. His horrendous beak opens in another ear-splitting *Screeeeeeeeeeeee!*

Arges pounds forward on all fours.

* * *

Tanuki reaches the safe room of the Lair of the Bull, a stone cell replete with shelves of provisions, sleeping benches and a round steel door like the vault of a bank. They've never had need of it, but The Bull insists they replenish supplies once a month. Each of them has a duffel bag in case the day should come that escape became necessary. Asterion has been more attentive about this in the last half century. The watoto are everywhere and their technology advancing at a frightening rate. Tanuki knows The Bull has feared they'd soon have to abandon their home. Now that day has come. *But this isn't how it's supposed to happen. Not like this!*

Tanuki frantically checks his bag, but of course everything's there. He lifts his satellite telephone but has no one to call. The Turkish authorities and his Japanese contacts would be useless. Tanuki pauses, trying to think, but thinking is useless as well. He shoves the phone back into the duffel bag, snatches up a flashlight and spare staff, and dashes from the room.

* * *

Arges and Xeco barrel toward each other in the great stone hall. Asterion launches into a sprint, straight at Ziz, faster than any creature his size should be able to move. The hooves of his toes chip the floor with each step.

He suddenly alters his course to intercept Xeco before he can reach Arges, sweeping low with his horns and arms at the Terror Bird's legs – but Xeco is too fast. He leaps into the air, gnarled arms held out for balance, clearing both the grasping Bull and the charging Rhino.

Arges tries to halt himself but gains little purchase on the polished floor. He scrabbles desperately, skidding directly toward Ziz, who rears up and strikes. Arges is yanked out of the way just as Ziz's beak pounds the floor, sending stone fragments flying.

Asterion pulls Arges to his feet, back and away from the enraged Quetzalcoatlus. Ziz shrieks, pounds the pillars again with his shoulders. Xeco rounds Arges and Asterion, moving toward Ziz.

"Is Tanuki away?" Asterion asks.

"Yes."

"Good, this is no place for the pup."

Xeco stands guard while Ziz hunkers down, tucks his wings in front of him and squeezes between the pillars into the hall. He unfolds himself, dull scaly skin, mottled gray with crimson detailing along the bones of his wings. His head rises to nearly sixteen feet above the floor.

Arges groans, "Great."

"No," says Asterion. "It worked, he's inside."

"That was a ploy?"

"Of course."

"Now what?"

"We inflict as much damage as possible," Asterion replies. "If necessary...," he nods almost imperceptibly toward the terrace, "we jump."

"As good a plan as any." Arges claps Asterion on the shoulder. "For life."

Asterion returns the gesture. "For Father."

Ziz raises his wings, cries his klaxon cry. Xeco, circling back around in an attempt to force them toward Ziz, releases another *Screeeeeeeeeeeee!*

Aster and Arges crouch, roar together, and charge.

* * *

Tanuki bounds down the stairs of the dark tunnel, the beam of his flashlight bouncing over glistening wet stone. His mind races. *Arges is older than Xeco, heavier and stronger – but the Terror Bird is so very fast.* Sleipnir, the horse-monster of Asgard, is amazingly fleet of hoof, but it has been speculated that only Sekhmet may be capable of outrunning Xeco. *And Xeco has that fireman's axe of a beak and those talons – the talons that tore the eye from The Rhino.* Tanuki was there. The popping and ripping, the howl of agony, the blood and black ooze. A shiver shoots along his spine. *Run, Tanuki, just keep running. Breathe, and run.*

* * *

Ziz advances on Asterion, snapping with his beak, swiping with his wings. The Bull jumps, ducks and rolls, avoiding the blows. Chunks of rock from shattered shelves, tables and chairs fly everywhere.

Arges and Xeco circle close to one another, The Rhino trying his best to grab hold of The Terror Bird, to land a fist, to get his arms around him. Xeco escapes every grasp and blow.

Gods, he's fast, Arges thinks, *but if I can just get a hand on his filthy neck it will be over.* But Xeco knows it too, and Arges has to protect his eye to keep Xeco from his intended prize.

Asterion grabs the tip of Ziz's wing but it's snatched from his grasp. He leaps, trying to get close to his opponent's body, but is blocked by a wing and tossed to crash into the wall, smashing a lamp. The flame is snuffed out. Gas flows from the torn fixture, invisible and deadly.

Xeco escapes a punch thrown by The Rhino and counters with a strike of his foot. The fearsome claws make no mark on The Rhino's thick hide, but Arges is pushed back, off balance. Xeco lunges, the hook of his beak landing solidly on Arges's shoulder. It glances off without leaving as much as a scratch. Xeco leaps back, screeching in frustration.

* * *

Tanuki continues down the tunnel stairs. *Asterion is of mighty stock and a brilliant combatant.* He's gone head to head with older Firstborn before, and, against all odds, been victorious. *But he's only three.* Xeco is older, and Ziz is *old*, even for a Firstborn, one of the True Ancients, the handful of Firstborn who survived the Cataclysm. Most all the True Ancients were assumed to be long gone. *But if Ziz still lives...* Tanuki shudders, pushes the thought from his mind, concentrates on the dark steps beneath him.

* * *

Struggling to rise, Asterion hears Arges shout a warning, but before he can turn The Terror Bird is upon him, opening an ugly gash in his back with his cruel beak. Xeco rears to strike again but abandons the attack as Arges closes in.

Suddenly Ziz has hold of Arges's shoulder and neck, his wing claws crunching deep. Arges grunts, beats at the wingbone with a fist, tries to push it away with his other hand, but to no avail. The claws only tear his flesh even more. Ziz slashes The Rhino's chest with his other claw, opening a gruesome triple wound. Then Asterion's hands are on the wingbone. With a great ripping sound, one of his horns pierces the leathery membrane.

Ziz cries out and releases Arges, who stumbles back, spinning, just in time to see Xeco striking at Asterion. Arges uses the momentum of his turn and swings a roundhouse at The Terror Bird's beak. This one connects. Xeco hits the ground hard, his head bouncing off the floor. Arges bounds toward him, but Xeco is already flopping away.

Ziz yanks his wing from Asterion's grip and slams it back into him just as quickly, sending him sprawling across the floor, blood from his back smearing the light-colored stone.

* * *

Tanuki stops short on a landing, where one set of steps proceeds downward through the mountains to the north while another goes up to the right.

Aster, Arges, my brothers.

Asterion is wise. He will see reason. He and Arges will come to their senses, submit and be spared. But Tanuki knows how deep The Rhino's hatred of The Terror Bird runs, and he saw the look in the eyes of The Bull, as if Aster knew what Tanuki fears to consider. *There will be no sparing of lives today.*

He looks back the way he came, then down the stairs, then up. *What have I done?*

He sheds his duffel bag and bounds forward – and upward.

* * *

The top of the curving stairs dead-ends into solid stone. Tanuki searches with flashlight and fingertips for a crack in the wall, finds it and pulls. The hidden latch comes outward with a *clunk*. A portion of the wall grinds to the side. Weak moonlight, fresh air and snow rush in. He stumbles onto a ledge, hears grunts and crashes of battle in the distance. *Arges and Asterion still live!*

At a steep angle below, not a hundred feet away, is the terrace outside their home. There's a sound like a rasping foghorn and Ziz comes backing out of the hall, shoving awkwardly between the pillars. He unfurls to his full height and howls at the cavern entrance.

Asterion emerges, gashed and bleeding, but undaunted. Tanuki hears a screech from the Terror Bird inside the hall, cut short by a colossal *whump.*

Arges staggers onto the terrace, blood flowing from his wounds. Ziz attacks with a wing. Asterion ducks, but Arges takes the brunt of the blow. He slams into a pillar with such force that it snaps. Asterion rushes to his aid – but not fast enough – Ziz skewers Arges through the stomach with his beak, pinning him to the stone.

Tanuki wails silently, *Arges!*

Asterion tackles Ziz at the beak, tugging it from Arges's body. Ziz whips his head, flinging The Bull away. Asterion hits the terrace, rolls, and drops over the edge, causing Tanuki to gasp in fright.

But Asterion catches the lip of the terrace with one hand. With a tug he's back up, facing his enemy. Ziz swipes with his wing, aiming high this time. Asterion ducks the blow, bellows and springs with all his might, angling his head to drive a horn into the heart of the beast. His aim and timing are perfect, but his horn snaps on impact and dangles from Ziz's hide, having barely pierced the skin.

Tanuki stifles a cry. *A horn of The Bull. Broken!*

Staggered by the blow, Ziz trips backward off the edge, but flaps his wings and rises in the air with Asterion clinging to his neck. Ziz reaches up with one leg, grasps Asterion in a gigantic claw and wrenches him off. With the other foot, he snatches the broken horn from his chest, then yowls and stabs it deep into Asterion's shoulder at the neck. Asterion roars.

Whether he breaks Ziz's grasp or Ziz lets go, Tanuki can't tell, but Asterion falls, plummeting toward the monastery a thousand feet below. Ziz shrieks in triumph and plunges after him. From this angle, Tanuki can't see the ground below the terrace, or what happens there. He can only imagine the worst.

What he can see is Arges struggling to get up, but unable to, bleeding profusely from the hole in his gut, his preternatural strength waning fast with the loss of his Firstborn blood. Tanuki makes up his mind to run back, to return to Arges, regardless of his own safety, but Xeco stalks onto the terrace and he freezes. Xeco shakes his head violently as if to clear it, then saunters toward Arges with infuriating self-assurance.

The snow continues to fall, flakes melting to tiny droplets on Arges's torn body, disappearing in his steaming breath, merging with his flowing blood. Xeco pounces, grasping with claws that now dig into weakened flesh. He raises his beak.

Tanuki can't bear it. "No, Xeco! Stop!"

The Terror Bird spies him and laughs, a grating, unearthly chortle. He turns back to Arges.

Tanuki shouts, "Nooo!"

Xeco strikes, again and again, chopping mercilessly at Arges's neck. The Rhino's body convulses with every blow, and then he is still. The Terror Bird wrenches back and forth until the head comes free.

Tanuki falls to his knees, "No..."

Xeco clutches the head with one foot, a toe in Arges's silent mouth, and digs into

The Rhino's remaining eye with a twisted clawed hand. The eye comes loose with a sucking *pop*. He tosses it to his other hand, looks up at Tanuki for a long moment, then throws his prize into the air and snatches it with his beak. He swallows it in one gulp and watches – watches Tanuki push himself up on shaking legs, grasping at the stone wall for balance, and totter into the mountain.

Xeco laughs and laughs, the ghastly hollow sound echoing in the cold mountain air.

FLOWERS & FIGS 6

There's a *beep* from a monitor on Sarah's desk, where Stan looks back at her from the booth in the lobby downstairs.

"We've got someone here to see Peter," he reports. "Is he available?"

"Did you say 'Peter'?" she asks dubiously.

"Yes ma'am."

Sarah checks a schedule on her computer. "He's in music hour. Just started. Can they wait?"

* * *

In the lobby, Kleron heard Sarah through the security booth speaker. "Music hour?" he says. "Wonderful! The old man has always been fond of music." He turns to his companions, drumming his black-gloved fingers on the counter, then back to Stan. "We quite enjoy a good tune ourselves. Perhaps we could join him?"

* * *

Bob pivots the microphone stem of his headset below his chin and asks Sarah, "Has anybody ever come to see Peter?"

"Nope," she responds, "and we've got no contact information or next of kin on file for him either. It's a damn shame they haven't come to see him before now, if you ask me." She waves down a nurse who's walking past. "Emily, are you going back to the offices?"

"Yeah, whatcha need?"

"Can you tell Dr. Williams that someone's here to see Peter?"

"Sure," Emily replies, then enters a door just past Sarah's counter.

Sarah swivels to face Bob. "Maybe they'll know something about Peter's medical history, or at least be able to give us his last name."

* * *

In the third floor security booth, Joe "hmphs" to himself, watching the screen. He pivots to look out to where Zeke still plays for the old folks. "Hey Lisa," he calls to the guard at the door. "Get Fi, will ya?"

Out in the rec room, Fi notices Peter's hands trembling and his head nodding erratically, like an old man's does sometimes, but cocked as if he's listening to something other than the music.

* * *

"I just need you to fill these out," Stan informs Kleron, sliding a clipboard through a slot below the glass. "Are you family?"

The man smiles broadly, though his eyes remain lifeless. "Why, yes. Very much so."

"And the rest of your group?"

"They are, in fact." He waves a hand at the two dark-haired pale young men in designer shirts. "These are my children's children, Derek and Tod." Derek and Tod nod in greeting.

"Over there are their cousins," Kleron gestures toward the two bearded fellows, who seem uncomfortable with being pointed out. They wear buttoned vests over long sleeved shirts of colored patterns, and though their beards meet their sideburns, their cheeks are shaved and they have no mustaches. "Their names are Henri and Didier." The two men shuffle and fret, then turn away and face the wall.

Kleron raises an eyebrow to Stan. "Don't mind them. They're French, you know. Traveled quite a distance for this visit. Could be the jet lag."

Kleron spreads his arms dramatically to introduce the tall men in fur coats. "And, of course, my half-brothers." The men turn their heads in unison to eye Stan through their sunglasses. They're the same height, at least 6' 6", and though they look like twins, one of them has the right sleeve of his coat removed and sewn over to compensate for a missing arm.

Kleron points at the one with both arms. "This is Wepwawet." Wepwawet removes his sunglasses to reveal eyes of startling primary blue.

"And his brother, there, is Surma." The one-armed man pushes his sunglasses up onto his head. His eyes are yellow, and not just any yellow, but the color of a bright canary.

* * *

Fi observes Peter with growing concern. It's like he's having a minor fit of some sort. She places a hand on his trembling knee, but he takes no notice.

She's thinking maybe she should get a doctor, when Lisa leans down and whispers, "Joe wants to see you."

"Me?" Fi replies, confused. "Okay." She decides that she shouldn't leave Peter, though, given the way he's acting.

Zeke watches as she pulls Peter's wheelchair back from the group. Billy, who's leaning against the wall behind Zeke, gives her a questioning look. She shrugs, trying to hide her mounting anxiety, and wheels Peter toward the security booth.

* * *

Dr. Williams thanks Emily for informing her about Peter's visitors, but as Emily leaves her office, panic sets in. She pushes herself up from the desk, turns to the mirror above the couch behind her. *It's got to be a coincidence*, she assures her reflection. *No one knows about last night* – but her inner voice is not so confident. It makes no sense, what she did, and she reviles herself for it, but she *just couldn't help it!*

She's felt inexplicably, irresistibly drawn to Peter since he first arrived. *An old man. A patient.* But there's something so intensely sensual about him – his smell, his warmth, his *whole being.* When it became clear the feeling wasn't going to pass, she tried to stay away from him. She couldn't shirk her medical duties entirely, though, she had to tend to him occasionally. She doesn't know why she finally lost control last night, but she did, *completely.* She'd gone into his room to check his chart, and it just *happened.*

She silently repeats, as she has a thousand times today – *It will never happen again.* She fixes her hair, straightens her lab coat and name tag, then goes to her cabinet for Peter's file.

* * *

Stan drags his eyes from the disturbing gaze of Wepwawet and Surma, and clears his throat. "Each of your family members needs to fill out a form as well," he instructs Kleron, sliding more pens through the slot.

"More forms?"

"Yes sir, and I'll need to see IDs."

"IDs, you say?" Kleron considers. "Let's see..."

* * *

Fi leaves Peter just outside the booth and waits in the doorway. Her brain, always over-active and today piqued by the events of the last 24 hours, feels like it's pinging off the inside of her skull in a mad effort to escape. *Do they know what happened in the pool? Is this about Dr. Williams and Peter? Maybe they did find out about my seizure. Is it Uncle Edgar? Has something happened?*

"Hey Fi," Joe says, pointing at the monitor where the lobby is enlarged on the screen. "These guys are here to see Peter."

That's it? But still... "You're kidding."

"Nope. They say they're family."

She steps up next to Joe for a closer look. "Weird."

Joe moves a volume slider on the screen. Now they hear Kleron, as well as see him.

"I have identification, of course," he says to Stan, "for every occasion."

Unnoticed by Fi or anyone else, Peter grips the arms of his chair and inhales sharply.

* * *

Kleron inspects the security booth through the glass, drumming his fingers again, then looks at Shane, who now has his hands on his hips near his mace and nightstick, before turning back to Stan.

"Your dedication to the safety of the patients here is admirable – " he peers at the name on Stan's security badge, "Mr. Stan." Kleron's smile is suddenly gone and his eyes become deathly cold. "But we won't be needing any identification." He leans close to the window, his breath forming crystalline frost on the glass. "And we certainly won't be filling out *any fucking forms.*" His lips curl menacingly and he emits a shrill, clicking squeak.

Shane is just reaching for his nightstick when Surma, the one-armed fur-coated twin, bolts across the room and slams him into the door with a resounding *bang.*

* * *

Bob yelps and topples over backward in his chair. Sarah spins around at the commotion. "What the hell, Bob?"

* * *

Peter jerks in his wheelchair. Fi and Joe gasp, staring wide-eyed at the screen.

On the monitor, Surma catches Shane as he slumps and tosses him away from the door. The two bearded men, Henri and Didier, pounce on him, snarling like crazed animals.

* * *

Stan reaches for the alarm on the security booth counter, lifts the plastic cover that prevents accidental activation – but before he can flip the switch the security glass crumples inward with a booming *crunch*, a hole punched right through it, and Kleron has him by the wrist.

* * *

Fi's hands go to her mouth. Joe gapes at the monitor. They see Kleron make a quick twist of his hand. Stan's arm snaps at the forearm and elbow and his shoulder dislocates. He shrieks.

Kleron yanks him and the entire crackled window out over the counter and tosses them both to the floor.

* * *

In the lobby, Derek, one of the dark-haired pale young men, rushes at Stan, lifts him and slams him into the security booth door – and goes straight for his neck with his teeth.

The other pale young man, Tod, dives over the counter into the booth. He reaches up under the counter, fishes around and rips out a bundle of cables. All the lights on the panel dim and the monitors go to static.

* * *

The screens in Joe's booth remain in operation. "Jesus Christ," he mutters under his breath. He flips the alarm guard and hits the switch on his control panel. Nothing happens. He flicks it back and forth, with the same result. He taps a different section of the monitor. "Station Two!"

Bob can be seen in the reception booth, Sarah trying to help him up from his fallen chair. He shoves the chair out of the way and scoots to the panel on his knees, headset askew in his tousled hair.

"Joe," Bob yells. "What the—!"

"Bob, is your alarm operational?"

Bob fiddles with something below the camera, accompanied by the sound of ineffectual clicks. He shakes his head. "No! What do you—"

Joe taps the lobby screen again, cutting him off. He picks up the handset of a phone on the counter, jabs a few buttons on the receiver, waits... "Dead." He slams it down, turns to Lisa. "Call 9-1-1," he shouts. "Tell 'em we need an ambulance and police, *right now.*"

Lisa rushes out of the security booth, cursing and stabbing a finger at her mobile phone.

Peter stares at the monitors, still gripping his wheelchair just outside the booth, lips trembling.

* * *

Tod bounds back out of the lobby booth. Derek releases Stan's body, allowing it to flop to the floor. Blood drips from his face, the fine white-on-white embroidery of his designer shirt soaked in red. He wipes his mouth on his sleeve.

"Well done, gentlemen," Kleron commends them, placing a hand on Derek's shoulder. He suddenly squeezes and Derek squeals, dropping to his knees. Kleron leans close to his ear. "Even if I am very entertaining, Derek, never, ever, laugh again."

"Yes, *Master!*"

Kleron helps him up by the arm, pats him on the shoulder. "Good boy."

* * *

Joe and Fi watch in horror as Henri and Didier rise to their feet over Shane's mauled carcass. Blood runs down their faces and dribbles from their hands. Gobbets of flesh cling to their beards. They raise their faces to the ceiling, and let loose an unearthly howl.

"I can't get through, no signal," Lisa calls out, hurrying back into the booth, holding up her useless phone. "Nobody else has one either."

Fi pulls her phone out of her pocket and Joe retrieves his. She hits a one-button call. *Uncle Edgar* appears on the screen, then she hears the telltale *beep-beep-beep*...

Joe drops his own useless cell on the counter, glances at the view of the lobby.

The men are just standing there, as if waiting for something. Then they see what. More pale men and bearded men filing into the lobby from the street. At least twenty of them pack the room and more are arriving by the minute.

Joe checks readouts on his computer. "The entry doors are disabled but the interior is locked down. That's reinforced steel, three hinges, double bolted. They won't get through."

Lisa points to a different monitor. "What about them?"

Joe taps a view of one of the stairwells. It enlarges, showing two more pale young men coming down the stairs. Unlike Derek and Tod in the lobby, these two are blond.

"Must've come from the roof deck," Joe remarks. "How the hell did they get up there?" Then he adds in reassurance, "Same kind of doors in the stairwells, all secured."

The pale blond men descend beyond the camera and Joe is about to tap the next lower view of the stairwell when a small figure drops onto the landing, wearing three filthy coats and four pairs of sunglasses. He tosses something down next to him – a body.

"That's John!" observes Lisa in despair.

Joe curses, "Shit."

"That's him," Fi says, pointing at the little homeless man.

"Who?" Joe asks, then remembers the report Stan gave him earlier. "The guy who grabbed you outside?"

"Yeah. He said his name is Max."

Peter stares hard at the monitor from behind them, quaking in his chair. His mouth moves silently, as if trying to say something, trying to remember how to speak, trying to recall what speaking is...

On the screen, Max disappears quick as a flash, outside the view of the camera – but he isn't on the section of the monitor above, which shows a higher view of the stairs, or the one below.

"Where'd he go?" Lisa asks.

Fi, Lisa and Joe all jump as Max's face appears right in front of the camera, which all of them know is placed in a high inaccessible corner of the stairwell. Max moves his head to inspect the camera through different lenses of his multiple pairs of sunglasses – then his face thrusts forward, mouth open, covering the lens. The stairwell monitor goes to static.

Joe rages in frustration, "God dammit!"

* * *

Kleron looks over the group in the lobby. He says something very calmly, in a language that Joe, Fi, and Lisa, who are listening upstairs, have never heard – because it hasn't been spoken in a thousand years – not by human beings.

Wepwawet, the fur-coated twin with both arms, shoves past Henri and Didier to the door where Shane stood guard. Surma steps aside. Wepwawet jams one hand through the wire reinforced glass of the small window, grabs the handle with the other, and wrenches the massive steel door right out of the frame.

The others duck as he swings back around and flings it across the room at one of the security cameras in the corner.

* * *

In reception on the second floor, a section on the lobby monitor erupts in static.

"Fuck!" Bob is still on his knees, hands on the edge of the console. Behind him, Sarah stares at the monitor, one hand on his shoulder, the other to her mouth.

* * *

Joe glares at the screen. "Fuck!"

People are beginning to gather outside the booth. Zeke has stopped playing and come over to stand behind Peter's wheelchair, trying to see the monitors.

Fi jumps as Billy knocks on the booth window. He holds his palms up and mouth's, "What's up?" He must have missed the action on the monitors. Fi shakes her head. He heads for the booth door.

Joe lunges from his chair and goes to the door, arriving before Billy. He spots a young nurse in running shoes, the same one who was talking to Billy earlier. "You, go out the side emergency exit."

She points to herself. "Me?"

"Yes you," Joe commands. "If we're lucky it'll sound the alarm. You have a phone?"

She answers reluctantly, "Yeah."

"See if you can get a signal outside and call the police. If not, find someone who has a phone that works. Flag down a car if you have to. Go!"

She runs to the door at the far end of the room.

"Everyone else, stay calm," he says. "Get these people back to their rooms, now." They just stand there. "Move!"

The staff hustles to their patients – except for Billy, who remains uncharacteristically silent near the door, one hand resting on Peter's shoulder, the other fingering his necklace.

Joe comes striding back into the booth, snatching his keys from his belt. He opens a long panel on the back wall that looks like the cover of a breaker box, presses a series of numbers on a keypad on another door behind it, and tugs it open. It's a gun safe. Lisa steps up next to him.

Joe pulls out a couple of 9mm pistols, hefts them, puts them back, then retrieves an M4 Carbine assault rifle and a Kel-Tec KSG bullpup-style shotgun. He hands the rifle to Lisa, who takes it with hesitation.

"Joe," she says, "Who are those guys? What—"

"Don't know. Don't care," he snaps back, checking the shotgun to make sure it's loaded. "Get your soldier pants on, Corporal. They're hostiles, that's all that matters. We've got men down, no backup in sight, and civilians in danger. You've been here before."

Lisa sets her jaw. "Yes sir." She releases the clip on the assault rifle, checks it, slaps it back into place and actions the bolt.

Joe drags another screen up beside the image of the lobby. In one window they see the group of attackers funneling through the torn open door, on the other, the first of them are already moving past the elevator to the stairs to reception. Joe hits another section of the screen and Bob is there, sweating profusely.

"They're on their way to you, Bob."

"I can see that!"

"Secure that door, right now!"

"Okay, Okay!"

On screen, Bob scrambles to his feet and off camera. Joe turns to Fi. "I want you to take Peter down to the shelter, all right?"

Fi looks at Peter, trembling in his chair. "Why would they want Peter?" She asks the question of herself as much as Joe.

"No idea," Joe answers. "Just get him to the shelter, and don't open it for anybody you don't know, got it?"

Fi nods, "All right."

Joe pats her on the arm and heads for the door. "Billy, go with her."

Billy steps in front of him. "I'm going with you."

"No, you're not."

Billy stands straight, squaring his shoulders. He makes Joe look small. "Yeah, I am."

"Billy, don't," Fi protests. "You didn't see what they—"

"If my people are getting hurt," Billy cuts in, "I'm gonna hurt back. That's how we do it where I come from."

Joe regards Billy's stern expression and massive physique. "Okay, but stay behind us, and if shots are fired, get the hell out."

"Got it." He steps aside for Joe to pass.

Zeke addresses Joe, his voice unsteady but resolute. "I'll go with her."

Joe puts a hand on his shoulder. "You're a good man, Zeke. If I were you I'd run like hell."

Zeke's eyes find Fi and he swallows hard.

Lisa hands Billy her baton. "At least take this."

Billy hefts it. "Thanks."

Fi strides to him and takes him by the arm. "Billy, what are you doing?"

"Hey, remember?" He leans close. "The only thing I like better than suckin—"

"Yes!" she interrupts. "I remember, but—"

"I'll be fine. You just get yourself and your old buddy to the shelter, okay?" He slaps the baton into his palm, smiles his ornery smile, and follows Lisa.

Fi watches through the glass as they round the booth and join Joe. Billy holds the door for Joe and Lisa to enter the hall to the stairwell that leads down to reception. He waggles his fingers at Fi in a wave, and she offers a reluctant wave back. He gives her the thumbs up and enters the hall.

Zeke pushes Peter in next to Fi in the booth. They both watch the hallway door close.

* * *

On the other side of the door, Billy's face goes flat. His buoyant charm is gone. He saw everything on the monitors. All of it.

* * *

Dr. Williams comes down the hall from her office carrying a clipboard and file folder. The door to Sarah's booth bursts open behind her.

"Out of the way!" Bob shoves past, carrying a metal brace and pushes through the door to reception.

Lost in her own thoughts, Dr. Williams catches the door and follows him through. Sarah's standing behind the counter.

"Are they here?" Dr. Williams asks, oblivious. "The people to see Peter?"

Sarah just stares at her.

* * *

Surma and Wepwawet have reached the landing outside of reception. The two pale blond men, Hedwig and Curt, whom were seen on the upper stairway cameras, are there as well. The door from the stairwell hangs broken open behind them.

Kleron joins them from the steps below. He glares at the blond men. "What took you?"

Max creeps through the stairway door, humming a carefree lullaby and dragging the body of John the security guard.

Hedwig jerks a thumb at him. "He stopped for a snack."

"And you?" Kleron asks.

Hedwig shrugs. "He wouldn't share."

Kleron shifts his attention to the little homeless man. "Leave it, Max, will you please? There's plenty where that came from."

Max offers a little bow, says, "As you wish, Master," then tosses the guard back into the stairwell, and grins.

* * *

Fi and Zeke watch the last of the staff and patients leave through the door at the opposite end of the recreation room. Peter shakes in his wheelchair below them.

Fi can't resist turning back to the monitors. She reaches a trembling finger to the screen, raises the volume on two opposite views of the combined reception area and waiting room.

Bob is seen struggling to shove the heavy metal brace into brackets on either side of the door to the landing above the lobby. It finally slides into place and he leans on it in relief.

Bang—the door flies inward, flattening him. Dr. Williams drops her clipboard and her files. Sarah screams.

* * *

On the far side of the hospital, the nurse in running shoes bursts into the alley. She stops, breathing the fresh air, looking to the sky. The clouds are getting darker and it looks like rain.

She checks her phone for a signal, but has none. She runs to the front of the building and sees two white vans and a school bus parked along the street to the right. One looks like a news van, with a satellite dish and extendable microwave antennae on top. There are two men next to it – and one of them is a policeman, in helmet and sunglasses, leaning on his motorcycle.

The nurse sprints toward them. As she approaches, she hears them arguing, but in a language she doesn't recognize. It sounds a little like French but also like German. "Officer," she shouts.

The other man wears blue overalls with a telecommunication worker's tool belt at his waist. He leers at her, blowing smoke from his cigarette. The embroidered patch on his overalls says *Luc*. He has a beard but no mustache.

"Is there a problem, ma'am?" the policeman asks.

"There are men, inside." She points at the building. "We're being attacked!"

"I know," the policeman replies with a smile – a smile that flashes translucent white teeth and needle-sharp fangs.

The nurse screams, but the sliding door of the van whips open, a hand claps over her mouth and she's dragged inside. The door slams shut, followed by sounds of a struggle, then silence.

The policeman grins at his bearded companion. "It was nice of them to send lunch, eh?"

* * *

Sarah cowers below the reception counter as Surma and Wepwawet enter the room. Kleron steps in between them and goes straight to Dr. Williams. Derek and Tod enter as well, followed by the reinforcements from the lobby, who disperse themselves throughout the waiting room. Max, Hedwig and Curt are nowhere to be seen.

Kleron comes very close to Dr. Williams, who's trembling but stands her ground. He stares into her eyes. "Where is he?"

* * *

"Who are they?" Zeke asks, his voice unsteady.

Fi doesn't know what to think, let alone say. "I don't know," she answers, the words barely audible from her dry mouth. "They said they're Peter's family."

"Really?"

She looks down at Peter, his gaze locked on the monitor, mouth hanging open, lips quivering. If only she could ask him. She places her hand on his cap. "Yeah... I need to get him to the shelter." Still, she doesn't move, other than to look with trepidation back to the monitors.

* * *

In reception, Dr. Williams gulps. "What do you want? Who are you?" She starts to back away but Kleron grabs her by the hair and pulls her to him.

His face is only an inch from hers, his mouth slack, their breath mingling. He tilts her head back and slowly moves his face down her neck, his lips brushing her skin, then reaches with his other hand and tears open her lab coat. Her blouse and bra come with it, leaving one breast exposed. He continues moving his face down. She takes a shaky breath, goose-bumps rising on her bared flesh.

Kleron moves back up to the other side of her face. "You stink of him," he breathes.

Dr. Williams stutters, trying to speak.

"Tell me," he hisses. "Where is this person you call Peter?"

* * *

Fi and Zeke watch in fright and fascination.

There's movement on another monitor – a view of Joe, Lisa, and Billy cautiously descending the steps to the waiting room door, the one on this side of the room.

On the views of reception, Wepwawet whips his head to the door, listening. He flashes past Kleron and Dr. Williams without a word.

Fi and Zeke jump at the sound of both Joe and Lisa opening fire from their positions on the stairs.

* * *

The weapons don't even slow Wepwawet down. He bounds up the steps, grabs Joe by the face, splatters his head against the wall and chucks his body over the railing. He reaches for Lisa – but Billy snatches her out of the way and front-kicks Wepwawet in the chest. Wepwawet soars back down the stairs to smash into the wall, cracking concrete with his back.

Billy shoves Lisa behind him and gives her the baton. "Get back upstairs."

"But—"

"*Now*, Lisa." Billy's eyes flash red, actually *flash*. She backs up the steps.

Wepwawet pauses, observing Billy clearly for the first time. A wicked smile creeps over his face. His voice is gruff and deep. "You've cut your hair."

Billy smirks. "Flowing locks are way out of style, shithead. Like fur coats." He points two fingers at his own two eyes. "Still got these, too." His expression becomes oddly reminiscent. "Nobody believes those old stories, anyway."

* * *

Watching the monitors upstairs, Fi and Zeke are dumbfounded.

Fi squints to make sure what she's seeing is real. "Billy?"

* * *

Wepwawet begins to take the steps up. Billy reaches into the V-neck of his scrubs, clenches the pendant of his necklace and jerks it from its cord. He blows into his fist and the pendant *begins to grow*, sprouting a handle as it increases in size.

Wepwawet halts, his smile fading at what he sees in Billy's hand – a single-bladed battle axe of gleaming copper.

Billy's face is severe. "This ain't no jawbone of an ass either, *bitch*."

* * *

Zeke's mouth works in silent incredulity. "Wha... what?"

Fi's normally bouncing brain lays there like a lump, stunned into submission. Peter frets violently, rattling his chair.

* * *

Billy looses a battle cry and launches himself down the stairs. Wepwawet barely escapes the sweep of the axe, which shears through the metal railing with a shower of sparks and explodes cinder blocks to powder.

* * *

Wepwawet comes crashing through the door to the waiting room, gaining the immediate attention of everyone in the room.

Billy steps in through the dusty air, eyes tinged red, the cords of his neck and muscles of his arms tensed for combat.

Dr. Williams, still held by Kleron, blinks at the imposing figure. "Billy?"

Kleron smirks. "I was wondering when you'd show up."

Billy's been wondering how they found Peter, why they've come, and now, how they knew Billy would be here – but none of that matters anymore. "I'm here now, *Kleron*."

"Why don't you save us all a lot of trouble. Take me to him and I'll let the parvuli live."

Billy brandishes his weapon. "How 'bout you get the hell out and I won't have to put this up your ass."

"The Axe of Perun. I doubt even I would enjoy that. Somewhat surprising, I thought it destroyed ages ago."

Billy smirks. "Nope."

"But it's not really an 'Oh no, run for your lives!' kind of surprise, is it?" Kleron remarks. "More like, 'Would you look at that, isn't it interesting?'"

"Come take a closer look, then."

Kleron appears to be disappointed. He addresses his band of marauders. "Take him alive, if you can."

"Never happen," says Billy.

"Either way. Your choice."

Billy tightens his grip on the haft of the axe. "Yeah, it is." Kleron shrugs and backs away, dragging Dr. Williams with him. Billy moves to follow but

Wepwawet and the others close in to block his path. Meanwhile, Surma circles to his flank.

Kleron raises his voice over the snarling of his troops. "You never saw the Holocausts, child. There's no hope for you here."

Billy braces for the assault. "There's always hope."

"You couldn't be more wrong, boy. You couldn't be more wrong."

At the far side of the room, a pale young man runs in from the hall to the lobby stairs, shrieking something indecipherable. He stumbles into the back of the group, jostling them against each other.

Derek grabs him to shake him out of his hysterics – then sees that he's bleeding profusely from the stump where one of his hands has been torn off. The man points back through the door, then squeals and shoves himself away. Derek and those nearby press back as well when they see what's stalking up the landing.

* * *

"Fi, is that your *dog?*"

There on the screen, bloodied jaws twisted in a ferocious snarl, sandy hair on his back bristling, is definitely—

"*Mol?*" Fi tries to process what she's seeing. "What's *he* doing here?"

Zeke scans the view of the lobby. Half a dozen pale and bearded men, posted to guard the front door, lie in pools of blood with their throats ripped out.

* * *

Billy can't see what's causing the commotion at the far door, but before he can take advantage of the distraction, Wepwawet advances on him. The nearest pale and bearded men follow his lead.

On the other side of the room, Mol attacks.

* * *

This can't be real. Beads of sweat glisten on Zeke's forehead. *Can it?*

Fi's fingernails go to her mouth. She used to chew her nails, a habit she thought she broke years ago at her Uncle Edgar's behest. Somehow, subconsciously, she resists the temptation.

Momentarily forgotten, Peter becomes increasingly agitated.

* * *

The reception waiting room is a tempest of flailing bodies and blood. Billy thrashes pale and bearded men with axe and fist while fending off Surma and Wepwawet, who are much quicker and stronger than the others, but more cautious and cunning.

Mol wreaks havoc at the other side of the throng, dragging men down with savage fury, slashing throats and limbs. They dive on him but he snaps and spins, throwing them off, a whirling dervish of claws and fangs.

Billy keeps his back to the wall, lunging out when he can. The pale and bearded men leave not a scratch on him. Neither Wepwawet nor Surma holds a knife or other weapon of any kind, yet they inflict nasty cuts on his forehead, arms and thigh.

Surma retreats from a brutal swipe of Billy's axe, clutching a gash in his shoulder. Bearded men jump in to take his place. Surma glances at the ruckus on the other side of the room, then shoots a look at Kleron, who stands in the far corner holding Dr. Williams, an expression of cynical amusement on his face. Surma grumbles and forces his way through the melee.

Wepwawet howls, a fresh groove cut across his chest. Billy pushes forward and his attackers back away.

Surma knocks two bearded men out of the way with his one arm. Mol doesn't hesitate to spring straight at his face. Surma sidesteps swiftly, clutches Mol by the scruff of the neck in full lunge, then spins and flings him out the door. Mol hits the far wall of the landing with tremendous force and drops, stunned. "Now!" Surma roars. Derek leads a half dozen bearded and pale men to pounce on Mol en masse.

* * *

"Oh my God," Fi cries out. "Mol!"

Zeke simply can't believe what he's seeing.

* * *

Full-automatic gunfire thunders through the waiting room. Pale and bearded men shudder and yowl, red blooms sprouting across their bodies.

Billy shouts, "Lisa, no!"

But she keeps firing from where she stands in the doorway, screaming her rage and terror.

A lightning sprint and Wepwawet strikes. Lisa flies across the room, slams into the wall and flops to her back. Her chest is a gaping hole, ribs sheared, lungs and heart splashed on walls and floor.

Billy roars in anguish, raising his axe for vengeance. An aberrant blur of darkness appears out of nowhere right in front of him. Blood streaks the ceiling.

* * *

Zeke and Fi both jerk away from the screen as crimson droplets spatter the camera.

Fi screams, *"Billy!"*

* * *

Billy gapes, "Fuck... me..."

The copper axe drops from his hand. It pings to the floor, shrunken back to a necklace pendant.

Kleron whispers in Billy's ear. *"No. Hope."*

Billy gurgles and falls, his entrails spilling on the floor.

* * *

Fi's hands tremble at her face. "Oh my God. Oh my God."

Zeke's shock is suddenly superseded by his will to survive – and save Fi. The fight-or-flight response. In this case, definitely flight. He takes her by the arm. "Fi, we've gotta go."

Peter is shaking so hard that the wheelchair sounds like it might fall apart in his grip, his face showing signs of some terrible internal struggle.

Zeke grabs the chair, spins him away from the monitors. "Fi, come on!"

But her eyes are glued to the screen.

Kleron backs away from Billy. Wepwawet stands over him, roaring in triumph, and snatches up Billy's body.

Billy manages to lift his eyes to the security camera. He clearly mouths, "Run."

Kleron follows his gaze.

Wepwawet bites down on Billy's neck and inexplicably severs his head from his body in one savage rip.

Fi and Zeke both gasp in horror and disbelief.

Billy's head clunks to the floor and the surviving pale men and bearded men cheer so loudly the speakers crackle – but Fi and Zeke can hear it resounding through the building as well.

Kleron steps to the camera and looks up into it.

To Fi, it's like he's looking right at her. He smiles.

Zeke grabs her by the arm again. "Fi, let's go!"

* * *

Derek hustles back into reception, wiping blood from his face with his sleeve. Several of the others follow, covered in wounds, their clothing torn to shreds. One of them has an ear missing and another lost a large chunk of his face.

"It's gone," Derek reports, sucking air. "Badly injured, I think, but it escaped."

Kleron's eyes narrow. "Unfortunate, but not critical." He nods toward the reception booth. "Check the monitors, see if you can spy the old man."

Derek vaults over the counter. There's a squeak, then rustling sounds. He sees Sarah, balled up underneath with her hands over her face. He whistles and snaps his fingers. Henri and Didier, who are recovering from their beating by Billy and already healing from the gunshot wounds inflicted by Lisa, rush to the counter, sniff, then jump over, one after the other. Sarah shrieks.

* * *

Zeke pushes Peter's wheelchair fast down the third floor hall.

Fi jogs along beside them, traumatized. "Billy..."

"And *Mol.*" Zeke adds, still doubting his own sight.

"And Mol..."

They pass rooms on either side where patients and staff are hiding. Through a window in one of the doors, Fi sees an orderly duck as they go by.

"What about all these people?" Fi asks, regaining some semblance of her wits. "Shouldn't we—"

"You heard them, Fi, they're after Peter."

"I know, but..."

"I understand how you feel," says Zeke, trying to sound confident and reasonable, "but we can't get them all to the shelter. And what could we possibly do against those... whatever they are?"

Fi takes a breath, "You're right." She steps ahead and hits the elevator call button. "You know where the shelter is?"

"No, actually—"

"Basement, past the pool."

The one time Fi has been inside the shelter was during a tornado drill over the summer. It was originally designed as a bomb shelter, incorporated into the plan of the building when it was built back in the 1950s when Americans lived in fear of a Soviet nuclear strike. Seems like such a ridiculous thing to worry about now. But then again, so does an attack on a hospital by monstrous men with supernatural strength looking for a half-catatonic old man.

The elevator *dings*.

"Let me take him." Fi tries to shove Zeke out of the way as the elevator doors open.

"Fi, I can—"

But she's adamant. "Zeke!"

"All right!" He steps away, allowing her to wheel Peter in. "All right."

Just as the elevator closes, the door from the stairwell slams top-down into the hall at the farther end, Max riding it to the floor. Hedwig and Curt rush in behind him. Max hurries along the hall but stops at the elevator, sniffs the air. Then he's off like a shot, heading for the recreation room, the pale blond men hot on his trail.

* * *

"*Shit.*" In the reception booth, Derek tries to make sense of the many security screens. He catches movement. "There!" He touches that section of the screen, enlarging it. It's just Max, Hedwig and Curt entering the empty rec room. "Wait," he retracts, "it isn't them."

"Keep looking," Kleron says calmly. "He's here somewhere."

Derek continues searching the monitors. What he doesn't notice are two blank sections at the bottom of one of them where white graphics over static read, *Aquatic Center*.

Kleron shoves Dr. Williams down over Billy's corpse. She struggles, whimpering. Her knees slip in the slick bodily fluids and one of her hands goes into his spilled intestines. He pushes her face to only inches from the lifeless eyes of Billy's severed head.

"Now will you speak?"

Tears fill her eyes. Her voice is no more than a whisper. "*Never.*"

Kleron lifts her face and studies it closely. "You love him."

She sobs, "Yes!"

"A senile old man, worthless and weak." He sighs. "Misguided creatures. Always placing your faith in the wrong hands." He looks to the fur-coated twins. "Will they never learn?"

Surma sneers, baring shining white teeth.

"It's in their nature to resist," says Wepwawet. "Just like the rest of us."

"Very well, then." Kleron drags Dr. Williams through the door next to the reception booth and pulls it shut. After a few moments there's a blood-curdling scream.

* * *

The elevator opens in the basement. Muggy air descends on Fi, Peter and Zeke as they exit.

"There," Fi points out.

The main lights are off, the room now lit only by spotlights in the rafters, but Zeke can see the familiar tri-part yellow and black shelter symbol marking massive metal doors at the far end of the room, beyond the length of the pool. He wonders if they'll be safe in there, if the doors will hold, at least long enough for help to arrive.

Peter jerks so hard in his wheelchair that Fi stops short – then she and Zeke see why.

There's something up in the corner near the shelter doors, climbing down a heavy drain pipe. It reaches the floor and steps into a patch of light. Spiky black hair, long black fur coat, the spitting image of the two fur-coated men they saw on the monitors upstairs – only this one is even bigger. He removes his sunglasses and glares at them with searing red eyes. A low growl crosses the expanse between them, rumbling like distant thunder.

Peter shakes violently, his chair clattering in his grip.

The man starts toward them. Fi backs up fast, pulling Peter with her. Zeke frantically hits buttons in the elevator.

"Stop!" the man roars in a voice that shakes the room.

The elevator begins to close.

The man rounds the corner of the pool. To Fi and Zeke's amazement he drops to all fours and bounds forward. Now he's coming very fast.

"STOP," he roars again. Pool water ripples at the sound.

The elevator shuts. Like everything else in this refurbished building, it's of the latest design and begins to rise immediately. And, luckily, these new elevators are fast. It just clears the floor when—BAM—the elevator shakes, followed by sounds of rending metal and vicious snarls from below. Fi grips the handles of the wheelchair to keep from falling and Zeke catches himself against the wall. They look at each other in astonishment.

* * *

The big red-eyed man glowers up at the receding elevator. He backs out of the shaft and looks to a point high on the wall. A security camera dangles there, mangled and broken. He gazes back up the elevator shaft, and begins to climb.

* * *

Kleron re-enters the waiting room from the hall to the offices, irritated and perplexed.

"Did you rape it?" Surma asks.

"You brutes and your raping," Kleron replies with scorn. "When will you realize, an effective seduction is the true measure of prowess."

"Trueface, then?" Wepwawet queries.

Kleron nods contemplatively. "Usually works. They'll tell me anything." The brothers shift position to look into the hall. Tod, who has survived the brawl with Billy, leans around them to see as well.

Dr. Williams sits on the floor against the wall, stiff and motionless, hands to her frozen face, fingers crooked, mouth agape, eyes wide. She's been literally scared to death.

Kleron shakes his head. "Not this time." He stalks to the counter. From below come the sounds of Henri and Didier's grisly feeding on Sarah. "Anything?" he asks Derek.

"No!" Derek snarks. He catches himself, eyes darting to Kleron. "I mean... not yet, Master."

Kleron offers a smile that quickly fades, then speaks to Surma and Wepwawet. "Search the building. Question all until he is found. Kill anyone you like."

* * *

Fi and Zeke burst out of the elevator with Peter, into the fifth floor hallway. They halt, looking both ways, then catch each other's gaze.

At the same time, Zeke asks, "Where do we go?" and Fi says, "What do we do?"

Fi thinks for a moment. "We've got to get to an exit. The stairs, maybe?"

"I can carry him," Zeke offers.

"*We* can carry him."

* * *

"There!" Derek taps a section of the monitor. It expands, showing Fi, Peter and Zeke. "Fifth floor hallway. An old guy in a wheelchair, some dude, and a girl."

"What color is her hair?" Kleron asks.

"She's a redhead, looks like."

"That's them," he confirms to Surma and Wepwawet.

Surma barks. Not 'barks an order,' but barks, loud and commanding. Henri and Didier bound back over the counter, covered in fresh blood. Derek vaults after them. Surma waves to the door where Billy entered and they and the remaining pale and bearded men rush through.

* * *

Fi pushes Peter toward the end of the hall but the wheelchair comes to a jarring halt, causing her to bang into it from behind. "What the...?"

"What's wrong?" Zeke asks.

Fi sees what the problem is. Peter has hold of the wheels. She hurries to the front. His whole body is shaking, brow furrowed, eyes blinking in fits.

Fi crouches, putting her hands on his. "Peter, we have to go." He snatches her hands. She tries to pull away, but he's too strong. "Peter, please!"

Zeke tries to help. "Peter, come on guy, we have to go, right now."

There's a *bang* from the elevator shaft and the sounds of shredding steel.

As Zeke tugs on Peter's wrist to break his hold on Fi, Peter releases one of Fi's hands, then, fast as a striking snake, snatches Zeke's.

"Jesus," Zeke shouts. Peter's grip is like iron.

Peter rocks back and forth, gasping for breath, mouth contorting.

"Peter, they're coming," Fi pleads. "We have to go!"

The racket from the elevator is getting louder.

Fi and Zeke attempt to pry Peter's fingers away. It's no use.

Then Peter speaks.

"H-a-a..." His voice is barely a whisper, but the sound hits Fi like the report of a gunshot. "...h-a-a-ve... to g-o-o-o..."

"My God..." Fi exclaims. "Yes!" She sobs, a tear streaming down her cheek. "We have to go."

There's a great shearing of metal from inside the elevator. The doors *boom* and shudder.

Peter says, "G-o-o... with *m-e-e?*"

"Yes," Fi cries. She snuffs hard, tears coming faster, touches the wetness on her cheek with her free hand. *How can this be?* She doesn't remember the last time she cried. She didn't even cry at her mother's funeral. But she's crying now, and after everything that's happened, it feels good. *Really* good. "Yes, Peter. We have to go, with you!"

Peter squeezes his eyes shut, expressing his own welling tears. He's fighting, fighting hard, striking at the brambles in his mind, heaving on the barbed wire, flailing at the clinging fog.

Bang. The elevator doors shake harder.

Peter's lips twitch and he manages to emit an audible "S-s-s..." Unseen by Fi or Zeke, his right foot inches forward on the foot-rest of the wheelchair. He presses his lips tight, then opens them again, the "S-s-s-s" coming stronger.

"Peter," Fi reassures, wiping tears from her eyes with her free hand then placing her palm gently to the side of his face. "Don't be sorry."

More clearly now, "S-s-s-s..."

"There's nothing to be sorry about!"

Another louder *bang* and Zeke sees the elevator doors bow from within. "Fi, we're just going to have to carry him."

"S-s-s-s..."

The elevator doors buckle.

Fi pleads, "*Peter...*"

Peter looks into Fi's eyes. His foot rises laboriously, creeping forward.

"S-s-s-*slip.*"

His foot hits the floor.

* * *

The red-eyed man rips open the crumpled elevator doors and shoves himself through.

At the other end of the hall, the door shatters inward. Max comes bounding through but halts suddenly, causing Hedwig and Curt to almost tumble over him from behind. Kleron pushes past them and glares toward the red-eyed man.

There's nothing in the hallway between them but Peter's empty wheelchair. It creeps backward, squeaking softly, and comes to rest against the wall.

ORDER OF THE BULL 6

The Lair of the Bull is a shambles. All is silent except for the rush of gas from broken lamps on the walls. Flames still burn in remaining lamps and lick at the fireplace hearth.

On the terrace outside, the head and body of Arges lie motionless beneath softly falling snow and moonlight. Far below, torch bearing monks scurry about the ruined monastery like frantic swarming fireflies.

Suddenly the hall belches a fireball of tremendous proportion, a concussive *crack* and *boom* that shakes the mountain to its core. The entire cavern collapses and the mountainside crashes down in an avalanche of dust and stone.

* * *

Hunched next to his duffel bag on the landing of the tunnel stairs, head in his hands, Tanuki swears he can still hear the horrible laugh of Xeco, the Terror Bird. How long he's been sobbing here in grief he doesn't know.

Arges is dead. The fabled cyclops, metalsmith and armorer to the ancients. The original Hephaestus, so badly maligned by the *petit* gods of Hellas.

Asterion, gone. Mighty Apis, whom the ancient Egyptians knew as the Herald of Ptah, a living manifestation of Amun, the first being, who according to their myths was self-created, without mother or father. Whatever the stories say, Tanuki knows that for many thousands of years The Bull was never far from Ptah's side. In India it was the same. Long before the Vedic Period, when The Bull was called Nandi, he was the right hand of Shiva. As Vohu Mazda, the Zoroastrians believed him to be a divine spark of Ahura Mazda, an aspect of creation itself.

The tunnel shakes abruptly, accompanied by a deep rumble. Tanuki grabs the wall and holds on until the tremors cease. Dust loosed from cracks hangs silently in the air.

The Lair of the Bull is gone, Tanuki presumes. *But what does it matter? My brothers are dead.* He sobs harder. *What am I going to do?!*

The words of Arges come ringing back, *"Find him, if you can. Tell him what has happened here."*

Tanuki takes a deep uneven breath, rubs the tear-soaked fur of his face, and braces himself.

However it turns out, whatever the consequences, Tanuki will find him, and tell him everything. He grabs up his duffle, throws the straps over his shoulders to carry it like a backpack, clutches his staff, and bounds down the stairs.

He will find Ptah, Amun, Shiva, Ahura Mazda, or whatever he might be calling himself these days. For Arges, for Asterion, he will find Father.

PART II

IL CAPRO

"There is nothing more difficult to take in hand, more perilous to conduct, or more uncertain in its success, than to take the lead in the initiation of a new order of things."

(Il Capro, as told to his pupil,
Niccolò di Bernardo dei Machiavelli)

T *hings have not turned out quite as expected.*
It's a good thing he didn't have a plan. Plans are inflexible. They can go wrong. That's why he tries not to make them.

But at this very moment, Baphomet simply can't move. He doesn't feel the bindings of rope or chain. Then again, he doesn't feel anything. He's not even sure he's breathing. No sense of smell, taste or touch. He thinks he can hear a distant droning, a soft thrum in his inner ear – and is that a sniffle, from far away? A whimper?

Oh dear, I hope I'm not making that sound. If it is a sound...

His eyes perceive nothing. They may be closed, he just can't tell. He tries to rationalize his blindness. He's either in complete absence of light, hooded, under a spell, or dead...

Is this it? The hereafter? Or is he waiting in some limbo of sensory deprivation for the afterlife to begin? Perhaps it will be a new life...

I'm losing my mind...

Cogito ergo sum! (*I think, therefore I am!*). The parvuli may credit Descartes for that, but he didn't come up with it. *Hell, I, The Goat, heard it when I was a kid.* He chuckles in his head. "Goat," "herd," "kid." *I think I laugh, therefore I am – amused...*

Insanity. Maybe he *is* losing himself, his personality being erased as his life essence prepares for rebirth – as a fungus, an amoeba or slug most likely, if karma holds true, given the manner in which he's lived this life. Perhaps he will be a kinder, gentler slug...

His brilliant mind, slipping away, what truly makes him *The Goat*, even more than his magnificent horns (which he does love dearly). An individual. Distinct. One of a kind. *I think, therefore I am* – Baphomet*!*

How did it come to this? Whatever this *is?*

Think. Reason. Rational thought. Logic!

And The Goat knows logic. Oh yes. His grasp of it far exceeds the meager accomplishments of the parvuli. But logical examination, though a marvelous exercise, will only get one so far. A warm up to the real game. *Strategy.* And that is where Baphomet truly shines. Anyone can plan, but a good strategist thrives under conditions of uncertainty, views setbacks not as failures but fresh opportunities to reexamine probabilities, reevaluate possibilities, adapt to emergent contingencies and exploit them to his advantage. Remain flexible in all things. Keep the bigger picture in mind. And expect the unexpected.

The drawback of most parvulus approaches to strategic theory is that rationality and logic are taken as givens. Far more fascinating is the *irrational*, and superior to logic, the *illogical*. It may not be scientific, but it's infinitely more compelling. Mathematical probability goes out the window. Intuition takes over. In a way, one must have faith. Faith in oneself. A shrewd gut, phenomenal instincts, transcendent inspiration, authentic natal impulse, as well as cunning, cynicism and duplicity. These are the tackle of the true schemer.

When it comes to strategy, The Goat has few equals. Father is, well, *Father*, and Myrddin Wyllt was a force to be reckoned with. Asterion isn't bad. Calculating, decisive, but insipidly predictable. More of a tactician, really. Ganesh would be a worthy opponent if he took an interest in such things. But they are all hampered by their beliefs, hobbled by the two greatest impediments to conceiving and implementing truly effective plots. Ethics and morality.

Ethics can be dispensed with entirely as far as Baphomet is concerned, and the master strategist's morals must be both pragmatic and pliable.

And Master Kleron? Moral issues don't concern him, obviously. He's one of the greatest strategists of all time, as was his master before him. But he suffers from another tragic hindrance to the design of genuinely exceptional stratagem, a most deadly Achilles heel (that boy did have bad feet). Kleron has a *cause*. So did his master. Undeniably brilliant, both of them. They each mounted the most ambitious campaigns this world has ever seen, in the forms of the First and Second Holocausts. *But they lost.*

The Goat played no small part in both those debacles. Yet here he is, on the same side again...

Baphomet blinks – and he feels it – cogitation is doing the trick. He still can't move freely or see, and he has no idea where he is, but his wits are returning. And he remembers. He's not dead, in no ethereal limbo.

He's a prisoner.

He recalls clearly now, the mission with Ao Guang and Dimmi. The cave of purple obsidian, and his own final words before he blacked out – *Mother Witch.*

Now that his brain's synapses are firing at full capacity there are many things to consider. But most critically – *how am I going to worm my way out of this one?* What nefarious scheme, what devious plot, can he possibly devise against *her?*

17

FLOWER & FIGS 7

F i and Zeke have stepped on glare ice, both of them feeling that jolt of adrenaline that comes at the instant when all traction is lost, when you realize you're going down hard and there's absolutely nothing you can do about it. And they can't see anything. Nothing but gray.

Then the gray is gone, an ethereal curtain ripped aside. They regain their footing, hearts pounding, and they almost do fall.

Peter is still between them clasping their hands, but his wheelchair is gone. They struggle to keep their balance, pulling him up and clutching him between them in a hug. They look at each other in amazement, their faces only inches apart over his shoulder.

"What was that?" Zeke exclaims.

Fi shakes her head frantically. "I have no idea."

They take in their surroundings. They're still in the hall on the fifth floor of the hospital. Sort of.

The paint on the walls is peeling, the tile on the floor cracked, half of it missing. No lights are on, what illumination there is comes from a broken window at the end of the hall. The few doors that remain on the patient's rooms hang loosely on broken hinges. Mildew stains the walls, water drips through moldy cracks in the ceiling. They jump at the whistling wing-flap of a pigeon flying in the window. It spies them and wheels around, retreating back the way it came.

Fi searches the face of the frail old man between them, but it offers no answers. His eyes are vacant and cloudy as ever. "Peter?"

He grips their hands harder. "S-s-slip."

Gray fog, frantic scrabbling to gain purchase on the nothing beneath their feet, then the mist disappears once more. Pounding rain under a dark stormy sky – and now they *are* falling.

They flail in the air, screaming as they plummet.

Plunging into dark water, bumping the bottom, pushing upward, dragging Peter with them, reaching the surface.

Zeke gasps, "Fi!"

She sputters, "I'm right here," and points to the edge, thirty feet away. "Swim!"

Paddling and kicking, towing Peter between them, keeping his head above water the best they can. Reaching land and crawling up the slick muddy slope, rain pelting. They drag Peter to shore and lift him from the ground, their bodies buzzing from shock and exertion.

They appear to be standing in an excavation site, but there is no equipment and there are no people. Then bursts of lightning reveal the buildings around them – tumbled, charred, twisted – and the water-hole looks more like a bomb crater.

"S-slip."

Gray fog, no traction, sliding, *slipping*.

* * *

They jerk as their shoes catch on solid ground. This time the grayness gradually dissipates. Wind gusts and recedes. Wisping lacy fog veils and unveils their surroundings. The sky is a milky white ceiling that illuminates everything in a flat even glow. Powdery white sand swirls in eddies at their feet. Silvery windswept dunes extend as far as the eye can see, then fade into a pale haze.

Neither Fi nor Zeke have any sense of temperature, and though the wind moves their hair and wet clothes they can't feel its touch. Sounds and scents come to them on the unfelt breeze. Each sound, each smell, is individual, distinct, but indiscernible from one another. There's wind and lapping water, but they also hear music, birds, traffic, voices, all mingling as if from a great distance. Each voice is vaguely familiar – they've heard the words before, spoken by people they know and have known, but if they concentrate on any of them they're gone.

They see the look of amazement on each other's faces. Then Fi realizes they are alone. "Peter..."

He's no longer between them.

They scan the landscape for any sign of him, spin to search behind them, and realize they're standing on something like a beach.

Before them is what looks like a cold, arctic ocean. A heavy vapor hugs its surface. Waves the color of weak milk crest and recede between glinting flows of ice, which form, then sink, form, and sink, in rapid succession. Across this expanse, at a distance impossible to determine, is a vast range of mountains, glittering crystal peaks piercing the cloud-covered sky. But the mountains move, avalanching into the sea as new peaks are thrust upward to replace them in a constant cycle of destruction and renewal.

A cloud of low fog wafts aside. Twenty yards away, a wilted figure in sleeping cap and ratty blue robe is dragging himself toward the white sea.

Fi and Zeke shout at the same time, "Peter!"

They charge toward him, but their feet sink in the sand. Fi falls forward, her hand going deep. She forces herself upright, tugging her arm free, but her feet sink further.

Peter crawls into the surf. She calls out, "Peter!"

Zeke pulls one foot after the other from the sand, fighting toward Fi, grunting with every step. They reach for each other and grasp hands.

"Come on," Fi shouts.

Using one another for balance, they trudge forward in the sucking sand. Ahead of them Peter flounders, then pushes himself to stand waist deep on wobbling legs and wades further out. The muscles of Zeke's thighs are burning. "Peter!"

"Peter, stop!" Fi cries.

He topples forward and plunges beneath the surface.

Fi shrieks, "Peter!" She clenches Zeke's hand, and with renewed effort pulls him with her. She groans through clenched teeth as together they plow their way to the surf.

When they finally reach the edge there's no sign of Peter. Zeke pulls back on Fi's hand in hesitation.

She releases her grip. "I'm going," she says resolutely, and wades in.

Zeke sets his jaw and follows. The ground becomes more solid under his feet as he enters. Instead of icy cold, a strange warmth rises over his ankles, up his legs to his waist. His hand touches the surface. It isn't wet, more like incredibly dense steam than water. Fi dives. Zeke groans, takes a step further, and drops unexpectedly into the depths.

The light is dim, the same all around, and there are no bubbles by which to orient himself. He thrashes and kicks, weightless in the swirling gray. His head pounds with his heartbeat. The sound of blood rushes in his ears. His lungs scream for air. He thrashes harder, hoping for a glimpse of Fi or Peter. Nothing but gray. He can't hold his breath any longer.

This is it!

His mouth pops open against his will and he inhales deeply.

A blinding burst of white light, followed by a dizzying progression of sights, sounds, smells, and tastes. He's bombarded with emotions—thoughts—ideas—dreams—heat—cold—comfort—pain—sadness—ecstasy—loneliness—joy—rage—terror. He sees and feels everything he's ever experienced, everyone he's ever known, everywhere he's ever been. In a dizzying montage he's reliving his entire life, all out of order, jumbled like pieces of a jigsaw puzzle tumbling through space. One image suddenly stands out, though it's fuzzy, as if seen through foggy glasses.

A soccer field. A young girl, no more than five or six, in oversized shin guards. She kicks the ball, looks right at Zeke, and smiles. The soccer ball pings off her head of wild red hair and she's bowled over by a throng of players.

Zeke squeezes his eyes shut. The girl's gone, but images assail him faster and faster, the sounds getting louder and louder. He presses his hands to his head to keep it from splitting open and screams, but there is no sound.

Something touches his hand, solid and real.

He opens his eyes. Centered in the blitz of images is Fi's face, obviously shouting at him, though he doesn't hear her. She grabs his wrist with both hands and pulls.

* * *

Zeke is dragged roughly from the white sea and dropped heavily on the sand. He rolls to his back, coughing, sputtering, mist puffing from his mouth and nose. Fi stoops over him.

"Jesus, Zeke." She takes him by the hand and helps him to his feet. He leans on her, legs shaking. Vapor steams from their bodies.

Zeke jerks his head up, remembering. "Peter..."

Her lips quiver. She slowly shakes her head, then presses her face to his shoulder.

Zeke holds her tight, closing his eyes. He'd never have wanted it to happen under such insane, fucked-up circumstances, and he feels guilty for even thinking it, but just having her close, holding her like this, he feels *whole*.

Unfortunately, there are more pressing matters to consider. Like the fact they're lost, alone, and have absolutely no idea where they are.

The desperate reality – or unreality – of the situation is fully dawning on Fi as well. She breaks their embrace and surveys the bleak topography.

Over Fi's shoulder, Zeke sees a disturbance in the misty ocean, a soft effervescence different from the waves. "Fi..."

She looks to him quizzically. "What?"

The disturbance becomes a rolling boil. He takes her by the shoulders and turns her toward it. "Look."

The area of churning vapor creeps toward them, a shadow moving just beneath the surface. They grip each other tight, holding their breath. The shadow comes within a few feet of the shore, then stops. The roiling subsides, the surface returning to tranquil waves. They breath again, a mixture of relief, loss, and fear.

Then something erupts from the mist, sending a great spout of sea gushing upward. Zeke and Fi clutch each other harder, shrieking at the top of their lungs.

Standing there, up to his thighs, is a man, his fists clenched, eyes screwed shut, chest heaving. The surface of his body glows with the same light as the mist, but fades as the vapor flows down his body to rejoin the sea. Long brown hair streams over his muscular shoulders, framing a face with wide-set eyes beneath a thoughtful brow, high cheekbones and strong jawline partially obscured by a thick brown beard that goes to the middle of his powerful chest.

Fi gawps at the sight. *Peter?*

But this is no withered old man. His body is... *perfect*. The physique of a world-class athlete at the peak of fitness, rippling with muscle beneath smooth mid-tone skin that glistens with moisture. And Fi can see all of it. His tattered baby-blue robe hangs open, leaving nothing to the imagination. If she wasn't suffering from shock and awe, she'd definitely blush.

The man suddenly thrusts his fists into the air, raising his face to the sky, and *roars*.

Fi and Zeke both shriek again.

The man's voice is deep, clear, and *very* loud. A sound both human and animal. Cosmic. Primal. A trumpeting of giants. The vaporous surface of the sea flees from him in concentric waves and the mist retreats from its onslaught.

Fi and Zeke stop screaming before he does, and then he is silent. The mist returns to a mere wisp on the wind, the surface of the sea to its incessant peaking and falling.

Breathing deeply, the man drops his hands, lowers his face from the sky, and opens his eyes.

Fi breathes in sharply.

"Whoa," Zeke exclaims.

The irises of the man's eyes churn with color, changing from gray to brown, then red, orange, yellow, gold, hazel, green, blue, indigo and violet. The colors continue to cycle until they finally settle on a brilliant emerald green. And he looks right at them.

"Fi!" he shouts with unrestrained enthusiasm. Fi and Zeke practically jump out of their skins.

He rushes toward them, arms outstretched, eyes gleaming, the widest of grins on his face. They try to back away, but he's too fast. The sand doesn't suck at his bare feet as it did theirs when they approached the surf. He snatches Fi and lifts her high into the air.

"Fi," he shouts again, exuberant. She squeaks in answer.

The man spins her around, once, twice, then sets her lightly on her feet and kisses her hard, right on the mouth.

The odors of rose, jasmine and lavender envelope her senses. She tastes licorice on her lips, feels her face turn pink, her whole body flush with desire. When he lets go, she's barely able to stand.

The man whips around, his eyes falling on—

"Zeke!"

Gaping and helpless like tiny cornered prey, "Uhh..." is Zeke's lone reaction, his only defense. The man advances on him and places both hands on his shoulders, absolutely elated.

"Zeke," he says softly, touching Zeke's cheek and examining his face. The man moves his hand behind Zeke's head, fingers in his hair.

Oh no he isn't, Zeke denies silently. The man pulls him closer – *Oh yes he is!* – and plants a forceful kiss on his lips.

Zeke isn't sure what a swoon feels like, but this must be it. He tingles from his mouth right down to his toes. He would never have thought you could taste patchouli, ylang-ylang or myrrh, but he does, and it's unbelievable.

The man pulls his lips away with an audible *smack* but doesn't let go, for which Zeke is grateful because his knees are wobbly weak.

The look on the man's face changes from glee to worry. "Are you harmed?" he asks earnestly. He runs his hands over Zeke's shoulders and arms, inspecting him for injury.

"Uhhh, yeah," Zeke hears himself say. "I mean, no!" He squirms and dances as the man gropes his body.

"Are you certain?" the man presses. "You were not injured in the fall? From the hospital? Into the water?"

Finally recovering from his swoon, Zeke jumps back, holding a hand out to fend the man off. "I'm fine. Really!"

The man's wide grin returns. He looks back and forth between Zeke and Fi, hands on his hips.

"I'm... okay too," says Fi.

"Good!" The man nods happily. "Good." Then he looks at the ground and is suddenly lost in thought.

After a long moment, Fi ventures to ask, "Are you?..."

The man reacts immediately. "Peter! Yes. I'm back. Thanks to you. Both of you." He looks intently at Fi, as if trying to figure something out. "Especially you. I think..."

His eyes move back to the ground. "I've misplaced my slippers," he says, wiggling his toes in the sand. And he's lost in thought once again.

Zeke gestures to the sea of mist. "Peter... Sir... Where are we?"

"Hmm? Oh. Memory," Peter answers absent-mindedly. "World Memory." He waves a hand aimlessly at their surroundings. "Sands of time, winds of change, peaks of present, sheets of past, etcetera, etcetera."

Fi and Zeke exchange looks. Not exactly the answer they were looking for. Peter doesn't move as Zeke steps cautiously around him to join Fi, then he suddenly looks up.

"We have to go." He steps between them, takes their hands in his.

Fi feels a hot sense of rage rise within her. She yanks her hand out of Peter's grasp, stepping back. "Wait! Wait a goddamn minute."

Peter is taken aback. So is Zeke, but Fi's sentiments are his, exactly. He pulls his hand away from Peter as well, mostly to show he's siding with Fi, but also because it feels weird to be standing on a beach holding hands with a dude.

Fi's surprised at herself as well, but she isn't stopping now. "Tell us what the hell is going on?" she demands. "People are being killed! Our friends are dead, and we want to know why." She jabs a finger at him, glaring. "And who the hell *are* you?!"

Her eyes flit over his glorious naked body. She catches herself and looks away. "And, close your robe already, will ya?"

18

MENDIP HILLS 2

A massive paw-hand swipes branches aside. Bödvar Bjarki, The Bear, squeezes from the hole that's been his daytime den here in the Mendip Hills of England. He stretches in the cool night air, sneezes, and farts. He wipes the slime from his nose and looks up through the trees, scratching his scruffy neck. All traces of daylight have left the sky.

Finally, he huffs to himself. That may have been the longest day he's ever spent. And that's saying something.

* * *

He approaches the base of the limestone cliff he found last night, checks his GPS one more time. He doesn't need the device. He easily recognizes the place and can smell the trace of his own scent, but he really doesn't want to fuck this up. Baphomet and Master Kleron are counting on him.

He leans the thousand pound hammer against a boulder, draws the enormous greatsword Kladenets from his back and drops it to clatter on the rocks. The rucksack he sets down much more gently. It begins to hum again, but Bödvar decides it doesn't matter anymore. He's about to make plenty of noise himself.

Very soon Myrddin Wyllt, The Madman, will finally be free. Free, and dead.

* * *

With a single blow, Kladenets chops halfway through the first of the two ash trees that stand before the rock face of the cliff. Bödvar jerks the sword free, tears hunks from the trunk with his claws, then squeezes behind the tree, braces his back against the stone, and shoves. The wood groans in protest but surrenders with a *crack*. The tree topples, limbs snapping and scraping against others as it goes, and crashes to the ground. He repeats the process with the second tree, then wrestles the trunks further from the base of the cliff.

He retrieves his hammer, scans the surrounding forest. A mist carpets the ground, crawling sluggishly down the hill. The moon, still practically full, beams like a bleached skull on black sand. Sensing no presence of troublesome parvuli, he sets his feet and swings the hammer with a fearsome grunt. The conical spike on the head of the hammer hits the rock face like dynamite.

* * *

Myrddin Wyllt wakens in the darkness. At least he *thinks* he's awake. He thought he heard something, felt a vibration in the gritty stone floor on which he lies. Then it comes again.

Phoom.

Is it possible? After all this time?

Years, decades, centuries. It has to be. Can it be a millennium? It's possible. Feels like an epoch. Could he live that long, locked away? Sealed in the cave, he's had no way to keep track of time. No sunlight or stars, no regular schedule for meals. No meals at all. Just a lick of condensation off the walls now and again, a bit of lichen scraped with his teeth.

Phoom.

Myrddin reaches stiffly from where he lies, feeling for a small pillar of rock that he carved long ago by scraping other rocks against it, just for something to do. In the old Brythonic tongue he croaks aloud, "Perhaps, a little light."

Phoom

He taps the stone gently with the tips of his fingers while muttering incomprehensible words under his breath. The stone emits a dim glow. Compared to the void of the cave, it seems bright as the sun. Myrddin squints his crystalline gray eyes, eyes that have lost none of their brilliance in his ages of captivity. His tangled white beard sprawls in the dust on the floor. He peers past the lit stone, through the greasy colorless hair that hangs over his creased and pitted face, toward the far wall.

Phoom!

FLOWERS & FIGS 8

Fi can't get used to the sheer helplessness she feels when her feet have no purchase. The electric shocks of adrenaline. The spastic gymnastics of her stomach that accompany each "slip."

And they just keep slipping, world after world, a curtain of fog between each. Rain, darkness, sunlight. Forests, deserts, mountains, shorelines, prairies, crowded cities and empty streets, even a raging battlefield, and many scorched and barren landscapes – empty, alien-looking, uninhabitable. A few times they walk for awhile in whatever world they're in, then slip again.

After the first dozen slips Peter ceased to utter the word with each, but Zeke says it every time, under his breath. "slip..." "slip..." "slip..."

They received no satisfactory explanation from Peter after his miraculous transformation back on the beach. "World Memory," he called it. Said something about it being "everywhere" but they were "between" worlds so they were able to perceive it "somewhat directly." *Whatever the hell that means.*

Peter assured them he'd explain more later but insisted they leave the place right away, stressing that "Friedrich was not wrong when he wrote, 'when you look into the abyss, the abyss also looks into you.'" Then he took their hands and a step and said "slip" and they were gone. The only other thing he told them was that when they "slipped," as he called it, they weren't traveling in time, as Zeke speculated, but shifting dimensions to other earths, "incompossible worlds," spun off from the original earth, their world, due to conditions of "contingent possibility" and events that spawned "incompatible futures."

Fi thinks she's going to throw up.

Peter pulls them up short in a familiar city with a partly cloudy sky and steady breeze. Fi checks street signs and store fronts. She recognizes them all. It even smells like it should. Not a good smell, but welcome nonetheless. She never thought she'd be glad to be back in downtown Toledo.

She turns to Peter. "Were we lost?" But he's gazing at Zeke in what can only be described as pure wonder.

Zeke hasn't noticed. He's busy surveying their surroundings, also realizing they're back. He checks the sky. Early to mid-afternoon, he'd guess. He catches Peter staring at him.

"What?" he asks.

Peter doesn't take his eyes off Zeke, but he answers Fi first. "Yes, Fi. I was a bit disoriented, I must admit. I've never recovered from a patermentia so quickly and am still a little groggy."

"A 'pater'-what?"

"It's just a term," Peter offers in explanation. "Something the condition is called by those who know me. An affliction I suffer from time to time. Entirely debilitating and impossible to prevent."

Fi wants to press him further because he doesn't seem capable of answering a question without spawning a dozen more, but his full attention is back on Zeke.

"Zeke," he asks, "what did you just do?"

"Uhh..." It seems to be Zeke's response of the day. "Nothing?"

"I did not make that last slip. I did not bring us here." He looks into Zeke's eyes, as if trying to find a splinter or a bug. "*You* did."

"I did?" Zeke flusters in denial, "No I didn't."

"It wasn't Fi," Peter insists. "I'd be able to tell. Have you ever done this before?"

"I don't even know what we were doing, but I'm pretty sure I've never done it before."

"Hmm..." Peter stands motionless and silent.

Zeke frets under his shrewd gaze. *Does he ever blink?*

Finally, Fi says, "Hey, Peter."

He focuses entirely on her. "Yes, dear?"

Fi's eyes widen. In that moment, with those words, Peter sounded just like her Uncle Edgar (but without the English accent), which brings something to mind like a sharp blow – she grabs Zeke by the arm. "I need to call Edgar. And we should call the police."

She shoves her hand in her pocket. Her clothes are mostly dry after their plunge into the waterhole while slipping away from the hospital, but when she pulls out her phone, water drips and the screen is badly cracked.

"Is it in service?" Peter queries.

"Oh, I don't think so."

"Good."

"Wha?—"

"We could be tracked."

"No way."

"Yes... *way*."

Zeke shakes water out of his phone. "Mine's trashed."

"In fact..." Peter takes both their phones and drops them through the grate of a storm drain.

"What the hell?" Fi exclaims. Zeke emits a short involuntary laugh at the absurdity of Peter's actions. Fi scowls at him too.

Peter is unaffected. "You said they didn't work."

"Yeah," Fi complains, "maybe, but—"

"Right," Peter interrupts. He glances up the street.

A group of middle-aged women exits a neighborhood restaurant amidst peals of laughter. They're all dressed up in their Sunday best, clutching fancy hats against the wind, gripping faux designer handbags.

"Wait here," says Peter.

Fi is about to protest, not only because she doesn't like to be told what to do and she's mad about her phone, but also because Peter looks ridiculous in his bare feet and frayed baby-blue robe – though at least now it's closed in front and tied – but Peter shouts first,

"My dear ladies!" He approaches boldly. Their reactions range from surprise to contempt.

Fi and Zeke can't hear what Peter is saying, but apparently it's disarming, even charming, because in short order the women are smiling and conversing with him. He says something to one of them that actually makes her blush. She reaches into her purse and hands him her phone, giving him a lingering pat on the hand.

"You've got to be kidding," Fi remarks. Zeke just shakes his head.

Peter gives Fi a wink, which incenses her for some reason, then steps to a recessed doorway out of the wind. The women giggle amongst themselves.

"Who do you think he's calling?" Fi asks.

"I don't know," Zeke answers distractedly.

After a minute, Peter finishes a call and dials another number. Fi pushes a strand of hair behind her ear. Her fingers hover close to her lips.

"Zeke, what did you do?" she asks.

"What do you mean?"

"How can you do... what he does, that *slipping* thing?"

Zeke rolls his eyes. "I didn't know I was doing it, if I even was. Honestly, I have no idea."

Fi grunts in frustration. When she looks back to Peter he's returning the woman's phone with an extravagant bow. The woman blushes again and her friends laugh.

"Hey," Fi shouts, but Peter's already hurrying back. "I wanted to use that. I need to call my uncle!"

"Not now," he responds coolly.

Fi glares at him. "Look, *Peter*, or whoever you are. My Uncle Edgar is going to hear about what happened at the hospital, if he hasn't already. And his dog was there and might have gotten hurt. He's going to *freak*."

Peter places a hand on her shoulder. Her first reaction is to pull away – but she doesn't. He's smiling in a way that isn't in the least false or condescending, his green eyes glowing with compassion. Soothing warmth radiates from his touch – and his breath – her favorite fragrances in the world.

"Fi, your uncle will be fine." His voice is soft and sincere. "I'll get you to him as soon as I possibly can."

She bites her lip. Zeke comes closer, pretending not to listen. Peter reaches nonthreateningly and pulls him nearer, throws his arms over both their shoulders and walks them down the sidewalk – an intimate gesture that happens so naturally neither of them realize he's done it.

"Who did *you* call?" Fi asks.

"Someone who can help us," Peter reassures them. "Someone we can trust. More than anyone."

Fi ponders, *But can we trust you?* "Did you call the police?"

"I did, against my better judgment." Fi gives him a look. "But they had already been informed and are, how do you say, 'on the scene.' Hopefully, Kleron discovered I was no longer at the hospital and vacated the premises straightaway. I'd hate to see a confrontation with the authorities lead to more needless death."

Fi and Zeke saw what the men at the hospital could do, and what little effect guns had on them. Peter's right.

"What did they want?" Zeke asks. "Those... *men*, at the hospital."

Peter speaks as if it's obvious. "Most likely to capture me while I was afflicted with the patermentia and drag me off to a new Tartarus."

Once again, Fi has no idea what Peter is talking about. She's beginning to think he's making shit up.

Zeke, on the other hand, knows what "Tartarus" is. The bottomless hell-pit of Greek mythology. *But that's just crazy.* "Why would they want to do... *that?*"

"That's a very good question, to which there is no pleasant answer." His brow furrows. "Unfortunately, my friends, they've seen us together. They may now be after you as well."

Fi looks stricken. "Why?"

"To get to me. And they will stop at nothing, I assure you." He holds them more snuggly as they walk. "I can protect you, but you must stick close and do as I say."

Fi looks to Zeke, but he's staring at the sidewalk. A few more silent steps and she ventures to ask Peter, "Who are they? They can't really be your family, like they said."

Peter's expression is grim. "They are my children."

* * *

Fi wants to call bullshit. Zeke's agitated, and thinking hard about something. He opens his mouth several times to speak but says nothing.

"What about Billy?" Fi asks.

Peter breathes out sadly. "My son as well, yes."

She scoffs silently.

"I hadn't spoken to him in quite some time. We didn't part on the best of terms. In the depths of the mentia, I didn't realize he'd come to my side..." His voice trails off.

"Samson," says Zeke. It just slipped out and he regrets it immediately.

Peter stops him in his tracks, his countenance hardening. He doesn't shout but his voice has a tone that sets Zeke's bones ashiver. *"Why do you say this?"*

"I didn't – I don't..."

"Did he tell you?"

"No."

Fi is struck by Peter's mercurial change in demeanor.

Peter backs Zeke firmly to a wall. "Explain yourself!"

Zeke's teeth rattle at his command. It's been twisting in the back of Zeke's mind since the incident in the stairwell with Billy, but he felt stupid just thinking it so he didn't dare say anything. Now he spits it out as fast as he can.

"The big scary guy with blue eyes – when they were on the stairs – he said something about Billy having cut his hair – which doesn't mean anything – then Billy said he still had both eyes, too. It sounded familiar, but it didn't occur to me – then he said something about a jawbone of an ass. I thought it was some kind of joke. They seemed to know each other."

Fi doesn't understand what Zeke's talking about, but she shares his distress. Peter might look like a raggedy redneck in a crappy blue bathrobe, but his presence is formidable. She touches his arm. "Peter..."

He ignores her, pressing Zeke further. "Go on."

Zeke's voice rises an octave. "According to the Book of Judges – Old Testament, right? Samson got his strength by letting his hair grow long and he had his eyes stabbed out when he was captured by the Philistines. It also says he killed a thousand men in a battle using nothing but a mule's jaw, the jawbone of an ass!"

Peter still glares.

"But then," Zeke sputters on, "that Kleron guy – he called Billy's axe the Axe of Perun. When I tried to put it all together it didn't make any sense, but..."

Fi doesn't know about any "Perun," but she's familiar with the story of Samson and Delilah – she saw the TV movie – it's ridiculous.

"Peter!" she appeals, "Zeke studies history and mythology. He's nuts about it but he's just kidding. Aren't you Zeke?"

Peter's taut features relax, but Zeke flinches as he places a hand on his shoulder. "You are full of surprises, Mr. Prisco. And you are correct, Billy's Truename is..." his expression saddens, "...*was*, Samson."

"Not the *real* Samson?" Fi asks dubiously. "From the Bible story?"

"The same."

"That's... impossible," Zeke murmurs. But then again, how much of what he's seen today with his own eyes is even remotely possible?

Peter eyes him keenly. "If there's one thing I've learned in all my years, it's that *anything* is possible."

Before they know it they're walking down the street with Peter's arms over their shoulders again. Fi notices this time. *How does he* do *that?*

"Much of what you've read about Samson is false," Peter expounds. "His story was passed generation to generation by word of mouth, which has never been particularly reliable. And the quality of any tale is affected by the motivations of those telling it." Pedestrians give them odd looks as they pass by. Peter takes no notice. "Samson's hair had nothing to do with his strength, of course, and he never lost his eyes, though his captors tried and claimed they were successful. He did have a jawbone of an ass when he laid waste to the army of 1,000 men, but it broke. Mostly he used his bare hands."

Now Fi *really* wants to call bullshit.

"I'll tell you something else," Peter adds, "which I believe you will heed without judgment since you seem to have been his friends. Delilah was *not* a woman."

Fi trips over a crack in the sidewalk.

Peter steadies her. "Careful, there."

Peter might be truly crazy or a great liar, but Zeke can't help wanting to hear more. "And the axe"?

"I gave it to him years ago, after his celebrated adventures." He halts abruptly, removes his arms from their shoulders and claps his hands together. "So!"

"So... what?" Fi asks.

"I should acquire some proper attire," he answers matter-of-factly, "don't you think?" He nods down the street. "There should be a thrift store around the corner."

"There is," Fi replies. "I think, but—"

"Do either of you have any cash?" he interrupts. "I promise to pay you back."

"Um..." Fi pats her pockets. She left her money in her backpack.

Zeke peels wet bills from his wallet. "I've got twenty-five, thirty... thirty-six dollars."

"That'll do nicely," says Peter, snatching the cash. Without checking for traffic he jaunts across the street, dragging Fi and Zeke by the hands like little kids.

* * *

Zeke stands by a bent rack of *Pre-Loved* stuffed animals, hands in pockets, contemplating his loafers.

"He's changing clothes," Fi says curtly, arriving from the back. "Says not to leave the store."

Zeke nervously runs a hand through his hair. "Okay."

She grabs him by the shoulders and shakes him. "Zeke. *What the fuck?*"

"What?"

"What do you mean, 'what'? This. Everything! I mean, is that really *Peter?*"

"You'd know better than I would. Is it?"

Fi pauses. "Yeah, it is. But who is 'Peter' *now?* And what's all that crap about those guys being his children? And Billy? *Samson? Really?*"

Zeke shrugs, as much at a loss as she is.

"We need to get out of here," Fi says. "Find my uncle. If anyone would know what to do—"

Zeke interrupts, "We... Fi... we can't just leave him here. I mean... Jesus. This is crazy, yeah, fucked up... *really* fucked up. But it's amazing too."

Fi's shocked. "Amazing? You think today's been *amazing?*"

She has a point. The attack on the hospital, the murders, Billy dead, and who knows what happened after they left. "Fi, I don't think we should—"

"No, you shouldn't."

Fi jumps and Zeke looks up with a start.

Peter stands in the aisle a few feet away. "Well?" he says in a more cheerful tone, and right here in the store performs a perfectly executed pirouette, stopping to face them with a graceful bow. "What do you think?"

It takes them a second to realize he's asking about his outfit. Checked flannel shirt tucked into patched green cargo pants, and oil stained ox-blood boots. He dons a camouflage baseball cap, pulling it too far down over his brow. The ensemble makes a fine compliment to his messy brown hair and unkempt beard.

Fi sighs, walks to him and untucks his shirt, tugging it down to smooth it over his hips, then adjusts his hat. "That'll do, I guess."

Peter leans close, genuine affection in his eyes. "Thank you."

She says, "You're wel—," but her voice cracks. She clears her throat and tries again, "You're welcome." Peter puts an arm over her shoulder once more. It should still feel odd to her, people don't usually do that sort of thing – certainly not her Uncle Edgar. But with Peter, whom she's found out she doesn't really know at all, it seems perfectly normal. Almost comforting. He walks her over and embraces Zeke as well, moves them toward the front of the store.

"What next, then?" Fi asks.

"The bank," Peter replies. "I owe Zeke some money, and I always pay my debts."

* * *

"But it's Sunday," Fi protests as she and Zeke hurry along the sidewalk, trying to keep up with Peter's purposeful stride. "The banks are closed."

"We'll see about that," Peter responds.

Ahead of them, three rough looking young men in sideways baseball caps, droopy drawers and gold chains come around the corner. Each of them leads a dog. Two heavily muscled American Pit Bull Terriers, one on either side of a massive Rottweiler. The Rottweiler is muzzled, but that doesn't keep it from trying to snap at the Pit Bulls, who snarl back. Hefty as he is, the man leading the Rottweiler is barely able to hang on to its leash. They take up the entire sidewalk, and it doesn't look like they're going to move.

Fi and Zeke slow down.

Peter halts and throws his hands up. "Puppies!"

The men with the dogs stop, giving each other a look that clearly communicates this hillbilly redneck must be bat-shit crazy.

"Peter," Fi cautions, "let's just cross the street."

Peter's answer is to lean forward and pat his knees. "Come on!"

Zeke keeps his eyes on the dogs, who cautiously sniff the air in their direction. "Fi..."

"I know," Fi snaps at him under her breath. "I'm very aware of the situation, thank you." She raises her voice, "Peter?"

Peter turns his head, still leaning on his knees. There isn't the slightest hint of concern or annoyance in his voice, "Yes?"

The dogs suddenly leap forward with such force they yank their leashes free. The man with the Rottweiler manages to hold on just long enough to be pitched forward onto the sidewalk with a curse.

Peter stands straight as the dogs barrel toward him.

Zeke utters, "Shit..." Fi grabs him by the arm.

Peter grunts, a noise that sounds a lot like "ruff." One of the Pit Bulls jumps up on his leg. The Rottweiler hits him full in the chest with its front paws. Peter doesn't budge.

"Hi there!"

The first Pit Bull licks madly at his shirt and arm. The Rottweiler buries its head in his chest, snorting with pleasure. The other Pit Bull cowers at Peter's feet, tail wagging, making little whining sounds, sneaking furtive peeks up at him.

The dogs' owners' mouths fall open, the big guy still lying on the sidewalk. Fi and Zeke are stupefied. Peter fusses with the muzzle on the Rottweiler.

The big guy pushes himself up. "Hey man, I wouldn't do that!"

"You don't need this," Peter coos at the Rottweiler, "do you boy?" He removes the muzzle. Immediately the dog slathers his face with its tongue. "Yeah, that's better." Peter tosses the muzzle to the big guy, who catches it, his gape renewed.

Peter rubs the head of the Pit Bull at his waist. "Well, hello." He leans to the meeker Pit Bull at his feet, pets it as well. "You too, sweetheart. You're a good girl, huh?"

Fi and Zeke hear more dogs barking from all directions, growing louder. Some run up the sidewalk behind them and push past, almost knocking Zeke down. Others round the corner across the street, a middle-aged man and woman racing behind them, shouting and waving small plastic bags.

"Hi! Hi!" Peter greets them all. The Rottweiler jumps down and growls at the newcomers, but Peter "ruffs" again and all aggression ceases.

Then Peter starts jumping up and down, swinging his arms and spinning, all the while shouting exclamations like "yay" and "woo-hoo!" There are close to a dozen dogs now, and more are arriving by the moment. They bark and bounce around him, some hopping on their hind legs, others whirling in circles, all yapping gleefully.

One of the Pit Bull owners says, "What—the—fuck?" He's still incapable of closing his mouth.

Peter beams at Fi and Zeke from the center of the doggie melee. The look on Fi's face sobers him. He glances around to see people stopping in the street to watch. More come out of storefronts, others lean out of upper story windows.

He sees the meek Pit Bull face away from him in a submissive squat, her tail cocked to the side. "O-o-o-kay," he says. Then, loud enough to be heard over the barking, he looses another commanding "ruff." All the dogs immediately sit and become silent.

Peter waves Fi and Zeke toward him. They approach with trepidation. Surprisingly, the dogs scoot out of their way. Peter puts his hands on their shoulders when they reach him. They proceed up the sidewalk, the dogs parting as they go. The owners of the first three dogs stare after them as they pass.

When they round the corner the dogs leap up to follow, but Peter leans back around, holds out a hand and whistles softly. The dogs all lie down and put their heads on their front paws. The female Pit Bull whimpers.

Halfway down the next block, Peter feels the eyes of Zeke and Fi upon him. "Dogs like me," he retorts. "I can't help that, can I?" They don't look at all satisfied with his answer. "Well I like cats too."

20

MENDIP HILLS 3

"It's thicker than I thought," Bödvar says aloud, then realizes he's speaking to his rucksack, which still sits on the ground against a nearby tree. These are the first words he's spoken to his hidden "partner" on the entire mission, other than "hush" and "be quiet." Eerily sweet humming emanates from the pack in response, accompanied by the muffled slosh of water. *Oh, what the hell,* Bödvar concedes. "Almost there," he tells the sack.

He's bashed a hole five feet deep in the face of the cliff. *How much more can there be?* He kicks away rocks, claws out loose chunks, then resumes hammering in rhythmic, tireless strokes.

The rucksack hums in time with the percussive blows, a different tune than it did before. This one sounds like a funeral march.

* * *

Phoom! Phoom!

Myrddin forces himself to his feet, completely naked and frightfully thin. The dim light of the glowing rock illuminates him from below in a most unflattering manner. Dust sprinkles from the ceiling of the cave, shaken loose with each pounding beat. He listens, then titters to himself and claps his hands, imagining an enormous heart beating in the earth. The heart of his beloved, beating for him. He does a little jig, shuffling in a circle, stops and gazes at the area from which the sound originates.

Could it be her? Finally, after all this time, come to set me free? A single word escapes his thick dry lips, "Nyneve..."

Myrddin blinks, his eyes glaze...

* * *

Sunlight through autumn leaves dappled his robe and the path beneath his feet as he walked through the wooded hills. No, not walked. Skipped. And he was singing. His beloved had sent him a message, received clandestinely in his study, received with a leap of his heart. Then he was there, at the mouth of the cave, their secret place. She had set out a picnic of roast chicken, a loaf of bread and wine. Lovely beyond description. The Lady Nyneve. She'd been his apprentice until things turned amorous. Until *he* turned amorous.

He attempted a kiss, but she was coy and turned her cheek with the slightest smile. When they finished their meal, he ushered her into the cave to describe once again his plans to transform it into a spectacular home for them, a veritable mountain palace. She listened kindly. Then she told him he could have his kiss, the first of many to come, if he would prove that he loved her as much as she loved him, that he trusted her – if he would tell her the last of his secrets, the ancient words that were the key to unlocking the mysteries of his grimoire scrolls.

Though he had sworn a blood oath to his mentor not to tell anyone, he revealed them to Nyneve. She kissed him on the lips for the first time, and the last. She placed a hand against his cheek and smiled – but there was a sadness there, too. Then she spoke just two words and he couldn't move. Gently, like a nurse undressing the wounded, she removed his shoulder bag of "magical" items, the ones he kept near at all times, including his scrolls and precious gambanteinn. She even lifted the talisman from around his neck, the one made by his mentor, his teacher, his friend, The Prathamaja Nandana.

Nyneve stepped lightly out of the cave, placed her hand on the stone and spoke archaic words. His words. The stone flowed and hardened, sealing in the darkness. The darkness, and The Madman. The Old Fool.

Once he'd overcome the shock at Nyneve's betrayal, Myrddin tried every arcane phrase he knew, then brute force, to escape this prison, but there was no undoing the incantation that trapped him here. Not from within.

Though he knew the risk of winding up stuck in solid ground, he tried to slip away. It didn't work, no matter how hard he tried. By some method even Myrddin cannot fathom, she'd stripped him of that rare gift along with his freedom.

* * *

Phoom!

Bits of rock fall as the steady assault continues. *Is that a crack, forming in the wall? Do I imagine the slightest glimpse of natural light?*

The last time Myrddin saw the sun, moon or stars, it was an agonizing time for the kingdom. Not because there was war, there had been a rare lull in the otherwise continuous fighting that beleaguered the land. The drought and famine saw to that. There was nothing to feed armies. Or the king's people.

The king slouched in his throne, worried and wasted away. Myrddin knew the hard times would pass and tried to convince him. If there is one truth Myrddin has learned in all his many years, it is that things *always* change. But the king didn't always heed Myrddin's counsel. He sent his knights out on a foolish, dangerous quest – including the best of them, the one most dear to Myrddin's heart. A kind, brave boy who did not know the real secret of his father, Launcelot, or who his grandfather *really* was.

Myrddin drops to his knees, clasps his hands and presses them to his broad wrinkled forehead. In Latin, he prays, "Dear God, if I do escape this place, if my wretched life is to be saved, I will devote the remainder of it to finding the boy and telling him the truth. This I swear to you, O Lord."

If the boy still lives, it occurs to him. He squeezes his eyes tight *"Dirige, Domine, Deus meus, in conspectu tuo viam meam"* ("Direct my way in thy sight, O Lord, my God"). He drops his hands to the floor, his dirty hair and beard hanging almost to them. A single tear drops in the dust.

Myrddin has always been a little mad. Maybe a lot. But right now he truly fears for his sanity. The betrayal, longing and loneliness have taken their toll. *And the guilt.* He wonders if he is imagining things at this very moment. *Is anyone here at all? If so, perhaps they've come to punish me for my sins. My many, many sins.*

With a mighty *crack* a portion of the wall gives way. Moonlight pierces the darkness, a beam in the billowing dust that freezes Myrddin Wyllt like an escapee pinned by the searchlight of a prison guard.

* * *

Bödvar watches the opening he's made in the cliff warily, sniffs at the stagnant air. The scent is unmistakably that of The Madman. And he's alive. But not for long.

He hoists a stone and wedges it into the hole, scoops rubble to hold it in place. Myrddin Wyllt has always been a tricky bastard and is not to be underestimated. He looks to his oversized rucksack, which is now eerily silent, and heaves a fretful sigh. It's time to let it out.

* * *

Bödvar gingerly sets a sizable urn on the ground, constructed of hard white oak, banded in iron, stained with dark water, mildew and dried blood. The key turns reluctantly in the antique padlocks that hold the lid into place. A moment of hesitation, then he tugs the hasps loose, lifts the latches and stands back. With a glub and gurgle the lid begins to rise. An iridescent vapor creeps out.

Bödvar backs away a bit more. He's never actually met this Firstborn. It never traveled openly or often, and hadn't participated in the Magnificent Holocausts. It also preferred hot wet climes, and The Bear kept mostly to cooler regions of the world. He's passed near to where it dwelt a few times, but went out of his way to make sure he didn't come *too* near.

It's Bödvar's understanding that this is possibly the most repulsive of all Firstborn, and though by no means the oldest, one of the most feared. He has nightmares just from hearing folks tell of their nightmares about it. In fact, he feels like he's having one right now.

The lid slides back in the ghostly moonlit mist and drops to the dirt. A thick glob of milky gray flesh slithers out, covered in translucent mucus, wet with water from the urn, and puddles on the ground. Finally the last of it slops down the side.

Bödvar takes yet another involuntary step back as one end of the creature begins to rise. When it reaches five feet, the top blooms and sucks in sharp gargling breaths, the swaying body expanding and contracting as it respires. The open mouth turns toward Bödvar, wet breath rasping across concentric rings of yellow, scalpel-blade teeth. The mouth closes, to Bödvar's relief, and he sees that it has full thick lips, soft and moist, of the palest pink. Nostrils slit open above the mouth, then two lumps bulge and open to reveal bloodshot eyes of light blue, with thin white eyelashes that wriggle like tiny tentacles.

Bödvar can't tell if there is a single bone in its body, but it does have limbs – rubbery and fluid with undulating strips of flesh for fingers at the ends of its ribbony arms. Viscous eyelids blink sluggishly as it gazes at him.

Then she smiles.

So this is Lamia. Bödvar shudders. *This is The Leech.*

21

FLOWERS & FIGS 9

"Excellent, it *is* here," Peter observes with gratification.

The impressive signage on the twenty story building reads *Empyrean Transnational Bank.*

"I thought it was a Third Fourth Fifth Bank," says Fi, "or Buffington Trust Credit Union."

"Yeah," Zeke responds, "banks change names once a month these days, I swear." Then he sees another sign, in the front window. "See, they're closed," he tells Peter. "I really don't need that money right now, I told you—"

"Nonsense," Peter scoffs. He hurries along the sidewalk to a young woman with thick glasses who is encouraging passersby to sign a clean air petition. He interrupts her spiel, "I'll sign!"

"Oh, okay," she replies, as if surprised anyone would, and hands him a clipboard and pen.

He flips over the top sheet with signatures, tears out the blank one below and hands the clipboard back to the woman. "I'll be back," he promises. "You have my word," and he bolts across the street.

Watching Peter dodge traffic, Fi observes that he moves with powerful grace and poise, perfectly balanced, self-assured and completely at ease. She and Zeke aren't quite so physically adept, so they're much more careful crossing. They arrive as Peter bangs on the glass double doors.

"Peter," Fi admonishes, "you can't just knock on a bank door."

A uniformed guard approaches from inside, shaking his head and mouthing the words, "We're closed."

Peter scribbles something on the back of the petition, presses it to the window. The guard squints through the glass and reads a single word, *ROSTRUM.* He frowns and says, "Go away."

Peter scribbles on the paper again. *Please call the manager.*

The guard mouths again, "No."

Peter calmly writes, *Contact your manager now or lose your job*. The guard snorts but pulls a radio from his belt and speaks into it. After a few moments he apparently gets a reply – and not the one he expected. Obviously perplexed, he clips his radio back to his belt and holds one finger up to Peter – not the middle finger, as Fi and Zeke would've thought, but his index finger, in a gesture to wait.

Peter grins and bobs his eyebrows at Fi and Zeke.

Across the polished granite floor of the lobby, an office door at the end of the empty tellers' booths opens. A pudgy man with a mustache peeks out, speaking urgently into a mobile phone while peering at the front door. He finishes the call, straightens his tie and approaches. Meanwhile, the guard unlocks the doors and pulls them open. Peter steps right in.

The man with the mustache finishes clipping a name tag to his lapel with jittery fingers. It reads *Robert Jenkins, Manager*. He eyes Peter's bushy beard and ratty apparel. "This is quite unexpected, I—"

"They're with me," Peter interrupts, indicating Fi and Zeke while grasping Jenkins's hand and shaking it. "They will receive every courtesy afforded to me."

"Of course..." Jenkins wipes his forehead with a handkerchief. "Absolutely, sir." He seems every bit as confused as the security guard, who closes and locks the doors behind them.

"This way, please." Jenkins shepherds them to a half circle of plush leather chairs. "You're very lucky to have caught me here on a Sunday, I just stopped by after a church function to..." but he sees by the look on Peter's face that he isn't interested. "I'm, er-—not familiar with this particular—procedure—you understand—but I phoned my superiors and have been instructed to make you as comfortable as possible and afford you every courtesy... as you said yourself..." The poor man is terribly flustered, but Peter is gracious.

"I thank you for your kind hospitality," Peter offers with a small bow, which seems to distress Jenkins even more. "How long do you think it will be?"

"I've been told no more than half an hour, sir." He mops his forehead again. "Can I get you anything to drink?"

Peter grins, "Bourbon on the rocks?"

* * *

Apparently some banks do indeed serve liquor, to Fi and Zeke's surprise. Peter has downed three drinks and Fi and Zeke a cup of coffee each when the elevator at the opposite end of the lobby *dings*. Jenkins is greatly relieved.

A tall man with gray hair steps out, wearing a charcoal sweater over a pink shirt. Following him is another man, stockier and bald, in a jacket and tie, carrying a thin metal briefcase. They beeline across the lobby, the tall man scrutinizing Peter, Fi and Zeke, the expression on his face revealing no opinion of them one way or the other. He walks straight to Peter, holds out a hand.

"Welcome to Empyrean Transnational," he says. "I'm Kenneth Hashi, Vice President, North American Op—"

"We're in a bit of a hurry, Ken, if you don't mind," Peter interrupts, shaking Hashi's hand firmly.

"Of course," Hashi replies. "May I first inquire as to your name?"

"No, you may not," Peter answers without malice.

"Very good sir," says Hashi, giving Peter a knowing nod.

"I'm Kalb, Regional V.P. of Security," the stocky bald man says, offering his hand. "It's a pleasure to serve you, sir." Peter greets him in return.

Hashi addresses the manager. "We'll be using your office, Jenkins. With me."

"Yes sir. Whatever you..."

But Hashi is already striding away, Peter right behind him. Fi and Zeke hurry to keep up. "One of these two will be your party's witness?" Hashi asks.

Peter turns to Fi. "Will you do the honors?"

"The honors of what?"

"Just watching."

She looks at Zeke, who shrugs.

"The young man should be comfortable here," assures Hashi, indicating chairs against the wall next to the door, then ushers Peter, Fi, and Kalb into the office and follows, closing the door behind him.

Zeke sits, a little jealous he's being left out of whatever it is they're doing in there.

Jenkins offers him a weak smile, clears his throat, "Another coffee?"

"That would be great, thanks," Zeke replies.

Jenkins wipes his sweaty palms on his jacket and hustles off.

Zeke groans and rubs his face, then looks at a newspaper laying on the seat beside him. The headline reads: *Nicaragua Votes for Statehood.*

"What?" he says aloud. He picks it up and reads further: *Final Central American territory achieves majority vote for a petition to Congress. If accepted, Nicaragua will become the 73rd U.S. State....*

He checks the date of the paper. It's today's. He glances at the guard, who's watching him warily from his position by the door. Zeke heads toward him, clutching the paper. He's planning to ask what the hell this news story is all about but stops dead as something else catches his attention.

On the sidewalk outside, a lanky young man with the hood up on his sweatshirt is sauntering past the windows. The blood drains from Zeke's face.

The man stops, setting a guitar case down to light a cigarette. He turns toward the glass to shelter his lighter from the wind. In the flare of the flame, Zeke sees enough of the man's face to make his insides squirm cold. The man retrieves the case and walks away. Zeke rushes the guard, his heart beating like mad.

"Open the door," he shouts. "Open the door!"

"Hold your horses," the guard replies. He slips a key into the lock and barely has it turned before Zeke shoves through.

* * *

Inside the manager's office, Peter sits at the customer's side of the desk next to Fi, typing energetically on a secure briefcase laptop Kalb has given him. Sitting in Jenkins's chair, Hashi leans close to a monitor, reading the screen. "So, there's a series of 36 questions, each randomly chosen from a pool of 100 that you yourself have created and entered answers for."

Peter keeps typing, questions flashing on the screen, appearing and being answered faster than Fi can read them.

"Then there will be a series of 13 passcodes of 13 characters each," Hashi continues. "Please remember that uppercase characters are recognized. It says here that the entire process should take between twenty and thirty minutes, depending on—"

Hashi's computer *beeps*. He stops speaking. On his screen, *ROSTRUM Protocol: Authorization Complete - ACCESS GRANTED* blinks in green letters. He glances at Kalb, who is surprised as he is, then Peter, who's sitting back in his chair, hands folded in his lap, and smiling.

"All right, sir," Hashi acknowledges. "Shall we proceed to the vault?"

* * *

Peter puts a hand on Fi's shoulder as they exit Jenkins's office. "I'll be right back," he tells her. "Don't go anywhere."

"So you've said," she retorts. She sees the row of empty chairs. "Where's Zeke?"

Immediately on alert, Peter scans the lobby, then nods toward the doors. "There."

Zeke enters past the guard and shuffles toward them, head down, hands stuffed in his pockets.

"Where did you go?" Fi asks, more irritated than worried. Then she sees his face – now she's worried. If anyone ever looked like they'd seen a ghost, it's Zeke. "What the hell?"

"It... it's nothing." His eyes shift evasively between her and Peter. "I just went out to get some air."

Fi touches his arm. "You're soaking wet."

"I... uh... quick downpour, that's all," he insists, but Peter is looking out the windows. There is no rain. He turns his penetrating eyes on Zeke, who shrinks under his gaze. "It's stopped now," Zeke adds.

Peter just says, "Hmm..."

Fi puts her hands on Zeke's shoulders, feels him shivering, "You're freezing."

"Jenkins," Hashi calls to the bank manager, who is just arriving with Zeke's coffee. "Get the young man a coat."

"Yes sir, sorry sir, I had to make a new pot." Fi takes the cup from him and hands it to Zeke.

"This way sir," says Hashi.

"Stay put, both of you," Peter states. It's not a request. He finally takes his eyes off Zeke and follows Hashi and Kalb toward the elevators.

Jenkins comes out of his office with a cashmere overcoat. Fi takes it, puts it over Zeke's shoulders and moves him to a chair. She sits next to him and leans close, then sees Jenkins still hovering nearby. She glares at him until he retreats to a more discrete distance.

"Okay," she asks Zeke, "what happened?"

"Nothing," he replies. "Really. I just got caught in the rain, that's all. Sorry to make you worry."

"Uh huh." Fi is unconvinced. "You still think this is 'amazing?'"

He manages a feeble laugh but the accompanying smile fades quickly.

"On second thought—" They jump to see Peter standing over them. "Why don't you two come with me?"

* * *

The elevator doors slide open to reveal a domed atrium of polished granite. Fi and Zeke have no idea how far they descended below the lobby, but it was pretty damn far.

Hashi and Kalb enter codes simultaneously on either side of a circular strongroom door. There's a resounding *clunk* and Kalb spins the operating wheel. The door tugs open with a soft rush of air.

They follow the two men into a room with safe deposit boxes lining the walls, a slim counter down the center. Hashi and Kalb go to the end and face the wall on the right. They each open a safe deposit box with a key, one up to the left, the other low to the right, then nod to each other and pull the boxes out together. There's another *clunk* as a section of boxes separates from the rest. Kalb swings the panel out – a facade for another vault door.

"We'll wait for you here, sir," Hashi tells Peter.

Peter raises his eyebrows at him, because he's standing in the way. Hashi backs away apologetically. Peter enters what seems to be a tremendously long passcode then holds his eye to a scanner. The scanner beeps and the door swings silently inward.

Lights blink on overhead as they enter. This room looks more like a morgue than a vault, with a stainless steel table against the left wall and safe deposit boxes, much larger than normal, stacked to the right. Peter crouches to a box on the lowest row. He enters a code on the front panel, subjects his thumb to a scan and slides out the drawer.

Fi isn't sure she should look, but Peter's making no effort to conceal anything. She feels Zeke lean over her shoulder to peek in as well. Peter retrieves an old canvas backpack and tosses it on the table.

Due to his avid fascination with all things historical, Zeke recognizes it as a World War I vintage military haversack, dirty tan canvas replete with the faded black letters, "U.S.", stenciled on the flaps. Peter rummages inside, retrieves stacks of cash from various countries held by paper bands, peels off a 100 dollar bill and hands it to Zeke.

"There you go," he says with a smile.

Zeke looks incredulously at the money. "That's too—"

"Far too little to compensate for your aid and kindness, I know," Peter interrupts, "but I'll make it up to you." Zeke opens his mouth to speak, but thinks better of it and stuffs the bill in his jeans pocket.

Peter shoves some of the cash, a wallet and several passports from the haversack into his pockets. He pauses, then gingerly reaches into a side pocket of the pack and pulls something out. He opens his palm and studies it. Fi and Zeke crane in for a closer look.

It appears to be a rod of gold, about the size of a roll of quarters, rounded smooth on both ends with arcane glyphs engraved along its surface. Peter whispers a single word Fi and Zeke can't make out. The object vibrates with a soft hum and begins to roll slowly in his palm. Peter mutters the same word and the vibration and humming cease.

"What is that?" Fi ventures to ask.

"It's been known by many names," Peter says casually. "The Spear of Rudra, Grid's Rod, the Lightning Bolt of Zeus – the *true* Zeus, mind you, not that *petit* god of the Greeks." The corners of his mouth turn up slightly at the look of puzzlement and doubt on their faces. "It was originally fashioned for the All-father by Arges, the greatest metalsmith of all time. He dubbed it Gungnir, Odin's Spear."

Zeke lets out a nervous laugh. "Yeah, right."

Peter's expression sobers. "There's something you should know, both of you." He shoves the thing into a cargo pocket on his pants. "I may not always tell the whole truth, but I *never* lie."

* * *

Peter offers a stack of cash to the nervous manager, Jenkins. "Will two thousand dollars be sufficient for the coat?"

Jenkins's eyes light up but Hashi holds up a hand, "That won't be necessary, sir." Jenkins is clearly disappointed.

"It's been a great pleasure," says Hashi, shaking Peter's hand. "Empyrean Transnational appreciates your business."

"The pleasure is mine," Peter replies.

Hashi nods to Fi and Zeke. Fi offers a wave, then feels like an idiot for doing so. Zeke smiles feebly. The guard holds the door for them while they exit.

Jenkins lets out a groan of relief, wiping his forehead one more time.

"Who *is* that guy?" the guard asks, watching Peter depart, his haversack now on his back. Kalb glares at him for his impropriety.

Hashi answers anyway, with complete honesty, "I have no idea."

* * *

Peter takes the clipboard from the young woman soliciting signatures, signs, and hands it back, along with the pen he'd borrowed. She thanks him and they continue along the sidewalk under a dreary sky.

"Zeke," says Peter with authority.

Zeke cringes as if trying to hide in the upturned collar of Jenkins's coat. "What?" he asks, his voice cracking.

Peter studies him intently, then reaches a hand toward his. His voice softens. "Let's go home."

Zeke hesitates, but takes it. He offers his other to Fi.

She wavers, looks to Peter. "You mean, this isn't our world?"

To her surprise, it's Zeke who answers by shaking his head, *No*. She narrows her eyes at him, but places her hand in his.

"Think about nothing," Peter instructs Zeke. "It's very close. Just feel out with that empty part of your mind."

Zeke takes a deep breath as they continue walking, then closes his eyes. His expression compresses into one of utter concentration, then the muscles of his face relax,
"Slip..."

* * *

An elderly couple, holding hands, stops at the spot where Peter, Fi, and Zeke had vanished. Caught up in conversation they saw nothing of their disappearance, but something else has captured their attention. A hum in the air, of the air itself, growing louder by the moment, accompanied by a vibration of the ground at their feet. The windows of the buildings shake, throwing their reflections out of focus.

They flinch from a sudden blinding flash and are rocked by a searing concussion like the sky itself being ripped apart. When they dare to look, they see an inverted cone of yellow light at the edge of the city, going from the ground to miles in the sky. At the very top is a seething black cloud. The light disappears with a rumble of thunder, but the cloud remains. It spreads and extends dark swarming tentacles earthward.

The hum increases to an unbearable cacophony of buzzing, clicking, and clattering. The first of the swarm reaches beyond the buildings several blocks away. The couple hears glass shatter, car alarms blare, metal scraping, rasping on concrete, all punctuated by scattered explosions. Then they hear the screams.

* * *

Fi's vision is blurred by fog and her feet slide beneath her, then the sensation is gone—
HOOONK.

She jumps at the sound. Zeke's eyes snap open. They leap back from the street as a fire engine roars past, blasting its horn.

Fi claps a hand on her madly beating heart. "I don't know how much more of this I can take."

"You're doing astonishingly well, Fi," comforts Peter. "Better than most, I'd say."

"So... are we back?" Zeke asks.

Peter pauses a moment, as if feeling out with his mind himself, just to make certain. "Yes. We're back."

Zeke breathes in relief, then realizes he alone still stands on the sidewalk holding Peter's hand. He lets go and shoves his hand in his coat pocket.

"Zeke, are you a man of honor?" Peter asks earnestly. Zeke gets an expression like he doesn't understand what he's being asked. Peter rephrases the question. "Are you a man of your word?"

"Yeah, I guess so."

"Are you, or are you not?" Peter asks again.

Zeke straightens. "Yes, I believe I am."

"Then promise me you will never do that again."

"You mean that..." he makes a sliding motion with his hand.

"Yes, that," Peter confirms, making the same motion. "Swear that you won't do it again until we've had a chance to discuss it at length. Understand?"

Zeke nods tentatively. "Yeah, I think—"

"Then swear, on your honor."

Zeke looks to Fi, then back to Peter. "I swear, on my honor, that I won't do it again until we've talked about it."

"At length," Peter repeats.

"Until we've talked about it at length," Zeke adds.

Peter grins, suddenly not so serious, and gives Zeke's shoulder a squeeze. "I don't know about you two, but I need a burger." His eyes light up. "And a *beer.*"

22

MENDIP HILLS 4

Bödvar would really like to be holding his Mighty sword Kladenets right now, but it might appear threatening and he would rather not provoke The Leech. He's also heard she can absorb a slash or jab from all but the highest class of Astra blade, anyway. Mortal and Mighty weapons supposedly slide right off. No one can grip her. She can't be crushed. Except by Father.

Bödvar simply has to trust Baphomet's word that he's safe with her. Or trust the pledge Lamia has made to Baphomet and the Master, more precisely. Bödvar wonders what they promised to persuade her to join their cause. Maybe freedom from persecution, or a lifetime supply of tender parvulus babies to suck on. Perhaps it's the life of The Madman himself. Bödvar knows the story. They all do.

Father had taken Myrddin's parvulus mother while frolicking in a bog, waist deep in black water. Neither were aware that a leech had attached itself to her thigh. Nor would they probably have cared. Father's seed overflowed the woman, swirling in a milky cloud and enveloping the leech, which was swelled with the blood of the woman.

When Father noticed the parasite on the woman's leg an hour later, his curiosity got the best of him. Instead of pinching it to oblivion he placed it in a basket of tightly woven reeds filled with water. Within days, a single soft cocoon had formed on the leech's ventral surface, and eight months before the birth of Myrddin Wyllt, The Leech was born. She grew strong and healthy, fed by Father on rodents and fish. Then one night, she escaped.

Though only a foot long at the time, she followed the heat and sound to the infant Myrddin, newly born. He lay mewling in his sleeping mother's arms when Lamia attached herself to his chest. The child made no sound, but the mother woke and raised the entire tribe with her cries. Father tore Lamia from the babe, but couldn't bring himself to kill the wretched thing. Instead, he sealed her in a vessel made from a gourd, trekked to the coast and threw her into the sea.

No one knows where the currents took her, where she might have washed ashore and escaped from that gourd, and Lamia is one of the few Firstborn who does not tell tales. There are stories of her from many parts of the world, however, that others have been all too happy to convey. Perhaps the most famous of these comes from her time in the region of Africa now known as Libya, back when it was a tropical and damp place. Though she's had many names, she was worshipped there by her Truename, Lamia. Cloaked as a human, she reigned as their bloody queen, reviled and supreme, for a thousand years. Then Vidar, the *petit* god who had stolen one of Father's oldest names of Zeus, discovered her true identity and drove her from her throne.

Since then she's been hiding in dark wet places of the world. When the Master and Baphomet found her almost a year ago, she was deep in the bayous of Louisiana where she'd been feeding on wayward Cajuns, lending credence to local folklore of the Cauchemar, the "Nightmare Witch."

Lamia takes quick slithering steps toward Bödvar, leaving a slick snail trail behind her. Bödvar fights the urge to run like hell.

"Greetings brother Matuno-s-s-s-s-s," she sputters in a language last spoken by predecessors of the Ancient Berber tribes of Northwest Africa.

Bödvar isn't sure how to respond, so he keeps it simple. "Lamia." And respectful. "Ma'am."

Lamia bats her eyes and giggles. It's more like a gurgle, but he takes it as a giggle.

"We h-e-e-r-r-r-r-r-e? He h-e-e-r-r-r-r-r-e?"

"Yes, Lamia." Bödvar nods toward the cave. "Just give me some time to clear the entrance."

"Take you tim-m-m-m-e, brother Bear-r-r-r-r."

Bödvar has the most serious case of heebie-jeebies he's ever experienced, bar none. He forces himself to take the few steps to the blocked opening of the cave, but he can't control the shiver that runs through his body.

"You cold, brother Bear-r-r-r-r?"

Bödvar nearly jumps out of his skin and whips around to find Lamia standing right behind him, stretched tall enough to look him in the eye. "Uhhh... No ma'am." He controls another shiver with a great force of will. "You might want to stand back, though. I've got to move these rocks."

"Of cours-s-s-s-se." She shimmies to the rucksack, shrinking back to five feet in height as she goes. "Thank you for thinking of me s-a-a-a-fety. This g-o-o-o-o-o-d?"

Bödvar wants to shout the most vulgar Old Germanic obscenities that come to mind (they sound so nasty in that language), as loud as he possibly can. Instead, he says "That should do it. Thank you." He's going to be *very* glad when this job is done and she's back in that urn.

He tugs the boulder out and chucks it down the hill. Lamia could squeeze through a hole even smaller than the one he's already made, but Bödvar wants to be able to enter as well. He's not going to miss this. He picks up his hammer and swings away. Lamia hums a happy tune while she waits.

* * *

Stone shatters and topples into the cave. Except for the rocks strewn on the floor and the dirt in the air, the entrance is clear.

Myrddin remains on his knees, his palms pressed to the floor. The rock beneath his hands is the only thing he knows is genuine. He thought he saw the light of the moon before, smelled the fresh air of the forested hills. Then it was gone. Now it's back, and the entrance is open. But for how long? Is it real, or just another twisted dream?

Then there's a glow in the dusty haze, a light that's other than diffused moonlight. A figure approaches, glimmering white, then blue, red and yellow. The colors chase each other, up, down, around. Myrddin squints to see. The dust is dissipating, carried away by the outside air. His vision clears and the figure takes shape.

"Nyneve?" he asks.

It *is* Nyneve. He sees her now. As lovely as ever. *She hasn't aged a day.* His good sense alerts him to the fact that his beloved is, *was*, nearly human and couldn't possibly be alive – unless he hasn't been trapped here nearly as long as he thinks. *Is that possible?* Incompatible thoughts grapple with one another. Until she speaks.

"Yes, my love. I am here."

It's *her* voice. *Her* beautiful voice. There's no more question in his mind. Tears streaming, he forces himself up on trembling legs. "Nyneve," he sobs, "my darling Nyneve."

* * *

Bödvar can't wait any longer. The last of the dust wafts out of the cave as he ducks his head and enters. Once inside, he can stand upright, and there he sees an amazing sight – Lamia's gleaming body swirling in psychedelic eddies of every hue, The Madman in her slimy embrace.

According to Baphomet, Lamia can manipulate chromataphore pigmentation in her skin to create multiple color combinations, like certain frogs. Her flesh is also bioluminescent, which gives her the ability to emit light, even in complete darkness. Bödvar didn't give a shit when he first heard it, but now he understands Baphomet's fascination.

The Goat also explained that the clear mucus she exudes from her body magnifies the colorful light show and contains chemicals that have euphoric and hallucinogenic effects on those she touches. When she was queen of Libya, she'd share this substance with her most loyal subjects in drug induced orgies of sex and blood.

Myrddin shudders with pleasure. The warmth of her, the pressure of supple breasts on his chest, soft hands on his shoulders, luscious lips pressed to his. The feel of something other than clammy stone. The touch of his dearest Nyneve.

Bödvar observes as Lamia slides one slippery hand from Myrddin's shoulder down his chest and stomach to his groin. In spite of his age and condition he throbs to life. With her other hand she grabs his wrinkled saggy ass and squeezes hard. Myrddin moans.

Humming her little song, she lowers her face to his breast, where her lips and pallid tongue find the scar that never fully healed, the one she gave him when he was a babe. She slathers him with slobber that contains both a powerful anesthetic and an anticoagulant that will keep his blood from clotting. Her mouth expands and she suction-cups her lips to his chest, her naturally lubricated hand still working his Mad-manhood.

Bödvar is enjoying this. After all the times Myrddin Wyllt has misled him and made him look the fool, this death through deception is sweeter revenge than killing the bastard himself.

Lamia slides her hand up from Myrddin's butt to brace his back. Her rings of razor teeth slice into his chest. Blood flows into her gullet. Then she stops. He's helplessly, hopelessly, under her spell. She releases the hold she has with her teeth. Blood trickles freely from the ring of incisions on his chest. She looks him in the eye, revels in his glazed expression of false ecstasy.

Lamia has waited for this moment all her life. She and The Madman not only share a father, but The Leech's mother had Myrddin's mother's blood in her when Lamia was conceived as well. By her reckoning, they are truly brother and sister. But when they were new to this world he had been coddled, nursed at a warm teat, cooed at and cherished, while she was kept in a basket and fed on rats. Then Father cast her away like trash and embraced the whelp of a parvulus whore as a true Firstborn child.

Lamia remembers, oh yes, Lamia remembers. She hates The Madman. And she loves him. Now she has his blood in her once again. Sweet, sweet nectar, the most delicious she's ever tasted. The first time she fed on him was no accident. This time he will die, *and he will like it.* Some grudges last that long. Some vengeance worth waiting for.

She will outlive her brother, and when the Deva are defeated and Father cast down she will be a queen again. The Madman will be only a myth, forever, like so many before him, and she will be free.

She moves her dripping mouth to his ear. "Hello brother-r-r-r-r-r," she whispers. "Me am no Nyne-e-e-e-ve. No-o-o-o-o-o. Me am you sister-r-r. L-a-a-a-a-m-i-i-a-a-a-a..."

"Not... Nyneve?" Myrddin mumbles. He opens his eyes, but all he sees is Nyneve.

"Me love you, brother-r-r..."

"Lamia?" It still doesn't register.

"Me love you to *death...*"

In Myrddin's blurry sight, the image of Nyneve's beautiful face dissolves to the visage of The Leech – but he's too far gone. There is nothing he can do to stop her. Nothing he *wants* to do to stop her. She licks blood from his chest, attaches her sucker mouth to him once more, and begins to hum.

"Ohhhhhh... Lamia..." Myrddin closes his eyes. If it's to be for the last time, he just doesn't care.

* * *

Mesmerized by the shimmering rainbow of her body and the lilting melody of her song, Bödvar watches Lamia drain the life from The Madman. It's a wonder to behold.

All Firstborn can see the cloak of another, but they can also see through it with little effort. Firstborn of a human mother, however, like Myrddin Wyllt, have the parvulus frailty of mind. A master of the art of cloaking such as Lamia can fool them easily. And she is one of the best. In addition, it is said she can hypnotize parvuli with her songs, fluttering eyelashes and wavering body – and even overpower the faculties of Firstborn who are *not* born of a weakling parvulus. For this reason, Bödvar knows he shouldn't look directly at her for too long, but he's loathe to turn away.

Entranced as he is by the bewitching allure of The Leech, the ordinarily ultra-vigilant Bear doesn't notice the breeze that ruffles the fur on his back, is barely conscious of the shadow that flits past his shoulder to form an inky blot on the cavern wall beside him. The soft voice is his first real clue that anyone is there at all.

"*Matunos...*"

Bödvar's consciousness twitches in its hypnotic haze. Someone has spoken his Truename, which none have used in over a millenium. Altar stones raised by the earliest Brythonic Celts still stand in honor of that name in High Rochester and Risingham here in England. He considered visiting them after this mission is over, if time and duty permitted, just for old times sake. The name Bödvar Bjarki is a recent appellation, one he took when he fought as a sellsword for a Norwegian king after the fall of Attila the Hun. He's kept it ever since, having always liked how it rolls off his floppy bear's tongue.

Who said that? His eyes try to focus on the shadow. *Who's there?* He's turning to see what might be blocking the light of the moon when a thin blade pierces his chest. Pierces deep. Without a grunt or moan, he slumps to the floor.

23

FLOWERS & FIGS 10

Fi and Zeke have barely touched their burgers and fries. They're seated at a table in a downtown establishment that calls itself an Irish pub and boasts the "best burgers in town." Peter obviously thinks they're good enough. He's devouring the second of two giant jalapeno cheeseburgers. Three empty beer mugs sit in front of him and the fourth is nearly gone. Zeke hunches in his chair, the bank manager's cashmere overcoat wrapped tightly around him, sucking soda through a straw. He isn't as chilled as he was, but his color hasn't fully returned.

They haven't spoken a word since they ordered, Peter having spent the intervening time between then and the arrival of the food chatting up a couple of attractive and well attired businesswomen at the bar. Since then he's been busy eating but incredibly alert, scanning TV screens above the bar and the crowded tables, studying everyone and everything. Every once in awhile he'd close his eyes as if listening.

He's watching people texting on their smart phones at the next table when Fi leans forward and speaks quietly, "Peter, you shouldn't..." He looks at her inquisitively. "It's rude."

"Just catching up on the latest *patois*," he responds, unabashed. ""*Lol, lfmao, rotfl*, those I know, or can figure out. But, YOLO!" he shouts. Nearby patrons look at him. "I'm assuming it means 'you only live once,' correct?"

Fi answers, embarrassed, "Yes, it does."

"Not entirely true, but..." He waggles his head, thinking about it, then stuffs his face with the remainder of his chili fries.

Fi takes a sip of her water. She loves a good burger, but she isn't hungry. Just exhausted and overwhelmed. She'd like nothing more than to wake up from this bizarre nightmare in her comfy bed, wrapped in her favorite quilt, and start the whole day over again. Without realizing, she lets out a dramatic sigh.

Peter pops the last bit of burger in his mouth and washes it down with the rest of his beer, some of which dribbles into his beard. He clunks the mug down and lets out a loud wet belch of satisfaction. "Pardon me," he says with a grin.

"Oh, I don't think so," Fi retorts. "That was disgusting."

He watches her languidly stirring ketchup with half a fry. "Fiona?"

She drops her fry onto the plate and gives him a squint-eyed, dirty look. Only her Uncle Edgar and Mrs. Mirskaya call her Fiona, and she likes it that way. "Finished?" she asks briskly.

"You're not tired, are you?" Peter asks, ignoring her question.

She sits back, wiping her hands on the napkin in her lap. "Well, yeah. I am."

Peter gives her the same scrutinizing look he gave Zeke earlier. "Hmm..."

"*Hmm* yourself," she snaps, tossing the napkin on her plate.

Peter grins wide, greatly amused for some reason. He wipes his mouth on his sleeve then notices the two women he was talking to earlier shooting furtive glances his way. "If you'll excuse me, and stay put, I need to use the little boys' room." Without waiting for an answer he drops a 100 dollar bill next to his plate and walks away along the bar.

Fi and Zeke sit quietly. There's so much to say. And nothing at all.

Zeke notices she's chewing her nails. "I didn't know you bite your nails."

Fi flashes him a look and shoves her hand in her lap. "I don't. Or, I *didn't*."

He changes the subject to what's really on his mind. "Well, what do you think?"

"About what?"

"Anything. *Everything*."

"You don't believe any of that stuff he told us, do you?"

"I honestly don't know what to believe. He did say he never lies."

"Which is exactly what every pathological liar says."

"I know, but still..." He leans closer. "Who do you think he is, I mean *really?*"

"Every time I think about it my stomach ties up in knots."

"Yes! It's exactly the same with me."

"Yeah?"

"Hell yeah. But... I can't help but think..."

Fi watches, waiting.

"I mean, there was a moment there, after we first did that slipping thing," he makes the sliding motion with his hand, "when he came out of that ocean of memory, or whatever it was. I thought maybe..." he laughs uneasily, "he could be God."

Fi feels like she's going to retch – out of anxiety, disgust, or both. She'd considered the same thing. But *Peter? God? No way!*

Zeke sees it on her face. "Or... you know, he could be *some* kind of god. He said he gave Billy the Axe of Perun – that grew out of a necklace, by the way – you saw it too. Perun was a Slavic deity who saved the world by defeating a dragon named Veles. But he also said that thing he got from the bank is Odin's Spear. Odin! The supreme god of the Norse pantheon, the All-father—"

"I know who Odin is," she retorts, holding her stomach. "I'm not completely clueless."

"Sorry." Zeke knows he's grasping at straws, but there has to be *some* explanation. "An angel? Or an alien... maybe?"

She shakes her head, incredulous.

"I mean, he can't be a *man*. Not a normal man, anyway. Can he?"

"I'm still trying not to think about it too hard," she groans. "I'm really hoping I'm just having, like, the most messed up dream *ever*."

Zeke reaches under the table and pinches her leg.

"Hey!" she shouts, jerking in her seat.

"Did that hurt?"

She gives him the dirty look. "No. You just startled me."

He tries a different tack. "Think about when he first came out of that sea of mist—"

"Naked," Fi interjects.

"Okay, naked," he concedes, "but *changed*. What was your first thought?"

"I'm pretty sure it was '*Ahhhhhhh!*' Just like yours."

"Well, yeah. But seriously, the first real thought, or word, that came to mind?"

Fi thinks about it. *What was it? What did I think?*

Zeke looks over his shoulder to check and see if Peter's coming back. All clear. "Come on, we'll say it together, on three, ready. One. Two. Three—"

At the same time, both of them say, "Beautiful."

They stare at each other.

"Really?" she asks. "You thought that?"

"Yeah. But I almost said 'perfect.'"

Fi remembers – she thought that too.

They gaze at each other for what seems a very long time, then realize what they're doing and look at their plates.

"Zeke," she says softly after a few moments. "This *has* to be a dream. Otherwise, the world's completely different from what we've always thought it was. What *anybody* thinks it is. And... a lot of people are dead." He looks at her with empathy and remorse, then focuses on his hands in his lap.

Fi stares at her plate. *Peter*... What happened to her special old man? The gentle dementia patient who loved flowers and figs and gazing at the stars? The quiet helpless guy who could brighten her whole week with an occasional faraway smile? It's strange, but she misses him.

She takes a deep breath, scans the restaurant. "Where *is* he?"

* * *

Fi and Zeke squeeze down the narrow hall of the pub to the restrooms. They come to the women's room first. "I'm going to stop in here," says Fi. Zeke nods, then halts. From the other side of the door comes a distinct smack and a woman's muffled groan. They share a look of alarm and Fi shoves the door open.

At the far end of the galley-style restroom Peter and the two women from the bar are pretzeled in a way that seems almost physically impossible – yet somehow Peter manages to hold both women up with a little help from the sink. Clothes are strewn everywhere. There's the same groan as before – but it isn't a sound of distress.

Fi and Zeke just stand there, gawking.

Peter smacks one of the women on the butt.

"Ohhh, yes," she groans. "Say it again!"

"You really like that?"

"I do. Do it. Say it!"

"Okay then, *Who's your daddy?*"
"You are. You are!"
Zeke reaches past Fi and pulls the door shut.
"We're leaving," she says firmly.
"But..."
"*Now.*"

* * *

Fi storms out of the pub, Zeke stumbling after her. Daylight has given way to night and it's begun to drizzle. Oblivious to the wet and cold, Fi darts across the street, weaving through traffic.

Zeke calls after her, then mumbles, "shit." He raises the collar on his coat and follows, dodging angry drivers who hit their brakes and honk.

"Fi!" he shouts again. "Come on. Think about—"

She halts on the sidewalk and spins on him so abruptly he almost runs into her. "I'm going home, to find my uncle. You can come with me, or you can stay with..." she waves back toward the pub, "*him.*" Zeke runs his hands through his hair apprehensively while she glares up at him. Having waited long enough, she figures, she turns and hurries up the sidewalk. Zeke groans and follows.

"Okay," he says, catching up to her as she crosses the street at the next corner. "But, maybe we can come back, after..."

"Maybe," she says brusquely, without slowing.

"Look, we could get a cab—"

"Just wave one down? In Toledo? Good luck with that."

"You know, your uncle sounds like an interesting guy and all, but can you really tell him about all this?"

Fi keeps striding along, making her way through downtown, headed toward home. She hadn't considered what Uncle Edgar's reaction might be. She's just assumed he'd believe her, and would know what to do about it. Now she wonders.

She wipes her eyes, glances up without stopping. At that moment there's a break in the gray sky and the moon glares down upon the world. The clouds blink it away and she shrugs off the eerie feeling of being watched.

"Fi," Zeke puffs as he jogs to keep up. "What if Peter really is somebody – important – and we just left him—"

"I think he's doing fine all by himself," she responds harshly. "And he isn't really *all* by himself, is he?" She checks for traffic and crosses another street. In spite of her mood, she hopes Zeke didn't see her almost twist her ankle in a pothole.

"But what if he *is* telling the truth?" he asks.

"What truth? He hasn't really told us anything. Nothing that makes sense. And if you want to think of it that way, have you considered your *angel* or *god* or whatever, might actually be a *demon?*"

"Those people who are after him," Zeke counters, "they sure don't seem like *good guys* to me."

"Yeah? How do you know? Maybe they are demons, but maybe there's some sort of coup going on, a fight for control over hell or something."

"Come on, Fi..."

"Well?! It isn't any crazier than—Oh!" In her haste, she trips off a curb and stumbles into the entrance to an alley. A car slams on its brakes and comes skidding right for her on the wet pavement.

"Fi," Zeke shouts, sprinting to tackle her. They tumble onto the far sidewalk as the car squeals to a stop.

The driver's door flies open. Fi swipes at the damp hair clinging to her face, shields her eyes from the headlights and rain. Out steps an elderly man in a windbreaker and slacks, with a hooked nose, braided ponytail and mutton-chop sideburns.

"Uncle Edgar?"

MENDIP HILLS 5

Myrddin Wyllt is having the most wonderful dream. It must be a dream, because he's making sweet love to his beloved Nyneve.

Or is it his sister, Lamia? It doesn't matter. Then, through the fog of carnal lust, he sees something watching. A pitch black shadow, hovering over... a bear?

Yes, a dream, but what a dream. And like all good dreams, he knows it will be interrupted before he can finish. It's already happening.

The shadow floats toward the pair in their lovers' embrace, flings a handful of sparkling crystal powder. His dream-beloved jerks away and screams the most horrible scream.

Myrddin crumples to the floor. *Nyneve!*

* * *

It's about time. Bödvar should be fighting for his life, lashing out at his attacker with his final breath. But he isn't. He's just lying there, blinking at the dim ceiling of the cave. *It's about damn time.*

With tremendous effort he turns his head to the cave entrance. He sees the moon as if for the very first time – and it seems to be looking back.

His thoughts are becoming startlingly clear, as if a sediment stirred by hate has always clouded his mind and is now settling away with his newfound stillness. The strangest thought occurs to him. *I wonder if I actually prefer the company of men?*

Gods know, most Firstborn will hook up with anything. They get it from their father. But Bödvar doesn't mean it *that* way. Here at the end of things, he realizes he's always preferred the company of parvuli – humans – *real* men. *How strange...*

Maybe he's spent his entire life, a life of epochs, fighting on the wrong side, pretending he believed something he didn't, that he was someone he was not. Unlike most Firstborn, he was born when the parvuli were already around. Thinking back, he can't imagine his life without them. He doesn't hate the humans. He *loves* them.

Bödvar's sister, his only littermate, always adored the humans. She lived among them often, taught them things, even carried them around on her back, something Bödvar would never tolerate. They adored her. Bödvar they respected, even admired, but always feared.

Their mother belonged to a long extinct species the humans have named the South American Short-faced Bear, also called a Bulldog Bear, of the genus *Arctotherium*. She stood eleven feet tall when raised up on her hind legs and was mean as hell, always smacking Bödvar around at the slightest provocation. He's sure he deserved it. His sister was just as tall as their mother when full grown, and born before Bödvar by a few minutes. As big as he is, he'd always been the runt, the "little brother," in size and birth order.

His sister was the polar opposite of their mother in disposition, and of him. Good and kind. Too much so, he always thought, to the point of weakness. *She was ferocious when riled though, phew!* It just took a hell of a lot to make her mad. They'd never come to blows on the battlefield, Bödvar is glad of that. She was stronger than he. Female Firstborn always are, given the same breeding and age.

For millennia he and his sister were inseparable. He tried to drive her away many times but she wouldn't leave him, no matter how miserable he made her. Then, one night, she'd finally had enough of his shit – his foul demeanor, his cruelty to the humans – and she deserted him.

Deserted? Where did that come from? I wanted her to go, to leave me be. Didn't I?

He came in contact with her only once after that, the day she died. As his Firstborn lifeblood drains away, Bödvar sees her clear as day.

It was twenty-thousand years ago. The last Great Ice covered much of the planet, and the final battle of the Second Magnificent Holocaust raged. She'd sided with Father, of course – she was always Deva, his sister, Devi to the core. Her Truename was Artio, but at the time she was known by the humans as the Vanir giantess Jörd. When Bödvar saw her she was armored in a massive breastplate, with great golden wings on her helmet, spattered with gore – but beautiful.

She was kneeling in the mud, clutching the broken body of her dying child, the boy she'd named Thor. She cast up her eyes, seeking aid for her son, and looked upon Bödvar for the first time in many myria. There was no hatred in those eyes, no blame, just the tears of a mother wracked with grief. She spoke only one pleading word. "Brother." He saw his Asura comrades approach her from behind. He did nothing, gave no warning. Her head fell from her shoulders. Blood sprayed scarlet plumes over the snow, speckling Bödvar's face and fur...

That's odd. Spreading from the wound in his chest is not just blood – there's also a radiating warmth, a comforting sense of *relief*. He's gotten what he deserves. It's over. The unease, the depression, the hate, the regret, and yes, the fear that's been part of him since he can remember, is leaving him. He feels at peace for the first time since he was a cub, settling down to sleep on feathery ferns, his face nuzzled in his mother's fur. The only tears The Bear has ever known well up in his eyes.

He wonders if there really is an afterlife, of any of the varieties that humans believe in. At that thought a soft sound that might be a laugh escapes his lips. *How trite I am.*

He's pretty sure there will be no fluffy clouds, no fanfare of trumpets or plucking harps, and he knows that the horror stories of a burning, torturous hell are just primordial memory fragments of the rule of the first Master and other terrible times in the pre-history of the parvuli. But who knows? Who is The Bear to say? Is it possible he will see Wiglaf once again? Or Valentine?

Bödvar's eyes widen, ever so slowly, as he lets out a long, soft breath.

Will my sister be there? he wonders. *Will she forgive me?*

* * *

Myrddin watches the flailing mass of gray flesh that was his beloved Nyneve, frantically twisting, coiling and uncoiling, mist rising from its blistering skin. It emits an ear-splitting scream that goes on and on.

Then it's upright, shrieking. *"It b-u-r-r-r-r-r-n-s-s!"*

The shadow swiftly unfolds a thin arm, impossibly long, and smacks at the creature, sending it to slap against the wall of the cave. From the shadow's core an opalescent globe appears, then flies through the air as if of its own accord. It shatters on the wall, splashing blue liquid on the wriggling thing. A spark flicks in an arc and the creature is engulfed in flames. The screaming and writhing increases in intensity.

It takes supreme effort for Myrddin to push himself into a sitting position. "Lamia," he finally comprehends. Then, with loathing, *"Lamia!"*

Suddenly she's up and hurtling at Myrddin with a shrill cry. The shadow lashes out and she slops to the ground, severed in two.

The flames are dying, but The Leech isn't dead. The bottom half of her quivers, tail and legs wriggling like worms. The top half lies in a steaming mass, breathing with short ragged breaths.

"Brother-r-r-r-r-r," she moans. "Help m-e-e-e-e-e."

The shadow occludes her from Myrddin's sight and there are sounds of slicing wet meat. Lamia could have healed from the burns, perhaps even lived out her life as an amputee without legs and tail, such is her genetic makeup. But when the shadow moves away she lies slashed to ribbons. There will be no recovering from this.

The dark shape approaches Myrddin, and like black smoke blown away in the wind, the shadow cloak is gone.

Myrddin gapes. "Fintán mac Bóchra..."

"Good greetings, Myrddin Wyllt," says The White Watcher. "We thought we'd lost you forever."

* * *

When Myrddin last had contact with this Firstborn, Fintán had been hiding himself away since the time of the ancient wars over the island of Éire. The loss of his wife Cessair in The Deluge had taken a dreadful toll on him, but it was the plague that wiped out the Partholonians which finally sealed his despair. He'd sworn never again to take part in the affairs of the world.

Over the millennia he gained the fabled epithets of White Ancient and The Witness, the ageless observer of the unfolding history of Ireland and indeed all the British Isles.

Myrddin, however, had begun addressing him, not without some derision, as The White Watcher.

Myrddin smiles, an affectionate gleam in his eye. "Fintán my boy, as I live and breathe." He speaks in Caithness Norn, a lost language once spoken in the far north of what is now called Scotland.

If there ever was a being who looked like a true mythological god of old, it is Fintán mac Bóchra. When he appears in mtoto cloak, both men and women swoon. He's *that* handsome. A true Adonis. More than Adonis himself ever was.

In Trueface, as Myrddin sees him now, it's no wonder he's known to his fellow Firstborn as The Falcon. His mother wasn't exactly a falcon, but one of the first raptors of the *avialae* clade, a predecessor to the diurnal birds of prey that populate the world today – and much larger. Fintán stands nearly seven feet tall and his wings span over 14 feet. Built somewhat like a man, he has extremely broad shoulders – actually, *two* sets of shoulders – one higher and wider for his arms, the other lower and set farther back for his wings. To accommodate both arm movement and the rigors of flying, his chest is tremendously thick, with rippling pectoral muscles that taper to his waist.

His head resembles that of a modern day eagle, with ivory feathers tipped gold, though his beak is more severely curved like a falcon's. The rest of his body is bare, with deeply bronzed skin, except for his white feathered waist and thighs. His legs are roughly humanoid in shape and function, but his feet are entirely bird-like with wicked curving talons.

Fintán removes his hand from the grip of a dagger sheathed at his hip, cocks his head to survey Myrddin with an eye the color of a golden citrine gem. "As you live and breathe, truly, by my grace." He has no human mouth, but his tongue and the lower part of his beak move when he speaks.

"By your grace," Myrddin replies with a nod of gratitude. "And what kept you, old friend? The Leech almost put me to an end."

"I had articles to fetch," replies Fintán, reaching into a cloth bag that hangs from a strap over his shoulder.

Myrddin gazes at the steaming heap of Lamia. "Salt, oil, and flame."

"And this." He tosses bunched fabric to Myrddin, who catches it and holds it up. A hooded gray robe of worsted wool. "I thought you might want for cover."

Myrddin stands, shaking, holding his hands out to steady himself on the air. Once he is relatively sure he isn't going to topple over, he dons the robe, runs a hand up one of the sleeves. "Many thanks, and more."

Fintán removes the cap of a plastic water bottle and hands it to Myrddin, who takes it hesitantly, having never seen such a thing.

"Water," Fintán explains.

Myrddin sniffs the bottle's contents and drinks cautiously. He smacks his lips. "Delicious." The effect of his encounter with Lamia, the loss of blood and so many years without food or drink suddenly washes over him. He puts a hand to his forehead, wavers, and begins to fall.

Fintán catches him easily in his strong arms. Myrddin's eyes flutter at the edge of consciousness.

"I have food as well," Fintán informs him. "You'll need to take it slowly."

Myrddin's voice is a ragged whisper, "There are... so many things..."

Fintán answers thoughtfully, "Over 1,500 years have passed since you were imprisoned here. Much has changed, but much has not. Many searched for you. When they desisted, I persevered, but in vain. How these beasts found you is beyond me. Nor do I know what it portends." Then, after a pause, "Nyneve is gone. As is your king." He studies The Madman. 1,500 years is a nighttime to Firstborn like he and Myrddin Wyllt. Somehow it must seem very different, however, when there is no escape. Still, it should be no surprise that Nyneve is dead. She was Fifthborn, nearly mtoto-kind. And Arthur was merely human.

After a long silence, Myrddin asks, "And my people?"

"The men of science today have uncovered their bony remains. They call them *Homo habilis*." Myrddin's countenance falls. "But some do survive, yes." Relief washes over Myrddin's features. "But what you really want to know..."

Myrddin searches The Falcon's features. *Does he know my deepest secrets?*

"Launcelot is dead."

Myrddin closes his eyes. *Of course he does. He* is *The White Watcher.*

"But his son lives."

Myrddin's eyes snap open. He gazes at Fintán in wonder.

Fintán lowers him to sit on the ground and strides to the entrance of the cave. Myrddin checks his wound. A red ring from the bite of The Leech has soaked through his robe, but the flow of blood is assuaged. He crosses his arms over his knobby knees and looks to Fintán, who stands over a bulky motionless form. "The Bear?" he queries.

Fintán crouches next to the body. "Yes." Bödvar's eyes are open, but there's no life in them.

"Young Matunos."

"Younger than you, perhaps, Old Madman, but senior to me. The Bear has always been a savage foe, and time was of the essence. I waited for assurance this was indeed where you were entombed, and better he to open it than I. I also did not know their true intentions until it was almost too late. There was no time for propriety of combat." He gently closes Bödvar's eyes. "Be that as it may, let it be known that I announced myself and did not stab our brother in the back."

"You did what had to be done," Myrddin reassures him. "There would be no reasoning with The Bear, and certainly not with The Leech. I owe you my life."

"Consider it a debt repaid. One of many." Fintán removes the dagger from its sheath and severs Bödvar's head from his body with one swift motion.

Myrddin doesn't even wince. It isn't necessary to decapitate a Firstborn to kill them, but it isn't a bad idea, just to make sure they stay dead, and it has become a grisly custom. But he does notice Fintán's weapon.

"Is that what I believe it to be?"

Fintán wipes it on the hair of Bödvar's chest. Long for a dagger, short for a sword, it's forged all in one piece with no hilt. The blade is a triangular spike with runes inscribed along all three sides – symbols older than Enochian, older than mankind, older than all but the most ancient of Firstborn – runes of the First Language.

Fintán utters the weapon's name, "Carnwennan."

"Pratha's Athamé." Myrddin looks to Fintán with circumspection. "It must have been given to you freely for you to wield it as an Astra blade, to cloak in shadow even to Firstborn who are not of mtoto blood, such as The Bear."

Fintán stands. "Arthur passed it to me upon his death. Excalibur went back to the lake."

"That is a story you must tell me, one day." Myrddin forces himself to his feet, shuffles to Fintán. "How do you suppose these devils found me, when all others failed? What incited them to commit such an act? I know well how Lamia despised me, and I have never been kind to Matunos, but to make this journey... And she and The Bear *together*, I cannot imagine..."

"They could not have done this of their own volition," Fintán responds. "Someone put them up to it." Together they regard the bodies of The Bear and The Leech, contemplating the grim implications.

After a long moment, Myrddin studies Fintán's regal bird face. "And what of you, Fintán mac Bóchra? Why have you come to my aid? Why has The White Watcher broken his solemn vow to never again take part in the affairs of this or any world, to observe only, and forever?"

Fintán shoves the Athamé into its sheath. "The time for watching is done."

PART III

FLOWERS & FIGS 11

On the rain-slick sidewalk, Fi and Zeke struggle to unravel the knot of arms and legs they've tied themselves into.

"Fiona Megan Patterson," Edgar exclaims in his familiar English accent. He grasps her arms and lifts her to her feet. "You've been trying to give me a heart attack since the day you came into my care. But this!"

Fi's shocked to see him here, but also taken aback by her imperturbable uncle's sudden ire.

Then he smiles affectionately. "It's good to see you, dear." Standing there with his hands on her arms, Fi feels safe for the first time in what seems to be a very long time. She moves in reflexively for an uncharacteristic hug, but he brushes past her to Zeke, ignorant of her need.

"Young man," he says, taking Zeke by the elbow and hauling him up, "are you all right?"

"I think so," Zeke replies, rubbing his knee.

"Are you certain?"

Zeke shakes his leg tentatively. "Yeah, I'm good. Thank you."

"I'm okay too," says Fi, crossing her arms. "In case you were wondering."

"Of course, dear," Edgar responds. "Into the auto, then." He strides to the old blue Bentley. "You too, lad," he urges, opening the back door.

Zeke hesitates, but Fi nods in encouragement. When he looks in at the back seat, there isn't much room—"Fi!"

"What?"

"Look."

She gives her uncle a questioning glance over the roof of the car then whips open the passenger's side rear door.

Lying on the seat is Mol. "Oh my God," Patches of blood soak through bandages that wrap his torso and front leg and he has freshly cleaned cuts on his face, but he grunts in welcome and wags his tail. "Mol." She hugs his big furry head. He groans in her embrace.

"Where'd you find him?" she asks Edgar. "Is he going to be all right?"

"He'll be fine, dear. He arrived at the house shortly after I returned and I dressed his wounds. Then I heard something had occurred at the hospital and left as soon as possible to find you."

"I'm so sorry," she says. "You had to be really worried. I wanted to call, but..." Her eyes flit to Zeke.

"You're here now," Edgar reassures her, "and all in one piece. That's the important thing. Now, get in out of this rain, both of you." Zeke hesitates. "Don't worry, lad, you won't hurt him."

That's not exactly what Zeke's afraid of. He cautiously presses himself in next to the big dog, who actually scoots over to give him more room.

Fi climbs in the front, turns to Zeke. "You okay? I can sit in back."

Now that he's in and Mol hasn't torn his arm off or even growled, he feels relatively safe. "It's all right, thanks."

Edgar addresses Zeke's reflection in the rearview mirror. "You must be the fellow who plays guitar at St. Augustine's."

Zeke sits up straight. "Yes sir."

"Oh, shit," says Fi, realizing she's made no introductions. "I mean, sorry. This is Zeke – wait – how do you know who he is?"

"Fiona, you don't think I am completely unaware of your life outside the house, do you?"

"You've been spying on me?!"

"Absolutely not," he replies indignantly. "There is quite a disparity between *spying*," he says the word as if it tastes awful, "and attending to your safety as a proper guardian should."

The only things Fi can think of to say aren't very nice, nor would they be productive in the present situation, so she remains silent. Luckily, Zeke speaks up.

"Um, I'm assuming you're Fi's Uncle Edgar. It's a pleasure to meet you, sir. She's told me a lot about you."

"She has, has she?" says Edgar. "Nothing good, I hope. I wouldn't want anyone ruining my hard-won reputation."

Zeke laughs anxiously, unsure whether he's joking or not.

"So," Edgar states, "explain yourselves, you two."

Fi's eyes go straight to Zeke, whose mouth hangs open. *Could he possibly know about them dating?*

"Uh..." she stammers, "explain...? You mean...?"

Edgar is reassuring but determined. "Fiona, what occurred at the hospital?"

"Oh!" she responds, relieved. Then the events of the day flood back like the memory of a nightmare. She bites her lip. "Please don't think I'm crazy..."

It's beginning to rain harder, pattering on the windshield, tapping the roof of the car. Edgar turns on the wipers. "Tell me everything," he says, putting the car in drive and exiting the alley.

* * *

Fi relates the story of the attack while Edgar drives unhurriedly along back streets, then makes his way to the river and across it via the Cherry Street Bridge. Zeke interjects on occasion, to clarify or add detail. Edgar listens without a word, keeping his eyes on the road. Fi thinks she sees his weathered hands tighten on the wheel when she describes the group that came after Peter, then backs up to tell him about the homeless guy grabbing her on the street before she got to work and showing up later with the rest.

Her voice quavers as she tells him about the guards being killed, and Billy. Edgar grows thoughtful when she describes what Billy did, and his axe, and how Mol showed up and fought and even killed some of the bad men. "I have no idea how he got out of the house," she says, "or why he would've come."

The only time Edgar looks at her is when she explains how they escaped from the hospital. What Peter did. The "slipping" thing. The strange misty beach, and how Peter changed. When she speaks of Zeke being able to "slip," Edgar regards him with circumspection in the mirror. She tells Edgar that there are other worlds, what Peter told them about Billy, about going to the bank, the little gold rod that Peter retrieved from the secret vault – and what he told them it was – and admits that this must all sound *completely* insane.

She leaves out any mention of her seizure last night and the dreams about the baby, and the part about the vision in the swimming pool. She also doesn't tell him the reason they left Peter at the bar was they caught him in a ménage à trois in the women's restroom.

"I was worried, I just had to leave," she says in conclusion. "I had to find you."

Edgar pulls into a deserted gravel lot that overlooks the Maumee river to downtown and stops the car. Fi watches him, hoping for some reassurance. For long moments he stares out the windshield, the wipers beating rhythmically against the drumming rain.

Deliberately, Edgar removes his hand from the wheel and places it tenderly on hers. She looks at it in wonder. "You've done well, dear," he says in the kindest voice she's ever heard him use.

"You believe me, then? You don't think I'm crazy?"

"Your sanity has always been questionable, dear." She frowns. Edgar gives her hand a squeeze. "Of course I believe you," he assures, "of course I do." She smiles weakly. Edgar returns the smile then looks back out the windshield in contemplation.

Distant lightning blinks the city skyline into ghostly silhouette, followed seconds later by the faintest rumbling of thunder.

"I don't think it would be wise to return home," Edgar says. "If the men who came to the hospital know who you are, and have truly associated you and Zeke with Peter, their next move may be to find out where you live, if they haven't done so already."

Zeke sits up in the back seat. "You think so?"

"It's what I would do."

Fi refrains from biting her nails. She nibbles on her lower lip instead. "Where will we go?"

"Somewhere safe. Where we can gather our wits and you can rest."

Zeke shifts in his seat. Fi turns to meet his gaze. She bites her lip harder, addresses her uncle. "What about Peter?"

"From what you tell me," Edgar replies, "the old man sounds perfectly capable of taking care of himself."

* * *

Rain continues to fall, lazy but consistent, as Edgar maneuvers the Bentley along a dark two lane road that winds southwest along the river away from the city. After passing through the small town of Rossford into a more sparsely populated area, large homes begin to appear on their right, between the road and the river, interspersed with upscale gated communities.

Zeke realizes he's been unconsciously petting Mol, who is sound asleep and snoring softly. His eyes roam the once plush interior of the old Bentley T1 Saloon. The fine upholstery, now cracked and faded. The finish of the hand-crafted wooden dashboard, crackled and dull, with circular analogue instrumentation. It smells like old leather, motor oil, and dog.

Fi has the knuckles of one hand pressed to her lips, wanting desperately to nibble her fingernails. She can't stop her mind from playing back the day's events. The bad men, the violence. Peter, Billy's death, and the murders of all the others. But in her head it's like it happened to someone else, like she's watching a movie she's seen before and is only half paying attention to. She knows she should be wracked with grief, having a breakdown, crying her eyes out, but she's spent so much of her life not allowing herself to dwell on pain, loss and loneliness, pushing heartache away instead of dealing with it, shoving it deep down inside and locking it away, she isn't sure *what* she feels now. She cringes at the numbness in her heart. *What's wrong with me?!*

She brushes her hair over her ear, sits on her hands to keep her fingers out of her mouth, takes a long, deep breath, and looks out the rain-spattered window on her side of the car.

A stone wall rises and falls with the rolling wooded landscape. Something about it looks familiar. Edgar slows the car, steers to the right onto a gravel drive. They continue through the trees to a wrought iron gate in the wall.

Fi sits up. "I know this place."

"You've been here before," says Edgar. "It's my employer's residence." He enters a code on the lighted keypad of a remote he retrieves from the glovebox. The gates swing open. "One of them," he adds, driving through.

"We'll be safe here, you think?" she asks.

"Trust me, dear. This is the safest place we could want to be." They wind through the wooded grounds of the estate, Edgar quietly whistling "Swing Low, Sweet Chariot" with what seems to Fi to be a slightly nervous air.

They come over a rise and Zeke exclaims softly, "Wow."

"It's not a palace," says Edgar as he brings the car to a stop, "but it is impressive, nonetheless."

Zeke is first out of the car. The house is three stories of brown stone that spread well over two hundred feet before them, illuminated along the front by in-ground lamps. His eyes wander the hipped and gabled slate roofs, copper gutters with green patina, and ivy that winds its way between tall windows.

Fi steps out, shielding her eyes from the rain, which has diminished to a meager drizzle. She hasn't been here since she was probably eight years old, when renovations were being completed and her uncle would bring her on weekends when the workers were away. To romp the grounds, swim in the pool, and bowl on the three lane alley in the basement. It still looks like what she always thought it did – a really big mausoleum.

"Fiona, dear," Edgar calls to her. She meets him at the front of the car. He hands her the house key. "Would you take Mol and open up, please?" he requests.

"Okay." She lets Mol out, who climbs down stiffly and follows her to the house.

"Zeke," says Edgar, moving to the back of the car. "Would you give me a hand, lad?"

"Sure."

Edgar opens the trunk and hands him an enormous blue backpack, military style, with a tent and bedroll attached. Zeke almost drops it – it has to weigh 50 pounds. He gets one strap wrestled over his shoulder and Edgar gives him an identical pack, except this one is pink – but just as heavy.

Zeke is wondering what Edgar is doing with these, and why anyone would make a military pack in pink, when Edgar lifts an oddly shaped black case with shoulder straps out of the trunk and leans it against the bumper. It looks like a custom case for a musical instrument, wider at the top and smaller at the bottom, with a long thin pocket running down the center of the front, like for a bow string or a pool cue, or maybe collapsible ski poles. *That's it*, Zeke muses, *Fi's Uncle Edgar is a closet snowboarder.*

Edgar pulls out a beat-to-hell, stained canvas duffel. It's much longer than the packs Zeke has and bows in the middle as Edgar places the strap over his shoulder.

"That's it, lad," Edgar says, shutting the trunk. "Many thanks." He lifts the weird black case and heads for the house.

Zeke struggles after him under the weight of the two packs. He careens up wide stone steps to the lit columned portico, lurches to the oak double doors, painted red and reinforced with black iron bars wrought in the shape of a tree. The tree splits in half as Fi swings the doors inward.

She finds a knob on the wall and light fills the formal two story foyer. When she was here last, there was scaffolding, visqueen plastic sheeting, paint cans and plaster dust. Now the place is immaculate. The floor is white marble streaked with silver, as are the sets of stairs to either side that curve upward to a balconied hallway that looks down from the second floor. The ceiling is domed, of the same white stone, with a glittering golden chandelier at its center. To either side, Greek statues stand on pedestals in front of colossal mirrors with gilded frames.

"Wow..." Zeke says again.

"Yeah," Fi agrees.

Ahead of them, between the stairs, is an archway to the back of the house. Edgar heads toward it. "This way, please."

Zeke lets Fi go ahead of him – mostly so she won't see how much trouble he's having with the packs. They pass through the arch as Edgar raises a bank of faders on the wall. Zeke stifles the urge to say "wow" one more time.

They've entered midway along an expansive great room. The ceiling must be twenty feet high, Zeke figures, and the room itself at least sixty feet wide and forty feet deep. To the right and left, hallways fade in darkness to other areas of the home. The floor where they're standing forms a rectangular border along the walls, because the central portion of the floor is about a foot higher, with an intermediate step that runs all around the edge. The centerpiece of the raised area is a gleaming white Steinway grand piano. Chairs and divans of various designs, from sleek contemporary to the most ornate antique, are arranged around it. More chairs, loveseats and chaise longues are placed in various sitting areas around the room. Behind him, above the arch, the upstairs hall is open to the room, creating a balcony on this side as well.

Edgar steps up to set the long duffle on the floor and leans the oddly shaped black case against a chair. Zeke's glad to be relieved of the heavy backpacks, which Edgar plunks unceremoniously on a highly polished burl-wood coffee table.

"What's all this stuff?" Fi asks, eyeing the packs and bags.

"Oh," says Edgar, rubbing his hands together in what occurs to Fi to be an unchar-acteristically anxious manner, "just some things I thought might come in handy."

Zeke removes the coat he received from the bank manager and Edgar takes it politely. Zeke realizes his clothes are almost dry and his chill gone, aided by the soothing warmth of the room. He stretches his shoulders and neck and surveys the space.

The wall to the left is covered with bookshelves built around a wide contemporary gas fireplace with glass doors. Mol laps water from a bowl and makes himself comfort-able on a plush sheepskin in front of it. Zeke wonders if he should say something about Mol getting bloodstains on the rug, but Edgar doesn't seem concerned. He wanders toward the back of the room, checking out the piano on the way, and looks out high wide windows that take up the center of the back wall.

Fi comes up beside him. "Edgar went to the kitchen."

"Okay," he responds, preoccupied. Distant lightning pulses through the clouds, revealing the texture of treetops that slope down and away from the house to the rippling glint of the river below. Zeke's never been inside such a home. He turns to Fi and smiles, then something at the other end of the room catches his attention. "Whoa..."

He steps down from the raised area of the floor and walks along the windows. Fi follows, stopping momentarily to pluck a string on a gorgeous harp that stands in the corner. Zeke peruses the collection before him with incredulity.

All manner of guitars and their ilk cover the wall. There's a mandolin, lute, banjo, even a vihuela, but by far the majority are guitars. Three of the electric variety and at least twenty classical acoustics. Gibson, Fender, Yamaha, Hanika, a couple of Hausers and Martins, all hung with padded hooks and in pristine condition. Zeke plays a Martin himself, though his is of a much lower series than those displayed here and he bought it used – which reminds him with a lurch in his stomach – he left it at the hospital. He sighs, then his eyes fall on a guitar with an extra wide neck and ten strings hung directly over a gracefully carved buffet that sits at the center of the wall.

"Beautiful, aren't they?"

Fi and Zeke both whirl to see Edgar holding a tray with a teapot and cups. Neither of them heard him come in. "Uncle!" Fi scolds.

Edgar wrinkles his brow, not understanding how he might have incurred her wrath. "Yes, dear?"

Fi shakes her head, scowling at him for startling them.

Zeke turns back to the guitar over the buffet. "Yeah, they're incredible." He reaches for it, then stops himself and turns back to Edgar. "Do you think your employer...? I mean, may I?"

"I don't believe he'd mind, lad" says Edgar, then his eyes flit to the hall that leads from the great room behind them. "However," he continues with a mixed expression of anticipation and wonder, "you could ask him yourself."

A man pads into the room in bare feet and tan khaki cargo pants, vigorously rubbing his head with a towel. A white cotton dress shirt is thrown over his shoulder and he carries a vintage stenciled haversack.

He wipes his face and lowers the towel to find Fi and Zeke gaping at him. He beams back at them. "There you are!"

This man has shorter hair, mussed by the toweling, and no beard, but there's no mistaking the strong features, those brilliant green eyes, and – Fi can't help but notice – that perfect sculpted torso. It's Peter, freshly groomed and showered.

Fi and Zeke both make mindless mono-syllabic noises like "um," "er," and "uh."

Mol leaps up in spite of his wounds and trots to Peter, tail wagging.

"Mol!" Peter greets him. He dumps the haversack on a chair, tosses the towel and shirt on top of it, then stoops to grasp Mol's face by the jowls and kiss the top of his head. "Good, brave Molossus." Mol makes happy doggie noises and wags his tail harder.

Fi and Zeke exchange puzzled glances.

Peter's grin spreads even wider at the sight of Fi's uncle. "Edgar..." he says with obvious affection.

Slowly, Edgar sets the slightly trembling tray on a coffee table, then lowers himself to one knee and bows his head. "Milord." Fi is dumbfounded.

"I really wish he wouldn't do that," Peter mutters. He bounds to the raised floor. "Edgar, rise!" He takes him by the hands and pulls him up. "On your feet, my good man."

Edgar raises his misty eyes to Peter's. "Welcome back, sir." Peter grasps him by the shoulders, then wraps him in a hug. Edgar embraces him in return.

"Dumbfounded" is *not* the right word for Fi's reaction – because there is no word for it. She has never seen her uncle in such a state, and no one hugs Uncle Edgar, let alone gets hugged back! What's even more bizarre – *they know each other?*

"Good to see you, Edgar," says Peter, releasing him. "You look well."

"As do you, sir." Edgar leans in and lowers his voice. "But, how...?" With an almost imperceptible movement of his head, Peter indicates to Fi. Edgar's eyes go to her. "I see," he whispers, a proud smile creeping over his face.

Peter moves a hand to the side of Edgar's neck and pulls him closer. "Quickly, what have you learned?," he asks quietly.

Edgar glances briefly at Fi, as if uncomfortable speaking in her presence, even in a whisper. "Kabir – Zadkiel, is missing," he bemoans. "Last night, in Detroit." He clears his throat softly. "And still no word from Mokosh."

Peter's face falls. "I am... very sorry to hear that." His brow furrows as he considers the events of the day in light of this news and his eyes well up. "Samson is gone as well."

"So I heard. Very unfortunate, indeed."

"Did you call upon him?"

"He came of his own volition several months ago, said he wished to make reparations. When he learned of your condition, he swore to watch over you until the paternmentia passed, no matter how long it took. I apologize, milord, I had no idea that Kleron—"

"None of us did." Peter's expression is pained. A single tear escapes down his cheek. "Though I should have."

"There's no telling how widespread this may be," Edgar continues. "I tried to call Freyja and her lads, but there's no response. The last time I spoke to The Twins was several years ago. Their phone is no longer in service and other methods of communication defunct. I've no manner of expeditiously contacting any of the others. We lost touch with them long ago, as you know."

"Yes, I know..." Peter considers for a moment, then gives Edgar's shoulders a squeeze. "Good work, as always. And thank you, for everything."

Someone clears their throat dramatically. Over Peter's shoulder, Edgar sees Fi cross her arms. He nods to Peter and takes a short step back.

Peter wipes his cheek and spins to face Fi and Zeke, his grin returning. "So!" he says, clasping his hands with a loud clap. He bounds down to join them. "You like my collection, Zeke?" he asks, taking his shirt from the chair and sliding his arms into the sleeves.

"It's... unbelievable."

Peter points to what looks like the three oldest guitars, aligned in a row on the center of the wall. "Do you recognize these?" he asks, buttoning his shirt.

Zeke studies the first of them, which is longer and thinner than a regular guitar, and shakes his head.

"That's a Stradivarius," Peter tells him. Zeke is stunned.

"I thought a Stradivarius was a violin," Fi interposes, not entirely happy with the direction the conversation is taking. She's got questions. Serious questions. And they've got nothing to do with guitars.

Zeke gives her a quick shake of his head and mutters, "Hm-mmm. The Stradivari made these too, but not very many. They're extremely rare."

Peter points to the second of the three. "A George Louis Panormo," and the third, "Antonio de Torres Jurado."

"Damn," Zeke exhales. *The history of the modern guitar on one man's wall.*

Peter finishes buttoning his shirt. He smooths it down, leaving it untucked, and smiles at Fi. She just looks annoyed.

"They must be worth a fortune," Zeke comments.

Peter is more interested in how Zeke wears his shirt, with the sleeves rolled up below the elbows. He folds his own up the same way. "I wouldn't know," he shrugs lightly. "They were gifts." He snatches the wide-necked guitar from above the buffet, turns and tosses it into the air, giving it a speedy horizontal spin, and catches it.

Zeke is taken aback at his handling of the precious instrument.

"Ten strings, obviously, extended range," says Peter. "The brainchild of the maestro Narciso Yepes, designed and manufactured by José Ramirez."

Fi's glare of disbelief and incredulity at the mini history lesson going on while the world as she knows it has completely shattered doesn't seem to sway Peter or Zeke in the slightest. Zeke prattles on like an enthusiastic appraiser on Antiques Roadshow.

"...With string resonators for C, as well as A, G and F sharps, giving it authentic chromatic resonance like a sustain pedal on a piano."

Peter gives him an approving nod. "Allowing for the transcription of compositions for baroque lute—"

"Without having to delete transposed bass notes," Zeke finishes, then looks embarrassed at having interrupted him.

Peter isn't bothered in the slightest. "Exactly!" He plops into a chair and gently strums the guitar. A sound of magnificent beauty floats to Zeke's trained ears. "Still in tune," says Peter, pleased. He begins to play. Mol sits nearby, listening contentedly. None even notice Fi's growing frustration.

Zeke's mouth drops open gradually... *my God...* He lowers himself to sit on the edge of the raised floor.

Peter is playing Bach's "Solo Violin Partita No 2," also called "The Chaconne," probably the most difficult piece of music to play on guitar, *ever*. Zeke's heard that even the greatest of classical guitarists can take years to master it. After introducing the main theme, Peter goes into a medley of sorts, choosing the most striking segments, and hardest to play, of all five movements of the piece. His quick but seamless transitions make Zeke dizzy. Peter grins gleefully, bobbing his head with the music, plucking away with his fingertips and extra long fingernails. Zeke can't believe it. *He makes it look easy!*

Fi's still standing there, arms crossed, completely ignored by the boys. Even the most beautiful music in the world won't soothe the questions simmering in her brain. She turns her wasting glare from the musical bromance and scowls daggers at her uncle instead.

Edgar stammers, "I'll fetch some biscuits for the tea," then bolts for the kitchen.

She rushes after him, muttering under her breath. "Oh, no you don't..."

* * *

"It was you!" she accuses, catching up to Edgar as he reaches the hall at the opposite end of the great room. "When Peter borrowed that phone today, he called you!"

He pushes through a swinging galley door to the kitchen, which is bright and roomy. White walls and cabinets, granite countertops, top-of-the-line stainless appliances. He proceeds to one side of the central island counter, Fi to the other.

"And it's been Peter, all this time," she presses. "*He's* your employer!"

Edgar crouches to a cabinet and comes up with a package of ginger nut biscuits. He sighs deeply, avoiding her condemnatory glare. "Please understand, Fiona. I have been under oath, and I hope you know by now that I'm the kind of person who would take an oath very seriously. This has been extremely difficult for me. Perhaps the most arduous task I have undertaken in all my life. But whatever you may think of me, I am a man of honor." He pauses in solemn contemplation. "At least, I used to be..."

"An oath? To *him*?"

"Yes."

"But why? Who is he, Uncle?"

Edgar sighs again, reaches to a cupboard behind him and retrieves a serving platter. "*That* he will have to tell you himself, dear."

"Part of the oath," she scowls, tearing at the package of biscuits.

Edgar leans on the countertop, studies the palms of his hands like a map – a habit he picked up from his father, he recalls, and it's not the most pleasant of memories.

* * *

The last notes of "The Chaconne" fade away. Zeke drags his eyes from the strings to Peter. "Jeez..."

Peter grins. "I'm a little out of practice." He holds the guitar out to Zeke. "Give it a whirl?"

"Umm..."

"Go on," Peter insists.

Zeke takes it gently, brushes his fingertips along the curve of the body, up the sleek neck. He turns it over – and sets it firmly in his lap because of what he sees written on the back, afraid he might drop it. He took only a year of Spanish in high school, but his months in South America doing volunteer work gave him enough experience with the language to interpret the faded pencil markings: *Dearest Pedro, truest maestro, we are forever in your debt. Muchas Gracias.* Beneath it, in two different scrawls, *Narciso Yepes* and *José Ramirez III.*

"I... uh..." He hands the guitar back to Peter, wipes his sweating palms on his jeans. "I wouldn't know how to play it. Thank you, though."

"You're most welcome."

* * *

"Fiona..." Edgar's voice is strained.

She pauses while arranging biscuits on the platter at the sight of her Uncle Edgar, her rock, her protector, so emotional and torn. He won't even look at her.

"I failed you today," he continues. "I was not there, in your time of greatest need. After all the years in your service, when you needed me most, *I was not there.*" Fi doesn't know how to respond, and now her uncle's hands are quaking. "I have deceived you all these years, and it has caused me more anguish than you can imagine. Nothing erodes the soul like secrets and lies. God forgive me."

Fi can't stand seeing him this way. He looks like he might actually *weep*... She takes his hands in hers.

"Uncle," she says softly, "you've *always* been there for me. You *are* a man of honor."

Edgar isn't so sure. Treachery runs in his blood. In an attempt to overcome it he devoted his early life to goodness, truth and faith. He bows his head further and wonders – perhaps he *is* his father's son, after all.

* * *

"Ah." Peter shakes a finger, "more of a six string man, ay?"

"Well," Zeke's eyes unintentionally dart to another Ramirez hanging on the wall behind Peter, "yeah, I guess."

Peter retrieves the guitar, somehow knowing exactly the one Zeke was looking at. He hands it to him. "Excellent choice."

Zeke holds it like it might crumble in his hands. It's one of the most exquisite things he's ever seen. He gingerly turns it over. In Spanish, it reads: *To Pedro, my teacher, my friend, with utmost gratitude*, signed *Andrés Segovia Torres*. Zeke thinks he might pass out.

"It's just wood and wire," Peter encourages. "Play something."

Zeke positions the guitar delicately. He thinks a moment, then begins. If you could hear golden flowing honey, it would sound like this guitar. The song he's chosen is "Greensleeves." Peter regards him with mock suspicion, trying to hide a smile.

Zeke notices Peter's expression and presses his palm softly against the strings. "You seemed to have a real affinity for that song when you were..." he lets the statement trail off, not sure how to finish.

"Old as dirt?" Peter asks. "An invalid? Out of my ever-lovin' skull?"

Zeke expresses a brief anxious laugh.

"Well, I should think I'd like it," Peter grins. "I *wrote* it."

Zeke's shocked and confused at the same time. *He can't be serious... Can he?*

Peter's jovial demeanor is suddenly replaced by one of focused concentration. He moves his head as if feeling the air with his face. Mol's ears perk and he looks intently toward the front of the house, throat rumbling.

Peter's eyes narrow. "Edgar."

* * *

In the kitchen, Edgar jerks his head up, instantly alert.

"What?" Fi asks. "What is it?"

* * *

Zeke starts at a sudden mechanical chirping sound. Lightning sparks through the great room windows, accompanied by a clap and rumble of thunder.

The light plays across Peter's stern features. "We have company."

26

FLOWERS & FIGS 12

Fi squeezes her uncle's hands, shouts to be heard above the piercing *chirp! chirp!* "Is that an alarm?"

Edgar responds flatly, "Motion sensors," then strides purposefully out of the kitchen. Fi hustles after him.

They enter the great room and Edgar makes a beeline for a wide rolltop desk built into the shelves in the corner beyond the fireplace. He reaches beneath it, presses something and the alarm is silenced. At the other end of the room, Peter replaces the ten string guitar over the buffet, then hurries to them. Zeke, the six string Ramirez still in his hands, walks cautiously to the piano in the center of the floor.

Fi joins him. "Now what?" she asks under her breath.

"Who knows," he replies, then lowers his voice. "But Peter just told me he wrote 'Greensleeves.'"

"What?"

"That's what *I* thought."

"Well, apparently my uncle's been working for *Peter* all these years and I never knew."

"Does he know who Peter is? Or – *what* – he is?"

"I think so, but he won't tell me anything."

"Why not?"

"Some stupid oath." She pushes her hair nervously behind her ear. "I don't get it, Zeke. This just keeps getting more and more fucked up." Her trembling fingers go to her lips. "I think I'm gonna lose it."

He takes her hand. "Well, you won't be alone. I'll be right there with you."

For the first time since all hell broke loose at the hospital, it dawns on her that Zeke *has* been right there with her, the whole time. It's selfish, she knows, since it means he's caught up in this insanity too, but she's glad.

The wind can be heard whipping up outside. Rain hammers the high windows. Fi and Zeke both notice their palms are sweating. Edgar moves books on the shelves above the desk, seemingly at random, sliding them out one at a time and pushing them back in forcefully. A soft *whir* and the shelves above the desk retract into the wall to be replaced by sliding panels of flat screen monitors. At the same time, the rolltop of the desk lifts to reveal more monitors, keyboards, lighted buttons and all manner of communication equipment.

Zeke groans, "Now it's the freakin' Batcave..."

Edgar's fingers fly over the keyboard and touchscreens in a staccato stream.

"Great," says Fi. "So much for Edgar not knowing how to text." She recalls his reaction in the kitchen. "I get the feeling he's not hard of hearing, either."

"I guess there's a lot about your uncle you didn't know,"

"You *think?*" There's no mistaking the sarcasm.

Images blink to life on the monitors, angles on various areas of the estate. Edgar touches an empty space on the desk and a 3-D image of the house and grounds appears. He pokes, pinches and waves through it, causing the image to shift, expand and zoom, then gives Peter a look of affirmation.

Fi and Zeke move closer. A chill runs up their spines at what they see. A holograph of Kleron, approaching through the woods with a group of the men from the hospital.

"Shit," says Fi. "That's not good."

"You *think?*" Zeke replies, returning the sarcasm.

Peter places a hand on Edgar's shoulder, who reluctantly relinquishes the chair.

"You're going to wipe the system," Edgar states, ill at ease.

Peter is already typing away. "Kleron has located us twice. He may have found a way in."

"Which nodes will you—?"

"All of them."

Edgar exhales his regret, but quickly recovers his bearing and moves to the table where the backpacks that they brought from the car are sitting. "Yours is the blue one, Zeke," he points out.

Puzzled, Zeke unzips the pack. Inside is a variety of clothing, toiletries, all the necessities. He checks the tag on a shirt, then a pair of pants. They're the right size. "How'd you know?"

"Peter told me you were with him. I did the best I could in the limited time available. Better safe than sorry, they say."

Fi's listening and just as puzzled as Zeke, but she's drawn more to what Peter's doing at the computers. She peers over his shoulder. He's typing password after password. Words like *erase* and *purge* appear, as well as cautions that these operations cannot be undone and data will be irretrievable.

"I'm sorry to do this," Peter says without looking up. "Every bit of intelligence and knowledge we've collected in electronic form, everything on our worldwide holdings, as well as our backdoor entry to government and corporate networks, all of it is accessed through this system."

Fi shakes her head but says nothing, surprised Peter is speaking so freely.

"Edgar and I began the project together, but he continued refining the system while I wallowed in the self pity and depression that brought on my latest bout of patermentia." He sighs, continuing to deftly manage mouse and keyboard. "But now it's a distinct possibility the network's been compromised. We've taken great pains to keep our identities and whereabouts secret over the years, but in this day and age, if one wishes to live among the watoto, that is becoming increasingly difficult to accomplish. Perhaps impossible."

As usual, Fi has no idea what he's talking about. *Watoto?* She's about to ask what it means when she sees a folder entitled *The October Foundation* pop up on the screen.

"Do you know of this?" Peter asks.

"Just that they funded St. Augustine's," Fi replies. "You?"

Peter shakes his head. He checks a monitor above the desk where red dots designate Kleron's group making its way across the estate. They appear to be moving slowly, deliberately taking their time. He opens the folder, revealing documents for the foundation as well as funds transfers for the hospital.

"Sly bugger." Peter says with appreciation.

Fi's mouth drops open. Edgar *is* The October Foundation. And he's *rich.*

"I remember now," says Peter. "It was Edgar who placed me on the front steps. He built St. Augustine's for me." He marks the folder for deletion, then adds casually, "He most likely arranged for your internship as well."

"What?" Fi asks. "Why?" Peter doesn't answer. Fi gazes at her now even more enigmatic uncle.

Peter considers the blinking words on the computer screen: *Are you sure?* He speaks as if to himself. "Kleron must have amassed considerable resources to prepare for this day. If there's a chance he has accessed any part of the network, we have no choice."

Fi pulls her eyes from Edgar to listen to Peter, though she still doesn't understand what he's talking about.

"I just hope it isn't too late." He clicks *Yes.* Series of bars appear, ticking up from green to red.

* * *

All over the world, in hidden vaults, secret government installations and shadow corporation basements, drives smoke and sizzle, others burst into flame, still more are subjected to electro-magnetic pulse. Every one of them is eradicated. Except one.

Conduits eject from a gleaming crystal cube in a shower of sparks, and there it sits, softly pulsing, deep beneath the earth.

* * *

Peter offers Fi a sly smile. "Luckily for me, I have an excellent memory." He hits a button and the rolltop and shelves return to their hidden state.

Fi realizes something – at St. Augustine's, Peter's mind was basically gone. "You *remember* being at the hospital?"

He rises from the chair and faces her. "Now that the mentia has passed, I remember *everything.*"

Fi's eyes involuntarily dart to Edgar and Zeke. *Uh oh.* For the past few months, when she needed someone to talk to about things she couldn't tell anyone, she'd talk to Peter.

He smiles tenderly. "And I know, now. It was *you*."

"What was me?"

"You brought me back."

Zeke and Edgar have noticed their conversation and listen with growing interest.

Peter takes Fi's arm and walks her closer to them. "You talked to me, read to me, took me out to see the stars. You gave me flowers and figs." He grins knowingly. "And I remember what happened in the pool."

Fi gulps, sees the questioning looks from Edgar and Zeke. She takes a deep breath. "Last night, I had a seizure." She's surprised by the lack of alarm on Edgar's face, but continues. "I dreamed about a baby floating in the ocean. I just remembered it today. And I remembered I've had that dream before. I know women dream about babies—" then off Zeke's look, "—it's not like that, Zeke!" He hastily returns his attention to the blue pack. "There were volcanos and meteors and stuff. But I saw it again, while I was *awake*. This afternoon, with Peter, in the swimming pool at the hospital—but I didn't have a seizure—it just—happened. I didn't tell anybody because it sounded crazy, but now..."

Peter takes her by the hands, smiling tenderly. "You were kind to me, your comforting presence tangible and profound, but I don't dream, Fi. Not ever. Not *alone*. It was *your* dreams, your visions, that caused my recovery. You were with me, in my memories, my past, in the beginning. You helped me remember who I am. The trip to World Memory expedited the process, but you began it." He steps closer. "You drew me and I followed, to today." They're silent for a long moment, staring at each other.

Zeke awkwardly zips up his pack, perhaps more loudly than necessary.

Edgar's jaw has grown slack. He clears his throat softly. "Clairvoyant, milord?"

"I believe so," Peter replies. "Though of what order and magnitude remains to be seen." He gives Fi's hands a squeeze. She realizes she's feeling very wobbly.

He releases her and addresses Edgar. "Now, however, we have uninvited guests to prepare for. When the time comes, we'll make for the hub chamber. If we are separated, meet me there."

"We're not leaving now?" Edgar inquires.

"No. Kleron knows we will be aware of his approach, and he's brought a small troupe. He could be here to treat, and we may learn something. Regardless, he needs to see that I am recovered." He casts a thoughtful gaze at Fi and Zeke. "And I don't want these two out of my sight, not just yet." He puts his hands on their shoulders and moves with them to the piano.

"What are we going to do?" Zeke asks.

Peter eyes the guitar in Zeke's hands. "Do you know 'Brian Boru's March?'"

"The song?" Zeke asks. "Yeah, why?"

"You?" he asks Fi.

"I... I'm not sure."

"It is sometimes called 'The Irish March,'" Peter adds.

"Oh, I've heard it. What... You don't want us to *play* it?"

"It's true what they say, you know. 'Music calms the savage beast.'"

"Breast," Zeke interjects.

"Pardon?"

"I think you mean 'savage breast.'"

"Do I?"

"From 'The Mourning Bride,' by William Congreve," Zeke explains. "'Music has charms to sooth the savage *breast.*'"

Peter eyes him keenly. "Hmm..."

Is he fucking with me? Again?

"Edgar," Peter calls out, "if you please."

Edgar is already reaching into the pink backpack.

"Did you bring that for me?" Fi asks.

"Yes, dear."

She's always felt like she knew very little about her uncle, now she wonders if she knows him at all – but she's realizing maybe he doesn't know her all that well either. "Pink, Uncle? Really?"

"It's your favorite color, dear," he responds, convinced he was being thoughtful. "And," he adds, "so you can tell them apart."

She glares at him, then recognizes the object he's retrieved. A thin box, handmade of Bolivian Rosewood. She approaches and opens it. "My mother's flute." It's the only thing her mother kept that Fi's father had given her, a platinum Verne Q. Powell. As beautiful and perfect-sounding as it is, her mom never used it after he left. Fi's played it only a few times, having used her own much less expensive instrument when she was taking lessons. It's been buried in her closet for years.

"You'll see I've also stowed your iPod," says Edgar, who then turns to Peter. "The two things dearest to her heart."

Fi shakes her head. She hasn't used that thing in ages. She pokes through the pack. Definitely her clothes. She lifts some, uncovering the pictures of her mother. *Why would he bring those?* And beneath them are – *panties?* And – *Oh God* – Edgar bought *tampons...*

"So you're *clairvoyant?*" Zeke speaks quietly right next to her.

"Shut up." She quickly closes the pack. "I still don't believe it. Besides, you're a *slipper.*"

"Yeah," he concedes. "That is weird."

* * *

Lightning strobes the rain as Kleron stalks from the tree line toward the front of the house. His companions from the hospital emerge from the shadows behind him. Mist curls from their shoulders in the chill wet air, billows softly with their breath.

In attendance are the band of ruffians who first breached the lobby: the dark-haired pale young men, Derek and Tod, the bearded men Henri and Didier, and the fur-coated brothers, Wepwawet and Surma, now joined by the larger one who chased Fi, Zeke and Peter at the pool. Max is also with them, as are the blond pale young men, Hedwig and Curt, who accompanied him at the hospital. The nameless throng that piled in afterward are nowhere to be seen.

As they cross the driveway, Surma reaches beneath the front of Edgar's car with his one arm and flips it over with ease. It lands upside down with a loud *crunch* of metal and glass.

* * *

"That would be my Bentley," Edgar scowls. He drops the backpacks and his long bag at the corner of the hall that leads to the kitchen, then strides up to the black case Zeke thought might contain a musical instrument or snowboard and snatches it up. In one smooth motion, he slides one arm into a slot in the back of it and swings around in an about-face, his braid of gray hair flying, while reaching into the top of the long pocket on the front and drawing out something silver and shining that makes a high ringing sound as it arcs through the air.

Zeke looks on in doubt and fascination. A *sword?*

Edgar gives the case a shake and it falls to the floor, revealing an aged white shield with faded smears of red in the shape of a cross. The whole maneuver took only seconds and now he stands at the edge of the raised area of the floor, facing the arch that leads to the foyer.

Having paused in the process of assembling her flute, Fi recognizes the sword and shield as the dusty heirlooms that have hung over their fireplace mantle all these years – but she isn't sure she recognizes her uncle. The shoulder slouch and hunch of his back are gone, and his expression holds a deliberate intensity she's never seen. Mol, who has remained innocuous but attentive, assumes a protective stance next to him, showing no sign of discomfort from his injuries.

Fi opens her mouth to speak—

"Don't move," Peter utters from behind her.

She whispers to Zeke, "He says that a lot."

"I think I'll listen to him this time," he whispers back.

They peek back over their shoulders, but Peter is gone.

* * *

The motley crew of aggressors crowds around Kleron beneath the portico at the front door.

"So, we'll storm the place, bust in through the windows?" inquires Derek. "Maybe tear through the roof?"

"Such tactics have their place," Kleron replies, "but when one is not entirely certain what to expect, I have always found it prudent to simply use the front door." He surveys the group, meeting the eyes of the bearded and pale young men in particular. "Stick close, and make no move whatsoever unless I expressly command it." The bearded men seem nervous and confused. Derek looks disappointed. Kleron fixes him in his gaze. "Do you understand?" Derek nods. Kleron addresses the little hobo. "Max?" Max lets out a high pitched grunt that's difficult to read as agreement or not, but Kleron seems satisfied. "Let's proceed then, shall we?" He nods to the largest of the three fur-coated men, who pushes his sunglasses up from his bright red eyes.

* * *

Fi and Zeke jump as the front doors burst into splinters.

Through the arch, they see the big man step cautiously into the foyer. He casts his red eyes around the room, glares at Fi, Zeke, Edgar and Mol, then scans the stairs and balcony above and backs out the door.

Fi and Zeke both let out a breath, then gasp together as Kleron strides in with Max right behind him. The rest of his retinue follows, silent except for wet footsteps on the marble floor. Rain continues to lash the great room windows and lightning flashes through the house between them and the open front doors.

Kleron stops a respectable distance from Edgar on the lower level of the floor. The others flank him closely, except for Max, who crouches farther to the side, nearer the hall to the kitchen.

Fi and Zeke hold their breath while the intruders survey their surroundings. Edgar and Kleron consider each other, unblinking. Though the low steady growl in Mol's throat is barely audible, his posture and raised fur clearly indicate his readiness to spring at the slightest provocation. Other than the big man with red eyes, Fi and Zeke have seen the group only on security video in the hospital.

Fi's surprised to see that Kleron isn't all that tall, maybe 5' 8" – though he's far from unimposing. His wet hair is slicked back and his features not unattractive, in a sharp and swarthy sort of way. Rainwater trickles down the black leather of his trench coat, beads on the shining black clasps on his shoulders. Most striking, however, are his eyes. Completely devoid of color or light, like an abyss, or the coldest, darkest reaches of outer space.

Derek and Tod cast mocking glances at Edgar's sword and shield and nudge each other, smirking arrogantly. They and the two blond men would be extremely good looking, like fashion models, except there's no life in their eyes and their skin is so pale it's almost transparent. Makeup smudges their faces, smeared from the rain. It stains their collars, and spindly veins show on their cheeks and necks. A pink stain on Derek's white designer shirt is all that remains of the blood from Stan's unfortunate demise at the lobby security booth.

The odor that pervades the room is unmistakably that of wet animals. It wouldn't be entirely unpleasant, except for the choking stench Fi remembers so well. Her eyes are drawn to Max, still wearing the same grimy stocking cap, four pair of sunglasses and three coats covered with filth. And she sees now that his wretched hands are both the same – the last two fingers missing, leaving just two fingers and a thumb on each, caked in crud, fingernails ragged and black. Stock still, grinning madly, slaver dripping into his forked beard, it feels like he's looking right through her.

Zeke realizes he's gripping the guitar much tighter than he should. The air in the room is charged with tension. He'd swear there's a palpable, almost supernatural force emanating from this group – and not a benevolent one.

Kleron scrutinizes Edgar's sword, his mouth curling in a smile devoid of mirth. He speaks in Austro-Bavarian, a language Fi and Zeke don't recognize or understand – but Edgar does.

"You'll not touch me with that before I have your throat, *boy*."

Edgar answers in English, his voice grim but steady. "I might, lad, I might."

Kleron's eyes narrow and his body tenses—

"*Hello boys.*"

The voice fills the room, followed by a flash of lightning and a sharp crack of thunder. Peter steps from the dark hall to their right.

The group shifts timorously, watching him with care. For a brief moment, what could be disbelief and trepidation flash in Kleron's otherwise expressionless eyes. "It *is* true," he says softly, in English now.

Peter deposits something that glints gold into his pocket as he steps calmly to the raised area of the floor. He stations himself between Zeke and Fi, looking down at the intruders.

Kleron forces his mirthless smile and – to Fi and Zeke's amazement – goes to one knee. "*Pater.*"

Zeke recognizes the word. Most people would pronounce it in English as "pāter," with a long "a," but when Kleron says it, it sounds like "pah-t-ĕr," with an alveolar trill at the end – a little roll of the "r." In Biblical Greek and Latin, it means "father."

The three fur-coated men drop to their knees and bow their heads. The bearded and pale men are befuddled, then Kleron reaches down and taps the floor with one finger of a black gloved hand. Derek, Tod, Hedwig and Curt lower themselves reluctantly. The big man with red eyes grabs Henri by the arm and hauls him to the floor. Didier gets the idea and drops as well. Max just hunkers down further.

Peter looks the group over. "Cù Sìth," he calls out ominously. The big man with red eyes rises to his feet, keeping his head bowed, avoiding eye contact.

"Surma," Peter announces. The one-armed man with yellow eyes stands. "And Wepwawet." The third of the fur-coated men, the one with blue eyes, rises cautiously. "The Cerberus three, reunited, I see," Peter says lyrically. "Such an honor." But the hard look in his eyes clearly communicates this is no honor at all.

Fi catches Zeke looking at her, his face screwed up in skeptical perplexity. Is he thinking the same thing she is? *Cerberus?* She glances at her uncle to see what his reaction might be, but he remains intrepid, unvexed.

Peter directs his attention to the little homeless man, "Max." It's as if Max hasn't heard him, and he still doesn't take his eyes off Fi. "*Maskim Xul,*" Peter says more emphatically. Max finally acknowledges him. Peter glares back, but he appears unfazed. "Are you quite comfortable, Max?" Peter asks coolly. No reaction.

Peter turns to the high-collared man, his voice becoming venomous. "And *Master* Kleron."

Kleron rises. "Pater, it is—"

"Kindly introduce the remainder of your entourage." Peter cuts in, surveying the bearded and the pale young men. "The least you could do after destroying my front door and soaking my floor."

Wrath flashes across Kleron's features at the interruption, but then it's gone, replaced with the smile that doesn't reach his eyes. "They are of no account, truly." The bearded and pale men say nothing, but their displeasure at being discounted so easily is apparent. Kleron continues, waving off-handedly at Henri and Didier. "Howlers, obviously. Third or fourthborn, I suppose. *Loup-garous, de France.* These are from Alsace. Palantines, shunned by their own people, ex-communicated by Ammann himself."

Fi watches the bearded men. They're particularly agitated, hyper almost, jittery and grinding their teeth like they're jacked up on drugs. Under Peter's hostile gaze they shudder with intermittent tremors, vibrating almost imperceptibly – and in the blur,

Fi swears she can see their faces oscillate between those of men and wolves. She looks at Zeke and can tell by his expression he sees it too.

"I know *what* they are," says Peter. "Though I find it hard to believe even you would associate with weres on a phase of purnima, let alone bring them to my home."

Fi and Zeke edge closer together. *Loup-garous? Weres? As in "werewolves?"*

Kleron sneers. "I couldn't leave them locked up. That would just be cruel." He indicates to the pale pretty-boys. "These are—"

"Yours," spits Peter.

Kleron raises a thick black eyebrow and offers a shrug. "Wampyr, of course, but what generation, even I do not know." Derek, Tod, Hedwig and Curt smile maliciously, baring needle sharp, translucent fangs.

Fi and Zeke squeeze even closer. *Werewolves* and *vampires?!*

An uncomfortable quiet settles over the room while Peter and Kleron's eyes remain locked, each attempting to back the other down, or read his intentions, or both.

"Well!" Peter shouts abruptly and claps his hands, complimented by a serendipitous clap of thunder outside. All the intruders jump except for Kleron and Max. The pale young men are particularly annoyed.

"We were just about to play a song," Peter announces, as if to neighbors who've dropped by unexpectedly. "You don't mind?"

Kleron watches him for a moment, then nods deliberately. The fur-coated Cerberi, Kleron, and Max appear to be accustomed to this man's odd ways, but the French werewolves fidget and the wampyr pretty-boys exchange puzzled glances.

Peter snatches the back of a chair and hurls it at Kleron, who catches it easily. "Take a load off, little one." Kleron's eyes narrow, but he places the chair on the floor and takes a seat with a flourish of his long leather coat.

Peter drags a chair in front of the piano, then pulls Fi and Zeke close. "Once we begin," he says under his breath, "do not stop playing, no matter what happens, no matter what you might see, understand?" He doesn't wait for a response before pressing Zeke into the chair.

Zeke's knees were about to give out anyhow, so he doesn't mind the sitting, but the blood drains from his face at the prospect of playing for these villains.

Peter walks Fi back and positions her to stand behind the piano bench, then takes a seat on the bench.

Fi feels like she's moving in slow-motion as she raises the concert flute to her lips. Zeke looks nervously back at them. Peter holds a finger up for Fi to wait, then gives Zeke a reassuring smile and a nod.

Zeke takes a deep breath and focuses on the guitar. Rain splashes the windows behind him, driven by gusts of increasing intensity. Rivulets flash in relief on the glass like x-rays of arteries beneath living flesh. Thunder cracks and rolls. Without thinking, because he's sure if he thinks, he'll choke, Zeke begins to play "Brian Boru's March," one of the oldest songs ever written, to his understanding. The lush tones of the aged Ramirez drift through the room.

Kleron props his elbows on the arms of his chair, hands folded at his chin, fingers steepled over his lips. Henri and Didier are enrapt by the music, but the pale young men shuffle and cross their arms impatiently.

Derek brushes Kleron's arm to get his attention, casts his eyes eagerly at Edgar's sword. Kleron shakes his head. The movement is slight but the message is clear – *No.*

Peter positions his fingers over the keys of the piano and joins the song. Thunder shakes the windows. Zeke concentrates on his hands and doesn't falter. Peter nods to Fi.

She swallows hard. As if on auto-pilot, she licks her lips, waits for a good point in the song, then, with a great force of will, begins to play. The airy notes of the flute float above those of the guitar and piano. She's never performed this tune, but to her surprise it flows effortlessly, as if she's played it a thousand times before.

Except for the pale young men, everyone in the room listens attentively, their taut intensity seeming to dissipate. Fi can almost hear the slowing of their breathing, sense their shoulders relaxing – but she notices that none are as absorbed in the song as Kleron.

Lightning flashes much closer to the house this time. Kleron doesn't blink. His eyes flit to Fi and an icy-hot sensation rises in her stomach, spreads to her chest and limbs. Somehow, in some way, she feels drawn to him, pulled by the vacuum of his empty black eyes. Though he's looking right at her, his gaze is distant, focused on something long ago and far way.

Lightning flashes again, and Kleron remembers – *and so does Fi...*

* * *

Wind and frigid rain blast her in the face, drench her clothing where she stands on a hill overlooking the stony Field of Clontarf, in a country that today is called Ireland. How Fi knows this, she can't hope to guess, but her confusion about it is nothing compared to the burning question – *how did I get here?*

She realizes she's lost her flute. Peter's warning rings in her head – *do not stop playing, no matter what happens.* Her panic melds with coursing excitement, fear, and rage – but these feelings aren't *hers.*

It's a stormy night like tonight. On the battlefield below, opposing armies rush headlong toward each other through the mud and lashing rain, hurtling war cries. And somehow she knows – on one side are Viking mercenaries and renegade Irishmen, on the other the forces of King Bóruma mac Cennétig, known today as Brian Boru. The vanguard of Boru's forces are led by a small force of warriors – among them the big man with red eyes, Cù Sìth, who accompanies Kleron today, as well as bearded and pale fighters much like the French weres and the pretty-boys, though not the same ones. There are other men as well, large and very strange. One towers taller than even Cù Sìth, built like a bear. Fi knows his name. *Bödvar Bjarki. Matunos.* The group emerges from a blinding sheet of rain and mist, and suddenly they aren't men at all, but shrieking, howling monsters.

Lightning splits the sky—

Seeing through eyes other than her own, she approaches an old man, red-bearded and crowned, who is sitting on a carven throne. The king rises, meets her in the center of the royal hall. She reaches out with a black gauntleted hand to greet Brian Boru, and feels great affection for him.

Lightning blazes—

She's back on the Field of Clontarf, standing beside Kleron, who is armored in black enameled steel and boiled leather, with a high collared black cape. Next to him, Brian Boru is mounted in full regalia atop an armored horse, watching the battle. She hears the clash and clang of arms, stomping of feet, bodies hitting the wet ground, and screams of agony.

Thunder roars—

The old king is kneeling before an abbott in a monastery, kissing his ring. Fi is next to Kleron as he watches from the shadows, unseen, and she feels his outrage at the betrayal.

Thunder rolls—

The monster warriors stand among the dead Vikings and rogues, surrounded by the Irishmen they fought for. Exhilaration flows through her as they roar in victory, thrusting bloodied fists and weapons to the sky.

* * *

Lightning flashes again and Fi is back in Peter's house, her heart thrashing in her chest, somehow still playing the flute. No episode, no fit, no seizure – but she wants to scream. She looks desperately to Peter for some indication he understands, that he knows what's happening to her, but he's focused on the piano, mindless of her plight. She sees him close his eyes—

* * *

Back in Ireland it's still night, but the rain is now merely a drizzle. There's a white tent on a hill, a hand holding a sword over a yellow sun embroidered on the blue background of a banner that whips in the wind outside it. Oil lamps silhouette the old king as he kneels before a crucifix to pray.

A dark figure slips into the tent behind him. Lightning flashes again and again. A curved knife is raised. Immense bat wings unfold. The knife descends. An overwhelming sorrow washes over Fi, coming from the tent, but also – she's startled to see a man beside her, bearded and robed, standing beneath a gnarled leafless tree. He pulls his hood back in spite of the rain. His hair hangs drenched and bedraggled over sad, emerald green eyes—

* * *

Fi's suddenly back in Peter's great room. Nothing has changed. *How can this be?!* Lightning flashes again—

* * *

Her hand is black and clawed, scrawling musical notation on parchment with a feather quill. She reaches for a lira and begins to play the notes – the same tune that Fi, Zeke and Peter are playing now—

It's a foggy, dreary day. Fi stands beside a rocky path lined with people in peasant's clothing, all weeping and moaning. She hears "Brian Boru's March" performed with fifes, drums, and bagpipes. Out of the fog come the musicians. She lowers her head as they march past in deliberate cadence. Her hands are clasped before her, clad in black gauntlets. She feels rage, but great sorrow as well.

Then she is next to Kleron, watching him bow his head at the approach of regally clad pallbearers carrying a grand casket. As they pass, she catches sight of a bearded man in the crowd across the path, wearing a robe, hood up, his green eyes peering at Kleron.

* * *

Lightning strikes just outside the window, searing the great room with blinding blue light. Thunder shrieks and booms, shaking the entire house. The windows clatter in their casings, so hard it sounds like they'll shatter.

Fi almost drops her flute – *don't stop playing, no matter what you might see.*

Her eyes find Zeke. He hasn't missed a note on his guitar, but he's white as a sheet, his eyes fixed on the three men in fur coats.

As if emerging from their own reflections in a shaken mirror, the men are changing – and growing. One-armed, yellow-eyed Surma and blue-eyed Wepwawet now stand at least seven feet tall, massively muscled with straight broad shoulders, covered in long shining fur so deeply black it's almost blue. And they have tails. The one with red eyes, Cù Sìth, looks just like them, but he's over a foot taller and proportionately broader. The three of them stand so close together their fur intermingles – one enormous shaggy figure with three heavy muzzles full of long sharp teeth, three sets of tall bristling ears, and three glowing pairs of eyes.

Zeke can see it now – *Cerberus... Can this really be the mythical three-headed dog-monster that guards the gates of hell?*

Awesome is the first word that comes to his mind to describe them – but in his mind it has its original definition, "to inspire an emotion of combined veneration, wonder, and dread," as opposed to just meaning "really cool."

The knees of the creatures bend backward like a dog's, and their clawed feet are hinged in the middle, the front part shaped much like a dog's paw. Their fingers are long and thick, the backs of them rough and calloused except for a shining black ridge that runs along the top of each finger. The biggest of the brothers, the one Peter called Cù Sìth, clenches one hand and Zeke sees that the ridges are claws, four inches long at least, which extend from the second knuckle of each finger. With his hand closed like that, callous-padded fingers folded underneath, it *is* a dog's paw. Zeke recalls how he ran on all fours at the hospital swimming pool. At least *that* makes sense now.

Behind the Cerberus, or *Cerberi*, or whatever they are, the bearded men have changed as well. Unlike the monstrous triplets, who never really had clothing, they still have theirs, and though their bodies remain humanoid, they look like, well, *werewolves*, with tongues lolling from wolfish chops, dripping slobber.

Zeke focuses on the notes of the piano behind him, mostly to reassure himself Peter is still there, and turns to Fi, who is playing her flute, with her eyes glued to the leader of the villains, the one Peter called Kleron, as if she can't look away.

Like the Cerberus triplets and the bearded men, Kleron has also changed, only even more horrifically. The high collar of his trench coat is now wrinkled pointed ears, and the coat itself has become *wings* – bat wings – membranous black skin stretched over slender bone, draped from his shoulders down his back and sides, each terminating just above the floor in a single black claw. The crest of each wing is appointed with a talon that hooks over his shoulders. What was his brown angora vest is russet fur on a barrel-chest. His black, leathery legs culminate in slim bony feet with claws for toes. Folded at his chin are hands with shining claws at the end of slender knobby fingers. The eyes are the same cold glistening voids, but his head appears larger, the skin creased, the darkest gray, with an upturned and splayed snout. Raven hair flows back from low on his forehead, up over his scalp and down to his shoulders. His abnormally wide rictus grin is cracked enough to reveal translucent pointed teeth and vicious fangs.

Fi jerks suddenly at another report of thunder, blinks as if she's woken from a dream, but she continues to play her flute as if by instinct. She finds she can now tear her eyes away from the hideous visage of Kleron – and her thoughts go to her uncle, as they always have when she felt like she was in trouble or lost. Right now she's both.

Edgar hasn't moved a muscle, but his eyes are glued to the little hobo, Max. Max hasn't changed in appearance like the others, but he smiles broadly at having garnered Fi's attention. She quickly looks away. The pale pretty-boys haven't changed either, except they're now grinning, their fangs clearly visible.

Peter stops playing the piano, sustaining the last chords so they fade gradually. Zeke strums the remaining notes, sits silently amazed. Fi lowers the flute from trembling lips, and "Brian Boru's March" has come to an end.

* * *

Fi blinks to test her vision. Kleron and the rest are as they were when they arrived – just very odd, frightening men. She and Zeke look to each other for affirmation that what they've seen is real.

Peter rises from the bench, places a hand on Fi's shoulder, and smiles approvingly at Zeke, who responds with a look that screams, *What the fuck?*

Kleron rises slowly from his chair, clapping idly. "Well played, Pater. So you know the truth of Brian Boru's demise."

"I should have killed you then."

"Dear, dear Pater. You should have killed me long before *that*."

The wampyr are clearly perturbed by the inaction of their master. Derek glances at the others, emits a high pitched shriek and attacks.

Kleron reaches for him, shouting, "*Nein*," but it's too late. Derek and Tod launch straight at Fi, Curt and Hedwig toward Edgar.

The two Frenchmen, returned to their werewolf forms, attempt to dart past the Cerberus brothers. Cù Sìth clotheslines Henri, knocking him flat on his back, and snatches Didier by the back of his vest like a parent preventing a rambunctious child from darting into the street.

If Fi blinked she'd miss it, the pale men move so quickly. But Uncle Edgar and his dog are faster. Blood sprays the high ceiling as Edgar's sword slices through Curt at an upward angle. Edgar then immediately bashes him with his shield – and Curt catches fire at its touch.

Mol snatches Hedwig's face in his jaws, slams him down, eviscerates him with his claws and crushes his skull in his teeth.

Curt hits the floor in two pieces. His burning upper half slides to a stop at Kleron's feet, where he spits blood in utter disbelief and beats weakly at the flames. Kleron steps back to keep his feet, now appearing clad in shiny pointed boots, out of the expanding pool of red. The flames die out, Curt's eyes go dim, and he is still.

Peter was even quicker than Edgar and Mol. When Derek and Tod leapt, he stepped in and caught both in mid-air while Fi stumbled backward and Zeke tipped over in his chair. One hand is now thrust through Derek's stomach, fingers and thumb protruding from his back, clutching his spine, while he firmly clasps Tod by the throat with the other. Keeping his eyes on Kleron, he squeezes Tod's head from his body with a squishy *crunch*.

Fi lurches further away, almost falling over a chair, barely avoiding the blood that spouts from Tod's violently convulsing body. Peter drops the head on top of it.

Max cackles, high pitched like an old witch, his filthy teeth bared and curded in slime.

On the floor from his tumble from the chair, Zeke scoots away, clutching the guitar in front of him like it might protect him. He clambers to his feet and scrambles around to the back of the piano, where Fi meets him, both of them quaking in terror.

Recovering from his initial shock, Derek lets out an ear-splitting scream. Stunted pink bat wings rip through the back of his shirt, flapping ineffectively. He rams his fangs into Peter's neck – or *onto* Peter's neck is more like it, because he jerks back with a shrill cry, blood spurting from his shattered teeth.

Fi and Zeke grab hold of each other reflexively.

Kleron groans at the indignity of his progeny's actions. "Not... yet," he mutters to himself.

Max laughs harder, spittle bubbling on his lips, his little round body shaking with coldhearted mirth.

Derek writhes and shrieks and pounds at Peter with his fists. His forearm snaps on Peter's shoulder, making a new elbow, and he screams even louder. Peter's face is stony, eyes cold. He doesn't even blink. He tightens his grip, crushing Derek's spine. Derek twitches and folds over backward like a garment bag. Peter tosses the body on top of Curt in front of Kleron. "Take that with you," he orders, then kicks Tod's corpse and accompanying head onto the pile as well. "And those."

Zeke sets the guitar on the piano, drops down behind it and pukes.

Max laughs uncontrollably, both hands holding his stomach.

"Max," Kleron appeals, "some decorum, please."

Max's titters recede. "Oh-h-h, wampyrs..." After a final "tee hee," he is silent.

"My most humble apologies," Kleron offers Peter with a small bow. "But you understand, Pater, better than anyone. There is no accounting for blood."

Cù Sìth lets go of Henri, who is now back in human form and not at all interested in continuing the attack. Didier picks himself up off the floor and cowers at the back of the group. Fi helps Zeke up. He leans on the piano, almost as pale as the dead wampyr.

"What did you presume to accomplish here?" Peter asks of Kleron, speckles of blood on his face.

Kleron shrugs as if there's no reason not to tell. "We were going to make this easy on everyone, cast you down in your weakness, rule peaceably. But even in light of your miraculous recovery, there can still be mercy."

"You know nothing of peace or mercy."

"Not true, Father, not true. I propose an accord, sealed with a gift, and a proof." He nods to Wepwawet, who marches through the arch and out the front door.

Peter eyes Kleron askance, slides a hand surreptitiously into his pocket. "Be chary, little one."

Kleron observes him warily, but continues, "In the last 24 hours, just that tiny sliver of time, our Asura brethren – and sistren," he offers to Fi, "have struck in all four corners of this world, and many others. The Deva are broken."

Edgar glances at Peter.

Zeke mutters under his breath, "Deva and Asura..."

"Will you stand aside, Pater," Kleron asks, "allow what was always meant to be, *to be?*"

"You know I will not."

"This can go easily for you and yours, or very, very hard. We will destroy all that you hold most dear." His eyes go to Edgar and Zeke, then linger on Fi. "*All* will suffer."

"Did the Holocausts teach you nothing?"

"*Oh yes.*" Kleron replies. "This time we have might like you have never seen, an army, *nay, armies*, unprecedented in all the history of the worlds."

"You dare, Master Kleron," Peter challenges, "after all that has transpired?"

"*Now* you pretend to care." Kleron shakes his head in scornful condemnation. "It is time, and you know it." He fixes his gaze on Peter, red fire smoldering in black coals. "All the worlds of promise have fallen."

Peter's eyes narrow at the significance of Kleron's words. Fi and Zeke watch closely as they glare at each other, an arcane knowledge seeming to pass between them. A knowledge, it would appear, of which Peter did not realize Kleron was aware.

"Why should I believe the Lord of Lies?" Peter asks.

"It doesn't matter. You will see with your own eyes, and despair."

"You will fail, yet again," Peter cautions. "We will stop you."

"You will try."

Wepwawet returns, dragging a canvas sack that thrashes and snarls through the arch.

"Ah, here we are," Kleron announces.

Wepwawet steps between Surma and Cù Sìth, hugs the sack upright to his chest.

"I offer this charity," Kleron says with a wave of his hand. Cù Sìth rips the sack away.

Bound tight and gagged by silken ropes, is Kabir.

The gray suit and heliotrope tie he wore at the concert hall, where he was working as a bodyguard just this morning, are bloodied and torn. His upper lip is puffy and bruised, and one of his canine teeth is missing. He struggles, emits a muffled roar through the gag, then sees Peter. His shock and shame are evident.

Edgar gasps, "Kabir..."

Peter utters his Truename, "Zadkiel."

"*Zadkiel...*" Zeke mouths quietly. "This is... I..."

Fi sees Zeke shaking, obviously freaking out. And so is she. She can't even chew her nails, she's gripping the flute so tightly. *It's happening,* her voice cries in her head. *I'm losing it. Do something, Peter!*

"He is yours," says Kleron, "and those who still breathe shall be spared, if you pledge the yielding vow."

Kabir shakes his head adamantly and groans. Wepwawet presses the claws of one hand to his throat.

Peter gazes dolefully at Kabir. "That, I cannot do."

Fi can't stand it any longer – *all the violence and death and secrets and monsters and this macho posturing bullshit!*

She screams in frustration, anger and fright. Zeke attempts a feeble grab at her as she charges from behind the piano.

"Stop it!" she cries, approaching Peter, who doesn't take his eyes off Kleron. "Just stop it!"

Zeke stumbles up, takes her by the shoulder, "Fi," but she pulls away.

Edgar is dismayed by her outburst, out of fear for her safety. "Fiona…"

"No!" she shouts, pointing the flute at him. Then she jabs the instrument at Kleron like a weapon. "*You.* That's *enough.*"

Kleron grins darkly.

"Fi," says Peter, still watching Kleron. "Calm down."

"I won't. All of you. Just *stop it!*"

"*FIONA!*"

The voice isn't Peter's alone, but that of a thousand Peters. The voice of a *god.* The air excites with its power and the house shakes. Outside, the wind peaks at its call, rain pummels the windows and lightning strikes in rapid succession, blasting a tree to splinters and setting the trunk aflame.

All in the room feel the command of that voice. Especially Fi. She stares at Peter, cowed and amazed.

"Fi," he says coolly, "let me handle this. Please."

"Okay." She backs away trembling, an equally shaky Zeke guiding her so she doesn't fall over the piano bench.

Peter sizes up his opponents, calculating options, weighing the odds – then he catches a subtle shift in the stance of one of the Cerberi, a slight clenching of a fist, a brief meeting of the eyes.

He glares at Kleron. "You have my answer."

Wepwawet smirks in cruel satisfaction.

Kleron's voice is a chill whisper. "So be it. *Pater has spoken.*"

No sooner are the words out of Kleron's mouth than Cù Sìth backhands him hard, knocking him through the air, then spins, front kicks Surma into Henri and Didier, and rakes his claws across Wepwawet's eyes.

Wepwawet staggers back with a howl, releasing Kabir and clutching at the ragged wounds on his face. Cù catches Kabir and tosses him to flop at Peter's feet.

Kleron snaps out his wings to halt his trajectory and lands in a crouch behind Max.

He rises, showing no signs of injury – but his eyes burn red at Cù Sìth and his mouth twists in a caustic sneer. "*You...*"

Max grins madly. "Bad doggie!"

Wepwawet slaps the blood from his bright blue eyes, which blaze at the apprehension of what Cù has done. He and Surma roar in fury at their brother's betrayal. Cù roars back, deeper and louder – then everyone in the room freezes as a deep timpani thrum underscores all, charging the atmosphere with crackling force. The lights flicker and dim.

Peter's fist is a dithering blur. He uncurls his fingers to reveal the gold rod from the bank and utters a single word. To Fi and Zeke, it sounds like, "*Goongneer.*"

An arctic chill shocks the air. Electric blue energy surges over Peter's body and down his arm. Particles of light whirl around his hand and expand in a sparkling cloud.

Time stands still. The cloud implodes.

Icy wind buffets all as every bit of air in the room seems to be sucked into Peter's hand. The object springs into a shaft, six feet in length, with a long jagged spearhead. Electricity sizzles over Peter's arm and the spear, then extinguishes.

No one moves except Max, who poises as if preparing to flee, or attack. Either way, his grin has been wiped away. Any trace of a sneer is gone from Kleron's face.

Peter surveys the group, his visage grim and imposing. With all Fi and Zeke have now seen, they're exceedingly glad they're on the same side.

Kleron's eyes move from Peter to Cù Sìth, then Edgar and Zeke, and finally settle on Fi. "Until we meet again." He opens his mouth, impossibly wide, and emits a prolonged ear-splitting squeak of incredibly high frequency, at the edge of human hearing and beyond. Fi and Zeke recoil at the unearthly sound.

Crackling power of blue and gold spirals down Peter's arm, builds like a ball of static at his fist, but in the time it takes for him to aim the spear and discharge the blinding streak of lightning, Kleron grasps Max's shoulder, takes a small step back, and they vanish. Where they stood, the stone floor explodes and melts to fuming magma.

* * *

In the eerie silence that follows, Peter's eyes fall on Surma and Wepwawet. Cù Sìth loops to block their escape through the arch. They hunker together and snarl. Nearby, Henri and Didier make themselves as inconspicuous as possible.

"Traitorous bitch," Surma grumbles in a grinding tongue never known to human beings.

"That depends on one's point of view," Cù replies in the same language.

Henri and Didier dart for the arch, but Cù catches each by the head in his giant paws. He lifts them until their feet dangle, gives them a moment to consider their fate, then claps his hands. Brains splatter and their shuddering bodies drop at his feet.

Mol cocks his ears toward the windows and growls deep in his throat. Peter probes the walls with his eyes, listening – and all hell breaks loose as a shrieking multitude of wampyr and werewolves crash through the windows.

Edgar shouts, "Fiona." Zeke instinctively grabs up the guitar and they rush to

Edgar's side. Breaking glass and pounding feet can be heard from throughout the house. Wepwawet and Surma howl and fling themselves at Cù Sìth.

Peter remains surprisingly calm. He eyes the guitar in Zeke's hands, then strides to a chest, knocking attackers aside, kicks it open, pulls out a guitar case and tosses it to him. Zeke ogles him, questioning.

Peter nods in affirmation, then shouts to Edgar. "Go."

Zeke stows the guitar. Edgar whistles for Mol. They hurry toward the hall that leads to the kitchen.

Kabir grunts from where he lies wriggling on the floor. Peter frees him from his bonds with one deft cut of the spear, tugs him to his feet and rips the gag from his mouth.

"My apologies—" Kabir offers in his deep crunchy voice.

"Later," Peter cuts him off. "Time to fight."

Without another word, Kabir postures low, roars, and charges the ghastly host. Wamps and weres go down like bowling pins that scream and bleed.

While Mol stands guard, Edgar shoves Fi's flute into her backpack and lifts the pack to her, but wamps and weres rush around the corner from the hall. He drops the pack and keeps them at bay with sword and shield. Mol drags others down, shredding necks and limbs. But there are too many.

Edgar glances about for another exit. More fiends clamber in the great room windows while others charge through the front door and pour in from the hall at the other end of the room. Some run on all fours, others flap on fully developed bat wings. Packs of werewolves, colonies of wampyr, males, females, in multiple varieties, shapes and sizes, nightmarish subjects of folklore from around the world made flesh. Still more shriek down at them from the balcony above.

Edgar orders Fi and Zeke back and they retreat the only way they can, along the wall past the fireplace to the corner by the desk. Edgar protects their back and flank. Mol tears at all who attempt to block their path. Edgar presses Fi and Zeke into the corner and engages the enemy.

Peter stands like a statue bolted to the floor, gazing down while wamps and weres hurl themselves against him. They don't even affect his balance.

When he looks up, his eyes gleam red. He twirls. Gungnir's blade slices through the surrounding host as if they're made of little more than air.

* * *

Kleron tromps from the top of a rocky hill, away from a dry riverbed that lies behind and below. Max scampers alongside, chuckling to himself.

There is no storm on this world, but a raucous clatter and hum pervades the air. Flocks of violet shadows flit over the barren landscape, cast by a bloated yellow moon in a lavender sky. Kleron and Max pay no heed.

"So, Pater has recovered," spits Kleron in the rhythmic guttural tongue of the Tuatha Dé Danann, a clan of his wampyric spawn who once invaded ancient Ireland, long before the birth of Brian Boru. "Quite swiftly, I might add. This changes things."

Max snickers. "And he's got his spear, hee hee."

"It's no laughing matter, Max."

Max laughs anyway.

Kleron steals a glance at him. "I've suspected there may be another traitor among us, but one of the Cerberi? And Cù Sìth, no less."

Max snickers at that as well.

"What do you make of this trickery?"

Max shrugs. "We are a fickle lot, I can attest. But I'm curious to see if he is accepted, or if Pater slays him post haste."

"As am I." Kleron halts and takes Max's wretched hand. He scans the ground before him and then the horizon, as if seeking unseen landmarks, then closes his eyes. Slipping can be tricky business, even for one as experienced as he.

An exceptionally rare gift, maybe two dozen Firstborn have ever been able to slip, and only a very few parvuli. Even The Prathamaja Nandana couldn't do it, as magnificent as she was. Father has always had the ability, though it took him over an aeon to discover it. It takes an innate talent one must be born with. Then, in most cases, Father has to teach them how it is done. He showed Kleron when he was young, by accident, and Kleron took to it like – *what do the parvuli say in modern English?* – "like a fish to water."

Max waits patiently, humming "Brian Boru's March." Kleron raises an eyelid to see him swaying contentedly with the tune, then takes a step and they slip away.

In the sky above, a thousand multi-winged horrors await.

* * *

Wampyr and werewolves continue to pour into the house, providing Peter and Kabir with a seemingly endless supply of fodder. They throw their lives away, stupid with bloodlust, or more afraid of their master than death itself. Much of the first, no doubt, but assuredly the latter. The noise is deafening, a raucous discord of squeals of agony, howls of rage, mighty blows, body falls, breaking bones, and the reckless destruction of Peter's furnishings.

Cù Sìth pays them no heed. He has his hands full with his Cerberi brothers. All three are gouged and bleeding, but even two against one, Surma and Wepwawet have difficulty gaining the advantage. The blows they land resound throughout the room. The Master's minions avoid them as much as possible in the press.

Droves of wamps and weres beat like waves against the sea wall of Edgar's sword and shield. He thrusts and spins with impeccable skill, his blade trailing silver in the air and splashing blood in all directions. Severed heads clunk to the floor. Quivering bodies and limbs heap before him. Fi and Zeke huddle in a rising reservoir of red and are spattered in copious quantities of it as well.

Fi thinks she's imagining it at first, but even in this din she hears snatches of a familiar tune. Soft and steady, while he hacks at the enemy with a stolid expression that shows no signs of fear or physical distress, Edgar is humming "Swing Low, Sweet Chariot."

Her mind fixates on it. Except for her uncle's song, accompanied by the methodical thump of his shield and ring of his sword, all other sound becomes background noise. She watches as if in a dream.

Mol stands courageously over her and Zeke, ready to snap at any attacker who might get past her uncle, but none have succeeded so far. Corpses continue to pile around them in a gruesome bunker.

In the center of the room, Peter snaps Gungnir like a whip. A trail of fluid electricity fries several weres. He aims the spear along the hallway balcony above and an extended bolt of lightning leaps from the blade like a ragged blue laser, torching wamps and weres as they leap over in droves to join the brawl. Much of the ceiling and balcony are scorched as well.

Three flung wampyr smash through the glass hearth doors into the fireplace. Two of them lie dead and burning, but the third runs out screaming and flailing, engulfed in flame. Peter spin-kicks it to shoot out the window like a yowling comet.

Rain squalls through the ruined windows, flashed by sporadic lightning. The air grows thick with steam and smoke, the vigorous scent of ozone, coppery tang of vaporized blood, and acrid reek of burning wood and flesh.

Kabir is incredibly fast, sure-footed and assured, leaping effortlessly to snatch fluttering wampyr from the air and pouncing to crush his foes – but as effective as his methods are he appears brutish compared to Peter, who moves with nimble grace, irresistible, unrelenting, as if engaged in a deadly waltz. None appear capable of harming him, even if they manage to connect with fist or claw, nor do any within range escape his wrath.

Fi notices a rosy glint of delight in his eyes, his terrible crooked smile. *He's actually enjoying this.*

Zeke's in a similar state to Fi, anesthetized by Edgar's tune, numb to the violent commotion. An automatic response, he thinks, to the utterly surreal and perilous situation they've found themselves in, to stave off life-threatening shock and unconsciousness.

Kabir throws off a dog-pile of the enemy, flips the piano, sending it somersaulting through the crowd. It smashes wamps and weres to pulp against the wall in a cacophony of snapping strings and bursting wood. Through a brief break in the throng, he sees Cù Sìth is in trouble.

Wepwawet has him around the neck from behind and has pinned one of his arms. They go down backwards and Wepwawet locks Cù's legs with his own. Surma stomps Cù's free arm, then drives a knee into his stomach and punches claws-deep into the thick meat of his chest.

Kabir knows better than to tackle one of these monsters – all three together may not equal one Maskim Xul, but they're far older than Kabir and from a particularly frightful bloodline. He tackles Surma nonetheless, just as Surma goes for Cù's throat.

They tumble and roll. Surma shoves him off and they both spring to their feet. Kabir readies for swift retribution, but Surma only flashes him an irritated glance before sprinting back to his brothers.

Cù wrestles out of Wepwawet's hold, blood trickling at his neck from the near fatal swipe of Surma's claws. Surma hits them both as they shove against each other to stand. All three crash through the wall next to the arch. A section of wall collapses and they burst out the other side, through the stairs and into the foyer.

* * *

The wampyr policeman from outside the hospital smooths rainwater from his sopping hair. He sits atop a stack of kevlar cases in front of one of the white vans parked in a copse of trees that overlooks Peter's home. Other cases, open and empty, are scattered nearby. He lifts his face to the sky, opens his mouth, prominently displaying his fangs, and catches water from the light but steady rain. Without his motorcycle helmet he looks much the same as Derek, Tod, Curt and Hedwig – handsome, pale, and brooding. He raises a set of military grade hyperspectral goggles and peers through them to see a clearly defined, magnified image of the battle in the great room.

"These things are so freakin' cool."

A few yards away, a werewolf in Trueface, but still wearing his overalls with *Luc* embroidered on the breast, grunts impatiently. "Let me see."

"I said *no*. I have my job, you have yours."

"Mine eez done!"

"Then chill out, Frenchy. Go chase a deer or something."

Luc grunts in frustration, checks his watch. He snatches a wireless detonator from his belt, switches it on to make sure it's operational – for the tenth time.

"Would you leave that thing alone?" the wampyr growls.

Luc grumbles but toggles it off and puts it away. "Vere *are* zay?—*Argh!*"

Kleron and Max have materialized right in front of him. He trips and falls backwards over empty cases.

The wampyr snickers while Luc scrambles to his feet.

"Everything eez prepared, Master," Luc reports excitedly, taking the detonator from his belt and switching it on. "Zee charges are een place, but zay are all still in zee building."

Kleron holds a hand out to the wampyr, who immediately relinquishes the goggles. Kleron scans the house – Peter and Kabir handily dispatching his minions, The Cerberi family feud in the foyer, Edgar and Mol repelling attackers in the corner. He zooms in on Fi and Zeke huddled behind them, then focuses on Fi.

* * *

An especially determined group of fiends converge on Edgar. Two wampyr come shrieking over the heap of bodies straight at Fi and Zeke. Mol moves to block them, but they halt suddenly in mid-leap, then are yanked away and flung the length of the room. Fi and Zeke gape at the sight of the dusky half-big cat, half-human visage that turns upon them.

In Trueface, Kabir's suit has been replaced by dark gray fur with a purple patch where the knot of his tie had been. He inspects them with gleaming copper tiger-eyes and points with a stout clawed finger. "Are you damaged?"

Zeke gawks at the single saber-tooth that juts down over his sturdy square jaw, and the striped cat tail that twitches over his shoulder. Fi shakes her head quickly, *No*.

Kabir curls one side of his feline split upper lip, presses his tongue into the ragged hole where his missing tooth had been and sucks on it. He regards Mol and nods. "Molossus."

Fi would swear that Mol nods back. Kabir shrugs a werewolf off one sloping shoulder, untangling its claws from his gray lion's mane, and returns to the fight, snapping its neck as he goes.

"Machairodus *Kabir*..." Zeke mutters.

"What?" Fi asks.

Zeke absent-mindedly wipes the spattered blood from his face. "Edgar called him *Kabir*. The Machairodus Kabir were big prehistoric cats, like saber-tooth tigers."

"Wha-a-a-a-t?" Fi gazes at Kabir, who chomps on the back of a passing werewolf's neck and shakes it vigorously.

"Peter called him *Zadkiel*," Zeke adds. "Like the angel."

Fi won't believe it. "No way."

But Zeke is beginning to wonder. "*Maybe* way."

* * *

The numbers of the enemy are being depleted. Edgar has one of the last living were-wolves, a particularly big and ugly beast, pinned to the bookshelves with his shield. Engulfed in flame, it shrieks and flails until Edgar drags his sword across its throat and lets it drop. Mol bites it on the shoulder and tosses its barbecued body onto the surrounding heap.

* * *

Kleron lowers the goggles. "Send in Mahisha."

"Yes, Master." The wampyr policeman clicks the radio handset clipped to his shoulder and relays the order.

Kleron crooks a devilish grin. "Let's see what they make of this."

* * *

Fi and Zeke help each other to their feet and gaze out over the carnage. The floor is slick with bright red blood, strewn with organs and limbs and piles of burst and steaming bodies. A divan burns, roasting the corpses of wampyr heaped upon it. Plaster is stripped from charred patches of wall and ceiling.

Cù Sìth comes lumbering through the arch, dragging his beaten and bloodied kin by the scruffs. He clean and jerks them over his head, one in each hand, looses a triumphant roar, and slams them down hard enough to crack marble and tremble the floor.

Edgar looks Fi and Zeke over to ascertain whether any of the blood that covers them is their own. "Shall we go?" he asks.

They nod eagerly.

Unfortunately, the respite is all too brief. Enemy reinforcements rush in from all directions, easily as many as before.

Edgar groans and readies himself for more, but this bunch doesn't attack. They stay along the walls, clog the exits, block the windows, line the balcony above, and are strangely silent.

Fi and Zeke hold their breath once again. Waiting is almost worse than the earlier bedlam.

Suddenly the entire house is jolted by some unseen impact, followed by sounds of distant stamping footsteps and muffled destruction. Peter eyes the wall hung with guitars – which are mostly destroyed, Zeke observes with regret. The jolting impact comes again, and again, growing louder, and closer. The surviving guitars rattle nervously on their hooks. Then the wall on which they hang explodes, sending fragmented masonry, broken instruments and the ruined buffet flying.

Peter's face slackens at the sight of the huffing, slobbering beast that stands before him amongst the rubble and dust.

Cù Sìth glares, growling. Kabir trips over bodies and broken furniture to Peter's side, astounded at what he sees.

He mutters, "*Mahishasura.*"

Zeke mouths wordlessly, then out loud says, "The Buffalo Demon? From Hindu scripture?"

"It can be none other," Edgar replies. "But..."

More weres and wampyr flow in through the fresh hole in the wall behind the Buffalo Demon and span to flank him on either side.

Peter stares up at the 11 foot tall hulk. "Mahisha?"

Enormous baleful eyes, cataracted in weak milky gray, roll down in wet sockets to regard him. "Yes." His voice comes from the pit of him, hoarse and gurgling with phlegm.

"You're *dead*," Peter states flatly, clearly perplexed.

Mahisha has the build of a hairy thickset man with a tumid belly, but his back is severely humped and draped in thick curling fur and his shaggy oversized head is more buffalo than human, with upward curving horns. The straggling hair of his armpits is braided and held with golden ringlets, as is the inverted peak on his chest. In one thick hand he grips a black metallic mace with rows of runes damascened in gold and silver along its eight foot length, and wicked flanges at its head.

Thick fleshy lips crook in a lopsided grin that drools into his ragged beard. "*Yes.*"

Wepwawet coughs up blood and grumbles, "It's about time." He tries to push himself up, but Cù Sìth pounds him down with his fists.

Mahisha intones, "*Samavari Maya,*" while lifting his mace in both hands.

Cù Sìth halts in mid-punch.

Peter shouts, "No!"

The base of the mace's handle stamps the floor with the sound of a ponderous gong. Air ripples from it in visible waves – and now there's not just *one* Buffalo Demon – there are *six*.

Without hesitation, the one nearest Cù Sìth swings a leveling blow. Cù reacts fast enough to avoid the deadly flanges of the mace's head, but the handle below strikes him in the midriff, launching him as if from a catapult to bash through the balcony at the far end of the room and punch through the ceiling.

Another Mahisha says, "*Samavari Maya,*" pounds his mace, and there are twelve. The dozen Buffalo Demons bellow together and attack. The wamps and weres join in, howling their savage inhumanity.

Fi and Zeke huddle in their corner once again.

The Buffalo Demons are surprisingly fast for their bulk, but Peter dodges every blow, wielding Gungnir with supreme deft and confidence, reaping a leg here, an arm there. He opens the gut of one, loosing an avalanche of steaming entrails. Its mace dematerializes in a particle cloud, and as its body falls it commences to decompose. Flesh sloughs, bones crumble and it ignites in sickly green flames that burn cold. Before the Mahisha reaches the ground it's nothing but scattered dust and a spectral whorl of smoke. Peter frowns at the sight.

Kabir speaks at his side, "There is foul sorcery at work here."

Peter grunts in deliberation, then nods to Edgar's corner. "Would you?"

"Of course," Kabir replies, and begins to fight his way across the room. He dodges the blow of a Buffalo Demon's mace and it shatters the marble floor. He sidesteps the charge of another, slashes a tendon at its knee with his claws, then leaps on its back and bites deeply into its shaggy neck. The beast roars, smashes its back – and Kabir – into a wall. The first tugs its mace from the floor and swings in an attempt to remove Kabir from its clone, but Kabir sees it coming and drops. The mace crunches into the spine of the second Mahisha and it disappears in decay and green flame.

Kabir is of equal age with Mahisha, but The Buffalo Demons are a whole lot bigger, and buffalo are *tough*. He can take them in single combat and has in the distant past, but he must take care when they are in numbers, especially in these close quarters. Of greatest concern is Mahisha's mace. It not only gives him, and only him, the ability to multiply himself, but it is also a high grade Astra weapon, its razor sharp flanges capable of incapacitating a True Ancient and killing all others with a single blow.

The Mahishas, however, seem more intent on Peter. They rush him from all sides, swinging their maces overhead. He blocks and feints, but two strike down on his head and shoulders. Flanges bend and break and stone explodes beneath Peter's feet at the impact.

Mahisha's mace is capable of harming all but Father, that is. No sooner have they lifted their weapons for another blow than he's on the attack, completely unharmed. He splits one down the middle with his spear, grabs hold of another's lower jaw with his free hand and tears it clean off, leaving the Mahisha hacking, grasping at the gushing empty space where it had been. A third he springs over the top of, gripping it by one horn as he goes, bending it over backward, then spinning to knock down others with its body and flinging it into the path of another's mace.

But every time their numbers dwindle, another incants, "*Samavari Maya*," and pounds his mace to replenish their ranks.

Kabir takes a place alongside Edgar. Protecting others – its what he does – and he's always liked and respected the young *waeponbora*. He doesn't know the young man and woman who seem to be in Edgar's care, but it doesn't matter. They will live through this, or Kabir will die in their defense.

A sudden roar and a glimpsed black form above.

The Buffalo Demons and Kabir may be matched in combat, but the notorious Cù Sìth is in another class entirely. He descends from the balcony in an arms-out dive, right into the center of a pack of Mahishas. In short order they are disemboweled or dropping with throats removed to the neckbone, reduced to rot and smoke. His reaction to their uncanny decomposition is a rumbling grimace.

Even Cù Sìth is susceptible to the Astra mace, however, and he must take care. But this kind of battle is what the Cerberi have always lived for. Sheer mayhem and slaughter. Kabir is still shocked that Cù turned on his brothers and defied his Asura master – Kleron could dispatch Cù Sìth as handily as Cù takes out Mahishas – and especially that he saved Kabir's life. Shocked, but leery. It will take more than this for Kabir to trust Old Shuck, the harbinger of doom, the vile Gwyllgi, the treacherous Barghest, the dreaded Moddey Dhoo. By whatever name he's ever been known, Cù Sìth has never done a kind thing for anyone in his life. Not without evil intent.

The wamps and weres are merely a nuisance to Peter and Cù, like chipmunks on lions, and those who get in the way of the Mahishas are stepped on with no more thought than walking on grass, or swept aside by a mace like dry leaves before a broom. Yet they keep coming, throwing themselves at Edgar and Kabir with reckless abandon.

Peter and Cù Sìth take the Buffalo Demons down as fast as they multiply. But only as fast. The gonging sound comes again and again. Meanwhile, wave after wave of werewolves and wampyr continue to spill into the house.

* * *

Kleron hands the goggles back to the wampyr and calls up into the rain and darkness. "Robber!"

Something shifts high in the shadows of a wizened oak, gazes down between branches with an eye like that of a dead fish.

Kleron shouts, "Go."

It just stares at him, bereft of life.

"By authority of your master, do as you are bidden," Kleron orders. It still doesn't respond. Kleron's voice rises in the revolting invidious tongue of his old master. "Obey me. The one who has summoned you commands it!"

The creature blinks sluggishly, then hops from the branch and soars into the dismal sky.

* * *

Fi fears for Edgar. He fights on, but his clothing is torn and he's bleeding from scratches on his arms and face. Kabir helps tremendously, casting wampyr and werewolves aside like annoying chaff, but there are *so many of them.*

Zeke senses her anxiety. If there was only something he could do. He's never felt more worthless in his life.

Something shoots in high through the broken windows and circles along the ceiling, artfully dodging flailing maces. It moves too quickly for Zeke and Fi to fully identify, but it's not a wampyr. This has shining feathers of iridescent blue and green, and a long wide blur of a tail. It lights on a ruined section of the balcony and Zeke and Fi can now see that it's form is much like a bird with a craning neck, but its blue-feathered face is strikingly like a man's, with an unnaturally long and pointed (beak-like, in fact) white nose. Elegant stalks topped with blue puffs crown its head. Its eyes are like the Mahishas', with irises of milky gray.

"Hark!" it cries in a voice that sets Fi and Zeke's ears ringing. Louder than Cù Sìth's

roar or Kleron's terrible squeak, louder than the bellows of the Buffalo Demons, louder even than Peter.

The bedlam grinds to a halt. Buffalo Demons back away from Peter and Cù Sìth. Kabir dispatches the few weres and wamps that remain too close.

Edgar takes advantage of the break to check on Fi and Zeke. "All well?"

Zeke frowns. That's a relative question, deserving a relative response.

Fi gives it to him. "Okay, I guess, considering. But how are *you?*"

Edgar smiles appreciatively. "Right as rain, dear." He touches his bloody fingers to her shoulder. "Hang in there, you two. We'll get through this. Have faith."

Fi and Zeke wonder. Faith seems like a strange thing to worry about right now.

"Tengu-Andrealphus," Peter hails up at the new arrival. "You, too, are supposed to be dead and gone!"

"*I am,*" Tengu-Andrealphus replies, seeming doubtful of the fact himself.

His image ripples like a disturbance in still water. Sitting on the railing now is a stately looking man garbed in breeches and a shining blue blouse embroidered in gold beneath a silken green cape, wearing tall gilded boots and a slim sapphire crown. The eyes, however, remain the same.

"*Tengu-Andrealphus,*" Edgar says with a tone of dread. "The Peafowl."

The stately man's image ripples again. His features become less comely, his wardrobe less urbane. A simple green and blue tunic, hose, boots of sandy suede laced to the knee, a felt cone cap topped with feathers.

Edgar mutters, "The Nightingale Robber."

Zeke gapes in response.

Tengu-Andrealphus moves his gaze over the crowd, but his dead eyes focus on nothing. "No choice," he says almost to himself. His image shifts back to his bird-like Trueface and he fans out his impressive tail, which displays multiple false eyes of black, green, purple and gold. He sets them to subtle vibration and sway.

Edgar blocks Fi and Zeke's view with his shield. "Do not look upon his tail," he warns, averting his eyes as well. He regards them both very seriously. "And *cover your ears.*"

For the first time today, for the first time in her life, Fi sees fear in her uncle's eyes. She does as he says and squeezes her eyes shut, then opens one and elbows Zeke to do the same.

Zeke complies, but when hers are closed again, curiosity overrides good sense and he peeks around Edgar's shield.

The herd of Buffalo Demons stand at the ready, all dead eyes on Peter. Peter glowers at The Peafowl, curious and appalled.

The wampyr and weres are enthralled by the hypnotic movement of Tengu-Andrealphus's tail. So is Cù Sìth. His jaw sags and long furry arms hang loosely at his side.

Overcome by his own inquisitiveness, Zeke looks. The eyes of the bird-man's tail kaleidoscope in his vision, and he can't look away.

Tengu-Andrealphus's expression is blank and his gaze distant. "No free will," he whispers, the words sounding to Zeke as if they're spoken right in his ear. The Peafowl puffs out his bird breast, larger than should be naturally possible, and swells his throat.

"*Stop,*" Peter roars. He raises his spear to fire off a bolt, but a mace knocks Gungnir aside and Mahishas rush Peter in a bellowing mob. He slashes and throws them off, tries to leap away, but they crush in, slapping and grabbing to keep him down.

Kabir, who has purposefully kept his eyes averted from Tengu-Andrealphus, repeats Edgar's warning to Zeke. "You heard the man, cover your ears!"

The harsh earnestness of his voice jolts Zeke from his spellbound haze in time to see Kabir bolt to the nearest Mahisha. He bounds to its back and scrambles across Buffalo Demon heads and shoulders, hunching beneath the ceiling as he goes. A mace grazes his ribs, horns gouge his shins, but he keeps on his precarious path long enough to launch himself at Tengu-Andrealphus.

The Peafowl thrusts his head forward, throws his mouth open and emits a sound beyond that produced by any creature that's ever lived or machine ever invented. Kabir goes stiff in mid-flight, stunned by the auditory shockwave, and drops.

Zeke's head snaps back as if he's been hit by a club.

Shards of glass still hanging in the windows splinter. Plaster cracks. In the foyer, the chandelier explodes.

Cù Sìth collapses to his knees, clutching his head. He throws his jaws open in a roar but no sound can be heard over the devastating vociferation of The Peafowl.

Wampyr and werewolves shove and tug at their ears, howl noiselessly, stagger and fall.

All Kabir can manage in his defense is to lock his fingers behind his head, squeeze his forearms to his ears, and curl up into a ball.

Peter, however, is completely immune to the stentorian clamor. And by some effect of being already dead, so are the Mahishas. Their lips move and maces hit the floor. They tackle Peter, bounding over each other to bury him beneath a Demon Buffalo mass, packed in from wall to wall and piled nearly to the ceiling.

As soon as Tengu-Andrealphus loosed his clamorous assault, Edgar discarded sword and shield and threw himself on Fi, wrapped his arms around her head and pressed his own ear against her shoulder. She blindly found his other ear and now holds a hand against it while hugging Mol's furry head tight to her chest.

The Peafowl's cry carries such force that it's almost no sound at all, but the crushing pressure of ocean depths. Zeke's skull and teeth buzz. The skin of his face feels as if in danger of being peeled off by a thousand forces of gravity. His bones hum. Sickening waves of nausea wrack his body. He's certain he's about to be squashed to nothingness, or explode.

Then the sound suddenly alters – the *whine*, *whir* and *squeak* of frequency modulation, like the changing of an old fashioned radio dial.

* * *

"You've been bad again, Zeke." Sour beer breath and garlic sweat. "And you know what that means." A fleshy *smack*. Sudden searing pain on his bare behind. Zeke gasps his eyes open.

Naked, face down on a coffee table. The woman's hard hands holding his wrists over his head. He knows better than to struggle, but can't help squirming. Her mouth close to his ear, cigarette breath through tobacco stained teeth. "*Bad Zeke.*"

The man spanks him again. The *clink* of a belt unbuckled and *slip* of leather on cloth. The sting and burn of a whipping belt. A gut-wrenching rush of fear and pain. The total helplessness of a child.

Zeke remembers these people. He *knows* them. Their names, faces, where they live, what they eat. And how they abuse the children. Foster parents in a *very* bad home. Zeke's aware of it all, but he's of two minds. One is present with the child, in the moment, seeing through the boy's eyes, feeling with his skin, sucking breath through his teeth, thinking every terrified thought. But he is *Zeke*, too, completely aware of himself as an observer, mute, bound and helpless.

Z-z-zip. Zeke knows what comes next. "*Bad Zeke, bad,*" the women croons, her calm voice and twisted grin more frightening than rage could ever be. "Punish him, baby."

"Yeah..." the man grunts.

"Give it to bad, bad Zeke." And she laughs.

Heartbreaking torment, pitiful, tragic anguish of a child plainly and literally tortured.

"Bad Zeke! Bad Zeke! Bad Zeke! *Bad!*"

He squeezes his eyes shut, spilling hot tears and terror. "Please," his little voice cries. "I'll be good. I promise!"

It has nothing to do with being good or bad, Zeke is well aware, just young and helpless in the hands of sadistic psychopaths, the sickest strain of sexual predators humankind has to offer.

Zeke remembers it all, every agonizing detail – *but it never happened.* Not to *him.*

Whine, whir and *squeak...*

* * *

The pressure claps back like air rushing in to fill a vacuum after an explosion. Hands still clamped to his ears, Zeke fears if he opens his eyes they might pop out of his skull, but he forces them anyway. The nightmare of childhood trauma has come and gone in a split second. Fresh and raw as it is, the horror of what he has returned to is little better. In fact, this time he's sure it will be his end.

Everything's fuzzy, like the whole room is an oscillating vortex mixer in some ungodly laboratory, but he makes out Edgar, Fi and Mol still knotted together. Edgar gritting his teeth, and though he can't hear them, Mol howling and Fi screaming. Zeke can't scream. He can't even breathe. He's drowning *and* boiling from the inside out. His mind swims. Blood gushes from the ears and nose of a nearby wampyr. The blurry form of a werewolf staggers by, vomiting its guts out.

A Mahisha kicks through the heap of dead wamps and weres and looms over him. Its spittle-spewing roar makes no dent in the Peafowl's clamant wail. Zeke's conscious-ness fades. With his last smidgeon of awareness he throws his arms around Fi, as well as Edgar and Mol by default. The Buffalo Demon winds up to crush them all. Zeke finds the breath to cry out and cringes back.

The jagged spearhead of Gungnir pierces through the Mahisha's chest from behind before it can deliver the deathblow. Its mace dematerializes and the beast tossed aside to fester and burn – but when Peter looks to where Edgar, Fi, Mol and Zeke had been, there's no one there.

27

FLOWERS & FIGS 13

The horrendous ringing in Fi's ears subsides gradually as she floats to consciousness. Sweet, blessed silence. Just the whispering calm of a warm breeze. The dreadful bellow of Tengu-Andrealphus is gone.

She peels Edgar's arms away. He groans, opens his eyes. Mol levers up and shakes vigorously while they survey their surroundings.

It's the same house, but much of it has crumbled away long ago. The entire structure is canted, rocked back, the windowed wall and part of the ceiling and upper floors toppled out to spread in ruin on the slope behind the house. Moonlight sparkles with dust motes, illuminating the rubble. No furniture, guitars, or books on the shelves.

"Are you all right, Fiona?" Edgar asks.

"Yeah, I think," she replies. "What happened?"

He rises stiffly and his eyes fall on Zeke, who is leaned back on what's left of the empty bookshelves with his arm draped behind Fi. "Zeke..."

Fi slides over to peer at him. His head lolls from her shoulder. Blood trickles from his left ear. "Zeke!" She takes his face in her hands, pats his cheek. "Zeke!" But there's no response. "Edgar!" Her uncle crouches to help, but Mol crowds past him and licks Zeke lavishly.

"Zeke," Fi pleads. "Wake up!"

Mol barks forcefully, right in his face.

Zeke jumps and his eyes pop open. "What? Shit! Fuck!" He breathes in arduous gulps as if he's been held too long underwater.

"Oh God." Fi takes him by the shoulders. "What happened?"

In his stuporous trance, he recoils at the sudden slap of a belt, the sharp burning sting on his skin. *Bad Zeke! Bad!*

"Please don't!" he pleads, cringing. "I promise. Please!"

Fi exchanges a quick look of worry with Edgar, then shakes Zeke again. "Zeke! It's me. It's Fi."

His eyes focus in recognition. "Fi..." Mol laps at him happily. He sputters. "Aww. Yuck!" Mol backs off, wags his tail and barks.

"Looks like you've made a friend," Edgar says with approval, scratching Mol between the ears. "Not easily done, but none could ask for better."

Zeke eyes Mol dubiously, then sees where they are. The memory of Tengu-Andrealphus and the Mahishas hits him like a bucket of ice water. "Where are we?"

Edgar rises. "I was hoping you could tell *us* that."

"I did that, thing," Zeke realizes with trepidation. "I slipped us here."

"That is the only explanation."

"But I... I..." He looks like he's going to pass out again.

"Hey, calm down," Fi reassures him. "It's okay. We're okay."

"For now," Edgar adds.

Fi frowns at Edgar, turns back to Zeke. "You saved us."

"I don't know... I just..." He winces and reaches for his ear.

Fi stops him. "Don't, you should leave it alone. It was bleeding a little, but it's stopped. Does it hurt?"

There's a dull ache and the hearing is muffled, but it's nothing he can't endure. "No, not really." He tries to sit up, but can't.

Fi scoots out of the way. Zeke tugs at his arm, the one that was behind Fi, which disappears above the elbow through a hole in the wall between broken bookshelves.

"It's stuck," he groans, pulling harder. His fingers tingle and sting, like circulation prickling after the cold.

Fi takes his other arm to help him pull.

"Wait," Edgar warns.

"What?" Fi asks.

"It isn't stuck." Edgar's gaze moves along the shelves.

Fi sees what Edgar is talking about. "Oh my God. Zeke... your *arm*."

* * *

Peering through the goggles, the wampyr policeman reports that the three from the corner are gone, and the hound.

Kleron takes the goggles and looks. "Where did they go?"

"I don't know. They were there, then they weren't."

Kleron sees Peter spin from where he stood near the corner and return to the fray. "And The Pater?"

"They were gone when he came near."

"Slipping, Master?" Max posits.

"Hmm..." Kleron ponders. "Fascinating, and unexpected. But which one?"

"What do we do?" Luc asks.

Kleron contemplates. "We wait."

* * *

Zeke's heart pounds as he follows Edgar and Fi's line of sight. His arm isn't stuck in the wall, it's part of it – and the wall is part of him.

Grossly misshapen, oversized and far too long, it bulges like a serpent frozen in ice. Patches of the wall and shelves are the color and texture of his blue oxford shirt, while enormous raised veins throb in the cracked and moldy plaster in time with his hammering pulse. Sticking out of the upper corner are the tips of enormous fingers of gypsum and rotted wood.

Zeke swallows hard, concentrates on moving his hand. The monstrous fingers wiggle. A piteous moan escapes his lips. Blood roars in his ears. He pulls frantically, but his arm won't budge. And it *hurts*, as if all the nerves are stripped raw and exposed. *The whole wall hurts.*

"Stop it lad!" Edgar cautions. "You'll injure yourself."

"Your sword," Zeke implores. "Cut it out!"

"Zeke," Fi shouts. "Calm down."

"Just cut it off, I don't care!" Then Edgar and Fi's hands are on him, beseeching him to stop. He slowly returns to his senses. "*Oh God...*"

Edgar holds Zeke's chin with a steady hand, and his words are the very voice of reason. "Do not despair, lad. Listen to me."

Zeke looks into his eyes, deep, clear and wise.

"Do you hear me?"

Zeke takes a shaky breath and nods. "Yes. I'm sorry."

"Nothing to be sorry about. Just try to stay calm."

"Okay... Okay." He swallows, concentrates on his breathing. "Be calm... Be calm."

"Very good."

While her uncle's attention is on Zeke, Fi gnaws at the nails of one hand, clutching the fur on Mol's back with the other. "What do we do?" she asks Edgar.

"First, we must *all* settle down. Understood?"

She yanks her fingers from her mouth, forces herself to breathe deeply, and releases the dog from her fretful clutch. Mol groans with relief.

"Peter warned me," Zeke pants. "He made me swear, never do it again, *never*, not until we talked about it."

"At length" Fi adds.

"Yeah, that too."

"For good reason, lad," says Edgar. "From what I understand, slipping between worlds can be very dangerous. That you can do it at all is nothing short of miraculous, I must say."

Zeke eyes the results in the wall-arm, licks his lips. "Doesn't seem very miraculous to me."

"It could have been much worse."

Zeke gulps, trying not to let his imagination run with that thought. "What do I do?"

"I could not use my sword, even if it were here. Not unless you no longer desire the use of your arm." Zeke gulps again. "You're going to have to slip it out."

"What?"

"Your arm. I believe it may be trapped somewhere *between*. You need to bring it here, to you."

"Will that work?" Fi asks.

"To be honest, I don't know. I understand very little of the phenomenon, but if I recall correctly, it has been done."

"Okay," Fi says, trying to sound positive. "That's good. There's some hope, then." Zeke blanches. "I mean, it's *going* to work. If you can slip, you can do this, right?"

Zeke exhales, gathering his courage.

"Remember what Peter said," she urges. "Feel out for it, focus on that empty part of your mind."

Zeke takes a deep breath and tries – but there's nothing to feel out *to*, and no empty part of his mind, either. It's jam-packed and wriggling like too many eels stuffed in a Ziploc bag – all the attacks and violence and blood and Andrealphus's terrible scream and that horrible memory of childhood abuse and *my arm is stuck in a fucking wall*. He pulls. It won't budge. "It isn't working," he sobs. "I can't do it. I just can't!"

"Zeke, you have to relax, lad."

His heart races and he's hyperventilating. "My head... I..."

Fi tries to help. "Zeke—"

"I brought us here," he rants, "who knows where, and now I'm fucked. *We're* fucked!"

"What can I do to help?" Edgar offers.

"I don't know!"

Edgar scowls as he considers the options. He needs to get Zeke's mind off his arm. A thought registers. "I suppose, just a bit couldn't hurt. Not now."

Zeke's eyes dart to him. "What?"

Edgar sits, folding his legs. Fi crouches next to him. A conflicted expression crosses his face, but a decision is made. "Mahisha."

Now he has Zeke's full attention. "Yeah?"

"You know of Mahisha from the ancient Hindu Puranic texts, yes?" Zeke nods. "This is what I have been told," Edgar proceeds. "It's not as if I was actually there. It is absolutely true, however, I have no doubt." Zeke watches him anxiously. Fi bites her lip. "Mahisha's is a tragic story, but he brought his demise upon himself. The mace he carries was made and given to him by his benefactor to police the others of his kind when he was a trusted servant. With it he can multiply himself, as you have seen. He alone has the natural ability, which his benefactor recognized in him, and the mace focuses it."

"Magic," Zeke breathes.

Edgar's forehead knits. "The ancient magic, *real* magic, is simply science, a comprehension and manipulation of matter and energy like any other, only far more advanced."

Thoughts percolate in Fi's mind, of how Edgar's shield caught the wampyrs and werewolves on fire, and how he could possibly know these things. But now is not the time to press the issue. For Zeke's sake, she suppresses her curiosity and growing resentment over the secrets her uncle has kept from her all these years. For now.

"But Mahisha was corrupted," Edgar continues, "and he became known as Mahishasura, The Buffalo Demon."

Zeke tries to process what he's hearing. He tugs at his arm in exasperation. It doesn't move and hurts more than ever.

Edgar sees his pain, and all he can think of to do is keep talking. "Tengu-Andrealphus is quite another story. He was never good."

"*Tengu-Andrealphus*," says Zeke. "Even the name doesn't make sense."

"You expect anything to make sense now?" Fi can't help it, it just comes out. She glares at Edgar. "I get the feeling nothing's ever going to make sense again."

"Fiona, you're not helping," Edgar reprimands evenly.

"All right!" She calms herself. "Okay. Sorry."

Zeke says, "Tengu is a magical bird demon from Japanese fables."

"Yes," Edgar responds. "Not to be confused with 'Taingou,' the dog-like demon of the Chinese."

"And Andrealphus is..." Zeke's voice trails off as he tries to recall the details from his reading.

"According to the European *Goetia* and *Pseudomarchia Daemonum* grimoires, Andrealphus was a Grand Marquis of Hell. From what I've been told, he took that title himself, it was never bestowed upon him. His Truename is Tengu-Andrealphus, but he was known as just Tengu or Andrealphus in different places and times." Edgar pauses, then adds, "I hear he was also quite proficient in mathematics."

"Yeah... But you called him something else, too. The Nightingale Robber." Zeke squeezes his eyes shut, calling up his studies. "It's from a Russian folktale about a high-wayman in the forests of Bryansk." His eyes open in revelation. "And he could yell really loud."

"You *have* done some reading," says Edgar appreciatively.

Zeke's cheeks redden. "It's kind of what I do."

"An obsession, really," adds Fi. She's seen the piles of books in his tiny apartment, the one time she was there.

"The Russian stories name him Solovei-Razboinik," Edgar elaborates. "He's no nightingale, however, but a kind of peafowl. If you've ever heard a peacock's call, you know how voluminous and unpleasant it can be. Multiply that by decibels untold, and that's what we heard today."

"There's a poem that goes with the story," Zeke interjects. He wracks his brain to recall it.

"My translation may not be the most accurate," says Edgar, "but I'll give it a go." He recites the verse:

"He screams, the robber, like a wild animal.
From the whistle of the nightingale,
From the scream of the wild beast,
All the grasses and meadows are entangled,
All the blue flowers lose their petals,
All the dark woods bend down to the earth,
And all the people there lie dead."

Zeke slumps in cold apprehension. "It's real... it's *all real*..."

"Not all, lad." Edgar cautions. "Don't believe everything you read, though there are seeds of truth in most of the fables and folktales of old. As there are in the great mythologies of the world."

Zeke stares at him blankly.

Fi crosses her arms. *This is supposed to help Zeke relax, how?*

"Mahishasura and Tengu-Andrealphus were killed in the stories," Zeke says weakly.

"That's not true? Peter seemed pretty surprised to see them, and from what I can tell he knows all about this stuff."

"He does. More than anyone." Edgar pauses as if considering what to say next, what he *can* say, then shakes his head minutely and continues. "The Buffalo Demon was a prodigious enemy, as you can imagine, but in a momentous battle at the end of a great and terrible war, his benefactor took to the field and slaughtered a hundred thousand Mahishas in a day, down to the very last one."

"I've studied the Hindu Puranas some," Zeke says. "They say he was killed by Durga, maybe the most powerful of all the Hindu goddesses."

"No 'maybe' about it, lad. The ancient peoples of the Indus Valley who wrote the original Puranas, and the Vedas that preceded them, also knew her as Maha Nigurna Shakti and Chandika, and later, Kali. Her Truename was *Prathamaja Nandana.*" He pronounces the name with reverence.

It means nothing to Zeke, but sounds awe inspiring anyway.

"The story of The Nightingale Robber contains the true account of Tengu-Andrealphus's death."

"Ilya Muromets chopped off his head."

Edgar nods.

Zeke's insides are cold and empty. Ilya Muromets is a Russian folk hero who supposedly had the strength of ten men. *And he's real too.*

"I feel ridiculous even saying this," Fi pipes in, "considering those things shouldn't exist at all, but if they're dead, how are they here?"

A pall of gloom descends upon Edgar's brow and his voice is tenuous. "Blasphemous, unthinkable."

"What?" Fi urges.

"They've been brought back."

"From the dead?"

"Necromancy..." Zeke shudders.

Edgar winces at the word. "Eldritch science of the most dreadful variety, abhorred and strictly forbidden."

Fi observes Zeke's pallid complexion and shallow respiration. "I don't think this is helping."

Zeke tugs half-heartedly at his arm. "Me neither," he rasps.

"Try, Zeke, *really* try."

"I can't."

"Use your mind, not your body."

"I can't do it, I said!" He yanks at his arm as if defying it to come loose. With each pull it feels like his fingers are being smacked with a hammer. "Godammit. I can't."

"*Zeke.*" She shouts with such force and determination that his breath catches in his throat.

He sobs, wipes his nose on his sleeve. "Just go without me."

"Yeah, right." She nudges Edgar out of the way and kneels in front of Zeke. "Hush. That's enough. We're here, and we're alive, okay? Right now, we're *okay.*"

His eyes plead as he sputters, "That's, not really—"

"No, listen to me. I want to ask you something."

"Okay," he gasps, trying to get his himself under control. "I'm listening."

"Are you hungry?"

"What?"

"I am. We didn't eat much at that restaurant."

"No, we didn't."

"When we get out of here, when this is all over and *we get home*, we'll have a big fat Greek dinner. I'm buying."

Zeke chokes out a laugh in spite of himself. Despairing, perhaps, but a laugh.

"And we'll have a stupid-huge death-by-chocolate dessert, one for each of us, and Turkish coffee."

Edgar gazes at Fi with admiration.

"And we're going to do whatever we can to get you to your conference."

Zeke snorts. "I haven't thought about that since we talked this morning. Doesn't seem very important now. Was that really just this morning?"

"I know, right? Seems like weeks ago."

"A lifetime." His face becomes thoughtful.

Fi can tell he's thinking about their "breakup." "Sorry about that little tirade of mine. I *am* a train wreck, you know."

"No, you're—"

"Yeah, I am. Just ask my uncle." Caught up in Fi's tactic to help Zeke, Edgar bobs his head in agreement, but when she gives him a sidelong glance he shakes his head adamantly. "And it looks like you don't have a choice, mister," she continues. "You're stuck with me, at least for awhile, whether you like it or not. No 'break' for you."

Zeke smiles wanly.

"You know I've never asked. What's your favorite classical music?"

"Oh... I don't know. I don't have a favorite, I guess."

"While you think about it, I'll tell you mine. Bach's 'Jesu, Joy of Man's Desiring.'"

"Yeah? I like that too."

"My mom used to play it on her flute to warm up for rehearsal. I'd just sit and listen and imagine I was bouncing along on fluffy clouds." Fi feels the familiar constricting sense of loss at the memory of her mom, but swallows it down. *No time for that.*

She whistles the short bright notes of the song in perfect tone, then nudges Zeke, bobbing her eyebrows in encouragement.

He joins in, "da-da-da"ing along – and can picture what Fi described in the frolicking tune. The notes seem to chase each other up an Escher-esque staircase of clouds in a bright blue sky. He trampolines with them from step to step, and Fi's face is the sun.

Edgar blinks, his eyes moist. In his odd long life he's known the most exuberant joy and profound sorrow, the most extreme yins and yangs of human experience. Right now he feels them both in equal measure. His heart swells to bursting. *This* is magic.

Fi slows the tempo, leans close with those lovely lips of hers, and Zeke becomes lost in her beautiful green eyes. All the pain, shame and desperation of only moments ago drain away, driven by the warm glow of her face, like rays of a new dawn banishing the darkness and chill of night.

Fi gestures surreptitiously to her uncle. He gets the hint and averts his eyes, even covers Mol's, who doesn't like it much. But as she leans closer to Zeke, Edgar can't help but look, and Mol peeks between his fingers.

Fi shuts her eyes, prompting Zeke to close his. She inches closer. He feels the heat of the sun between them. She slides her hands to his face, stops whistling, and as their lips are about to meet, poised at the infinite crux of longing, bliss, and destiny, he embraces her – with both arms.

Fi's eyes fly open at his touch, accompanied by a sharp intake of breath. "You did it!"

Zeke flushes, confused. "What?" Fi's song and proximity still resonate through him and it takes a moment for reality to seep back. "Oh..." He sees, and feels, that his arm is free of the wall. "Oh. Holy fuck. How'd you do that?"

Fi gives him a peck on the lips, hops to her feet and offers a hand. He takes it and stands, gawking at his arm like he's never seen one before. "Whatever you did, it worked!"

Fi smiles and shrugs, then turns away and puffs out her cheeks at Edgar, an expression that betrays she had no idea it would.

Men are easily distracted, and she had to do something to stave off Zeke's panic. They couldn't leave him like that, and without him they were all 'fucked,' just like Zeke said. She pats Mol on the head and steps further into the room, Mol at her heels. Still, it was a cheap trick, using her feminine wiles, and she can't help feeling a little guilty. She still doesn't know how she feels about him (*who's had time to consider feelings?*), and she'd hate to have him think she was leading him on. But none of that's important right now, so she kicks the thought down the stairs of her emotional root cellar and trips the door.

"How'd she do that?," Zeke asks Edgar, baffled.

"First lesson, lad, don't slip near solid objects until you've had extensive practice and instruction. And second," Edgar pats him on the shoulder, "never underestimate the power of a woman."

Zeke blushes in understanding.

"Well, what now?" Fi asks, fixing her ponytail and grimacing at the blood and grime on her scrubs.

"My better judgment says we do no more of that dreadful *slipping*," Edgar replies, "but we must return to Peter. I'd recommend we remove ourselves to a safe distance on the grounds, then slip back and assess the situation from there. Agreed?"

"Do you think you can find it?" she asks Zeke. "And not get us stuck in another wall, or a tree, or something?"

Zeke runs his hand through his hair, then wipes it on his pants in disgust, then realizes his pants aren't any better. He resigns himself to being filthy. "Yeah, I think so."

"You think so, or you *know* so?"

He thinks about it.

"I mean," she adds, "what would I have to do to distract you *next* time?"

Edgar clears his throat.

Zeke blushes again. He concentrates, and responds with more confidence. "I know so."

"All right then," says Edgar. "Off we go." He heads for the nearest egress, the fallen window wall.

Fi follows, allowing herself some small satisfaction at making her stoic uncle uncomfortable. *Serves him right, the secretive old bastard. Just wait 'til we get out of this. He's going to have some serious explaining to do. And so is Peter!*

The four of them pick their way through the fallen remains of the back wall and upper floors laid out on the ground behind what's left of the house.

The sky is as clear as can be and the moon starkly bright. Its blue-green light illuminates the landscape like a sunlit seabed under shallow Caribbean waves. The twinkling river below is smaller than on their world and follows a more winding path.

It's uncomfortably warm. The only sounds the soft scratch of branches in the wind and rustle of dry leaves. Except there is no wind. The air is still as death. No trees either, just clear rolling landscape on both sides of the river.

Mol snuffs at the air.

"Do you smell that?" Fi asks.

"Smoke." Zeke replies.

A fiery glow rims a debris strewn knoll to the north. As they approach, the odor becomes stronger and they hear the distant laconic wail of sirens, the kind intended to warn of approaching tornados or other pending disaster. They crest the knoll and halt. The entire skyline is burning, searingly bright, most intense where downtown Toledo should be.

"Dear Lord," Edgar exclaims.

Ebony columns plume over the city, rimmed in silver by the light of the moon – but something else moves in and around the smoke. A living black cloud, swarming above the city, accompanied by a barely audible hum which rises and falls in pitch as it climbs, banks and dives of its own accord.

Perspiration erupts in beads on Zeke's forehead.

Fi's scalp tightens. "What is that?" she asks.

"I don't—" Edgar begins to reply, but stops short at the sound of a tense growl forming in Mol's throat and the sight of the hair rising on his back. Mol has his forepaws up on a masonry stone, peering at the valley below. They move forward to see what's got him spooked.

The ground beyond the rubble, down the rolling hill to the river and spread wide to either side, appears to be tiled with long tapered blocks in shades of brown, green, black and gold, metallic and satin-sheened like massive alien scales. Sprouting from one end of each is a pair of short segmented stalks, and all have taller spiky sticks rising from the cracks between them.

Edgar touches Mol. "Shh..."

A set of the segmented stalks nearest them twitches and begins to wave in a circular motion. The "tile" does a pushup on four bony forelegs to gaze at them with enormous multi-lensed oval eyes.

Fi freezes. "What... is *that?*"

Edgar is at a loss.

"It looks like a grasshopper," says Zeke.

The creature jerks its antennae forward then stands fully upright on skinny but powerful spiked back legs with back-bending knees. Nearly five and a half feet tall, it appears to be part biological, part synthetic, with an exoskeletoned thorax and abdomen, four jointed arms, saw-toothed claws of shining silver, and an ingrown helmet that gleams like golden chrome.

Fi gulps. "A really big grasshopper."

"This is no natural *orthopteran*," says Edgar. "I have never heard of such a creature. Except... but no..."

"Locusts from hell," Zeke whispers.

"*What?*" Fi asks.

"Revelation. The Apocalypse." Zeke gazes at the animate cloud above the burning city. "'Out of the bottomless pit, an army of locusts will come upon the earth, and to them is given power.' Or something like that."

"Something like that," says Edgar. "But these can be no such thing."

"You sure?" Zeke asks.

It takes a moment for Edgar to answer. "Pretty sure."

The standing locust tilts its weird insectile head and inspects them coldly. Animal, machine, both or neither, there's a sinister intelligence in its eyes.

"Guys," Fi says, "it doesn't really matter, does it? Whatever it is, it doesn't look friendly."

The locust works its multiple mouth parts then spreads its serrated mandible pincers and shrieks, sending black spittle flying – the shrill chirr of a monster cricket and aching creak of claws on slate.

Mol howls. Zeke, Edgar and Fi wince at the sound.

When it finally stops, Fi huffs, "I wish things would quit screaming at us!"

The locusts to either side of the one that shrieked push themselves up on their forelegs in unison. Behind them, the rows rise, wave after wave. Then, beginning at the river, they all stand up on their back legs in an undulant forward ripple. An army snapping to attention.

"Ohhh." Zeke takes Fi and Edgar's hands. "Ready?"

The lead locust spreads a double set of veined translucent wings at its back. Its fore-wings begin to vibrate. The noise they generate is like the wail of a cicada, but much louder and far more alarming. The furthermost row of locusts near the river hops into the air and flies forward, the rest of them rolling up ranks to follow. Combined with the call of the lead locust, the chitter, click and buzz of the swarm is deafening.

Edgar grasps Mol by the scruff. "Ready, lad."

As the flying locusts get closer, those in the nearest row drop back to their forelegs, readying to spring.

"Are you?" Fi asks Zeke.

Zeke shifts a little this way, then that, squinting into nothing. "Ready as I'll ever be, I guess."

Edgar watches the swarm close in. "Zeke, my boy..."

Zeke closes his eyes and exhales slowly.

The flyers are almost to the locust front line, which screeches and launches in a unified sailing grasshopper leap.

Zeke takes a baby step back from the oncoming host. "Slip."

* * *

Zeke opens his eyes and looks around. "Uh oh."

There's no house, only a bare rocky hilltop where they stand. And the river valley is an ocean as far as the eye can see. A metropolis of crystal towers rises majestically from its surface, gleaming in the moonlight – but shattering and toppling in glittering shards to splash in the waves under the assault of a hurricane of locusts. Flying glass cars plummet and crash, sleek watercraft founder and sink.

The light of the moon flickers and they hear a clicking, clacking, clattering whine. The sky is filled with locusts. Thousands of them. Tens of thousands. The cicada wail rises. The swarm turns in on itself and dives straight for them.

Fi shouts, "Zeke!"

"Slip."

* * *

A red rock landscape and they're in the contracting eye of another locust storm. Edgar takes a gash to the arm, but keeps his grip on Zeke and Mol. No time to say *slip*, Zeke just does it.

More worlds, one after the other, all infested with locust vermin.

* * *

They trip into a muddy forest clearing, the surrounding trees the size of redwoods. Livestock pens and a coop lie in ruin. Bits of skin, fur and feathers of the animals they once contained litter the ground. A wildfire rages through the underbrush. The acrid smoke-filled air seethes with locusts. Several fight over the remains of an elk, crunching its bones and antlers like breadsticks in their mandible jaws. Others shred greenery and bark from the trees.

Out of the smoke and noise a locust barrels into Fi, Zeke and Edgar from behind, knocking them to the mud.

The creature crashes and skids, rights itself, casts about with its antennae, scratches at its hard ocular shells to clear the muck and pine needles.

Zeke swipes mud from his eyes. Fi coughs and shouts his name. He fumbles in the smoke, finds her hand and they help each other to their feet.

The locust whips around, locates them, and screeches, but it slides on the muddy slope as it tries to leap. Others have heard, however, and take up its cry.

"Inside." Edgar scrambles toward them, pointing to their backs. "Get inside!"

Fi and Zeke turn and run without question, only then seeing a log cabin right where Peter's great room would be. They shove through the broken door and by the light of an oil lamp see what's left of what could be several people, including the bloody remnants of a child's dress hanging from a gorging locust's jaws. Fi chokes back a scream.

Zeke focuses intently on the next slip – as bad as it was in Peter's home, they have to get back, and *now*. He can't afford to make any more mistakes, for all their sakes.

The swarm is at Edgar's back as his hand reaches the door jam. The locust inside drops the shredded clothing and lunges. Zeke grabs Edgar's hand, pulls hard, and the locust shoots through empty space to slam headfirst into the wall.

* * *

In the corner of the great room near the desk, Zeke and Fi stumble backward, Zeke dragging Edgar as if out of thin air.

Cù Sìth's roar, grunts of Kabir, bellowing Mahishas, the slice and sizzle of Gungnir. Piles of werewolf and wampyr bodies lie in a crimson flood, none left alive. There are more holes in the walls than when they slipped away, and a portion of the ceiling has collapsed. But they're back. There's no unbearable cry of Tengu-Andrealphus – and they see why. Peter has a hand around his throat.

The creature looks up at him with lifeless eyes and croaks in an old Slavic tongue, "Thank you."

Peter says dispassionately, "Be at peace," then drops his spear, jams his arm down The Peafowl's throat and yanks out his guts, practically turning him inside out. The body crumbles and flashes to dust in his hands.

Fi blinks at the awful sight, then glances around and grabs Zeke's arm. "Where's Mol?"

"Dear Lord." Edgar scans the room and moans, stricken with the realization, "I lost Molossus."

"We left him!" Fi sobs to Zeke.

Before his better judgment can prevail, he pulls away from her. "I'll be right back."

Edgar lunges, "No, lad," but he slips away.

"Edgar!" comes Peter's resounding voice. He storms toward them, hops to the back of a Mahisha that blocks his path. Gripping it with his knees, he takes hold of its horns and twists, breaking its neck. It falls forward, burns and wafts away, leaving Peter to land on his feet without missing a step. He holds his hand out to his side as he comes, mumbles something, and Gungnir shoots from the floor to his hand in time to dispatch another Buffalo Demon.

He kicks bodies aside and glares at Edgar. "What in the name of all that is good are you doing? Where is Zeke?"

"He's gone back for Mol!" Fi answers.

"Gone *where?*"

Edgar looks sheepish and ashamed.

"Slipping!" Peter roars.

"The worlds are swarming, milord," Edgar warns.

Peter scowls, "Swarming?"

"With locusts," Fi replies.

Peter's features twist with skepticism and confusion. Quietly but vehemently he says, "I must end Mahishasura here, before he spreads like a virus." He jabs a finger toward Edgar and Fi. "You get to the chamber, *now.*"

"Not without Zeke," Fi protests.

"Fi, do *not* defy—"

"He saved us!" she cuts him off. "I'm not leaving without him!"

Peter's eyes flare. He growls like an animal. "Zadkiel!" he summons over his shoulder, then steps menacingly toward Fi. She draws away, taken aback by his aggressive rage, but before he reaches her, he disappears.

Kabir disengages from the brawl with the Mahisha, leaving Cù Sìth to it, and makes haste to Edgar and Fi. Buffalo Demons give chase. Edgar snatches up his sword and shield, climbs a heap of bodies, hacks the mace arm off a Mahisha, then spins and removes its shaggy slobbering head.

* * *

"They're back, but without the hound," the wampyr policeman reports, observing the great room through the goggles. "But the boy disappeared again, then the guy with the spear. Maybe to go after him. He didn't look happy about it."

"The *boy?*" Kleron snatches the goggles and looks.

"How can that be?" Max chuckles. "Hee hee!"

"I suddenly find myself intrigued by this parvulus man-child. He may not be as irrelevant as I presumed."

Max holds out a grotesque tri-fingered hand. "Master, may I?"

Kleron hands him the goggles. Max fumbles with them to find the best position over his multiple pairs of sunglasses. He finally gets them situated, holds still while he observes the pandemonium in the house, and giggles.

* * *

Coughing and waving his arms, Zeke emerges from the log cabin, which is now on fire. Locusts whiz through the smoke overhead, but the majority of the horde appears to have gone elsewhere.

He shouts, "Mol!" The crackle of brush fire and buzz of locusts are the only reply. He stumbles further into the clearing. *"Molossus!"*

He can't tell from what direction or distance it comes, but there is a frantic bark, followed by a heartrending yelp.

* * *

"Zeke," Peter cries, hacking at attacking locusts. He trudges from world to world, slip after slip, calling out for Zeke, leaving infernal insects cut to pieces in his wake.

"Dammit. Zeke!" Then he pauses at the sight of the crystal city crashing into the sea under a barrage of locusts.

Kleron's words hiss in his ears, *The worlds of promise have fallen.*

A stumbling slip and he sees a city burning in the distance, the smoke above it teeming with the aberrant creatures. An inverted cone of light flashes into existence on the horizon, from the ground to the highest reaches of the sky. It flickers and disappears, leaving behind another abominable swarm.

You will see with your own eyes, and despair.

Peter swears in disbelief. *"Great Élan..."*

* * *

Zeke dodges a zipping locust. "Mol!" Another bark and he glimpses the dog, beyond the clearing, running for his life in the smoke, crashing through burning brush, beneath low branches, winding around trees, barely evading the locusts in hot pursuit.

"Come on Mol. I'm here!" Zeke cries, then charges toward him. Mol breaks through to the clearing, bearing fresh wounds, his fur singed and smoking, bandages lost in the undergrowth – and a cloud of locusts swoops in between them, cutting them off entirely.

Peter hurdles roaring over Zeke's head, body and spear crackling with electricity. He whirls – locusts dice and sizzle, flaming wing-parts flutter – then vaults over Mol, flipping and spinning to clear the pursuing horde. As soon as his feet hit the ground he thrusts a hand toward Zeke. "Go!"

The swarm rises and hovers, momentarily baffled by Peter's arrival. Then the pitch of the hive whine rises and they attack Peter with greater fury than Zeke has yet seen, he and Mol apparently forgotten. Peter fights them off with fist and spear, but they continue to pour out of the sky like a diabolical waterfall.

Zeke calls to Mol but the dog remains where he is, barking desperately at Peter. Zeke steps toward him but is struck still by the sight of Peter, barely visible through the swarm. He's trying to make his way to Mol and Zeke, but the insectile horde is too thick. They pull him into the air. He frees himself and drops a short distance, but more swarm in and carry him higher.

Then he ceases to struggle against them. His gleaming red eyes find Zeke through the cyclonic horde, and over the deafening racket, his voice comes like thunder.

"GO!"

But Zeke only gapes as Peter is swept swiftly upward, far above the smoking tree-tops into the night sky. The dark mass grows larger and darker as more locusts gather around him, having abandoned all other pursuits. Mol barks wildly.

A great searing blast rips the swarm asunder. Zeke covers his eyes at the flash. When he looks again, a vivid coruscation of falling stars fills the sky, flaming locusts in a bright willow brocade, winking out as they fall. From the center a dark speck plummets – holding a blue rippling spear.

The ground shakes as Peter hits with both feet at the far edge of the clearing, his legs driving into the dirt to his knees. He wades out of it like it's water – and he doesn't look happy.

"You two still here? What did I say?"

Mol barks, takes a few steps toward him.

Up above, the surviving locusts have regrouped, more have arrived, and they're diving like a hive of angry hornets, faster than terminal velocity should allow.

Zeke points. "Peter—"

"I said *leave!*"

The locusts hit like a pile-driving column of black water, obliterating Peter from sight. They wash over the ground on impact, threatening to engulf the entire clearing.

Zeke shouts to Mol, who whirls and races toward him, just ahead of the oncoming flood wave of locusts. Zeke sprints to the flaming cabin. He reaches the door and spins as Mol jumps.

* * *

Fi cries out in surprise as Zeke comes flying backward into the room. He goes down like a sack of bricks under Mol's furry bulk.

The air rushes out of Zeke's lungs. "*Oooof.*" Mol slathers him with drool, which doesn't help him catch his breath.

Fi grabs the dog in a hug. "Mol, you made it!" She pulls him off Zeke. "Zeke, you did it!"

A wheezing moan is all he can manage in reply.

Edgar stands over them, shaking his head in gratitude and relief. "Thank the Lord," he mutters, then says, "Get him up, Fiona. We must away."

Fi steadies Zeke on his feet. "That was incredibly brave. And stupid."

Zeke tests his tender ribs with his fingers. "I'm going with 'stupid.'" Mol barks as if he agrees.

"Where's Peter?" Fi asks.

"Fighting locusts," Zeke replies.

Edgar hands Fi her blood-stained pink backpack. "He'll be along, don't you worry."

Zeke sees Kabir keeping the Mahishas at bay nearby, and Cù Sìth battling them in the center of the room. "They're still fighting?"

Edgar helps him slide his arms through the straps of the blue pack. "Their kind do not soon grow weary. This could go on for days."

While Edgar stows his shield in its case, Fi and Zeke watch Cù Sìth ravage the Buffalo Demons. The wounds he received from his brother Cerberi are already healing pink scars and he appears to have sustained no further injury. Kabir has taken more superficial wounds, but his zeal hasn't diminished in the slightest.

Edgar retrieves a sword belt from the shield case and straps it to his waist, then dons the case like a rucksack. "Hurry, now."

"Wait..." Zeke rolls a wampyr body out of the corner by the desk and retrieves the guitar case.

"Really?" Fi asks.

"Peter gave it to me," Zeke replies. "I can't just leave it."

Kabir meets them as Edgar slings on his long bag at the hall to the kitchen. He places a hand on Edgar's shoulder. "Fair thee well, good sir."

Edgar returns the gesture and replies, "Until the chance of our next meeting."

Kabir nods and readies to cover their retreat – just in time, because a Buffalo Demon is charging straight for them.

* * *

Edgar leads the way through the kitchen. A Mahisha's head crashes through the wall, smashing cupboards to splinters. It spies them and bellows its rage, then disintegrates and bursts into flame, the result of a deathblow from the other side of the wall.

Through a small door hidden behind a refrigerator at the far end of the kitchen and down curving steps to a cellar of mortared stone. Fully stocked wine racks cover all four walls, floor to low ceiling.

In spite of what he's been through, Zeke is oddly elated by their escape. "That's a lot of wine," he observes.

"Take some, if you like," says Edgar, moving to the far corner and pulling a bottle from the rack. He tosses it to Zeke, who catches it and inspects the label. Fi reads it as well. *Dom. Romane Conti, 1997.* The name means nothing to either of them.

"Not bad, but hardly worth the price, if you ask me," Edgar adds, reaching through the space where the bottle had been. He presses a stone, which recedes at his touch. There's a clunking sound and a segment of the wall, rack attached, separates from the rest. Edgar ushers Fi and Zeke through. "Après vous."

They find themselves in a tubular tunnel made of brick, angling downward. Dim electric lights strung from wires along the ceiling recede into the distance. Zeke unzips Fi's pack.

"Hey," she objects, her voice echoing.

"I can't reach mine," says Zeke, shoving the bottle in.

Edgar leads them deeper into the earth, Mol a few steps ahead of him. "These tunnels once went on for many miles, up and down the river," he explains as they walk. "Some went beneath it as well, all the way to the heart of the city. The oldest were part of a natural cave system used by primitive humans for tens of thousands of years. Later peoples dug more. The Native Americans used them for travel, trade, shelter and war. During Prohibition they were a smuggler's route."

They pass entrances to other tunnels on either side. There are also ladders leading up into shafts in the ceiling and down through the floor. Some are made of wood, others rusty metal, while still more are grooved into the bedrock.

"I've never heard of any of this," says Zeke.

"The few existing records report that they were all destroyed or caved in of their own accord before World War II."

"Cool," Zeke declares.

"You think so? It feels warmer to me..." He sees Fi and Zeke exchange glances. "Ah, I see. You mean 'cool' as in 'nifty,' 'neato,' perhaps 'rad,' 'badass,' 'phat,' or 'sweet?' In England we might say 'ace,' 'brill' or 'smashing.'"

Zeke grins. "Something like that."

"Whatever you do, do not attempt to slip from here. Understood?"

"No problem. I don't plan on doing that ever again if I don't have to."

"Well, just don't, even if you think you must, unless you relish an instant demise buried in stone. The tunnels are collapsed on all other worlds, or don't exist."

Zeke glances at Fi. "Okay, good to know."

* * *

A Mahisha hauls off to hit Kabir with its mace. In mid backswing it bursts like a water balloon. The mace flies free, knocking another Mahisha off its feet before it dissolves into the aether.

Having slipped right into the heart of the beast, Peter stands where the splattered Buffalo Demon had been, his tattered clothes covered in gore. Kabir spits Buffalo goo and tries to wipe it from his eyes, but it suddenly blazes green. He smacks out the flames while Peter lets the flash fire that covers his own body pass. More Mahishas close in. They turn back-to-back to defend against them.

Peter shouts over his shoulder. "Did the boy and Molossus return?"

"Yes, Pater. They've all escaped, as you wished."

Peter is relieved. "I must follow, but first we need to finish this. Keep close." He cuts down several Mahishas. "Cù Sìth, to me!"

Peter slashes through Buffalo Demons as he makes his way to the fireplace hearth, Kabir at his back. Cù Sìth leaps from the path of two charging Mahishas, leaving them to knock heads and lock horns. He catches hold of the broken balcony, swings clear of swiping maces and grasping hands and runs in a crouch. Peter kicks a charging Mahisha, sending it crashing back against the others, and scythes a clearing near the hearth with his spear. Cù Sìth jumps down next to him.

Electricity is already arcing along Peter's arm when he commands, "Get back. And get down."

The lights in the ceiling burst in showers of sparks. The nearest Buffalo Demons realize what's coming and frantically push back against their clambering fellows.

Multiple firebolts erupt from Gungnir and fork through the throng, followed by a flash of atomic proportions.

* * *

A supernova of blue light blazes from inside the house, setting it ashudder. Glass from the remaining windows is blown out. It tinkles, glittering on the grounds.

Luc exclaims, *"Putain!"* as he and the wampyr policeman shield their eyes. Kleron remains passive, unaffected by the blinding brilliance.

"Ohhhh," Max cheers, thrilled by the goggle flare that would blind a human being and seriously impair the vision of a younger Firstborn. "Pretty!"

* * *

The great room is dark except for the electric glow of Gungnir, the atmosphere as thick as dockside fog at midnight. A backup generator kicks in. Emergency lights blink to life at the exits and in all four corners of the room.

Peter glances over his shoulder at Kabir and Cù Sìth, who both had the good sense to cover their eyes as they crouched. They lower their hands and peer up at him. He raises an eyebrow and the corner of his mouth crooks up. They exchange glances and see what Peter is smirking about.

Even behind the blast, the power of Peter's spear would have killed any human. As it is, their fur stands on end, fluffy and steaming. They look like big scary teddy bears.

They clear their throats and smooth down their fur as they stand to assess the effect of Gungnir's fury. The greasy air is clearing through the broken windows. Charred streaks score ceiling, walls and floor. Bodies of dead wampyr and werewolves lie cooked, burst and fuming. Nothing remains of the Buffalo Demons but lingering wisps of their demise – except for two who lie moaning in the far corners.

Peter grunts in dissatisfaction. Kabir catches his arm. "Go to the others, Pater. We'll take care of this."

Peter's features harden, questioning.

Cù Sìth nods. "Go."

Peter studies him. "Are you truly with us, Moddey Dhoo?"

Cù places a hand on his heart and bows his head. "You have my allegiance, Pater, forevermore."

Kabir doesn't look convinced.

Peter deliberates, then gestures toward the broken windows. "There is an islet in the river below, meet us there, but do not delay."

"Yes, Pater," Kabir replies.

Peter spots his haversack in the debris. He shoulders it, saying, "Be nice, you two. I'll need you both before this is over." They eye each other warily. "I mean it," he adds, and runs out of the room.

* * *

"The person of interest has followed the others," reports the wampyr policeman, having retrieved the goggles from Max.

"Person of interest?" Kleron queries.

Luc explains, "Zat eez cop talk."

"I see," Kleron responds. "So, what are we waiting for?"

Luc is confused. "For your order, Master."

"Well, you have it." He and Max turn to watch the house through the trees. The wampyr moves closer for a better view.

* * *

A wounded Mahisha rises groggily. Cù Sìth swipes out its throat with his claws. It gurgles and dissipates in flame. Kabir snatches a mace from the reaching hand of the other. The haft is big in his hands and longer than he is tall, but he swings it with proficiency. Both mace and Buffalo Demon disappear as the flanges split its thick skull.

Kabir peers through wafting dust. Cù Sìth is nowhere to be seen. He growls at the assumed betrayal, then hears a mighty *crash* and *roar*.

Yet another Buffalo Demon, apparently the last, clomps through the gaping hole in the wall where he had remained hidden. He tears Cù Sìth from his back and flings him away.

The Mahisha regains his footing, grips the haft of his mace in both hands and raises it vertically before him. "*Samavari Maya!*"

Kabir throws himself into a feet-first base slide and catches the descending toe of the shaft on his shin instead of letting it hit the floor. The Mahisha roars in frustration and shifts the mace to crush him. Before Mahisha can strike, Cù Sìth's jaws are clamped to the back of his neck. Kabir attempts to drag himself out of the way but The Buffalo Demon's hoof stomps his injured leg. The grappling duo fall right on top of him.

* * *

Kleron watches expectantly. Nothing happens. He looks over his shoulder to see Luc, his finger poised over the detonator, watching Kleron eagerly. "For pity's sake, Luc," he says, "push the damn button."

"Oh," exclaims Luc. "I woz not sure—"

"Luc!"

KABOOM.

Luc pushed it all right. A gigantic fireball erupts from the foundation of the house, then another, and another. Flaming hunks of stone smash into trees. Edgar's Bentley is crushed and buried. Explosion after explosion sets the ground trembling beneath their feet.

"Primitive, this human technology, but effective under the right circumstances." Kleron grips the handle of one of the kevlar cases and beckons, "Maskim Xul."

Max gazes at the explosions for a moment longer, bursts of color reflecting in his multiple pairs of sunglasses, then hops to Kleron's chest and clings there.

Kleron says, "Let's see if we've had any luck with Plan C. Or is it D, now?" then launches into the air, flapping his great bat wings.

* * *

Zeke doesn't think they've gone all that far, but they've taken more twists and turns in the tunnels than he could keep track of. If he were to lose Edgar, he's sure he'd never find his way out.

"Zeke," Fi shouts. "You all right?"

He peeks around the corner of the earthen tunnel where he is taking a much needed pee. "Be right there!" He zips up and enters the passageway where Edgar, Fi and Mol wait next to a rusty iron ladder that leads down into a shaft in the floor.

"Sorry," Zeke apologizes. "I really had to go."

"When nature calls." Edgar replies, digging inside his long bag. He pulls out two flashlights. "We'll be needing these," he says, handing one to Zeke. "You've each got one in your pack as well, but I'm afraid I stowed them toward the bottom. If it begins to dim, twist the handle back and forth." He demonstrates, a whirring noise accompanying each turn. "In daylight, you can recharge them in the sun. The casing is photoelectric." He gives the second one to Fi. She and Zeke try the twisting recharge.

"Smashing," says Zeke.

Edgar "harrumphs" and returns his attention to the long bag.

Fi wonders how Zeke can joke at a time like this. She thinks she might understand, though. She's glad to be alive, too. Maybe it's some kind of post-battle, post-war high. If so, she's not looking forward to the crash. She watches him play with the flashlight like it's a Christmas toy. After all he's been through, he still has that insatiable curiosity of his. And she can't forget, he went back for her uncle's dog. What kind of guy does that? She's beginning to think – *maybe the best kind.*

Edgar lifts an electric lantern from his bag, closes the bag with straps and ties. *That ratty old thing must have been made before zippers were even invented.* "Uncle?" Fi says delicately.

Edgar stands and shoulders the bag. The tone of her voice has caught his attention. "Yes, dear?"

"I'm sorry, but seriously, what are we doing?"

"Why, evading mortal danger."

"What about work? School?" she asks. "Zeke's supposed to be going to a conference tomorrow." She takes a step closer. "When do we get to go home?"

Edgar ponders before speaking. "I had hoped and prayed with all my heart it would never come to this for you, but now that it is upon us, I believe you'll find there are many things we consider important, crucial to our very existence even, which become meaningless when confronted with the immediate and basic necessity of staying alive."

Zeke swallows hard. The possibility of prolonged mortal danger might be something everyone considers at one point or another in their lives, but now they're living it, on this very day.

Fi puts the flashlight in her back pocket and takes Edgar's hand in both of hers. "Then help me understand, Uncle. What's this all about? What's *really* going on?"

Edgar is struck by Fi's proximity. Her tender touch. But mostly he's moved by the sudden realization of just how grown up she is. *What happened to that troublesome child with the unruly hair? Where did she go? So quickly?* "I..." He doesn't know where to begin.

Fi considers, *My uncle, lost for words.*

Suddenly the earth shakes as if a giant has stomped the ground above – the result of the first detonation at the house. Dust falls. The lights flicker and go out.

"Bloody hell." Edgar switches on his electric lamp, snatches the guitar case strap from Zeke's shoulder. "Quickly now!" Bypassing the ladder completely, he steps over the edge of the shaft and drops into the darkness below.

* * *

Peter is just entering the tunnel from the wine cellar when the first explosion hits. The ground jerks, loosing bricks from the ceiling. He runs, sliding the haversack more securely onto his back. With the second explosion the cellar door blasts apart, sending splintered shelves and shattered bottles spraying into the tunnel behind him. The concussions continue. The tunnel begins to collapse.

Peter hits the ground and slides feet first to a shaft with no ladder and drops down. He lands in a passage lined with cut stone. This one is crumbling as well. He sprints, knocking falling rocks out of his way, hurdling rubble. He reaches another downward shaft and dives in head first. He hits the floor in the lower tunnel, rocks crashing around him, and bounds to yet another shaft. He stumbles over a slab and somersaults in. Fifty feet he falls, the walls collapsing around him, and splashes hard into a foot of water. And so does all the stone from above.

* * *

Edgar holds the lamp high to provide light for Fi as she climbs down the wrought iron ladder. A blast rocks the tunnel and the ladder snaps loose from the wall.

Zeke, shining his flashlight down from above, shouts, "Fi!" She screams on the backward falling ladder. The top slams into the lip of the shaft, jarring her loose from the rungs. Edgar drops the lantern and catches her in his arms.

"Hurry lad," shouts Edgar, setting Fi on her feet.

Fi pulls her flashlight from her back pocket and shines it up the shaft, calls out, "Come on, Zeke," while Edgar retrieves his lantern.

Zeke shoves the back end of his flashlight in his mouth and swings down onto the tilted ladder. Awkwardly but quickly he steps down the rungs like steep stairs and jumps the last few feet. Mol bounds down easily after him.

Another massive concussion. Edgar hands Zeke the guitar case, shoves him and Fi in the direction they need to go. "Run!"

They do, splashing through puddles, as fast as they can while burdened with their packs. A section of the tunnel caves in behind them.

"Bear right," Edgar calls out, bringing up the rear. "Go right!"

Fi and Zeke sweep their flashlights through the thick, billowing dust. Mol, now leading the way, barks up ahead. They find the tunnel and dart into it. The earth all round them rumbles and shakes.

"Now left," Edgar yells over the din. "Left!"

They dodge falling rock and almost pass a small entrance, but again Mol barks a signal.

"Fi!" Zeke grabs Fi by her pack, shoves her into the tunnel and bounds after her. He looks back to see the entire passage closing in like the throat of an enormous beast. A boulder falls right at him. He twists and it grazes his backpack, nearly knocking him to the ground. He catches up to Fi and sprints with her. "Run Fi. *Run!*"

But Fi *is* running, all the while fearing she'll trip over her own blundering feet like those stupid girls in the movies. *Don't fall,* she pleads with herself. *Please don't fall!*

Mol barks wildly, urging them on, but they can't tell from which direction in the rumbling quake and opaque dust.

Zeke pushes on blindly, his lungs burning. The muscles of his legs are on fire. They're going to give out any second now and he'll be buried alive, he just knows it.

Suddenly both of them are grabbed up by powerful arms, pulled into another tunnel and carried, feet dangling behind them, faster than they could ever run themselves. The walls fall in around them.

Then they feel fresher air on their faces and are thrown forward to tumble over and over each other, flashlights flying out of their hands as the passage behind them caves in completely, buffeting them with forced air and debris.

* * *

The quakes decrease in magnitude and finally stop. Illuminated by a flashlight lying on the floor nearby, Fi coughs and pushes Zeke off of her. He rolls to lie awkwardly on his backpack like a tipped-over turtle. He realizes he still has the guitar case gripped in one hand and gently sets it down.

Mol hovers close while Fi gets to her knees, shrugs her pack. She puts a hand on Zeke's chest. "You okay?"

He wipes the grit out of his eyes, breathing heavily. "Yeah. I think so."

The dust is receding, sucked away by a subterranean breeze. Fi picks up the flashlight, aims it at the clogged tunnel entrance – and is confronted by an extremely familiar but entirely unexpected sight.

"Mrs. Mirskaya?"

Vest, blouse and long skirt soaking wet and covered in dirt, the stocky Russian widow has her hands firmly planted on her hips and a look of harsh disapproval on her face. "Fiona, what did you do?"

Fi is flabbergasted. "I... What are you doing here?"

Mrs. Mirskaya points an accusing finger. "I should ask you same thing." She descends upon Fi, her countenance softening considerably, snatches her up and crushes her in a hug. "I am very happy to see you, *moya solnishka* (my little sun)."

Fi can't get her mind wrapped around the fact that Mrs. Mirskaya is here. Mol barks in greeting.

Mrs. Mirskaya releases Fi and gives him a cursory pat on the head, "*Da, da.* Good Molossus," then frowns at Zeke, lying there on his back.

"Oh," says Fi. She helps Zeke to his feet. "Mrs. Mirskaya, this is Zeke."

He offers a hand. "Very nice to meet you, ma'am."

Mrs. Mirskaya crosses her arms, eyeing him critically. "I know who is Zeke."

"What?" Fi asks. "How does everybody know about him?"

Mrs. Mirskaya shrugs. "Edgar tells me."

Fi jerks suddenly, "Edgar..."

"He was with you?" Mrs. Mirskaya asks.

"Yes," Fi shouts, frantically sweeping the beam of the flashlight.

They're in a circular chamber, approximately forty feet across and five stories high. At various intervals between here and the ceiling are walkways that circle the walls and cross the chamber itself, connecting tunnels at other levels with ladders and switchback stairs of various materials and construction. The walls and domed ceiling are reinforced concrete, and from the tunnel entrances look to be several feet thick. Two other passageways lead from the bottom level, where they now stand. One angles sharply off the chamber and upward into the surrounding earth. The other dips downward.

But there's no sign of Edgar.

Zeke retrieves the other flashlight and finds himself on the edge of a pit in the center of the room. He aims the light to reveal narrow stone steps spiraling down into dark running water twenty feet below. "Oh..."

Fi runs to the blocked passage where they entered. "Uncle?!" Mol barks, echoing her concern. She whirls on Zeke, blinding him with the flashlight. "Did you see him?"

He shields his eyes. "I didn't. He wasn't behind us."

She spins back to the rubble and screams, *"Edgar!"*

28

FLOWERS & FIGS 14

Fi screams again, her voice ringing through the tunnel hub chamber, "Uncle Edgar!"

Mol barks at the walkways above. There's a *clank* of metal, then "Swing Low, Sweet Chariot" being whistled softly. Fi trains the beam of her flashlight on the sound. A weak glow of light appears.

"I'm here, dear," says Edgar, carrying his electric lantern down a set of iron stairs.

Mrs. Mirskaya breathes with relief and Mol barks. Fi sprints to Edgar. She doesn't think about it, just catches him in an atypical but enthusiastic hug as he comes off the bottom step.

"Oh God," she gasps, tears trailing through the grit on her cheeks. "Don't do that!"

"What's that, dear?" Edgar asks, patting her awkwardly on the back. "Become separated from you, or come back?"

Fi pulls away and smacks him on the chest, sending up a puff of dust. "Asshole," she utters, then hugs him again, pressing her face to his jacket.

"I daresay that's the first time you've ever called me such a derogatory epithet. To my face, that is."

Fi steps back, hanging on to his sleeves. "Sorry."

"Rubbish. It's long overdue, if you ask me." Then he adds tenderly, "I'm just happy to see that you are safe." He looks over the group – Zeke, Mol, and then his eyes light on Mrs. Mirskaya. "All of you."

He hands the lantern to Fi, removes the strap of the long bag from his shoulder and sets it on the floor, then shrugs the shield case and leans it against the wall.

"What *was* that?" Zeke asks. "It couldn't have been an earthquake, could it?"

"No," Edgar replies, taking the lantern from Fi. "Explosives. The house, I'd say. Kleron's doing."

Fi lowers the shirttail of her scrubs, which she's been using to clear the wet dirt from her eyes. "They blew up the house?"

"That would be my guess," Edgar says, lowering himself to sit against the wall.

"What about Peter?" Fi asks. "You think he's all right?"

Zeke stops shaking dust out of his hair, ashamed of himself. Even though they were mostly destroyed already, the first thought that came to mind was, *all those guitars.*

Edgar answers, "Milord is always all right."

Zeke makes a feeble attempt to remove his pack but gives up, leans back against the wall and slides into a sitting position. "Is there another way back? Should we see if he needs help?"

"If he is delayed, there's nothing we can do to assist him, believe me. Don't you worry, he'll turn up." But his eyes meet Mrs. Mirskaya's, and there's something in his voice that isn't entirely encouraging.

* * *

Dust settles in the deep tunnel where Peter fell, revealing a wall of stone and earth, slanting from the ceiling into a foot of water. It is completely silent.

boom... ever so slightly the stones vibrate, dust curling lazily.

boom... a few pebbles are displaced.

boom... the water ripples at the sound. The sound of pounding deep within.

* * *

Zeke has finally squirmed out of his pack and sits leaning against it next to Fi. Arms wrapped around her knees, she's listening to Edgar and Mrs. Mirskaya converse heatedly in Russian on the other side of the chamber.

Edgar speaks Russian. More she didn't know about her uncle. And now Mrs. Mirskaya, the eccentric babysitter and friend of the family she's known forever, is in on it too. Whatever *it* is. *Who are these people? Have they been lying to me my entire life?* She doesn't know what to think or believe. *Could my whole life be a lie, too?*

Though she understands a little of the language, they're speaking too fast and hushed for her to make out much. She can tell he's catching her up on the day's events. Peter comes up a number of times and she hears the names of Kleron, Maskim Xul, Cù Sìth and Zadkiel, which surprise Mrs. Mirskaya, but nothing compared to her shock at the mention of Mahisha and Tengu-Andrealphus. Now they're arguing about something and Mrs. Mirskaya appears to be gaining the upper hand – which isn't at all surprising.

Mol nudges her shoulder. He's a bloody mess, singed and lacerated, hunks of hair missing, but he isn't bleeding anymore and doesn't seem to be in pain. *Tough old dog.* Fi throws an arm over him and holds him close.

Zeke chews the last of an energy bar and takes a sip of water from a plastic canteen, both of which he found in his pack. "So, your uncle speaks Russian," he says.

"Apparently," Fi snaps back.

"You didn't know?"

"Nope."

"Oh." He'd feel like the odd man out, even sorry for himself, if it wasn't for the obvious fact he isn't the only one having his world turned upside down. Absolutely crazy, impossible shit, all of it, and he still can't believe most of what's happened, but it's got to be even worse for Fi.

They haven't learned much more about what the hell is going on, or who or what Peter and those other – *things* – are, but Mrs. Mirskaya (whom Zeke doesn't think likes him very much), told them she was also attacked. Edgar had called her at the store to let her know that something terrible had happened at the hospital, but before she could leave to meet him a bunch of wampyr and werewolves (which she called *vampiry* and *oborotni* – *"Chort demony. Otvratitel'nyye sushchestva!"* she'd literally spat. Fi translated, something like "Damn little demons, revolting creatures!"), stormed the place with the Cerberus brothers (*'Cerberus brothers,' if that isn't insane all by itself*). She said she put up a hell of a fight and the store was completely demolished (something about the north wind and a flood, which Zeke didn't quite understand), but they finally overpowered her and threw her in a van. As they were driving over a bridge, she'd busted out a door, jumped to the river below and swam all the way here. There's evidently an underground waterway that runs through the hills here to the river and she'd followed it to the well in the center of the chamber. She'd just come out and was headed to the house when the explosions started.

Zeke would think her story was incredibly ridiculous – which it is – to swim upstream in frigid autumn water, all the way from downtown, then underwater from the river to here, wearing a long skirt, no less. But that, and the fact she knows about this place, and therefore obviously knows Peter, brings him to the conclusion that Mrs. Mirskaya is one of *them*. He doesn't have any idea what *they* are, but whatever it is, it isn't human.

And he can tell Fi's grappling with the same idea.

"Hey," he says quietly.

She offers a weak smile. "Hey."

"Looks like you really are stuck with me for awhile." He runs a hand through his grimy hair. "Sorry."

Fi doesn't know if she should laugh or cry, but there's a tiny flutter in her stomach and her heart lightens a bit. "That's okay, I guess." She can't help but smile a little more. "At least you're not too hard to look at."

"Thanks. I think." He manages a smile himself. "But if I look at all like I feel right now, I'm pretty sure it's like shit."

"Mmm, not really." She takes in the sight of her own filthy arms and hospital scrubs, runs a hand over her head. "Me, on the other hand. Ugh." She proceeds to redo her ponytail, shaking the grit out of her hair as she does so.

Zeke wiggles a pinky finger in his injured ear.

"How is it?" she asks.

"Annoying is all, really. And it itches."

She offers a sympathetic smile.

"Thanks again," he says. "If I ever thanked you in the first place. For helping me when I was trying to be Wall Man after doing that slipping thing."

"Don't mention it. We'd all still be there if it hadn't worked."

"Well, yeah, there's that, I guess." He pauses, takes a breath. "And, I just want to say again how sorry I am about last night."

Fi's surprised he's bringing that up now – though it is very sweet. Still, she'd rather not talk about it.

"I just... it isn't that I—"

"It's okay, really," Fi cuts in, trying to ease his anxiety, and hers. "I think I'm over it now." His face falls. "I mean, I guess it isn't all that important, you know? Considering everything that's happened..." She indicates around the room. "...Is *still* happening."

Zeke thinks for a moment. "Or maybe it's the *most* important thing." They gaze at each other for what seems like an age. A soft white glow rises on their faces.

* * *

The shuffle of hard shoes on stone and Edgar is standing over them with his lantern, next to Mrs. Mirskaya. He looks troubled.

"Uncle," says Fi, "are you all right?" Edgar doesn't answer. "Should we be worried about Peter?"

"No, dear," he replies. "Peter is quite self-sufficient, to say the least."

Zeke saw what Peter can do, especially how he survived the swarm of locusts. Still, he said he'd be here, and if he isn't...

Edgar pulls up his long bag and sits on it, but remains silent. Zeke and Fi exchange glances. There's obviously something on Edgar's mind. Mrs. Mirskaya takes a seat next to him and clears her throat with dramatic impatience, urging him to speak.

Edgar studies his hands and begins, "I deeply regret that you two have been drawn into this. Perhaps I could have been more vigilant, better prepared." He sighs, looks up. "But there's nothing for it now. Zeke, you'll have to stay with us for as long as necessary to ensure your safety. As dangerous as that may be in itself, if we were to simply let you go home, or even hide you the best we could, they'd eventually find you and interrogate you for what you might know. It wouldn't be pleasant, and you would not survive."

As weird and frightening as that sounds, Zeke appreciates Edgar's candor. The truth is, if given the choice, he doesn't think he'd *want* to go back. *Except for a crappy apartment filled with dusty old books, what do I really have to go back to?* And the only person he really cares about in the whole world is right here.

"Looks like you're not going to make your conference," Fi says apologetically. "I know how much the assistantship meant to you."

"There's always next year." He thinks about where they are and what's happening. *I hope.* "That paper I was working on seems silly now anyway, writing about myths as if that's all they really are, just made up old stories." He gives her a small smile, then replies to Edgar, "It's okay, I understand."

Mrs. Mirskaya crosses her arms and raises an eyebrow at Edgar, who clears his throat uncomfortably.

"You say you understand, lad," says Edgar, "but therein lies the rub. Neither of you do." He folds his arms on his knees. "What would you like to know?"

Zeke is stunned. There have been a bazillion questions buzzing in his head since this whole thing started, but now, with Edgar offering to tell them anything they want to hear, it's like he's walked into a super-mega store with unlimited cash and is faced with row after row of endless aisles packed with cool stuff. He knows there are a ton of things he needs, but his mind is suddenly blank.

"What about your oath?" Fi asks Edgar with a touch of sarcasm.

"Technically," he replies, "my vow of secrecy was to be kept until Peter's recovery and return, or an event occurred of sufficient magnitude to warrant its dissolution. Mrs. Mirskaya, who took the very same vow, has convinced me both criteria have been met."

"Oh," says Fi. "Okay." She's excited by the idea of hearing the truth, but scared too. Her understanding of the world, her entire belief system, everything she's ever known or thought she knew has been slowly crumbling away all day – her whole reality, like a protective eggshell she's lived in her entire life, cracking around her, leaving her feeling more and more raw, naked and afraid. *Maybe I don't want to know...* about Peter, and Edgar and his sword and Mrs. Mirskaya and all those creatures and what they want – but she has to.

Maybe if she starts with something easier – well, maybe not *easier* – but something that's been haunting her, a ghostly specter lurking in the dark corridors of her mind – a specter named Kleron. She can still see his eyes, looking at her, into her, through her.

Zeke opens his mouth to speak, but she beats him to it. "I saw something, when we were playing that song."

"'Brian Boru's March?'" Zeke asks.

"Yeah."

He looks to Edgar. "Peter told me he wrote 'Greensleeves.' Is that true?

"Aye, lad, he did."

Okay, that's crazy, but, "Did he write 'Brian Boru's March' as well?"

"No," Fi answers for Edgar, to the surprise of all. "Kleron did." She shoves stray hair back over her ear. "But Peter was there."

Edgar and Mrs. Mirskaya stare at her, stupefied.

Earlier, when Edgar told Mrs. Mirskaya about Fi's visions of the baby, she'd looked at Fi in wonder and said nothing. Now she asks, "How do you know this?"

"While we were playing, Kleron was looking at me with those horrible eyes and it's like I was suddenly *there*. It was so real. Sometimes I was myself, just watching, but sometimes it was like I was someone else, seeing things through their eyes, feeling everything they did." She shudders.

Mrs. Mirskaya leans closer, an almost manic interest in her eyes. She takes Fi's hands in hers. "Fiona, what did you see?"

Fi's focus becomes distant and she speaks softly. "Monsters. Fighting with men in the rain, on the Field of Clontarf. That Kleron – *guy* – and an old king, Bóruma mac Cennétig – Brian Boru. Then Kleron stabbed him in a tent and there was a funeral and they played *that song*. Peter was there watching, some of the time, in the end. He wore a robe with a hood, and he had a beard. He wasn't very happy."

Mrs. Mirskaya is beaming – which is making Fi nervous. Edgar doesn't seem quite so enthused.

Zeke speaks up, "I just saw what the guys in the room really look like, I guess."

"You saw their Trueface," says Edgar, though still preoccupied by Fi. "The song distracted them, relaxed their attention to cloaking themselves as human.

"Cloaking?"

Mrs. Mirskaya claps herself on the knees and grins at Edgar. She exclaims something in Russian Fi doesn't catch.

Edgar harrumphs, "Mirskaya, Fiona may be a seer, and an empath as well, but she is *not* a witch."

Fi's mortified. "What?!"

Mrs. Mirskaya retorts to Edgar, "Not *bad* witch, *durak* (fool)." Then to Fi she says, "Good kind. Very much good."

It doesn't seem "very much good" to Fi. Just thinking about it again has started the visions of Kleron and Boru playing over and over in her mind, like a demented movie projected behind her eyes, and she's suddenly got a throbbing headache.

"What was going on with Kleron and Boru?" she asks. "I can't get it out of my head!"

Edgar reflects for a moment. "I cannot address how or why you were able to experience the events that you did, because it would be mere speculation." Mrs. Mirskaya moves to speak but Edgar gives her an earnest look and she remains silent. "But I know the story of Kleron and King Brian Boru, if it would ease your mind."

Fi rubs her temples. "Yes, please."

Edgar leans on his knees, the light from the lamp on the floor casting odd shadows over his features. "In the days of Bóruma mac Cennétig, known today as Brian Boru, Ireland was called Éire by its people, but the Westland Isle by others. The Romans knew it as Scotia Major and Hibernia.

"At that time, Peter and Kleron had come to an accord – rather, to say Peter was tolerating Kleron might be more apropos. Kleron had come to Peter after centuries of exile, begging once again for forbearance. He claimed he wanted to help the peoples of the isle to keep the old ways, to protect those close to nature who worshipped the earth, sun, sea and stars. Kleron had been a frequent presence in those lands for thousands of years, since it was called Fiodh-Inis, the Wooded Isle. It was he who had led the Tuatha Dé Danann to drive the Fomorians and the Fir Bolg into the sea. He seemed to be doing right by the good peoples there."

Fi doesn't recognize the names – but Zeke does – ancient, barbarous, magical clans from Irish mythology. He forces himself to breathe.

"Peter felt that after all the evil Kleron had done, he might be rehabilitated. And this war in Éire seemed such a small thing – to permit Kleron to aid one small population in such a tiny part of the world – what harm could it do? There was some suspicion that Kleron had a hand in the earlier battle at Camlann, in England, but there was no proof."

Fi looks to Zeke, who says, "Camlann is the battlefield where King Arthur was killed by his nephew, Mordred, right? I mean, according to the legends."

"That is correct," Edgar responds.

"The stories are true?" Fi asks.

"Some parts."

"That really happened too?" Zeke asks. "There really was a King Arthur?"

"Oh yes," Edgar replies somberly, "but that's a tale I shall not tell today."

Zeke gathers from the tone of Edgar's voice that he'd better leave it alone, which he will. For now.

"Sorry Uncle," Fi apologizes for the interruption. She would've thought that what he's telling them might have the opposite effect, but her headache is actually receding. "You were saying?"

"Peter had a tremendous desire to believe in Kleron's reform, you see, in the possibility of real atonement for what he had done to humankind in the past. With all his heart, he wanted to believe Kleron could change – because if Kleron could, then anyone can.

"And so, in spite of Kleron's possible involvement in Arthur's demise in England, Peter allowed Kleron's alliance with Boru's forefathers. When Boru came along, he and Kleron became fast friends. That was genuine, from what I understand. It's been said Kleron loved the king, as much as he could love any man, which I don't believe is very much, myself. Be that as it may, Boru made a pact with a Catholic abbott behind Kleron's back, and in Kleron's eyes betrayed him utterly. The Church wanted dominion over the land and to do away with any and all worship they did not sanction."

"So Kleron murdered Boru and blamed it on the Vikings," says Zeke, almost to himself.

Edgar looks up at Zeke's quiet insight. "Exactly. After Boru's funeral," he proceeds, "Kleron disappeared without a trace, and Peter discovered, to his great dismay, that the whole time Kleron had been on the Isle he was clandestinely seeking ancient powers, lost technologies of domination and destruction. Peter had been blind. He spent years searching for Kleron, but to no avail. It's haunted him ever since.

"In the last century rumors have circulated that Kleron had returned, but that was all. There's been no hard evidence he was here or up to anything to be concerned about. Until today."

If Zeke's mind was a microprocessor it'd be clocking way too fast. "Mr... Edgar, sir, if you don't mind, from what I understand, Brian Boru would have been high king in Ireland in, like, 1000 A.D."

"He died," Fi interjects, "I mean, Kleron killed him, on April 23rd, Good Friday, 1014 A.D." Off Zeke's look she adds, "Don't ask how I know that. I just do."

Mrs. Mirskaya smiles approvingly, causing Fi to shrug.

Zeke continues after a quick blink and toss of his head, "And, as close as anyone can guess, the Battle of Camlann, when King Arthur was killed, might have happened five hundred years before that..."

"In the year of our Lord, 542," says Edgar.

"But the Irish legends of the Tuatha Dé Danann and the Fomorians, I mean, there's no proof, but if it actually happened, we're talking something like 1700 B.C., if not earlier. Kleron was alive? Back then?"

"Aye, that he was. Kleron is one of the oldest living beings on this earth, or any other."

"So..." Zeke queries, "like, thousands of years old?

Edgar doesn't answer.

Zeke hazards another guess, "*Tens* of thousands?"

Edgar glances at Mrs. Mirskaya. She nods in encouragement. Edgar doesn't seem entirely convinced he should tell them this, but he does anyway. "Kleron was born 63 million years ago."

Fi and Zeke blink stupidly. Zeke feels like the wind's been knocked out of him.

Everything he's heard is ludicrous, of course – *but a 63 million year old being? That can't be even remotely possible!* Then again, he can't believe Edgar would make up something so outrageous. Edgar could just be wrong, or have been lied to himself. But a part of Zeke – that wildly curious part from his imaginative childhood, when he'd read those old stories and be lost in them for days, then emerge depressed that he had to live in a world so lame in comparison and do chores and homework instead of slaying dragons – that part of him *wants* it to be true.

"Who *is* Kleron, then?" Fi asks with trepidation. "*What* is he?"

Edgar's face turns grim. "He's had many names, like all of his kind. 'Kleron' is a more recent nickname. Long ago he was known as Mechembuchus, and later Belial."

Zeke's eyes go wide, "But—"

Edgar raises a hand for patience. "The Dead Sea scrolls state, and fairly accurately, mind you, that Belial was High General of the Sons of Darkness. They read, 'for corruption thou hast made Belial, an angel of hostility. All his dominions are in darkness, and his purpose is to bring about wickedness and guilt.'"

Zeke finishes for him, reciting more of the ancient texts, "'And all the host associated with him are but angels of destruction.'"

Edgar nods, impressed once more at Zeke's knowledge and recall.

Fi's finding it very hard to sit still.

Mrs. Mirskaya speaks in an ominous tone. "In lands that were once my home, the peoples told stories heard from *dedushka i babushka*, who heard from *their* grandparents, and so on. They called him Chernobog, 'black god,' bringer of calamity, lord of darkness."

"He has also been known as Mastema, The Deceiver," Edgar continues, "and Merihem, as well as Neuntöter, purveyor of disease and pestilence. A single bite from him, if it isn't immediately fatal, carries the original strain of the bubonic plague, responsible for the agonizing end of untold millions of lives over the millennia. The Norse peoples called him Surtr, 'the swarthy one,' master of fire. You may recognize the name Mephistopheles, 'one who avoids the light,' or Abaddon, also known as Apollyon."

"The angel of death," breathes Zeke. "Described as having the wings of a bat."

"Aye," Edgar confirms. "The predecessors of the Aymara and Inca of Mesoamerica considered him a deity of death who ruled Uca Pacha, the underworld, and held dominion over a race of demons. They called him Zupay. Others in that part of the world knew him as the terrible god Tohil, also known as Tezcatlipoca, which is a derivation of the much older Huitzilopochtli. Later generations, those who weren't aware of his true history, named him Camazotz.

"There are other names, other stories about him, from every culture, old and new." Edgar pauses, takes a deep breath. "But his first name, his Truename..." his voice falters.

Mrs. Mirskaya sees his distress and takes over. "As story is told, Kleron was born in quiet of earliest day. His papa looked up with joy, saw bright star in sky, and named him *Lucifer*."

Edgar makes the sign of the cross over his heart.

"The Devil?" Fi blurts out, incredulous.

"The image or persona of The Devil that you may be familiar with," Edgar informs them, "is a conglomeration of a number of ancient beings, but primarily there are three: Kleron, yes, but also one who called himself Khagan, Kleron's master, who is long dead, and then there is Kleron's father."

"B-but," Zeke stammers, "Now you're talking about *God*."

Edgar responds emphatically, "No, I am not."

Zeke's eyes meet Fi's. She speaks first. "When Kleron came to the hospital today, he said they were Peter's family. Then later, Peter said they were his children. Billy too. I thought it was all crap."

"At the house, Kleron called Peter 'Pater,'" says Zeke. "I thought it could be another form of his name, but it also means 'father.' That can just be a title of honor, too, but... They really *are* his children?"

Edgar looks at them, one to the other, his eyes pleading. "Please do not think less of him, I beg of you."

* * *

The pounding deep within the collapsed passage where Peter is buried grows louder. The wall of tumbled rock shakes, stones loosen. A boulder splashes into the black water, sending frothy waves into the long darkness.

* * *

Zeke's mouth moves, but no words are coming out.

"But... how...?" Fi asks. "How can Peter be Kleron's father?"

"The three Cerberi as well," Edgar adds. "The legendary Cerberus has always been three brothers from the same litter, not one three-headed beast. And the dreadful Maskim Xul," he cringes just saying the name, "the one they call Max. They are all Peter's children, and they are called 'Firstborn.' But there are more, you understand, and not all are like them. Samson, for example."

The memory of Billy stabs at Fi's heart.

"And Kabir," Edgar adds "Or Zadkiel, I should say."

Zeke still hasn't closed his mouth, but he finds the ability to speak. "Is he *the* Zadkiel? The angel who stopped Abraham from killing his son?

"'Angel' is a misunderstood term, but it was he who staid the dagger of Abraham, yes."

"And the vampires? And werewolves? That's really what they are?"

"Yes. They are real. Always have been."

"Are they Peter's, too?" Fi asks.

"They are anomalies, as Firstborn progeny go. The weres are the result of some of Peter's children of the canine variety breeding with natural wolves, and amongst themselves. Somehow their bloodline retains more human-like traits, generation after generation. The wampyr are descendants of Kleron, who has a unique ability among Firstborn to breed with human women."

Just when Fi's face couldn't go any whiter, it does. She stands unsteadily, bracing herself against the wall. She's never thrown up, not since she would spit up as a baby. She felt like she was going to whenever they "slipped," but now she thinks she might actually do it. She paces, trying to catch her breath, to get her blood moving again. *This is completely insane!* But what really has her worried is something deeper, more than what Edgar has told them – sure, that's some crazy shit, incredible, ridiculous even – but what's really troubling is that *he knows all of this!*

Edgar watches her, sympathizing with her plight. He remembers what it was like when he was first told these things by his mentor, the woman who trained him when he was a young man. He looks to Zeke, who has his head in his hands.

Mrs. Mirskaya tells Edgar, "Maybe if you start at beginning."

Zeke looks between his fingers. Fi shakes her hands at her sides, takes a deep breath and comes back to sit down. "Okay," she consents, takes another breath. "As long as it doesn't start with 'Once Upon a Time.'"

Edgar smiles in spite of himself. "I cannot tell you everything, because I don't know everything, in spite of my occasional claims to the contrary, and I'm afraid what I say may not ease your minds, though it will, hopefully, clarify some things."

Fi scowls. Even now, her uncle can't just explain something, he's got to put a spin on it. "Uncle..."

He gazes at her, his expression difficult to read. "I only say this because, as outlandish as what I've already told you may sound, and even in light of what you've now seen with your own eyes, this will most likely seem... impossible. But I assure you, it is not. I only ask that you keep an open mind," he looks seriously at each of them, "and forget everything you know."

Fi and Zeke exchange looks of apprehension. Edgar rubs his forehead with long calloused fingers, pinches the pronounced bridge of his nose, trying to decide how to begin. "All right," he breathes, folding his hands in his lap.

"What he truly is or where he comes from, no one knows, not even he. His first memories are of when the earth was young and the oceans were first taking shape."

Fi suddenly re-experiences the vision of light on water and a baby floating in ruddy waves, his eyes all the colors of the world. Still, she hears her uncle's voice.

"At that time, he was simply matter and energy in continual flux, a shapeless entity of mass and light. He had no form because he knew no form. No knowledge, language, or recall, not even a name. Within him, however, was a locus of supreme consciousness and intellect. Unlike all else in the world, he was *aware*. He perceived what it was to be alive, and he rejoiced. That was almost four and a half billion years ago."

Fi snaps out of the vision. "Four and a half *billion* years?"

Edgar is sympathetic but insistent. "As I said, the world was new. He is as primordial as the earth itself."

Fi and Zeke stare in dumb silence.

"As years became millennia and passed to aeons, he explored the oceans and ever-changing landscape continuously, for his curiosity was insatiable. Though he can partake of them if he wishes, he has never required food or drink, or even air to breathe, acquiring all the sustenance he needs from the elements themselves. We can only strive to imagine the isolation he must have felt as he matured, this single solitary being, utterly alone except for the tiniest and most nascent forms of life, for, literally now, over three billion years."

He pauses to let this sink in.

Nope, try as they might, Fi and Zeke can't imagine it. Living completely alone, not even knowing what companionship might be like, that there could ever be such a thing at all – let alone for three billion years.

"In his solitude," Edgar resumes, "he would sleep, sometimes for millions of years at a time. Meanwhile, life evolved, becoming more and more complex, until eventually he had something akin to company. Just to watch, at first, but then large enough to touch and even to frolic with. Of course all of this took more hundreds of millions of years, but you can imagine his jubilation. Well, you can't, but you catch my meaning."

Fi thinks back on what she's learned about the evolution of life from her studies and finds her tongue. "The best anyone can figure is the first forms of life appeared in the oceans between three and a half to four billion years ago."

"Give or take tens or even hundreds of millions of years," says Zeke, surprising himself that he can speak at all.

"Well, yeah," Fi concedes. "Then cells with nuclei formed, supposedly about two billion years ago, and multicellular organisms, still just tiny, about a billion years after that." Edgar wags his head, roughly agreeing.

Zeke adds, "The earliest geological records of primitive animals, all of which lived in the ocean, date to approximately seven hundred million years ago."

"That sounds about right," Edgar agrees. "And they continued to evolve until species developed that were *anisogamous*, complex enough to require sexual as opposed to asexual reproduction. When they were advanced enough, and this is where things may seem to become particularly... peculiar... he discovered his ability to conform to the corporeal physicality of these life forms and procreate."

"What are you saying?" asks Fi. "He could have sex with animals?" She thinks about Kleron, the three Cerberus, Kabir, and the others. "*Any* animals?"

Mrs. Mirskaya snorts. "He is not *man*, Fiona."

"He *became* these creatures," says Edgar, "and when it happens, he feels what they feel, sees what they see. He *is* one of them."

Zeke considers the ramifications – to know what it would be like to actually *be* a dog or a cat or a bird – or a bat. "So, he can change into anything he wants?" he states.

"Not at will, no," Edgar responds. "It requires—"

Mrs. Mirskaya interjects, "True love."

"He can love animals?" Fi asks. "Like *that*?"

"He loves all living things," says Edgar. "Perhaps I should back up a bit. In addition to having been here since the beginning, he believes it was his very presence in the oceans, the vital spark of his own living being, which gave rise to the earliest forms of earthly life."

"Ohhh..." Fi groans.

"But to answer your question, yes, he can love any creature, like *that*."

"But—"

"Before we fly into moral outrage," Edgar cautions, "consider when this was occurring, and the kind of being we're talking about here. *There were no people*. And if you question the validity of what we are telling you," he stresses, "just remember what you have experienced today. Bear in mind, you two, that he has perfect recall of everything he has ever seen, heard, touched, smelled, even thought, and he is a brilliant scientist to boot. He could explain all of this far better than I. Everything I'm telling you was first related to me personally by my mentor, whom I trust implicitly, then by The Pater himself, and it has all been corroborated by other genuinely ancient beings – his First-born children."

Fi still needs reassurance on the whole subject of *reproduction*. "Okay, but, he never actually had sex with animals. In the form of a man, I mean."

"Mmm..." Edgar looks uneasily to Mrs. Mirskaya, who rolls her eyes. "I wouldn't say *never*..."

"Ugh. That's just—"

"Fiona," scolds Mrs. Mirskaya. "Don't be *blyustitel' nravov*."

"But this is about—hey. I'm not a prude!"

"You are being prude."

Then Fi realizes – if Mrs. Mirskaya really is one of them, she could be talking about Peter and Mrs. Mirskaya's mother – who might not have been a human person at all... *Oh God*, she thinks, *please don't let it be a muskrat...*

"Just to be clear," Zeke asks, "we *are* talking about Peter, right?"

"Yes," Edgar replies. "Peter is *The Pater*, the physical father of not only the ancient beings of which we speak, but quite literally all life on the planet."

FLOWERS & FIGS 15

In the deep dark tunnel, the wall of fallen rock heaves forward, toppling stone and earth into the water. Then it's pushed farther from within, more violently. A third time and Peter bursts forth into the tunnel. He feels around in the rubble, tugs out the haversack, now practically ruined. He retrieves a chemiluminescent glow-stick, its activating capsule already broken. Yellow-green light illuminates the rough walls, reflects in the water. He places it in his mouth, rummages through the sack, pulling out cash, identification, and stuffing them into the multiple pockets of his ragged cargo pants. Leaving the pack where it lay, he pats dust off his tattered shirt, brushes grit out of his hair and rubs it from his eyes. He checks his pockets once more to make certain the small metallic rod that is Gungnir is there, then listens, sniffs the air, and splashes down the corridor.

* * *

Zeke's mind is spinning. Fi crumples back on the wall, exhaling like a punctured tire.

"Before I go on," Edgar continues, "I must tell you, *no*, Peter is absolutely not the all-seeing, all-knowing, all-powerful creator of the universe. He is very strong, very smart, and by all accounts entirely indestructible, but he cannot conjure something from nothing, transport himself wherever he wishes, be everywhere at once, see all, travel through time, read minds or miraculously answer prayers. What, or who, the True Creator may be remains a mystery, and a matter of faith. But be assured, Peter is not The Devil either."

Fi isn't sure if that's a relief or it just adds to the greater quandary.

"It is the case, however," Edgar continues, "that all of the ancient religions and mythologies, some still known and many long forgotten, have a god or multiple gods based upon him, and he *has* mistakenly been believed to be God himself."

"Well sure, if he's been around for, like, *ever*—" Zeke catches himself, apologizes for interrupting, and leans back against the wall.

"No apology necessary," says Edgar. "I completely understand your—eagerness—shall we say." He addresses Fi. "And skepticism. But hear me out." Fi and Zeke do their best to contain themselves.

"As I mentioned earlier, the result of a union between The Pater and another living creature is called a Firstborn. They are a natural part of what we understand as evolution, but each of them can constitute a great leap in and of itself. Now, evolution proceeds as it always has, and The Father, or The 'Pater,' as the word came to be used for the same meaning in ancient Greek and Latin, began the process, but Firstborn can, and do, alter it as well. They are capable of breeding only with their mother's kind, or those species very close to it – with Kleron being one notable exception, as I mentioned – and though their progeny lose their mighty strength and longevity rapidly over successive generations, new species have evolved, many of which are still with us today.

"From the beginning, however, Peter realized his offspring were very different from their mother's kind. They gained from him incredible strength, immunity to disease and the elements, and unnaturally long lives, but they also had physical attributes he had never seen before. Some gained more of these than others—five fingered hands, two arms, bipedal locomotion, binocular vision, certain organ and brain configurations, warm bloodedness—attributes that only much later did he realize were collectively *humanoid*.

"He's never known why, or what this means, but somewhere in his unique, magnificent physicality, his cosmic genetic makeup, there is the blueprint for man—and woman, of course. From inception, dominant within his unexplainable DNA, has been the pattern for humankind."

"And he looks like a man today," Zeke interjects.

"He has not returned to his original shapeless state for a very long time, and except for a few isolated instances, for the last two and a half million years he's had only the appearance of a man. In fact, it seems that he can no longer take any other. His form has become fixed. He has, for many thousands of years now, remained human entirely."

"Maybe because he's finally achieved his true form," Zeke comments. "*Our* true form. What he was always meant to be."

"Perhaps. There's still much he doesn't understand, and perhaps never will. Strange as it may seem, he knows more about everything else in the world than he does about himself."

"He looks to be in his early forties, maybe," says Zeke. "Does he get any older, physically, I mean?"

"None are old enough to have seen much change in him, but he insists that he does indeed age with the passing of time, just not very quickly. In human form, he appears to have matured at the rate of approximately ten years of a natural human's life for each billion of his own."

"Why did he look so old when he was in the hospital?" Fi asks.

"Ah, the patermentia, or so it is called. This is the first time I've seen it, but he's been afflicted with it numerous times in his life. Entirely beyond his control, and completely debilitating, it's a condition brought on when depression progresses to despondence and finally despair. From what I've been told it can last for quite a long time. He either simply gets over it eventually or it is alleviated by an occurrence of great significance – but sometimes just some small seed of hope and love."

Mrs. Mirskaya smiles with proud affection. "This time, Fiona, *you* were cure."

Fi's not so sure about that, but Peter did say something about her bringing him back. "In my dreams, or visions, or whatever they were, why did I see him as a human baby?" she asks.

"Other than being precipitated by love," Edgar proffers, "he theorizes that his appearance may also be affected by what another creature's, or person's, perception of him may be, mapping their own understanding of themselves and the world upon him. In your case, you perceived him through your own sensitivities and perhaps even intuited his innate human form. When faced with the entirely unfamiliar image of Peter from his earliest memories, you may have sensed this newborn consciousness and your mind defaulted to imagining the persona of a child.

"This isn't much different from how Firstborn who are not born of human mothers can appear to be human, as you have seen, through a sort of illusion called 'cloaking.' There is a physical transformation, yes, but mostly it's us. We see what our minds are familiar with, what makes sense to us. And let's be honest, the natural appearance of a Firstborn of an animal mother doesn't make sense in the modern world. The Firstborn willfully give us a mental nudge to complete the impression, but in essence, we see only what we are ready to see, and what our limited minds can accept."

Fi has her fingertips pressed to her lips. She won't bite her nails while Edgar's watching, but she really wants to.

Zeke breathes a quiet, "Oh man." Shapeshifters appear in practically every myth he's ever read, men and women who can change into animals, or vice versa. It's called "therianthropy." There are many creatures that are part human, part animal, too. Most of them incredibly strong, living for unbelievable amounts of time. No wonder so many of the Firstborn were considered to be gods or supernatural monsters. And Peter himself... there are stories from all over the world of a supreme god who falls in love with a woman—or a female animal—and spawns more gods. Now Zeke knows where all these legends come from. The paper he was writing for the assistantship competition, where he proposed a common denominator between disparate mythologies, now seems absolutely validated – *and* incredibly naïve.

"Due to multiple factors," Edgar continues, "there aren't many Firstborn alive today. But the fact remains; they do exist. Some live secretly amongst us, cloaked as humans, but most abide quietly in remote places of the world."

"Or on other worlds." Zeke adds.

"Yes, but the majority remain here, on this earth."

"How many are there?" Fi asks. "Firstborn, I mean?"

"There have been millions over the epochs," Edgar replies. "But now only a few dozen, maybe more, maybe less." He looks to Mrs. Mirskaya for affirmation, who nods. "No one knows exactly, since they generally don't keep in contact with one another. Or with their father."

"Why not?" asks Zeke.

Edgar shrugs. "Old feuds, ambivalence, apathy, a desire for privacy, even fear for their lives. Firstborn are strong, as I have said, but they are not immortal, not entirely beyond injury or death. Some are benign and some benevolent, but there are those who are neither. You've met a few of the worst. The fact is, for a very long time all have been silent, relatively inactive. Until today."

Fi asks, "Why today?"

"I wish I knew."

"But why would they go after Peter?" Zeke queries.

"There are animosities that go back millions of years, and wars, terrible wars. But the last, which is referred to as The Second Holocaust, ended almost twenty thousand years ago. There has been peace between them, relatively speaking, ever since. Peter hoped the aggression had finally come to an end. That, however, does not seem to be the case."

"Wars over what?" Zeke asks. "What do they want?"

"You've no little knowledge of mythology. The Titanomachy and Gigantomachy of the Greek's, the Hindu's Vedic struggles between the Deva and the Asura, the Armageddon of scripture and the Norse Ragnarök (which have both already happened, by the way), The War of Heaven as described in the Old Testament, also called the battle between the Sons of Light and the Sons of Darkness. What do you think?"

"Control of the earth," Zeke ventures.

"Dominion over mankind," says Fi.

"Or," Zeke considers, "our annihilation."

Edgar and Mrs. Mirskaya look grave.

"You think that might be what Kleron's up to now?" Fi asks.

"It is entirely possible."

"I don't mean to sound rash or disrespectful," says Zeke, "but if that's what they're planning, if they're so awful, why didn't Peter just kill them all, up in the house? We saw what he can do. I mean, I appreciate that it might be hard if they're his children, for Christ's sake, but under the circumstances..."

Fi shoots Zeke a look. She never warned him about taking the Lord's name in vain around her uncle.

Edgar takes it well. "'Difficult to kill one's children, for Christ's sake,'" he repeats. "That's something to think about. But to answer your question..." He contemplates how to proceed. "I cannot begin to fathom all of Peter's thoughts or motivations, but even if he were to have taken them all on—and he could, make no mistake—chances would be very good that Kleron, the Cerberi, or more likely Max, would have gotten to either or both of you, or me, for that matter, while he was busy with the others. Then we would have been in a very tight spot indeed. In fact, that may be exactly what they were hoping for. Since none of us, including Peter, are sure of what Kleron intends, would the possible sacrifice of all three of us have been worth it? Also, if Peter would have managed to capture any of them alive, torturing them for information would do no good, not with this lot, and the weres and wampyr would certainly not have been entrusted with any information worth having."

"And Kleron knew that," Zeke realizes. "And he can slip. He could have just disappeared at anytime."

"Exactly. Most likely, Peter hoped that if he showed them he was back in full capacity they might cease and desist. He wouldn't *have* to kill them."

Fi shakes her head. "I still don't know why he wouldn't want to, after what they did at the hospital, and to Billy—Samson—whoever he is—*was*, he was Peter's son too... and a great guy."

Edgar sighs, "I appreciate your sentiments, and I am truly sorry about your friends, but The Pater does not do that sort of thing carelessly. Unless..." He and Mrs. Mirskaya exchange glances. "Unless he is afflicted by the mania."

"You mean like when his eyes were red when he was fighting?" Zeke asks.

"No, that is the bloodlust. All creatures have the capacity for it, to some extent. The patermania is something quite different." He studies his hands, continues with his previous train of thought. "There is something about The Pater that you must understand. He loves *all* his children, regardless of what they've done, when he is in his right mind. We've inherited our emotions from him, but he feels them stronger than we ever could. That doesn't mean he is always lenient, that he won't sacrifice one child to protect others, but it's a choice he does not relish, that he never takes lightly, and his remorse and guilt know no bounds, even when taking the life of a Firstborn is justified.

"When Peter was forced to slay the worst of them, responsible for the deaths of millions of Firstborn, his own brothers and sisters, as well as the near eradication of all humankind, still, The Pater wept." Edgar pauses. "Imagine if all your worst enemies were *your* children."

Fi and Zeke mull that over.

"Consider a family, a lifetime, measured not in years and decades, but in epochs, tens of millions of years, even hundreds of millions, where days fly by like seconds and ice ages come and go like winters. In lives like those, relationships are more complex than you can possibly imagine. There is love, yes, but there are also resentments, jealousies, hatreds that go deeper than humanly possible. In lives like those there is sea change, even war, *every day*."

Edgar rests a moment, studies his upturned palms on his knees. "I have a hard time grasping these concepts myself. I am a mere infant to them, no more or less than you two children." His voice wavers. "And I was born on April the 12th, in the year five hundred and three, *anno domini*."

Zeke's eyes jerk to Fi, who's staring at her uncle.

This is it, Fi thinks. When she discovered Edgar's association with Peter, she got an awful nagging feeling – an unthinkable notion that swelled dramatically at the first sight of her uncle so deftly wielding his sword and shield, and has been mounting into an ominous fearful anxiety ever since. And now...

She finally asks the question she knows she doesn't want the answer to. "Edgar, are you one of them? Are you Firstborn?"

Edgar closes his eyes, "Yes," shakes his head weakly, "and no."

"But you're not my uncle." It's not another question, but a statement of fact that wounds her deeply.

Edgar's eyes open. There are tears, and he can't bring himself to look at her. "Please understand that to tell you this pains me more than you can imagine. But it is also a great weight lifted from my heart. There is no worse burden to bear than deceit. I can finally be free of it, as you can now know the truth." He takes a deep, slow breath, gathering his courage. "No, dear, I am not your father's brother, nor his cousin. And my name has not always been Edgar. I am, or I was, *Galahad*."

Zeke's eyes whip from Edgar to Fi, then back to Edgar. "*Sir* Galahad? Knight of the Round Table? The only person to ever sit the Siege Perilous and live? The 'Perfect Knight,' who succeeded in the quest for the Holy Grail?"

Edgar nods, but it appears not to be in agreement, only shame. "I am Thirdborn, Peter's great-grandson. The illegitimate child of the betrayer, the adulterer, Sir Launcelot du Lac, God rest his soul. His father was not, however, King Ban of Benwick, as the legends tell it, but a lecherous Firstborn who tricked Ban's wife into bedding him, in much the same way he manipulated the Lady Igraine into sleeping with Uther Pendragon to beget Arthur.

"My real grandfather was heralded by many names. His first name, his Truename, given to him by Peter, his father, was Myrddin Wyllt. They called him The Madman, for good reason, but you might know of him best as Merlin, The Magician."

Zeke looks back to Fi, who sobs, tears flowing freely. He would think this revelation about Edgar was unbelievably cool – if Edgar and Fi didn't look so awfully miserable.

Mrs. Mirskaya's eyes are moist with sympathy for both of them.

"And you?" Fi asks Mrs. Mirskaya, her voice catching on the words.

"I am Firstborn, Fiona. Peter is my papa. My Truename, is Mokosh."

Mokosh... Zeke doesn't know a lot about Mokosh, only that she was a fabled deity of earth and water, invoked by ancient Slavic peoples for protection from their enemies, and the weather, because she supposedly held sway over the elements.

"My mother, however," Mrs. Mirskaya adds, "was not *muskrat.*"

A pang of guilt stabs Fi's heart. "You know about that?"

"*Mokosh* knows all." She grins. "Just joking. Is not a problem, Fi. Is appropriate, I think. And I have been called worse things in my life, believe me."

Fi can barely speak due to the painful lump in her throat. "I'm sorry."

"And a long and illustrious life it's been, Fiona," Edgar explains, taking small relief in talking about someone other than himself. "Mrs. Mirskaya, Mokosh, was born in what is now known as the Orinoco River Valley of Venezuela. Her mother was a prehistoric aquatic mammal that today's scientists have named *Phoberomys pattersoni.* Quite like a muskrat, yes, but *much* larger."

"The name 'pattersoni' is only coincidence," says Mrs. Mirskaya, "but you are Patterson too. Is funny, yes?"

Fi can think of a few things it might be, but 'funny' isn't one of them.

"If it makes you feel any better," Edgar says to Fi, "the predecessors of the Native Americans of the Pacific Northwest referred to her as The Beaver, and they revered her."

Fi's guilt isn't eased much, but she says, "Okay." Getting busted calling Mrs. Mirskaya 'Old Lady Muskrat' sucks, of course, but it's nothing compared to the weirdness of finding out what Mrs. Mirskaya really is.

Zeke's trying to imagine what Mrs. Mirskaya looks like uncloaked, or in "Trueface," as Edgar called it. He isn't having much luck. He eyes Mol. "What about him? He isn't going to stand up and start talking, is he?"

In spite of herself, Fi blurts out a sound that's part sob, part laugh. Years of no tears at all and now she's crying for the zillionth time in one day.

Edgar rubs Mol's head affectionately. "I'm afraid not, lad, but my old friend here is definitely not your typical dog."

Mol poses proudly while Edgar explains. "This faithful fellow is the last of a most noble bloodline called the Kelabim. Their progenitor, Mol's great-great-great-great grandfather, was Shvan, a gallant Firstborn warrior who perished long ago fighting for the survival of the human race. Mol's father was named Argos, not to be confused with Arges, the cyclops and armorer of the gods. You might remember Argos as the canine companion of Odysseus from Homer's *The Odyssey.*"

"Damn...," Zeke moans, eyeing Mol with newfound respect.

"Mol has chosen to remain by my side for quite some time, but I did not name him. He is *the* Molossus, the original Hound of War of the Greeks, present at the Battles of Marathon and Thermopylae, among many others, friend to Socrates and Plato, escort to the armies of Alexander the Great. It was his children and theirs who went to war alongside the peoples of Hellas, today known as Greece, for many centuries, and his line that has been reared into the largest breeds of dogs we know today." Mol slops his big tongue up the side of Edgar's face. Edgar wipes his cheek without fuss. "He is Fifthborn, though nearly 3,000 years my senior."

Fi stares at Mol through a haze of detachment, as if nothing more can astonish her.

Edgar addresses her directly. "I'm sure you've noticed, Fiona, I never hovered as you played in the yard alone, or showed concern for your safety when you walked the streets at night. Perhaps even wondered why. It wasn't that I did not care."

Fi shrugs flaccidly, sniffs. "I thought you were just letting me do my own thing, I guess."

Edgar places a hand on Mol's back. "It's because you've always had a guardian angel, following, watching from the shadows."

Fi doesn't even look up. *Too much. It's just too much.*

"Normally he would tail you from a distance, even in the day, on your walk to work, but today he was locked in."

"I was at the house," Zeke offers in apology. "He came outside."

"Not to worry, lad, but he must have sensed some time later that something was amiss, as is his way, broken out of the house in my absence and made haste to the hospital."

All Zeke can think of to say is *wow*, but it seems so incredibly lame he keeps it to himself. Then something occurs to him. "Mol's a dog though, right? Pretty much, anyway. No offense, but you look older than he does. Mrs. Mirskaya seems younger, too – though I'm guessing she's doing that cloaking thing."

Mrs. Mirskaya snorts. "Flattery gets you nowhere, *mal'chik* (boy)."

"Astute observation," Edgar replies to Zeke, brushing off Mrs. Mirskaya's brusqueness. "All the earlier generations in direct lineage with The Pater live very long lives, but all, even the Firstborn, age at varying and unpredictable rates. No one knows why. Mirskaya is indeed far older than I, but has aged more slowly. Firstborn always live the longest, regardless. And though I'm closer in descendance to The Pater than Molossus and he is older, and humans live longer than dogs, he may yet outlive me. It's a mystery."

Fi stirs from her daze, wipes her cheeks and rubs her eyes. "I don't understand." Her voice is pleading. "I've known you," she looks to Mol and Mrs. Mirskaya, "all of you, since I was a baby. And now all this with Peter..."

Edgar exhales in an odd mixture of sorrow and liberation. He's been dreading this moment since Fi first came into his life – but also looking forward to finally being able to tell her the truth one day. Now that day has come. "I was pledged to look after you since before you were born." Mrs. Mirskaya lays a hand on his wrist. "We both were." Mol barks sharply. "Mol too, I suppose."

Fi shakes her head in disbelief. "Pledged? By who?"

"Your father," Edgar replies. Fi just stares blankly. "I may not be your uncle, but we are related, you and I. I am, in fact, your *nephew*. Your great-nephew, to be more precise, because you are my grandfather's sister."

Edgar is fully aware that this revelation is ripping Fi's world apart, and his heart aches for her as she stares at him with her teary green eyes. Nonetheless, a touch of pride creeps into his voice. "You, Fiona Megan Patterson, are *Firstborn*."

Fi's jaw bobs inaudibly. Zeke's color isn't so good.

Mrs. Mirskaya weeps with joy. She envelopes Fi in a tender hug. "Welcome to the family, *sestrenka* (little sister)."

Blinking tears over Mrs. Mirskaya's shoulder, Fi manages to speak. "That's... but then... Peter?"

"You must find it in your heart to forgive him, dear," Edgar implores. "Forgive us all."

FLOWERS & FIGS 16

Fi is stunned, bewildered, confounded. *Me? Firstborn? Peter? My father? No fucking way!*

A bizarre sound echoes through the hub chamber, nearly inaudible in pitch but chilling to the bone. Goosebumps rise on Fi's arms. Zeke's injured eardrum jangles painfully and the hair pricks on the back of his neck. Mol whines and shakes his head, sending his ears flapping. Edgar leaps to his feet, sword ringing from its scabbard.

Mrs. Mirskaya curses softly, "*Chort vozmi.*"

It comes louder, a high-pitched series of ticks and squeaks.

"What's that?" says Zeke, with a shiver. "It sounds like..."

"A bat, aye," Edgar confirms. "*The* Bat. This can be none other than Lucifer himself."

* * *

Peter bounds from the top of a ladder into a tunnel of brick. He runs to another and leaps, catching it near the ceiling – but it snaps, sending him sprawling to the floor. He regains his feet and springs straight up the shaft, catching the edge of the tunnel floor fifteen feet above with one hand. With a single tug he swings himself over and hits the ground running.

* * *

Fi and Zeke snatch up their flashlights and jump to their feet. They hear the flutter of large leathery wings and skitter of many clawed feet.

Edgar watches the tunnels, including the levels above. "From the odor of it," he says, "The Spider as well."

Fi smells it too, the now familiar charnel stench. "Max."

"Max is a *spider?*" Zeke squeaks. He feels like he's going to puke again. "I really don't like spiders."

"Maskim Xul is not just spider," says Mrs. Mirskaya, "He is True Ancient, born 140 million years passed."

"140 million years..." Zeke mutters, still trying to comprehend such incredible spans of time. He sweeps his flashlight desperately across the various entrances. The sounds seem to come from everywhere.

Edgar dons his shield. "Behind me, quickly." Fi and Zeke back toward the wall. "You too, lad," he tells Mol. Mol hesitates.

"Do as you are told, *glupaya sobaka* (silly dog)," Mrs. Mirskaya scolds him. "They eat you alive." She takes a place beside Edgar. Mol reluctantly squeezes in behind her, but positions himself to defend both Fi and Zeke. She laments to Edgar quietly in Russian, "They might eat us all."

Fi doesn't translate the fearful words to Zeke. She still hasn't come to grips with what Edgar told her about who and what she, and her *father*, really are, but she can't help the words that escape under her breath. "Peter, where are you?"

* * *

Peter comes skidding around a corner and stops dead, faced with a stone slab wedged between the walls. He shatters it with a swift kick only to find a boulder blocking the entire tunnel behind it. A single punch and it crumbles, but the passage is still packed with rubble beyond. He grunts in frustration and dashes back the way he came.

* * *

"There," Edgar says, pointing his sword at the tunnel that slants downward from the chamber floor. Fi and Zeke aim their flashlights around him. There's the sound of scrabbling on rock. A dark umbral figure flits across the ceiling, then down the wall to the shadows below, where they can't see from their angle.

Edgar steels himself for the attack. "Fiona, Zeke," he whispers. "I must confess, I have never met foes such as these in combat. I would have you flee, but I'm afraid that would not be wise. They are very, very fast. Be ready, however, as a last resort."

"What are you going to do?" Fi asks.

"What I was born to do, dear," he answers firmly. "I will defend your lives unto my very death."

Fi blanches at the thought.

"But do not despair yet, young ones." He raises his voice so Max and Kleron are certain to hear. "I wield the Sword of David, taken from Goliath in the spoils of battle. It is one of the deadliest arms ever forged, an Astra weapon crafted by The Prathamaja Nandana herself, with the power to pierce hide and heart of even a True Ancient. I also bear the shield of Joseph of Arimathea, blessed with his own holy blood. No harm shall come to those under my protection while I still draw breath."

His tone resounds with confidence and clarity. "And hearken unto me, ye devils. *I, Galahad, doth ne choose to die this day!*"

* * *

Peter wriggles through a crack and finds himself stymied once again, the natural crevice before him clogged with stony earth. He crawls to the blockage, jams the glow-stick in his teeth, and shovels with his bare hands.

* * *

A melodic voice lilts into the chamber.

"Oh, the Incy, Wincy Spider,
Climbed up the water spout..."

Hearing the words to Max's song, Mrs. Mirskaya eyes the well in the center of the chamber, then the ceiling.

Edgar raises sword and shield. "Prepare yourselves."

Fi and Zeke press harder against the wall behind them. A slight breeze brushes their hair and they realize Mrs. Mirskaya is speaking quietly in a language that sounds a little like Russian, though it is actually much, much older – an ancient appeal only Mokosh can muster.

Here, deep underground, they hear a distant roll of thunder. Mrs. Mirskaya's voice rises and the wind increases, circling in the chamber. Near the ceiling, black clouds materialize, tumultuous and coursing with heat lightning. Raindrops fall, fat and warm on their raised brows.

The clouds spin in cyclonic fashion and the rain becomes a torrential downpour, but Mrs. Mirskaya raises a hand and it's blocked from them as if by a shield of curved glass. She raises her other hand and lightning bolts strike ferociously into each of the tunnel openings, again and again. The crack and peal would be deafening, but the invisible shield muffles the din.

The lightning ceases at Mrs. Mirskaya's command, but then she shouts her incanta-tion and a roaring geyser spouts from the well in the center of the room, up through the eye of the storm above to blast against the ceiling. More arcane speech and the geyser splits into branches that flood the tunnels with the force of a thousand fire hoses.

Zeke's awestruck at the realization he's witnessing something that most likely hasn't been seen in human memory – and no one would ever believe today. The super-natural power of the ancient deity Mokosh unleashed.

Fi's speechless. Then she hears another voice. Even behind the invisible barrier its foul timbre assaults her ears with striking clarity. A searing ache shrieks through her brain. From Zeke's groan, she can tell he hears it too.

Mrs. Mirskaya shouts her spell to repel the verbal attack, but the fell words only become more strident. Fi feels an unearthly chill and realizes she can see her breath. Mrs. Mirskaya struggles on, but through the frosty shield they see the geyser freeze solid. The dreadful words quiet, then roar to life once more. White hot fire blazes from one of the upper passages. The ice shatters and its shards boil to steam. The fire reels through the chamber and Mrs. Mirskaya's shield flares like the hull of a spacecraft descending through the atmosphere.

Fi and Zeke feel like they're being cooked alive. Mrs. Mirskaya fights on, but her hands tremble under the strain and her voice falters.

The vulgar incantation roars even louder and the shield is blasted to nothing. Mrs. Mirskaya cries out and slumps to the floor. The foul speech silences and the fire is gone.

"Mrs. Mirskaya!" Fi crouches over her, Zeke by her side.

Mol nudges the old lady's cheek. She's breathing.

"Oh, thank God," Fi exclaims.

"She'll be all right, Fiona." Edgar is shaken, but resolute. "We have other matters to attend to."

Fi and Zeke once again aim their flashlights at the mouth of the lower tunnel.

Max creeps toward them far enough to reveal his soiled stocking cap, soaking wet and steaming, their lights mirrored in his four pairs of sunglasses, and his savagely grinning mouth.

He chortles, "There ain't no rain can wash this spider out." And he changes...

The stocking cap is now a mangy tuft of gray hair above a face covered in patchy gray fuzz, matted with filth, his nose two seeping holes and mouth a wide slobbering crescent grin with yellowed and blackened fangs that protrude over rubbery lips. Each lens of the sunglasses is a lidless, yellow orb of an eye, eight of them in all, one pair above the other, each pair a different size. The black pupils are rimmed in red and all of them move in unison as he peers around the chamber. He inches forward, revealing more of his true form in all its hideous glory.

Zeke's insides turn to water at the sight. A ribbed thorax, black with red markings, and a bloated rippling bulb of an abdomen that expands and contracts as he breathes, with shabby peeling flesh sparsely covered in gray bristles. Attached to the thorax are eight legs, like any self-respecting spider should have, but the first set is more like scrawny arms with slender hands that each have two fingers and a thumb with curved black claws, and the back set is oddly angled in bony hips that afford him the ability to walk upright when he wishes. Each of the back six legs have a pair of hooked and sharply toothed claws, bristling with spiky hair. Crawling on the ground, as he is now, the knees – or elbows – peak above his head and back.

Fi covers her nose and mouth against the stench. Zeke gags. Both shrink behind Edgar but peer around him to keep the creature in sight.

Max crawls along the edge of the well, all eight eyes trained on Edgar. His voice is eerily whimsical and soft.

"Will you walk into my parlor?
said the Spider to the Fly,
'Tis the prettiest little parlor,
that ever you did spy;
The way into my parlor,
is up a winding stair;
And I have curious things to show you,
when you are there."

Edgar takes a bold step to block Max from Mrs. Mirskaya's prostrate figure, and Fi and Zeke are surprised to hear him finish the stanza.

"Oh, no no, said the Fly,
to ask me is in vain;
For who goes up your winding stair
can ne'er come down again..."

Max zigzags closer, side-stepping this way and that like a crab, his claws skritching on the stone floor. Edgar adjusts his stance with each movement, anticipating the coming assault.

"Sheathe your sword, young *wæpenbora*," creaks Max, "and I'll kill you quickly, I promise."

"I cannot tell you how many times I've heard that one, little Spider," Edgar scoffs, "and the word of Anansi is dubious at best."

"Alas," Max sighs, inching closer. "I have other tricks up my sleeve—Oh!" his hand shoots to his mouth and he looks at his arm, grinning like a fool. "No sleeves."

A high piercing squeal slashes the air, causing Fi and Zeke to jump. Edgar is distracted for an instant – just enough time for Max to strike, quick as lightning.

Edgar crouches, stabbing past his shield, straight at Max's eyes, but The Spider rolls sideways, avoiding the thrust by an inch, and propels himself upward with all eight legs, high into the air. Edgar raises shield and sword.

A phantom shadow descends from a walkway above. Fi tries to shout in warning, but before she can utter a sound Kleron sweeps Edgar's sword arm aside with his left wing and clamps Edgar's wrist with the claw at the peak of it, then grips Edgar by the throat with one hand, hoists him off his feet and pins him between shield and wall with a leaping shove.

Edgar exhales sharply, pain shooting through his chest and back.

Fi screams, "Edgar!"

With a lion's roar, Mol attacks. He clamps his jaws onto Kleron's leg and wrenches with all his might – to absolutely no effect. With less concern and effort than one might shoo a gnat, Kleron kicks him. Mol sails across the room, thuds against the far wall with a piteous yelp, and falls limp to the floor.

"*Mol...*" Fi wants to go to him, but she fears more for her uncle.

Kleron leers up at Edgar with his grotesque, bat-like Trueface. "What did I tell you, *boy?*" He clenches his wing-claw, snapping Edgar's arm below the wrist. Edgar grunts in pain. His sword clangs to the floor.

Fi screams, "Nooo!" and moves to help Edgar, but Zeke holds her back.

Kleron steps on the sword and kicks it backward into the well. Edgar squeezes his eyes closed at the sound of the splash.

Zeke tries to drag Fi away but she fights against him, shouting again for Edgar. A hideous cackling comes from above and she looks up to see what Zeke has been fretting about – Max, clinging upside down to the bottom of a platform overhead. They back away, but not fast enough.

Max drops, knocking both of them to the ground. He pounces on Zeke, swiftly lifts him with middle legs and rolls him over and over, using his back legs to guide a stream of milky thread that exudes from his abdomen. In seconds Zeke's wrapped from ankles to shoulders, arms bound to his sides, and dumped roughly, just as Fi aims a kick at Max's head.

"Ho ho!" Max shouts, easily deflecting the blow. He leaps on Fi, who lands on her back with a shriek. He pins her tight, pressing a disgusting hand over her mouth, all eight eyes and drooling mouth of pointed teeth hovering inches from her face. He presses his ghastly body against hers, paws at her with his claws – but he's careful not to harm her, not to damage her precious skin. Not yet.

"Little Miss Muffet, sat on a tuffet..." he breathes. The reek of his breath makes her eyes water.

Dizzy and nauseous from being spun in Max's web, Zeke sees the blurry image of The Spider perched atop Fi. He struggles in his bindings, tries to shout, but is forced to gag back his own rising gorge.

Edgar fights frantically in Kleron's grasp. "Do not touch her!" he gasps. Kleron presses hard against him, tightens his grip on his throat. Then both of them notice a wisp of smoke curling between them.

"Ahh," notes Kleron. "The blood of Joseph of Arimathea." He grips the edge of the shield with his free hand, moves back just enough to peel it away from his chest and wrench it from Edgar's arm. The fur on Kleron's chest is burned, the skin blackened and smoking in the shape of a ragged cross.

"That will leave a mark," says Edgar wryly.

"You did warn me," Kleron concedes. "The bloodline of Joseph may be toxic, but it is not deadly to one as old as I." He gives Edgar's broken arm a twist with his wing claw, causing Edgar to wince hard. "Tell me, how did Pater dispel the mentia so quickly? It is... unprecedented."

Edgar glares in response. Kleron loosens the hold on his throat, enough for him to croak, "Divine intervention. Unconditional love. Blessings The Accursed One will never know."

Kleron smiles his mirthless smile and gives Edgar's broken arm another twist. Edgar suppresses a moan. Kleron turns his attention to The Spider. "Max, enough," he reproaches.

"Yes, Master," Max says in disappointment. He lifts Fi and gives her the same web-spinning treatment he gave Zeke, though he wraps her more sparsely, with a few strands of web around her ankles and just enough to hold her arms to her sides. He drops her on her back, then proceeds to secure the unconscious bodies of Mol and Mrs. Mirskaya. When he's completed his task, he returns to hunker on top of Fi.

Edgar struggles in protest. Kleron leans close. "Begging your pardon, good knight," then suddenly releases him and steps back, holding his arms out in a non-threatening gesture, though still holding Edgar's shield.

"Children," he cries, addressing Fi and Zeke. "I'm afraid you have gotten the wrong impression of me. I have no intention of harming you." His human cloak returns. "I'm here to *save* you."

Edgar doesn't dare attack without his sword, but at least he can speak his mind. "Do not hearken the Lord of Lies!"

Kleron ignores him and addresses Max. "Maskim Xul, leave the young lady be, if you please." Max removes himself reluctantly, skitters to squat between Edgar and the well, blocking him from the others and all exits.

Kleron gazes at Fi with what appears to be heartfelt compassion. "I hate to tell you this, young lady, but Galahad, your dear Uncle Edgar, is little more than a well intentioned fool, guiltless of all but faith in a non-existent God, and folly in his devotion to a fickle lord. Peter is not who he pretends to be. He is The Father, yes, but one who abandons his children. He will bring you nothing but misery and woe. Woe to you, and all whom you love." He looks at Zeke for a long moment, then sets Edgar's shield against the wall and crouches next to Fi.

"We haven't much time, dear ones." He continues, switching to the language they heard earlier when the water from the well was frozen then decimated by fire – foreign beyond time and place, ugly, unintelligible, but he speaks calmly and without malice. The words morph, melt, and though they still echo in the background of their minds, Fi and Zeke also hear Kleron in English, his voice mellifluous, consoling.

Come with me, my children. Follow, and be free. You will know the truth, and everything you have ever desired will be yours.

Fi thinks she can hear Edgar shouting, somewhere, far away, but she's spellbound, lost in Kleron's voice and black eyes. Eyes like portals to another universe. Deep within them she sees a flowering meadow under the sun, and her mother, laughing with a toss of her hair, skipping, dancing, playing her flute. She can smell the grass, the flowers, her mother's perfume, see the sparkle in her eyes. And suddenly Fi is with her – not a young girl like she was before her mother died, but the age she is today. Together.

Zeke has a similar experience, but his visions involve a guitar, amorphous images of parents he never knew, and Fi.

This world will be the last, and it will be ours. Come with me, and live.

The pain, horror and grief of the day fade away, like a nightmare forgotten upon waking.

* * *

"FIONA MEGAN PATTERSON!"

Edgar's commanding voice rolls like thunder over the sunny meadow. Fi pauses, just feet from her mom. Her mother smiles, but her eyes are vacant, lifeless.

"This isn't real," Fi says softly, her own voice watery and faint.

"Fiona!"

"This isn't real," Fi says louder. She can still hear Kleron's voice, but it has returned to the harsh, terrible utterance it was earlier.

She whispers, *"Zeke."* She spins to the trees, then shouts to the sky, *"Zeke!"*

* * *

Zeke is seated at a large dining room table, family all around. And though Fi is sitting right next to him, holding his hand, he hears her voice from elsewhere.

"Zeke, this isn't real!"

He blinks. The faces around the table are vague, unfamiliar. It's a family he never knew. A family he never had. He looks to the Fi beside him. She smiles, her eyes void of the spark of life.

"Don't listen to him!"

Somehow, Zeke understands. He takes his hand from the fake Fi's, and begins to extricate himself from the dreamy web of Kleron's spell.

"Okay!" he replies to Fi's voice.

"Don't believe him!"

"I don't!"

"He's the Devil!"

"I know!"

"He's evil!"

"I got it!"

The illusions shatter into tiny splintering fragments, which fall to the floor of the chamber and vanish.

* * *

Kleron ceases to speak. He looks at Fi, to Zeke, then back at Fi, clearly puzzled. It takes a few moments for his false smile to return. "The Devil, you say? It was not *I* who tempted your Jesus Christ in the desert. That was *our father.* And I'm sorry to tell you this, but there is no such thing as *evil."*

"Whatever," Fi retorts. "Flowers in a sunny meadow? My dead mother? Is that the best you've got, *Lucifer?"*

Both Edgar and Zeke are shocked by Fi's bold defiance.

Even Kleron is befuddled. "Well, I..."

"Go to hell," Fi shouts.

Kleron's smile fades and his icy black glare drops the temperature in the chamber 50 degrees in an instant. "Better yet," his eyes glow hot, *"I'll take you with me."*

He growls, thrusting to his feet. Shedding his human cloak, he throws out his arms, clawed fingers splayed, spreads his horrendous wings and raises his face to the ceiling. His growl becomes a roar of the ghastly language from before.

This time Fi and Zeke hear no other words. They just *see.* And *feel.*

Kleron's eyes are blazing, his breath a yellow sulfurous fume. Flames curl from his nostrils. Smoke flows out of his ears.

The temperature rises so quickly that Fi and Zeke's clothes begin to smolder, then flame.

And they scream.

The chamber is engulfed in a vortex of fire. Edgar grits his teeth against the heat and howl of it. Wooden steps are set aflame, metal railings glow and sag.

And Fi and Zeke scream.

Kleron's fell voice becomes impossibly loud, a chorus of horrors from another world. His wings whip up the inferno.

A whirling pillar of fire erupts from the well, and within its flames a hideous face takes shape. Red, scaled and horned, yellow eyes with pupils like black fangs, flaming pits for nostrils – and two cadaverous mouths packed with scythes for teeth, twisted up in heinous grins on either side of a wicked scar, like an axe wound roughly healed. Both mouths speak with the infernal chorus, the same words as Kleron, but with a pitch even deeper and more primeval.

Edgar shrinks against the wall, squeezes his eyes shut and prays. "Satan, the Lord rebuke thee. I renounce all ungodly anger and give no place to The Devil..."

Fi and Zeke gag on the mephitic fumes, cough, and scream. Pain surges through Fi's head, threatening to split her skull.

Mrs. Mirskaya stirs, fights against her bindings, moans through the web that wraps her mouth. Mol shudders, wakes, and howls.

The chamber shakes. The walls and ceiling crumble and fall. They find themselves lying on a jagged promontory of stone overlooking an endless cavernous landscape of rock, magma, and fire, its high smoky ceiling glowing with a sickly nuclear radiance. There are hellish screams of multitudes in agony – not of the dead, but of the tortured and dying.

Edgar raises his voice as he draws strength from his supplications. "Devil, I resist thee! I loose myself from every bond of Satan in the name of Jesus Christ. I am delivered from the power of Satan unto God!"

His eyes snap open. "Fiona! Zeke!" he cries. "It's only an illusion. *It is not real.*"

But *this* feels real. Wholly different from the earlier delusions. Wholly *other*. Their clothing withers in flame, skin blisters and peels. All around them, for as far as the eye can see, thousands of people are being tortured – flogged, flayed, scalded, scorched, dismembered and raped. Some are attached to machines, both archaic and futuristic, abhorrent and unimaginable, on cliffs and plateaus laid out with butcher's tables, cables, rods, spikes, vials, crystals, and chemical vats, like an evil laboratory more despicable than anything dreamed up in a Nazi concentration camp.

Aberrant creatures stalk the cavern, abominations of parts taken from a variety of beasts, sutured and welded together, the subjects of vile experimentation. Some are recognizable from fable and myth – griffin, chimera, nue, baku, sphinx, ammit and tarasque. Others they have never seen depicted or described. But all are the substance of nightmares.

Hundreds of twisted demons with necrotic indigo skin and scorching sapphire eyes are herding the humans, manning machines, prodding, tormenting, brutalizing. Three are very close, skinning a man alive with their claws, driving wires and tubes into every orifice of his body.

Fi smells their purulent breath, observes with revulsion the sloughing skin of their gangrel bodies, the leprotic pustules and sores – and for some inexplicable reason, *she knows what they are.* They're called *Blues*. And they *are not here.*

She somehow calls up the courage and willpower to resist, tapping reserves of fortitude she never thought she had, and cries out, *"That's enough of that shit!"*

And the hellish landscape is gone, every trace of the conflagration ended. Nothing in the chamber is burned. It's not even hot.

* * *

Kleron stands fixed in Fi's furious glare, his wings still spread, arms wide, but looking, and perhaps feeling, a little ridiculous.

Fi breathes raggedly. She's still terrified, but she's also really, really pissed off. Maybe angrier than she's ever been in her life. "It's one cliché after another with you, isn't it? Cheesy illusions. Fire and brimstone? Get with the times, asshole. You're a *fake.*"

Max chortles, wheezes and coughs.

Kleron's wings fold behind him, arms drop to his sides. A range of emotions flit across his features as the red glow fades from his eyes. He's amazed, then impressed, and finally, amused. He addresses Edgar while keeping his eyes on Fi. "You've had your hands full with this one, eh, Galahad?"

Edgar makes no response. He's as surprised as Kleron.

Kleron studies Fi intensely. "And still so young..."

Zeke doesn't know what to think. He's mostly just relieved not to have been burned alive, for real.

Kleron picks up Edgar's shield. "Was my facile defeat of almighty Mokosh *fake?*" He holds it out to his side dramatically. "Is *this?*" He utters a single unhallowed word and the shield bursts into flame.

And Fi knows – *this is no illusion.*

She gapes in terror at the incandescent, unholy hue, feels the intense heat, smells the reek of *real* brimstone—

* * *

Through her own eyes, Fi tears her bedroom apart – but the hands doing it are black and clawed. She looks into the dresser mirror to find herself staring directly into the dead black eyes of Kleron. He smiles a crooked smile. Behind him, reflected in the mirror, are her antique brass bed with Mrs. Mirskaya's handmade quilt, her chair and closet door, her travel posters and books. And it all catches fire. The black hand strikes out and smashes the mirror.

Kleron's hand slides down the stairway railing of her and Edgar's home, igniting it as it goes. He strolls leisurely through the hall downstairs with his hands out to his sides and a sardonic grin on his face. Smoke and flame rise from his claws as they gouge wainscoting and plaster. He looks into the parlor as he passes. It's all on fire.

On the bookshelves, Bibles burn.

Hanging on the wall, a Latin cross burns.

From some disembodied perspective in the front yard, Fi sees Kleron emerge from the house, now a blazing inferno. One-armed Surma leans against a white van parked on the street, cleaning his teeth with a stick and sneering.

As Surma and Kleron drive the van away, the house explodes.

This happened.

* * *

Fi gasps, her sight and mind returning to the hub chamber, to the present.

What's left of Edgar's ruined shield crumbles from Kleron's grasp, smoking cinders and ash. He speaks to Max. "Prepare her." Max leaps atop Fi without hesitation.

"No!" Edgar lunges, but Kleron is on him, hand clamping his throat, slamming him against the chamber wall once again.

"And Max," Kleron adds, "do something about that insolent tongue of hers, will you please?"

Max grins wide. "Yes, Master." He grips Fi by the jaw with a disgusting hand, moves the claws of one leg to her mouth, clicking them together in a snipping motion. Fi tries to scream.

Edgar shoves at Kleron and groans.

Zeke yells, *"Hey! You mother—"*

Kleron realizes what Max is about to do. "Max!"

Max grumbles, then reaches to his bloated ass-end and pulls out a strand of web. "Where was I?" he wheezes. "Oh yes,

Little Miss Muffet, sat on her tuffet,
Eating her curds and whey..."

He wraps the web around Fi's head and over her mouth. The sticky strands adhere to her skin and hair like tape.

"Leave her to breathe," Kleron cautions.

"Of course, Master." Max snips the web, runs his filthy clawed fingers through her hair. He continues to croon his rhyme as he touches her cheek and neck.

"Along came a spider..."

He caresses her breasts through her shirt. She tries to protest, but it's no use. She sobs as the revolting hand moves slowly over her stomach. His voice becomes a scratchy whisper,

"Who sat down beside her..."

His hand slides down, down. Fi screams, again and again, as loud as she can through her gag of web. Edgar shouts his outrage, tears streaming. Mrs. Mirskaya struggles, helpless, and Mol barks wildly. Zeke writhes in his bonds, cursing Max at the top of his lungs.

Their cries do not go unanswered.

Peter's voice comes to them, fulminating through the tunnels. *"Lucifer!"*

Kleron's reaction, however, isn't quite what Edgar would have hoped for. Instead of dropping him and fleeing for his life, Kleron reaches into a small shoulder sack with his free hand and retrieves what looks like a smartphone. His bat ears twitch as he listens. Peter's voice echoes into the chamber again. Kleron eyes one of the tunnels above, slides his thumb over the touchscreen of the device, and taps it.

* * *

"Kleron!" Peter roars, racing through the tunnel. In his haste, he pays no heed to a small heap of stones against the wall. As he runs past it there's the triple-flash of a red LED accompanied by a quick *beep-beep-beep—BOOM!*

Peter stumbles and regains his footing, but another explosion rocks the passage, and another. The floor collapses beneath his feet. He falls, bouncing from wall to jagged wall, and plunges into black rushing water.

* * *

The tremors in the hub chamber subside. Dust billows from the tunnel above, wafts down gently over all. Kleron listens. Satisfied, he returns the device to his shoulder bag.

Edgar slumps in Kleron's embrace, realizing Peter must be trapped – there is no help on the way.

Max turns his attention back to Fi,

"And frightened Miss Muffet away."

He heaves her onto his back, where he holds her firmly with one arm.

Zeke cries out in despair, his voice painfully hoarse, "Fi!"

Kleron leans in, wings reaching forward, and whispers in Edgar's ear. "She will undoubtedly serve quite entertaining, your lovely *niece*." The wings creep around Edgar, pressing between his back and the wall. "Even if she does not prove to be useful otherwise." Edgar squirms, groaning harshly. Kleron clenches Edgar's shoulders with the single talons at the tops of his wings, while the claws at the wings' ends hook his ankles. He pulls the two of them even closer together, then very slowly opens his horrific mouth, pushes out his pointed blood-red tongue, and licks Edgar's face. Max watches, silently grinning.

"That was quite an impressive oratory you delivered earlier, gallant Sir Knight," Kleron says disingenuously. "Are you still so confident you will not die today?" Edgar grunts, unable to move or speak, so tightly is he cocooned in Kleron's embrace. "Let's put that famous prophecy of yours to the test, shall we?"

Savoring Edgar's helplessness, Kleron opens his mouth again, wide enough to engulf Edgar's entire face. He tilts his head and inches forward.

Edgar finds himself staring straight into The Bat's gaping maw. Dripping fangs, ridged black roof of his mouth, pulsating uvula in his throat, and vile red tongue.

Fi watches in horror from Max's back. *I'm sorry!* she wants to scream at the top of her lungs. *I'll go with you. I'll do anything you want, whatever you say. Just don't hurt him!*

But she can't speak. It's all one voluble meaningless rant with the gag in her mouth.

Edgar closes his eyes, and prays.

* * *

But the bite doesn't come. When Edgar opens his eyes, Kleron is leaning away, mouth hanging open, his expression one of intense concentration – and confusion.

Kleron turns his head to peer into the dark recesses of one of the tunnels that leads from this level, opposite from the way they heard Peter shouting. He peaks his ears and listens.

The others hear nothing, but then again, they don't have the ears of a bat – and a Firstborn bat at that.

The sounds are faint even to Kleron, the slightest trace of feet scraping stone. What concerns him more, however, is the whispering.

He dilates his broad nostrils, drinks in the air, but what breeze there is flows lazily out through the tunnel where he hears the sounds, away from the chamber, so he smells nothing. He swivels his ears this way and that. No sign of Peter. No sounds of digging, no shouting, no other footfalls. *Hopefully The Pater is trapped forever. Just thirty days would be nice*, which is all Kleron needs. But he isn't counting on it.

He retrieves his wings and removes the wireless detonator from his bag, scrolls to symbols for the explosive devices he and Max have planted, pinpointing the ones they placed in the tunnel from which the sounds originate. He taps one. Nothing happens. The device is capable of transmitting a half dozen types of signal. One of them should work, even below ground and surrounded by stone. He tries them all. Still nothing.

Kleron's grip on Edgar's throat slackens. Edgar shoves with all his might in a desperate attempt to free himself, but Kleron holds him tight.

And still Kleron listens. The sounds in the tunnel remain distant, but whatever's making them is coming this way – and from the whispers he has an inkling of the identity of this newly approaching horror. Dread twists in his gut. He shakes himself. *How can this be?*

He must think quickly. Failing capture of The Pater, the plan was to take the girl alive, but circumstances have now become dire. He can't slip with her, even if she went willingly or he could earn her trust. There are no equivalent tunnels or caves on nearby worlds. They'd be buried alive. He and Max are old enough and strong enough to survive. Their Firstborn bodies would simply open a space, crushing stone and compacting earth around them, but they'd have to keep slipping in the hopes of eventually coming to a world where there was open space, an underground river, deep canyon or some other manner of escape. It could take days, months, even years, if they found a way out at all. The girl would be killed on the first slip, and without quite a bit of luck, even he and Max could eventually suffocate and perish.

Since they must use the tunnels, taking the girl now may not be the wisest course of action. Max is extremely quick and agile, with his many legs. Carrying her wouldn't slow him much, but it may be enough, and being able to fly does Kleron little good when the tunnels are tight. But if there was something to distract his adversaries, to keep them busy while he and Max flee...

"May I, Master?" It's as if Max has read his mind.

"Yes," Kleron decides, "you may."

Max dumps Fi face down on the floor and pins her there. This is what he's desired since the first time he saw her, this morning on the street. To feed on her succulent, young, tender Firstborn flesh. Still, he hesitates. "Are you certain?"

"Do it," Kleron confirms. "Do it now."

Zeke and Edgar watch in horror as Max's mouth opens wider than any mouth should be able to. Slimy black fangs fold down, shaped like cat's claws, oozing droplets of cloudy yellow venom from needle-sharp tips.

He jabs them deep.

The searing agony is more intense than Fi ever thought possible. She hears herself screaming, Edgar wailing, Zeke shouting, Mol barking and Mrs. Mirskaya's moaned protestations.

Her vision blurs and closes in, all sounds fade. Then she feels nothing, and everything goes black.

FLOWERS & FIGS 17

P eter swims through the flooded tunnel, the green glow-stick clenched in his teeth. Something glints in the silt beneath him. Edgar's sword. He retrieves it and looks up to see a dim circle of light high above.

Peter scrambles from the water in the well. He spits out the glow stick, forces water from his lungs without so much as a choke, and bounds up the curving steps.

Mol barks a harried greeting. Mrs. Mirskaya groans in her fetters of web.

Zeke, wrapped like a mummy except for his head, has tears of anguish in his eyes. "Peter," he croaks. "Help her, please!"

Edgar sits misty-eyed, muttering prayers, rocking with Fi cradled in his arms. Peter sniffs the air and eyes the tunnel openings, then rushes to set the sword at Edgar's side. "Edgar, where are Kleron and Max?"

Edgar doesn't reply.

"They're gone," Zeke answers for him.

Peter hurries to Zeke and rips at the web that binds him.

What Zeke doesn't know is this web can't be torn by the teeth or claws of any First-born other than Max. It can only be cut by the highest class of Astra blade or broken by the hands of The Father. "Tell me what happened," Peter demands.

"Kleron was about to kill Edgar," Zeke answers desperately. "They were going to take Fi, but then they didn't—I don't know why. Kleron told Max to bite her and they just took off."

"Bitten..."

While Peter frees Mol and Mrs. Mirskaya, Zeke rushes to Edgar and Fi. Her face is deathly pale. She still breathes, but in shallow, ragged breaths.

Peter kneels next to Zeke. Mrs. Mirskaya and Mol crowd in opposite.

"Oh, Fiona," Mrs. Mirskaya mourns. She lays a hand on Fi's forehead, clenches her red rimmed eyes and mutters unrecognizable verse. Fi's breathing steadies but her pallor remains.

Peter shakes Edgar by the shoulder. "Galahad!"

Edgar forces himself out of his despair. "Yes, bitten." He moves to turn Fi over and Peter helps. Gaping puncture marks bubble with blood and yellow pus, one low in the seat of her pants and one in the thigh. "The bite of The Spider."

"No," whispers Peter, removing Fi's bindings. "No..."

He rips her pants from waistline to thigh, folds the cloth back to uncover the festering wounds.

Under normal circumstances Zeke would be seriously uncomfortable in the company of an unconscious woman with her pants torn down over her ass, but these aren't normal circumstances. He just wants to help. He reaches to wipe the poison from the wounds.

Mrs. Mirskaya snatches his hand. "*Nyet!* Do not touch," she warns. "Not if you want to live."

Peter wipes the secretion away himself. He shakes it to the floor where it bubbles and smokes, then examines the wounds, which are becoming swollen, purple and green around the edges. He smooths back Fi's hair, forces open each eye to see them rolled up in her head.

"Is there anything you can do?" he asks Mrs. Mirskaya.

She looks glum, helpless, ashamed. "I can ease her suffering, but that is all. My items of healing are destroyed in the store. But even if I had them... this Mokosh cannot mend." She sobs. "I have failed you Papa, and Fiona."

Peter brushes a tear from her cheek. "You've failed nothing, dear daughter." He lifts her chin to look in her eyes. "It's good to have you with us."

She sniffs, then wipes her face forcefully as if trying to erase the fear and regret.

"Here, hold her," Peter tells Edgar, positioning Fi face down across Edgar's legs.

"What are you going to do?" asks Zeke.

"Suck out the poison."

"Is that wise, milord?"

"It's all I can do for her," Peter insists. "That she's still alive is..."

"Miracle," Mrs. Mirskaya finishes for him.

"A testament to her strength and will to live, I was going to say," says Peter. "This may not be sufficient, but I will do it."

And so he does, drawing deep at the injury on her leg. He spits, the spatter again hissing on stone. He shakes his head as if to clear it, then moves to the other wound. He spits again, then leans back against the wall.

"Water, milord?" Edgar offers.

Peter shakes his head. "No, it won't help." He wipes his mouth with his sleeve. The venom burns through the cloth like acid.

Edgar turns Fi over in his lap, looks at her face. There's no change. He takes her hand in his. "Miss Fiona?"

Fi begins to convulse. Mrs. Mirskaya grasps her head in both hands and utters more ancient words, her brow furrowed in concentration. The spasms lessen in severity but Fi still breathes in sporadic rasps.

"Help her," Zeke begs. "Peter, do something!"

"There's nothing I can do," Peter bemoans. "I don't have the skills necessary—"

"Then we have to get her to a hospital," Zeke interrupts. "Right now!"

"The venom of Maskim Xul is like no other," Edgar explains. "She's beyond human care."

"If Max is a spider, isn't she just paralyzed? Won't she wake up eventually?"

"This is not that kind of bite," Peter replies.

"There's got to be *something* you can do," Zeke insists. "You're, like, the oldest being on earth. You're a *god*." He looks to Mrs. Mirskaya. "Both of you!"

Peter still breathes heavily from the effects of the poison. He has trouble focusing his eyes on Edgar, but the vexation there is clear.

"Yes, milord, I told them," says Edgar, without remorse. "My oath of secrecy holds no more."

Peter stares at him for a moment then looks to Zeke, "This requires a level of healing beyond which I possess. There are talents, aptitudes that only manifest in my children, in *real* creatures of this earth."

"But you're of this earth, as much as anyone," Zeke argues, "even more!"

"Am I?" says Peter, his temper flaring. "Am I? And you know this for a fact, young *mtoto*? Please, *enlighten* me!"

Zeke feels a great aura emanating from Peter, sees it in the steely glaze of his green eyes, now tingeing red, in the bestial tautness of his features and set of his jaw. And a scent permeates the air, penetrating straight to Zeke's brain stem, his alligator brain, his most primitive being, prickling his skin, turning his insides cold. The pheromones of the alpha wolf. The alpha of *all* species.

Zeke knows he should be groveling, throwing himself on his back, offering his throat in submission – but he isn't afraid, and that surprises him. He's just pissed off and desperately worried for Fi. He remembers the dogs on the street, how they reacted to Peter. They loved him. He forces himself to hold Peter's gaze.

Edgar intercedes in the tense moment. "Perhaps Freyja?"

Peter releases Zeke from his eyes. "Even on this earth she's too far away," he answers Edgar. "And she may have been targeted by Kleron's forces already. Either way, this is beyond her as well."

"The Buffalo Woman, then," Edgar suggests. "I've heard—"

"Impossible to locate," Peter snaps back. "Always has been."

"The Rat, Akhu?"

"This is beyond her capabilities as well. And no one knows on which world she dwells."

"Then, there is only one other..."

Mrs. Mirskaya looks up in alarm.

Peter is about to snap at Edgar again but stops himself. The crimson drains from his eyes. His words soften to a whisper. "She would be our best hope, yes. But you know very well she hasn't been seen nor heard from in almost two myria, nearly 20,000 years."

"Who?" Zeke asks. "Who can help her?!"

His eyes on Fi, Edgar speaks with an almost superstitious awe in his voice. "The Prathamaja Nandana." Mrs. Mirskaya's expression squirms between deference and disdain. "From what I know of her, she could be Fi's only hope."

Peter glares at him. "Be careful what you wish for, Galahad."

And then a new sound wafts into the chamber, an utterance flowing like a prolonged exhale, rushing water or gusting wind. Zeke hears it as much in his head as in his ears, and it's unlike any language he's ever encountered, even the terrible speech of Kleron. Edgar stiffens visibly, lifts Fi and clutches her to his chest. It sounds like chanting, a low murmur interspersed with clicks and grunts.

"*Bozhe moi...*" Mrs. Mirskaya marvels at the prospect.

Still affected by the venom, Peter uses the wall to steady himself to his feet. He reaches into his pocket, firmly grips Gungnir, and peers into the darkness of the tunnel that enters the chamber from a sharp angle.

"*Grozhdon kh-r-r-r-eeeeet!*"

That's what the words that come ringing into the chamber sound like to Zeke. Pain shoots through his head as if he's been cracked on the skull, he sees stars – and finds that he cannot move.

The chanting continues, but more softly. Edgar sits holding Fi, stock still. His eyes flit to his sword, but he can't reach for it. Peter's hand remains in his pocket.

The chanting stops, leaving a quiet emptiness that is somehow far more menacing – and there's light in the tunnel, weak at first, then growing brighter, off-white like the color of the stone itself.

Zeke can't speak, but his mind screams – *What now?!*

A slender hand, covered in shining blue scales with claws of red, slides around the corner. Light radiates from the stone at its touch. Zeke can't see the creature's face, but a shadow is cast on the far wall of the tunnel entrance – the shadow of a lizard-like head, which opens its mouth and hisses. The outline of a prehensile forked tongue flickers out to taste the air between sharp curved teeth. The creature moves closer. He wants to squeeze his eyes shut, but he can't. It steps around the corner.

Zeke would gasp if he could – not from fright – but because he's suddenly faced with the most beautiful woman he's ever seen.

* * *

Even if he could move, Zeke doesn't think he would, his attention is drawn so forcefully to the woman who just entered the chamber.

Nearly six feet tall, with an exceedingly slim waist and long slender legs, she could be a runway model – but different. *More*, somehow. Like royalty – no – a *goddess*.

Her feet are bare, toenails polished red like the fingernails of her hands. The same deep red as the pendant held at her neck by a fine golden chain. Her skin is smooth and glowing – and Zeke can see a lot of it. The floor length, shimmering blue robe she wears is near-nude sheer, hanging loosely from straight proud shoulders, clearly revealing high round breasts – and the rest of her.

Even though Zeke's paralyzed, he feels himself blush – so he concentrates on her face. She looks to be maybe fifty years old, but any lines in her face just make her more striking. Her hair is deep brown, almost black, held in a bun, and on her head sits a chaplet of finely wrought gold. She has high cheekbones, full lips, thin sweeping eyebrows, and eyes that tilt up slightly at the outside. Gleaming eyes of burnished gold. Sagacious, fierce, and ravishing. Eyes that can draw you in or pierce your soul.

She walks straight to Peter, moving with such grace she seems to float. Her bare feet make no sound. She stops inches from him and brushes his hair back with an elegant hand. There is no fear in his eyes, only astonishment.

"Pater," the woman purrs in a voice as lovely as the rest of her. She places a hand behind his neck, slips another behind his back, and pulls him into a deep kiss. She leans him back like a dancer dipping a partner until he's horizontal to the floor. The stone wall behind them glows with soft light, as does the floor beneath. After what seems an eternity she breaks the kiss, looks Peter in the eye. His expression hasn't changed – still astonishment.

"You taste like spider," she says, and drops him flat on his back.

The woman straightens, waves her hand and says three words that Zeke doesn't comprehend. He realizes he can move again – but he isn't sure he should. Edgar, Mrs. Mirskaya and Mol twitch, now free from the paralysis as well. Mol backs away and sits quietly, head bowed.

Peter sways to his feet. "Pratha..." he breathes, "how is this possible?"

She caresses his cheek. "I seem to remember someone very close to me, and wise, or so I thought, once telling me—"

"—anything is possible," Peter whispers.

"Milady?" Edgar speaks, his eyes wide in wonder.

"Sir Galahad," she beams. "It is good to see you."

"It is Edgar these days, milady," he croaks. "But you, my Lady Lyne, are... have always been..." He swallows to assuage the constricting dryness in his throat, *"The Prathamaja Nandana?"*

She nods ceremoniously.

Peter looks quizzically from Pratha to Edgar. "I wasn't aware you two were acquainted. How is *that* possible?"

Edgar looks sheepish. "Milord, I was sworn to secrecy, but even if I were to speak of it, I did not know milady was... who she is... until just this moment."

Pratha smiles at Zeke, who gulps, feeling his whole body flush. Her eyes fall on Mrs. Mirskaya. She nods curtly, "Sister," and offers a hand.

Mrs. Mirskaya eyes her warily, but takes it and stands. "Sister," she greets curtly in return and kisses Pratha grudgingly, a sharp peck on each cheek. There is obviously a deep seated sisterly friction between them, but Mrs. Mirskaya's concern for Fi over-rides her animosity. "We need your help," she says bluntly.

Pratha eyes Fi in Edgar's arms. "I see." Zeke scoots aside as she kneels. She places a hand on Fi's forehead, closes her eyes, mutters more incomprehensible words. Fi's fitful breathing slows, becoming deep and even. "Turn her," Pratha orders. Edgar does so. She examines the wounds while Peter goes to Edgar's long bag.

Zeke finds the wherewithal to speak. "She was bitten by Max." He clears his throat at the unexpected cracking of his voice.

"The Spider," Pratha retorts. "I can see that for myself, young man, thank you." Even when terse, her voice is seduction sonified, and her breath, the intoxicating fragrance of lilacs, eucalyptus, frankincense resin and musk. Zeke's head swims. She touches him on the arm and an electric shiver runs right to his loins. "Move away. Quickly," she commands.

Zeke lurches to his feet, staggers back. He shakes his head and his whole body follows. *What the hell?* He's been aroused plenty of times in his life, but he hasn't felt this way, all aquiver and light-headed, since he was twelve, a young boy in puberty, when fourteen year old Ginny Radcliff kissed him on the mouth and let him touch her breasts in the back seat of the school bus. He turns away to adjust himself in his pants.

"Galahad, leave her to me," Pratha says.

"Yes, milady." Edgar slides out from under Fi. Peter places a blanket beneath her head. Edgar gets to one knee, grunting at the pain in his ribs, supporting his broken wrist with his other hand. Pratha takes hold of his crooked arm, inspecting the unnatural lump and discoloration. "It's nothing, milady," Edgar dismisses.

Pratha takes Edgar's hand in hers, runs her other hand down his arm, saying more esoteric words. Without warning, she yanks, setting the bone back in place with a sickening *crunch*. Edgar doesn't wince. There is no pain.

"Boy," she calls to Zeke without looking up.

He knows she must be talking to him. "Yes... ma'am?" He cringes as his voice cracks again.

"Gather some of The Spider's web and bind Galahad's arm."

Zeke responds immediately, "Yes ma'am."

Edgar picks up his sword with his good hand and joins Zeke as he gathers the longest strips of web that Peter removed from him earlier.

Both of them keep an eye on Fi. Pratha licks her fingers and jams one into each of Fi's wounds. Fi groans. Zeke moves to protest but Edgar catches his arm, shakes his head. Pratha chants more strange words and Fi arches her back, inhaling sharply.

"How long ago was she struck?" Pratha asks Peter, who turns to Edgar.

"Seven minutes, fourteen seconds," Edgar answers without hesitation.

"And she still lives," says Pratha, impressed. She pulls her fingers from Fi's wounds, presses her hands over them. "There is no time to explain," she states firmly, "but do not be alarmed." Before Peter can respond, she shouts. If Zeke knew Sumerian, he'd know she said, "Come forward!"

From the shadowy corner of the tunnel where she arrived shuffle three odd looking men. The first enters in a stoop then straightens to what has got to be eight feet in height. He has sharp Asian features, a freakishly long face and lime-green eyes. The other two are maybe six feet tall, but one is dark skinned with big black eyes and extremely muscular, while the third, who stands between the others, has pink eyes, close-cropped white hair and a goatee. They're all dressed in khaki long-sleeved shirts, pants, and jungle boots.

Edgar tenses, gripping his sword. Mol commences to growl. Mrs. Mirskaya curses under her breath.

"Curiouser and curiouser," says Peter. The men avert their eyes as if pained by his scrutiny. "Trueface, gentlemen, if you please."

The men shimmer and turn into creatures the likes of which Zeke has never seen.

The giant Asian man now looks much like an alligator, but with a slimmer snout and standing upright. The ridged tail he drags behind him is almost as long as he is tall.

The dark muscular man is a monster right out of The Brothers Grimm or H.P. Lovecraft – covered in hair, with long claws, tall fuzzy ears, wet black nose and a horrible wide mouth full of jagged teeth. Zeke's first thought is that it's another werewolf – but this guy's much more frightening. He looks a lot like a hyaena, only uglier.

And the light-skinned man with the goatee – this one Zeke thinks he recognizes from drawings, literature, and old B-movies about Satan worship. He softly exclaims, "Baphomet."

Astounding Zeke even more, the goat-creature bows with a regal sweep of his horns. "At your service."

Edgar holds his sword at the ready. "Forgive me, milady, but I am not fond of the company you keep." Mrs. Mirskaya sets her fists at her hips and grunts in agreement.

"They are gifts, for Father," says Pratha, laying a hand on Fi's clammy forehead. "You have nothing to fear. We have an understanding. They do as I say, nothing more, and they do not die."

Peter lays a hand on Edgar's shoulder, who lowers his sword but doesn't sheathe it. He takes a bold step toward the creatures and all three drop to one knee.

Pratha has no patience for the formalities. "Idimmu Mulla, my bag." The dark hairy fellow with jagged teeth shivers and yelps, but speedily pulls a leather bag from his shoulder. He cowers until Peter nods for him to pass, then takes the bag to Pratha, careful to avert his eyes from both her and Peter – but his gaze falls on Fi and he's frozen in place. Pratha doesn't seem to notice, but Zeke does.

She takes the bag from the beast, then says, "Pitch the devices into the water." The creature yips nervously and shuffles to the edge of the well, pulling the strap of another shoulder bag over his head. Peter steps to him and he cowers again, holding the bag open for Peter to see. It's full of explosives that Kleron and Max had planted in the tunnels.

"I-I-I de-de-activated them myself," Dimmi stutters, still not looking at Peter. "I did it, I did."

"Dump them, Dimmi," Peter says. At these words, Dimmi lets his eyes meet Peter's, but he sees no kindness there. He yips again and up-ends the bag, spilling its contents.

At the sound of the devices splashing, Ao Guang leans forward ever so slightly to peer into the well. The vertical pupils of his eyes slowly contract as the smell of it reaches his nostrils.

Dimmi closes the bag and can't get behind Baphomet quickly enough. Once there, he crouches low, shaking uncontrollably.

Zeke might feel sorry for the beast, which is obviously terrified, if he hadn't seen how it looked at Fi.

Pratha retrieves a folded leaf from her bag, opens it and smears an amber greasy substance on Fi's wounds. "Boy," she calls again, and tosses the leaf to the floor next to him and Edgar. "Apply that to Galahad's wrist and wrap it tightly."

Zeke squats to the leaf. Edgar crouches next to him, making sure he has a clear view of Ao Guang, Baphomet and Dimmi, and that his sword is held between him and them.

Pratha speaks again. "Ao Guang, my kit."

The alligator-monster rises and shrugs to swing an ornately carved wooden chest he was carrying on his back into his enormous clawed hands. He lumbers past Peter to Pratha, gets down on one knee and presents it to her, bowing his head so the end of his long toothy snout nearly touches the floor. He rises, bows to Peter, who doesn't respond, then returns to his place.

Along the way, Ao gets a better look at the water below. From its dark tint, scent and movement, he can tell deep below is fresh running water. *A way out.*

Baphomet hasn't taken his eyes off the floor, but Peter watches him carefully. He addresses him in Latin, "*Et tu* Baphomet?" The Goat's eyes meet his. "After my tolerance following the treachery at Ragnarök, my faith in you in Éire, the lenience I showed during your millennial shenanigans in Old Europe and the Levant, you betray me, yet again?"

Baphomet nods obeisantly. "Only under threat of death, Pater."

Peter's voice has an edge of imminent reckoning. "And there's no threat here, I suppose?"

"I have betrayed no one, Pater."

Peter smirks. "Not *yet*." Baphomet begins to respond, but Peter cuts him off. "Silence! Wag your silver tongue without being asked and it will be removed. *Intueri?* (Understand?)"

"*Quidem, patrem meum* (Understood, my father)." He falls silent and returns his gaze to the floor.

Zeke doesn't know why it should be, after everything else that's happened, but it's really weird to see these creatures talk.

He begins applying the slimy foul goop to Edgar's wrist, glad to have something to keep himself busy. "What do you think this is? Smells like Brussels sprouts and rotten beef."

Edgar shakes his head. "I've found it best not to ask, lad."

Zeke picks up the strands of web. "Don't we need a splint?"

"Not necessary," Edgar informs him. "One of the perks of being Thirdborn. A simple break like this will be healed in a day or two."

Zeke binds Edgar's wrist, but his eyes keep flitting to Fi, and Pratha crouched next to her, who's pulling corked bottles of odd contents, herbs, and God knows what else from her wooden chest and mixing them with mortar and pestle. Peter sits on the other side of Fi, holding her hand, and Mrs. Mirskaya kneels next to him.

"Fiona is in the best possible hands, lad," says Edgar. "From what I understand, there is no healer more skilled in all the worlds."

"She'll be all right, then?"

Edgar watches Zeke work the web around his arm. "You have the right to know. It's said that none have ever survived the bite of Maskim Xul, not even Firstborn." Zeke tugs a little too hard on the makeshift bandage. "But," Edgar adds quickly, "none have had this level of care, and so soon after the wounding. We are truly blessed."

Pratha hands a small wad of leaves to Peter. "Chew this well." Peter unwraps what appears to be a big ball of wax and pops it into his mouth.

"Water," says Pratha as she holds the wound on Fi's leg open with one hand and applies the paste she's been preparing with the other. Peter removes a pink water bottle from Fi's pink pack and drinks some. "Not for you," Pratha admonishes. He recaps the bottle. "You're slipping, old Father."

"How so?"

"You were entirely unprepared for my approach, and you enchanted rather easily when I uttered the primal verse."

"Hmph," Peter scoffs. "You know I can't be enchanted, not even by you. I was, however, taken by surprise. In my defense, I had just tasted The Spider's venom, and I'm still recovering from a deep mentia which lifted only earlier today."

She raises a perfect narrow eyebrow. "Just today? Perhaps I misspoke. Still, you are fortunate it was only me."

"*Only you?* After almost two myria without so much as a note, allowing all of us to believe you were probably dead, you decided, today of all days, to pay us a visit – with The Gharial, The Hyaena, and *The Goat?* Or is it fate? Perhaps God's plan, as Edgar would have me believe? Maybe it was *magic.* We spoke your name out of dire need and —poof!—you appeared with your new best friends."

"All of the above," she replies with equal sarcasm. "Apparently these three were sent by their master to recruit or assassinate some unidentified beastie in the deepest darkest jungles of the Amazon rainforest." She flashes a sly smile. "They found *me.*" She eyes Ao Guang, Baphomet, and Dimmi, who quickly duck lower.

Zeke can hear Peter and Pratha conversing, but has no idea what they're saying. "What language is that?" he asks Edgar.

"One of the old Hindu dialects," Edgar replies.

"How many languages do they speak?"

"All of them."

"You're pulling my leg."

"I am not," Edgar insists. "I'm not kidding either."

"How many do you speak?"

"There are as many as 6,900 distinct languages still spoken in this world today. I can read, write and converse fluently in 637, plus many more dialects, but I understand them all when I hear them."

Zeke doesn't know why he should be surprised, but he is.

"It's quite easy for Firstborn," Edgar continues. "They're hardwired that way, so to speak. It's a little more difficult for me, and much harder for regular folks like you. No offense."

"None taken." Just learning the rudimentary Greek and Latin for his studies and the smattering of Spanish he knows was like having his teeth pulled. He ties off the bandage on Edgar's arm. He even made a sling, which he adjusts around Edgar's neck. "How's it feel?"

"Like new, thank you," Edgar replies. "You have some training in field dressing."

"A little, when I was doing volunteer work. Three months in South America, then three in Africa. I was kind of a free agent, setting up temporary care units mostly. Red Cross, some with Doctors Without Borders, local groups too."

Edgar lets out a low sharp whistle and Mol approaches. Edgar begins applying the medicinal goo to Mol's deeper cuts. Mol sniffs the stuff, sneezes and shakes his head, but tolerates the procedure.

Zeke helps, searching through Mol's hair to locate injuries, but continues to glance at Pratha, crouched over Fi, plying her magic, or practicing the most advanced medicine ever known. He gets the feeling it's probably a little of both.

Pratha opens Fi's mouth, sprinkles a mixture of herbs and powders on her tongue. "Pour," she says to Peter. Peter lifts Fi's head and tilts the water bottle to her lips. Pratha holds Fi's mouth closed and rubs her throat, forcing her to swallow.

"Kleron was here," says Peter.

"I have a sense of smell," she retorts. "Your glorious 'Morning Star.' Up to something fiendish, no doubt. And The Lier in Wait serves him?"

"So it seems."

"Maskim Xul has never followed another. He didn't happen to tell you why he's chosen to now?"

"I'm afraid not. Since the death of his wife there's no one to temper his cruel predilections, and he has even less love of the watoto."

"I received word of her demise."

Mrs. Mirskaya interjects sadly, "A terrible loss for us all." She speaks in the same language they do, with no trace of a Russian accent.

Peter momentarily gazes into the past, then continues. "Zadkiel, who is calling himself Kabir, was taken by Max, but he is with us now. He'll meet us shortly." He considers the explosions. "If he is able." He looks at Pratha, who is intent on her treatment of Fi. "Kleron has gathered an army of wampyr and werewolves, from more worlds than this, from the looks of them." Pratha shrugs as if they are inconsequential. "The Cerberi accompany him as well."

"I heard they had a falling out."

"Reconciled, or so it seemed. Cù Sìth appears to have come to our cause."

Pratha looks up in wary surprise. "Now *that* is curious news. And you trust him?"

"His actions support his claim, but there has been no time to interrogate him. I cannot say." He thinks back on what he remembered just before Cù Sìth attacked Kleron and his Cerberus brothers in order to save Kabir – Cù climbing down the drainpipe by the swimming pool, a broken security camera high in the corner above him. "Earlier today, Kleron assaulted the hospital where I was staying. I believe Cù may have been trying to help us even then, in his way."

"Come to think of it," says Mrs. Mirskaya, "it was he who distracted Surma and Wepwawet, making my escape from them possible. It could have been intentional. But this is *Cù Sìth* we're talking about." She grimaces and shakes her head. "Very hard to believe."

Peter is pensive, but proceeds. "We have no knowledge of who else Kleron may have targeted. Edgar – Galahad, Mokosh and I have had little to no communication with the Deva for some time. We know where only a handful abide, and have no way to contact most of them. Edgar attempted to get in touch with The Twins today, with no luck. The same for Freyja."

"I wouldn't be overly concerned about Freyja," Pratha replies, rubbing Fi's temples. "She is feisty, that one."

Mrs. Mirskaya grunts in agreement, then says to Peter, "Edgar tells me that Samson is dead."

"Yes," Peter says quietly. "An honorable passing."

Mrs. Mirskaya glowers at Pratha. "Of course you would not know our brother Samson. He was born long after you ran off."

"I heard tales of his deeds," Pratha replies flatly. "I am sorry for your loss."

By the dour look on Mrs. Mirskaya's face, she doesn't accept her condolences.

Pratha glances affectionately at Edgar. "I'm gladdened to see Galahad is with you."

Peter replies with fondness and gratitude. "He's been invaluable to me."

Pratha studies Fi's face like she's some kind of scientific specimen. "And who is this one?"

"Her name is Fi," says Peter. "Edgar's ward."

"Hmm," she hums, in much the same way Peter did when he wanted to annoy Fi and Zeke.

"Pater," Mrs. Mirskaya chides. Her speech slips back into English with a Russian accent. "It is no secret to Pratha. She can see." She addresses Pratha with glad pride. "This is Fiona Megan Patterson. Last of the Firstborn. Our new baby sister."

"The *last daughter*," says Pratha. "And she is a good one?"

Peter gazes at Fi's wan features. "The best."

"*Starshaya sestra* (big sister)," insists Mrs. Mirskaya, "you must do all within your power to save her."

Pratha replies curtly, "Of course. Why wouldn't I?"

Mrs. Mirskaya scowls at her and Pratha returns the challenge with a sternly raised brow.

Peter attempts to avert the pending sibling confrontation. "These attacks are meticulously coordinated," he tells Pratha. "There has been no open, organized aggression of this kind since The Second Holocaust – which you almost missed entirely, come to think of it." He watches her take a sheaf of leaves from her box. "I never got to say it then, though. Thank you for your help, in the end."

Pratha shrugs. "I was bored." She begins applying a sticky orange substance to the leaves. "Sounds like this is where the action is now," she says lightly, then raises her voice for Baphomet to hear. "I must thank The Goat for inviting me to the party. I might have missed this as well." Baphomet nods cordially as if that was his intention all along.

"Have you questioned him?" Peter asks. "He's long been Kleron's number one."

"Only enough to find out where you might be located," she answers. "I thought I'd leave the rest to you."

"How did you journey here?"

"In grand style, I must say, by mtoto standards. One of those flying machines called a helicopter, then a private jet and a large automobile – a limousine, I believe. The Goat has quite the resources, you know."

"No, I did not," says Peter, questioning the wisdom of isolating himself from the Firstborn and the goings on of the world for so long. "There is more you should know."

"And what might that be?"

Peter tells her about Mahisha and Tengu-Andrealphus coming back from the dead, and the locusts on other worlds.

For the first time since she arrived, Pratha's expression becomes grave. "Even Lucifer has not the lore to accomplish these things," she responds solemnly. "At least, he never had..."

Peter's eyes meet Mrs. Mirskaya's as they consider the grim possibilities.

Having finished treating Mol, Zeke and Edgar sit quietly, watching and listening, though Edgar still keeps an eye on Pratha's three companions.

"Edgar, sir," Zeke whispers, nodding at Pratha. "Who *is* she?"

Edgar replies in a conspiratorial tone. "Until today, I knew her only as the Lady Lyne. My boy, she was my mentor. She taught me how to be a knight. Truly taught me, like none other could, not even Launcelot, my father. The same as she trained Sirs Eglan, Reginus, and Ewain before me."

"And she's Firstborn?"

"Oh yes. I always suspected, but now I know it to be true. And if I am not mistaken, it was her presence that caused The Bat and Maskim Xul to beat such a hasty retreat."

"They're that afraid of her? Those two?"

"Oh yes."

"But they confronted Peter like that. I mean, he's the strongest, isn't he?"

"He is, by far. But she has powers that Peter does not, that he cannot. She's also—obviously—female, a daughter. Very rare. Very strong. And she's *old*, lad."

"Older than Kleron?"

"Aye."

"Older than Max?"

"I don't know what knowledge you have of geological history, but she was born when all the land mass of the earth was last together as one continent, what's now referred to as Pangea." He gazes at Pratha with reverence. "She is *The First Daughter*, perhaps the eldest surviving True Ancient, over 250 million years of age."

"Jesus Christ..." Zeke exclaims.

Edgar gives him a look, but lets it pass. "True Ancients are those who lived through what they've come to call The Cataclysm. You might know it as the K-T Extinction Event that destroyed the dinosaurs, 65 million years ago.

"What I know of her was passed to me by Peter and the handful of Firstborn I have met," Edgar continues. "She disappeared almost 20,000 years past, after the last of the Great Wars, The Second Holocaust, but stories of her were carried the world over by those who survived.

"It was she who inspired the Hebrew tales of Lilith, as well as the Babylonian's Tiamat, the Great Mother Serpent, described as both creatrix and beast of chaos, neither of which are entirely true. But they are not entirely false, either. The Sumerians of the same region revered and feared the memory of her as Ama Kashshaptu, 'Mother Witch.'

"To the tribes that became the Aztecs she was the fabled Coatlicue, Teteoinan, Cihuacoatl, and Toci, the last of which translates to 'our grandmother.' The earliest peoples of the Indus Valley knew of her as none other than Kali, The Dark Mother, but before that Saraswati, goddess of knowledge, and Satarupa, the one of 'a hundred beautiful forms,' in addition to Durga and Maha Nigurna Shakti – whom I mentioned as the benefactor and executioner of Mahisha. She was Naunet, Amaunet and Mother Snake Goddess to the Egyptians, and to the ancient Slavs, Baba Yaga, a magical crone of ambiguous nature, at once kind and dreadfully cruel.

"Her names are countless and legends abound, some more veritable than others – but that woman there, Zeke, my lad, is quite literally The Mother of Dinosaurs."

Zeke stares at the beautiful woman who is calmly applying leaves to Fi's wounds like bandages. His mind would be blown – if there was anything left to blow. "I guess I can see why Kleron and Max are afraid of her, then."

Edgar leans nearer, keeping his voice down. "There is more." Zeke listens closely. "Peter has been known to show forgiveness and mercy, qualities that some consider weakness and have taken advantage of in the past. From what I understand, these are traits The Pratha does not share.

"We have nothing to fear from her, but be wary, lad. In my time with her she always appeared in the form we see now. I have never seen her Trueface, but that is not it." Images of the scaly blue hand and the shadow of the toothy lizard head and forked tongue flash through Zeke's mind. "It is also said she can take the form of your innermost desires, or your darkest fears."

Both of them start as Peter raises his voice, speaking in English. "You know, you two, we can hear every word you're saying."

Edgar stammers, "Well, I just thought the lad—"

"You'll give away all my secrets, Galahad," purrs Pratha, speaking in English as well. Edgar is stymied.

"Fat chance," Peter scoffs.

"I understand that a 'fat chance' is synonymous with 'something that is not likely,'" she replies.

"That is correct. You haven't been completely out of touch with modern culture."

"I steal into the cities now and again." Then she adds coyly, "A girl has needs an anaconda cannot always satisfy."

Edgar sees the look on Zeke's face. He pats him on the knee and rises to his feet. Zeke stands as well, brushing dust from his pants. Then they both turn quickly away at the sight of Pratha yanking Fi's pants off.

"Humans, so bashful," Pratha derides.

Peter fishes a pair of sweatpants out of the pink backpack and Mrs. Mirskaya puts them on Fi. Zeke peeks to see that Fi's decent again, taps Edgar on the arm to let him know. Peter hands Pratha a thin thermal blanket from the pack.

"What about this?" he asks, pointing to his mouth, the gunk he's been chewing for her now a salty, bitter mush.

"Oh, we don't need that," she says, wrapping Fi in the blanket.

"It's not for the girl? To counteract the venom?"

"I needed it softened. It is very old."

"What is it?"

"Nasal mucus of sloth, mostly." Peter spits the glob onto the floor. "No need to waste it," she admonishes, scooping the glob with another leaf. She wraps it and places it in her bag while Peter wipes his tongue with the palm of his hand. "And don't be such an mtoto. You've had much worse in *that* mouth."

Mrs. Mirskaya nods in confirmation. "This is true."

Zeke is astounded. Fi is possibly dying, people are being killed by ancient devils, worlds are being destroyed by demon locusts, there are monsters in the room not fifteen feet away, Peter and his eldest daughter have just been reunited after a stupid-ridiculous amount of time – and they're clowning around, tricking each other into eating boogers.

"Can she be moved?" Peter asks.

Pratha sets her palms on Fi's chest, thumbs and index fingers touching, closes her eyes and expresses one perfect word.

"*Ommmm...*"

The air resonates at its flawless tone. The chamber itself seems to expand. Sparkles of light appear before her, suspended like golden glitter. She inhales them, then leans down and breathes them into Fi's nostrils and open mouth. Some of the pink returns to Fi's gaunt waxen cheeks.

Mrs. Mirskaya looks on with profound esteem.

Baphomet is spellbound. With one simple word, The Prathamaja Nandana has accomplished something the great and powerful Mokosh cannot, that Baphomet and even Master Kleron could never do, a feat beyond Father himself – summon healing power from the cosmos and bestow it upon another.

"She can travel," Pratha says in a weary voice, as if this brief deed has nearly drained her.

"Then we must leave here," Peter responds.

Pratha places her forehead between her hands on Fi's chest and mutters more "magic" words.

Peter rises, gazes down at Fi and Pratha, then approaches Edgar and Zeke.

"Is she going to be all right?" Zeke asks.

"It's too soon to tell." He peers at the floor as if trying to read something in the stone. "I'm deeply sorry for your trials this day, and for those to come. I can only blame myself. I have been lax in my vigil. In fact, I've paid very little heed these last centuries.

"And today, I now understand that Kleron foresaw the possibility I had emerged from the mentia. His intention was to take advantage of the murkiness of thought that accompanies my recovery, to raise my ire and cloud my judgment further. Perhaps I should have sent you into these tunnels before he arrived, but he obviously knew of them and planned on us retreating here in hopes of trapping me – in fact, he wanted us to know he was coming, perhaps hoping we would flee. When we did not, he was prepared to drive us here with his minions. He expected we might attempt to slip as well and covered our escape to other worlds with the swarms. What these locusts could be, from where they hail, or through what manner of infernal corruption First-born are being summoned from death, I cannot yet comprehend."

"You did what you thought best, milord," Edgar consoles. "That's all anyone could do."

"I am not *anyone*." Peter places a hand on Edgar's shoulder. "I may be limited in this form, but I am not diminished. Be assured, I will not underestimate Kleron again."

After a moment of silence, Zeke asks, "So, what's the plan?" Though he expects an answer, he's taken aback by Peter's brightly determined gaze.

"The Deva must be found," Peter pronounces firmly, his eyes burning with staunch intent. "*It is time to gather the Warriors of Old.*"

Edgar bows his head in honor and humility.

The intensity in Peter's eyes diminishes and he speaks in solemn trepidation. "If any still live."

Baphomet observes attentively. The parvulus boy, the Thirdborn cavalier and The Hound of War pose no threat. The wounded girl is Firstborn but young, an unknown commodity, and she may not survive. Mokosh and The Prathamaja Nandana, however – *two* Devi, female Firstborn who stand with Father – *and* The Pater himself... Formidable, very formidable. The odds may be rising against him, but as obstacles become clearer, so do possibilities to counter them. He strokes his goatish beard with the finger-hooves of one hand, recalling one of the most important lessons he taught his young apprentice, Niccolò Machiavelli: 'Whosoever desires constant success, must change his conduct with the times.' Baphomet will come up with something. He always does. He is, after all, *Baphomet.*

He notices Ao Guang staring vacantly into the well and gets the feeling The Gharial is about to do something very, very foolish.

Ao Guang's gaze, his whole being, is drawn to the water, his natural element. His reptilian-Firstborn brain squirms with his own plan. *I must escape and find Master Kleron. I will tell him what I have seen – and of the failure of The Goat. Baphomet will fall from the Master's grace, and I, Ao Guang, will be made Asura Khan in his stead!*

He launches himself and dives into the well.

Mol barks an alert; Edgar shouts, "Hoy!", but Pratha has already sprung into an acrobatic backflip and plunges after The Gharial. Peter rushes to the edge, followed closely by Zeke and Mol. Edgar moves more cautiously, keeping an eye on Baphomet and Idimmu Mulla, brandishing his sword, while Mrs. Mirskaya remains with Fi.

Dimmi whimpers, looking to Baphomet with wide terrified eyes.

Baphomet shakes his goat head coolly. *Very foolish indeed.*

A sudden violent thrashing sends water splashing up into the chamber. Zeke leaps back, but Peter stays where he is. Dimmi ducks behind The Goat. The pool becomes still. Tense moments pass before the surface is broken.

Pratha is only a fraction of Ao Guang's size but she treads easily up the steps, dragging him by the snout with one hand. She reaches the floor and flips him. His tail smashes a section of walkway above. The Goat and Hyaena duck their heads against falling debris. The chamber trembles with the impact of Ao Guang's long wet body slapping the floor.

That monster must weigh a ton, Zeke thinks, *but she handles him like he's just a stuffed animal!*

Pratha straddles The Gharial's back, trapping him between her legs. The crown of Ao's head is partially crushed and thick blood pumps from a ragged wound in his neck. Pratha glares at Baphomet and Dimmi and begins to speak an unspeakable speech. Not as diabolic as what was uttered by Kleron, but of greater portent. They shrink from her gaze.

The atmosphere in the chamber becomes oppressively hot and humid. Pressure builds in Zeke's ears as an ominous primal fog flows from the tunnels, oozes over the floor and fills the well. With it come thick rich scents of fetid water, rotting vegetation, musk, mud and blood. There's the odor of ozone as well, and a crackling energy in the air. The room tilts, the walls spin around him, Pratha goes out of focus. Zeke presses his hands to his ringing ears and clenches his eyes shut.

* * *

When Zeke opens his eyes, the group is standing in the dark glade of a swamp that can only be described as prehistoric, ankle deep in black water that slithers with unseen horrors. In a circle around them, where the walls of the chamber had been, glistening black megaliths project from the ground, deeply engraved with elaborate runes. A fire burns brightly in a rock-ringed pit in the center.

Eyes of red and yellow peer ravenously from the surrounding vegetation. Gargantuan trees draped in hoary vines, ferns the size of houses. Zeke removes his hands from his ears. The ringing is gone, replaced by hoots, growls and sounds of branches snapping in the undergrowth beyond the glade.

The sky sparkles with more and brighter stars than Zeke has ever seen. A monstrous webbed-winged terror looses a bone-chilling wail as it flaps across an impossibly large moon.

Peter and Mrs. Mirskaya are unfazed by the new surroundings. Baphomet and Dimmi remain cowering. Mol creeps timidly to Edgar's side, who's every bit as astonished as Zeke.

Pratha still straddles the alligator-monster she called Ao Guang. But she's changed. Completely nude, sheer gown and chaplet gone, her long dark hair flows freely over milky white shoulders. Zeke blinks and she has blue skin, a red bindi gem on her forehead – and four arms. She wears a tall headdress, a necklace of shrunken heads and a skirt of severed human limbs. In a flash she sports a square golden helmet, has shimmering blue feathers on her shoulders and along the outside of her arms, and a wicked, whipping tail. Another flash and she's robed in gold and has the head of a cobra. Then she's an old crone, then a coiled serpent. Other aspects flicker. Goddesses, demons and monsters from every age known to humankind, and many unknown. Then The Prathamaja Nandana appears in what Zeke realizes must be her Trueface.

She's built much the same as in her human cloak, svelte and long-legged, but covered in sparkling blue scales, lighter colored and softer-looking on her belly, breasts and neck. The claws on her hands and feet gleam red, and she has a tail, long, slim and lashing. A ridge of dark scales runs from the crest of her skull down the center of her back to her waist. Her face is lizard-like, her nostrils flared holes, teeth curved white razors, and articulate tongue forked and flickering. In the center of her forehead is a dime-sized dot of bright red scales. And she still wears the red pendant at her neck, as she has through all her transformations.

Her eyes are vertical ellipses, wider and less alien-looking than the thin reptilian slits of Ao Guang, but still golden, intense, provocative.

"Whoa..." whispers Zeke, completely unaware he's spoken aloud until Edgar whispers back,

"Aye."

Pratha grips The Gharial's snout as her incantation continues. His skin shrivels beneath her hands, blackens and splits. He struggles as the pestilence spreads over his head and down his neck, but cannot escape her grasp.

Peter only has time to say, "Pratha," before the Firstborn known as Ao Guang, god and monster of legend, a being who has walked this earth for 53 million years and could snatch the life from even Cù Sìth with a snap of his jaws, has his head ripped from his body with a single wrenching twist, like he's just a stuffed animal.

MENDIP HILLS 6

"Don't let go."

The White Watcher – Fintán mac Bóchra – The Falcon – stands near the base of the cliff, a long pack strapped to his back, Bödvar Bjarki's giant sword, Kladenets, secured beside it.

On top of them both, Myrddin Wyllt clings tightly. "Sound advice," he replies. "Obvious, but sound." He now has a snug woolen cap, like his favorite one of old, tugged down over his ears. Another gift from Fintán.

Myrddin glances back at the cave – or, where the cave *was*. After Myrddin had eaten, rested, and Fintán attended to the bite of The Leech, he'd laid hands upon the stone, spoken words and collapsed the entire cavern. The cavern that was his involuntary home for more than 1,500 years.

With a mighty hop and *whoosh* of wings they ascend into the dark sky over Somerset County. Myrddin watches the Mendip Hills recede below, sees bright clusters of lights where he knows there once were villages, and in places where there were none. Lights that spread for miles. *Things* have *changed*.

He would ask about it. He'd ask many things, but speaking with the wind rushing over them at this speed would be difficult, and needless. There will be time. There is always time. For now he's content with the first crimson glow of the sun about to rise, the cool wind on his face. The wind of freedom. And it is enough.

The Falcon banks and soars out toward the Atlantic. They aren't certain where their journey will take them, Fintán and Myrddin Wyllt. But they know one thing. They must find their father.

And The Madman has a sworn duty to seek out his grandson. Sir Galahad. The Perfect Knight. He promised.

FLOWERS & FIGS 18

Zeke watches his feet shuffle one after the other on the damp tunnel floor, thinking back on their preparations to leave the hub chamber.

After the gruesome beheading of Ao Guang, the prehistoric swamp disappeared and they were right back in the chamber. Edgar explained it was a hallucination induced by the archaic verse and psychic sway of The Prathamaja Nandana, a phantasm of memory and imagination like the vision of hell conjured by Kleron.

Pratha kicked Ao Guang's body to slither and splash into the well, then snapped off the end of his lower jaw, stored it in her ornately carved trunk and chucked the rest of the head in the water.

Zeke ponders the bizarre procession ahead of him. Peter, supposedly the oldest living being in the world, the progenitor of all life on the planet, and Fi's *father*, leads the way, wearing Fi's pink backpack and carrying her wrapped in a silver blanket in his arms.

Pratha walks alongside him, cloaked once again as a practically naked, beguiling woman, touching Fi's pale sweaty forehead occasionally and muttering her bizarre words in a language Edgar told him is the First Language, invented by Pratha and Peter together when she was young, almost two hundred and fifty million years ago. Then there's Fi's old babysitter, Mrs. Mirskaya, who owned a Russian Market but also just happens to be the ancient Slavic goddess Mokosh.

The legendary devil Baphomet, to Zeke an entirely fictional character until only an hour or so ago, follows them with his head held high – except when he ducks to clear his horns below an outcropping of rock in the ceiling. Beside him scuffles the grotesque hairy hyaena-thing they call Idimmu Mulla, Dimmi for short, sniveling as if he's being led to certain death. The two of them now carry all of Pratha's belongings.

Edgar, who Fi thought was her uncle her entire life but turns out to be a fucking knight from King fucking Arthur's court, follows a few paces behind them, the fucking Sword of David in his hand. His shield case, no longer needed, he left behind. Mol pads at his heels like any good dog would, except he's *the* Molossus, original Hound of War of the Greeks and something like four and a half thousand years old.

Zeke brings up the rear, backpack heavy on his sore shoulders, the handle of the guitar case containing a handmade Ramirez original clutched in his hand. His legs feel like lead, his head throbs, and his ear aches.

Before he knows it, Peter calls down an "all's clear" and they're climbing a ladder. Following the others, Mol ascends on his own, which at this point doesn't surprise Zeke in the least. Peter Pan and Tinkerbell up top passing out milk and cookies wouldn't surprise him now. *Shit*, he thinks, *before the day's out I might get to ride a unicorn...*

He's suddenly jolted by remorse so intense his knees almost buckle and his ribcage constricts to cut off his breath. *How can I joke like that? How can I even joke when Fi might be dying? She really might be dying. Right now.*

But he can't think like that either. He can't think like that at all or he's just going to curl up and die himself.

He squeezes his eyes shut, forces himself to swallow, to quell the dread expanding in the pit of him, threatening to engulf his breaking pounding heart and hollow him out forever. He tries to control his breathing, to muster what little strength and hope he has left.

"You all right, lad?" Edgar peers down with a look of tender concern.

Zeke manages a nod and meager smile. "Yeah. I'm good. Thank you." He hands the guitar up and climbs, his hands weak on the worn wooden rungs.

He emerges through a hatch in the floor of an expansive boathouse, in the center of which floats a pristine vintage yacht of gleaming wood with shining chrome fixtures. Edgar tells him it's a 57 foot Trumpy Flushdeck, manufactured in 1962, but he isn't listening.

As if in a dream, he watches Pratha usher Baphomet and Dimmi through the main salon of the boat, forward to the cramped crew quarters, speaking to them in words that can only be interpreted as a promise of fatal consequence should they misbehave. Edgar takes a seat outside their door, sword in hand, Mol at his side.

After depositing Fi on a berth in the owner's stateroom, Peter leaves Pratha and Mrs. Mirskaya to look after her. Not knowing what else to do, Zeke follows him out to the aft deck, watches him climb to the bridge and fire up the engines. The tall boathouse doors open automatically and Peter backs the yacht out into the muddy Maumee River.

Zeke has lost track of time entirely. It's still dark, but the rain has stopped. Through the mist and trees he sees a muted orange and yellow glow high on a hill, maybe a half mile upriver. The burning remnants of Peter's house. Tiny blots of blue, white and red blink around it, lights from emergency vehicles that must have arrived while they were busy trying to survive down below. Fallen trees crisscross each other over indentations in the landscape where sections of the tunnels have collapsed, like needles in a deflated pincushion.

Peter swings the boat about and heads upriver in the direction of the house under low throttle. Zeke fights off his weariness and joins him on the bridge. Peter angles the boat to a thin wooded strip of land that forms a small islet near the center of the river. He keeps the boat as close to the bank as possible, peering through the mist.

"Kabir?" Zeke asks.

Peter's throat rumbles but he says nothing. Zeke maintains the silence and keeps watch as well, listening to the soft splash of the bow and lap of the wake on the shore. They make a slow circle of the islet, search the far bank, cut back to the near, then out for another deliberate swing around the islet. No sign of anyone. As they round the side nearest the house, Peter pulls something Zeke can't see from his pocket, studies it in shadow, then flings it ashore. He guns the engines and the boat lunges downriver, heading north-east toward Lake Erie, which Zeke approximates to be about 20 miles away.

Peter stares straight ahead, deep in thought. Still and statuesque in the mist and moonlight, there's something about him that gives Zeke pause. He seems absolutely present but distant at the same time, both rock solid and ethereal, singular and infinite, as if Zeke can perceive with his feeble human faculties only a slice of something that exists in unfathomable dimensions.

In the face of such overwhelming presence and depth, Zeke feels tiny, fleeting, a speck of dust passing on the breeze, utterly humbled and insignificant. "I'm sorry," he breathes.

Peter looks at him. Zeke's breath catches. In those eyes he senses for the first time Peter's incomprehensible age. Eyes set in a skull far too finite to contain his immanent intellect and memory, reflecting thoughts that span back to the immeasurable past and ahead to a troubled future only Peter can envision or comprehend, looking right at him yet through him, lucid and enigmatic.

"I broke my promise," Zeke mutters. Peter's eyes narrow. "I slipped."

Peter's features fold into sadness, a profound sorrow for everything that has ever lived and died, or never lived at all. The burden of the world laid bare, shame and self-recrimination, ageless and inviolate.

Then he smiles. "Get some rest."

But Zeke doesn't leave. Instead, he squeezes the bracing bar at the bridge entrance to steady himself. "I know I can't be one of them..." he says, nodding below deck, but he can't bring himself to say more, already fearing the answer, any answer, though he has absolutely no idea what it might be.

Peter smiles again. "No, you're not one of *them*."

Zeke almost laughs, feeling ridiculous and relieved. But not entirely relieved. There's disappointment as well, and that makes him feel more ridiculous, even stupid.

There *is* something he can hold on to though, crazy, ridiculous and stupid, but *real*. "Then why can I slip?" he asks, doing that little sliding motion with his hand, again afraid of the answer.

Peter looks thoughtful. Zeke's heart skips and thumps as he waits. Then Peter says, "I don't know."

"Really?"

"Really."

"But... you must have a theory."

Peter ponders a moment, then shrugs. "Not really."

Zeke's confused. If Peter doesn't know... But then, there's something oddly comforting in that, as though, if Peter can't explain it, it's okay that he can't either. But that's confusing too. *Oh my head...*

Peter catches hold of him as he sways. The hand on Zeke's arm carries all the soothing, reassuring, all-encompassing power of a loving father cradling an infant child. That's what it feels like to Zeke, anyway. His head is clearing, just a little, and the strength returning to his legs.

Peter says, "You may be just a man, but I'll be keeping my eye on you, Zeke Prisco."

His smile is deep as the sea, firm as the foundation of the earth, radiant as the sun. Zeke blinks at his own bad cliches...

Peter winks. "Get some sleep."

Zeke descends wordlessly from the bridge. Having received no direction from the others and hesitant to knock on the cabin door, he makes his way along the rail to the foredeck where he drops his backpack and sits painfully against the divider between the front windows of the salon. He searches through his pack until he finds a thin insulated coat, and puts it on.

The moist air should feel good on his face. The low rumble of the dual diesel engines, the hush of the bow cutting the water, the subtle rise and fall of the deck should be comforting. But the feelings are lost on him. He's a wreck, absolutely exhausted, mentally and physically, his overfull and addled brain a sluggish morass mulling his own condition and the day's events – including the most mind-bending of them all – what happened when he chased down that man outside the bank, an experience shoved aside by everything else that's happened since, but he knows he'll have to deal with eventually. And tell Peter about.

For now, though, all he wants to do is sleep. But that's not true. What he really wants, would give anything for, is for Fi to be all right. To open her glorious green eyes and smile that Fi smile that beams sunshine, to walk and talk and laugh and kiss him, and never let go.

EPILOGUES

Not twenty minutes after Peter's boat has disappeared around a bend in the river, Kabir crawls from the flowing gloom onto the steep mucky bank of the islet. Muddied and bedraggled, he rubs his aching leg.

This isn't exactly what he had in mind when he considered taking some time off from work, even if he *did* find Father and *is* spending time with family.

"We're too late." Cù Sìth towers atop the rise in human cloak, his black fur coat and hair dripping wet. "They're gone."

Kabir groans. It took long enough to dig themselves out of the rubble of the demolished house, but Cù Sìth insisted on completing yet another task. Then the mtoto authorities arrived and had to be avoided with stealth and caution.

"But I found this." Between thumb and forefinger, Cù holds up a large gold coin, pitted and worn, framed by the ruby glint of his eyes.

Kabir recognizes the token at once, the odd glyph stamped on its face. A Deva sigil. A call to war that cannot go unheeded. Cù Sìth may have some inkling as to what the coin signifies, but the glyphs themselves would mean nothing to him.

Exposed on the precipitous slope in the shadow of the dreaded Moddey Dhoo, Kabir feels acutely vulnerable. He considers plunging back into the river. Not for his own safety, but to try and lose Cù Sìth, on whom he still can't bring himself to rely. But he needs to see the other side of that coin...

As if by providence, Cù flicks it with his thumb, sending it flipping into Kabir's outstretched palm. Kabir keeps his eyes on Cù, not allowing himself to be distracted. Cù drops a makeshift sack of sopping black fur, red and ragged at the edges, dripping incarnadine – the result of his grisly endeavors back at the house. Kabir braces for the assault, but instead of hurtling them both into the river, Cù grips a tree branch for anchorage and offers a hand. After a moment of conflicted deliberation, Kabir takes it.

Cù slings the carcass sack over his shoulder. Kabir inspects the flipside of the coin.

Now he has a clue as to where to find Father. The question is, how are they going to get there?

* * *

Tanuki ran. Over 50 miles, roughly north, through the bowels of the mighty Kaçkar Mountains. Twice the speed the fastest marathon runner could muster, clinging tight to the straps of his pack. Goaded by tragedy, whipped by demons of regret, through winding tunnels he raced, up and down steep inclines and endless switchback stairs, around sweeping ledges, across narrow stone bridges that spanned bottomless crevasses, never slowing until he reached the safe room hidden behind the mountain face that overlooks the Turkish city of Rize on the southern coast of the Black Sea.

He didn't consider opening the secret door to the forested slopes beyond, but dropped his pack, lit an oil lamp, and flew into a frenzy of anguish. Benches, shelves of supplies, a stone table, nothing but the lamp and stool on which it sat escaped his woeful wrath.

Finally he collapsed amongst the wreckage. His wracking sobs became whimpers and he drifted into sleep. But it brought him no reprieve. Tortured dreams of the horrific death of Arges at the hands of Xecotcovach, The Terror Bird. The fall of Asterion. The triumphant cry of Ziz as he plunged after him. And haunting all, like an apparition of contempt, the look on Father's face Tanuki is sure to see when he learns what has transpired.

How long Tanuki thrashed, gnashed his teeth and wept in fitful slumber, he did not know. Then the nightmare changed, and the terror deepened.

Something is coming.

Shuffling, sliding, huffing and wet. A sharp *crack*, then the sliding. *Crack*, and *slide.*

Sprawled face down on the rough stone floor, Tanuki opens his eyes. His sight is soft and uncertain. A stupor of sleep and bereavement, or still dreaming?

Crack, slide.

Paralyzed by dread, he turns his eyes upon the sheer blackness of the tunnel entrance. Burbling, rasping, *crack, slide.* Then the shambling horror breathes his name, the wheeze of death itself.

"T-a-n-u-k-i..."

Abject fear grips Tanuki's soul, but by some inchoate volition he flops over and scoots away in panic, bumping the stool and lamp. The wavering amber flame sets the shadow edges of the doorway quaking like Tanuki's own heart.

Crack, slide.

A tenebrous form nears the entrance, humped and malformed on the floor. *"T-a-a-a-n-u-u-u-k-i-i-i..."*

Wake up! Certain he's still dreaming, Tanuki chokes on bile that rises in his throat, screams in somnambulant depths of despair. *Wake up!*

A gory limb plunges into the light and stabs the floor.

Crack!

Tanuki can't believe his eyes. And this is *not* a dream.

A hand, clotted in grue, each finger ending like half a cloven hoof, clutching a horn with its tip driven into the stone. With a deathly groan, Asterion, The Bull, drags himself into the room, sliding on a greasy slick of his own Firstborn blood.

* * *

Far above the thin skin of atmosphere that shields the earth like a blanket protects a child from unknown terrors of night, the moon keeps its eternal watch in the cold silence of space. Through cloud, rain, and fog, roof, rock, sea and stone, the moon sees. And the moon knows.

The story continues in

PATERNUS: WRATH OF GODS
The Paternus Trilogy, Book 2

Available now on Amazon and Audible

Thank you for reading Paternus!
If you liked the book, please consider leaving a
review on
Amazon or **Goodreads**.
Reviews are incredibly helpful to authors!

Sign up for the
Paternus Books Media Newsletter
at paternusbooks.com
and get your **free** "Even myths have legends" character lineup computer wallpaper and
"Beserker" short story
(free stuff subject to change).
Your inbox will not be e-bombed and your email address will never be shared. Nobody
likes that.

Continue reading for a sneak preview of Wrath of Gods...

WAKE

"*He is dead.*"

"*Don't say that.*"

"*He looks dead.*"

"*Stop it. He's not dead!*"

"*Glupaya devochka, I am meaning 'dead to world,' not* dead *dead.*"

Zeke hears the voices, but it's like they're speaking from another dimension, in slow motion, through a garden hose.

He extricates himself from the sucking black sediment of deepest sleep, relief dawning in his sluggish mind—relief to be emerging from the hellish nightmares that plagued every moment of his slumber. He struggles toward the light of consciousness, then becomes aware of movement below.

Inky black tentacles swell from the void. One lashes out—*slap*, sting and burn. Another grabs his ankle and he's dragged back into the depths, ears ringing with a *whine, whir* and *squeak* like the sound of changing channels on an old-fashioned radio. He screams, soundless, swallowed by darkness.

* * *

Cheap booze. Abandoned buildings. Filthy blankets, flea bites and vomit. Playing guitar with strung-out bands in shitty bars reeking of piss and sour beer. Sticking needles in his arms with shaking hands. Fever sweats and hunger. Ribs cracked by boots in a cold alley. Despair.

* * *

"Come on, lad. You need to wake up now. Rise and shine."

The dull impact of a slap on the cheek.

He's Zeke, he knows it, and he's asleep, somewhere—but he's also someone else, in another place and time.

* * *

A parking garage at night.

A couple stumbles in, leaning on each other, laughing. It's them. The man and woman from earlier nightmares. Nightmares of childhood torment and abuse.

Stepping out in front of them. "Remember me?"

"Unbelievable," the man slurs. "You miss me, ya little fuck?"

The woman laughs. "Bad Zeke! Bad!"

The man laughs with her. "Bad Zeke back for the belt?"

The woman guffaws. A pistol lifts to her face and fires. An explosion of brain and bone.

The man begs. He gets a bullet in the stomach and crumples, whimpering. A knife is drawn and goes straight for the man's groin.

* * *

"Zeke. Wake up!"

Someone's yelling, shaking him. Someone he knows.

A dog barks.

"Milady, perhaps you could...?"

* * *

Scarlet neon. Sickly green light. Washing blood from his hands in a mildewed sink. Splashing his face with rust-brown water. Scrawny arms, tracked with sores. A broken mirror. Bruised and sunken chest, tattooed and pale. Raggedly shaved head and gaunt face. Teeth stained brown between cracked lips twisted in a fiendish grin. Eyes sunken in purple hollows, staring back at him.

Zeke's eyes.

* * *

The voices argue, vaguely familiar. A woman with a Russian accent, an Englishman, and a girl.

But not just any girl.

* * *

Her name clicks in Zeke's mind at the same time his bald double in the mirror screams, "*Fi!*"

Whine, whir and *squeak...*

* * *

Splash!

Zeke sputters, water running from his face and hair. He blinks it from his eyes.

He has a hard time focusing, but makes out the form of a woman standing over him, her lithe body draped in a diaphanous gown of shimmering blue. A pendant of deep metallic red hangs at her neck, and a slim golden chaplet sits atop dark hair pulled back in a tight bun. Sensuous lips quirk up at one corner and keen eyes of burnished gold glint beneath sweeping eyebrows. She bounces a canteen in her hand.

"Like magic," she says in a velvety voice. Zeke's foggy brain is pierced by a vivid memory of wonder and trepidation.

Prathamaja Nandana. The First Daughter.

Next to her is a stocky, dour-looking woman with long, stiff black hair, streaked gray. She wears an ankle-length skirt, blouse and vest. Her overly endowed, peaked chest, propped by thick crossed arms, seems to point at him in accusation.

Mrs. Mirskaya, Fi's old babysitter and employer—who also happens to be Mokosh, the fabled Slavic deity of weather and protection.

Fuck. From one nightmare to another. But this one is real.

Mrs. Mirskaya purses her lips, which causes the sparse hair on her upper lip to poke out like little whiskers, then clucks her tongue behind prominent front teeth. "*Lentyay,*" she says in Russian.

Zeke can barely hear her, doesn't know the word means "bum," "slacker" or "lazybones." Given Mrs. Mirskaya's general attitude toward him, though, he could probably guess.

An elderly gentleman leans in to unbuckle straps from Zeke's shoulders. Mutton chop sideburns, long braided ponytail, proud hooked nose and flinty gray eyes.

Fi's Uncle Edgar.

"Sorry to disturb you, lad," Edgar says. "We have a bit of a situation." But Edgar's voice is muffled and Zeke can't quite make out what he's saying. Edgar hauls him up from a flip-down seat that faces sideways, its back secured to the wall. Once he's certain Zeke isn't going to fall down, he hurries away.

Zeke sways on his feet. "Wait. Situation?" He's disoriented, his muscles stiff and sore to the bone, and his back hurts like hell. He's also shaking, feeling thin, weak, worn out. He pumps a finger in his left ear, which still bothers him due to the clamorous cry of Tengu-Andrealphus, The Peafowl, who attacked them at Peter's house. It doesn't help.

His nose registers mingled smells of plastic and tin, fuel and disinfectant, but his groggy mind can't place them—then the floor bucks and shudders.

Zeke catches himself on the top of the seat, shakes his head to clear his thoughts. His hearing remains weak in his bad ear, but his good ear squeaks and pops. Sound rushes in—the drone of engines and howl of wind. A relentless vibration runs through his heels up his spine. And he remembers.

He's on a plane.

They'd left Peter's estate outside Toledo on a boat, made their way up the river, then across the western end of Lake Erie to Canada. Edgar presented official-looking papers at a dock near Windsor and made a call on the dock master's phone. A black van picked them up and drove them to a remote airfield where the plane was readied. A decommissioned Alenia C-27J Spartan troop transport. Edgar told him he'd "bought it for a song."

Of course Edgar owns a military plane, Zeke's worn-out brain had mused. *He is Sir Galahad. Sir Galahad should own whatever the hell he wants, right?*

Too exhausted to ask questions, Zeke had gone to the hangar restroom to wash up and put on fresh clothes from his backpack. They'd placed Fi on a fold-down cot on the plane, unconscious, ghostly pale, breathing shallow and weak, perilously close to death. Then they were off on the long trans-Atlantic flight to Norway. Going to see Freyja, of all people. *The* Freyja of Norse legend, Edgar had assured him.

Unbelievable.

Well, more *of the unbelievable.*

Zeke rarely left Fi's side during the flight, and Mrs. Mirskaya was always nearby. Peter flew most of the time, but Edgar took over once while Peter sat with Fi, holding her hand in silence.

Zeke couldn't sleep. He didn't want to. For worrying about Fi, but also because every time he dozed off the nightmares of childhood torment and drug-induced misery returned. And memories of murder. Someone else's memories.

He must have finally succumbed, though, because here he is, having one hell of a time waking up. But how could he have let it happen with Fi in her condition? She's been bitten by Maskim Xul, and for all Zeke or anyone knows, she's dying. Aggravated, he shakes himself and slaps his cheeks.

"Hey sleepyhead."

Zeke jumps and whips around to find Fi standing behind him—*standing*—clutching the taut webbing at the back of another seat to keep her balance in the turbulence. Her smile is weak and her red hair a mess, but she's changed into clean sweatpants, tank top, light jacket and hiking shoes—and she's awake—and *alive.*

"Fi!" He grabs her and hugs her. "You didn't die!"

She grunts. "Nope." She hugs him back. "Careful, though. Little sore."

Zeke puts space between them but keeps hold of her arms. "Oh my God." He chokes back tears. "We didn't know if you were going to make it. You okay?"

"I guess. I mean, I feel like shit, and I can barely stand up." She touches the bandaged fang-wounds hidden beneath her sweatpants, on her bottom and the back of her thigh, and winces. "My ass hurts."

Someone brushes past, chortling. "She got bit on the butt."

Zeke and Fi cringe as Dimmi flashes a toothy grin. He's in human cloak, dark-skinned and black-eyed, wearing khaki shirt and pants, and jungle boots, as he'd first appeared in the tunnels beneath Peter's house. He giggle-barks at his own joke.

"Idimmu Mulla!" From near the back of the plane, Pratha's voice comes as a warning. Her golden eyes glare, though she smiles at the same time, as if she wants him to screw up so she can rip his head off. Literally. Just like she did to the alligator-monster, Ao Guang.

Dimmi yips and hurries on his way, carrying a crate in his hands.

"That guy's creepy," says Fi.

"That's Idimmu Mulla. They call him The Hyaena."

"Dimmi, I know. I woke up a couple hours ago. Edgar and Mrs. Mirskaya filled me in on what happened after Max bit me." She shivers at the thought.

"So you met Pratha and Baphomet, too."

"Mmm. Yeah." Fi gazes over Zeke's shoulder, her expression a mixture of contemplation and fear. "The First Daughter, and The Goat."

The plane is entirely open, cabin to tail, the interior nearly eleven feet wide and over seven feet high. It's mostly empty, with red canvas troop seats folded against the walls. In the tail section, Edgar, Baphomet and Dimmi are hurrying to pack a truck that rests on a skid.

Like Dimmi, Baphomet is "cloaked," as Edgar called it, taking on human form. Most likely to keep his horns from inhibiting his movement in the plane's cramped quarters. He's dressed the same as Dimmi, but is extremely light-skinned, with short white hair and goatee—and pink eyes. Fi saw their Truefaces earlier, though, and she's discovered, if she squints and thinks about it, she can see his Trueface now too, like a superimposed image. The backward curving horns that rise above Baphomet's caprine face nearly reach the ceiling, yet they're ethereal, their sharp points somehow passing through the conduits and cabling as he efficiently, almost gracefully, goes about his work with slender fingers that terminate in tiny cloven hoofs, crouching on back-bending legs with cloven feet. Dimmi works on the other side of the truck, and Fi can see his grotesque fuzzy face and big black eyes, high peaked ears and wide mouth full of jagged pointed teeth. She blinks, and they're in human form once again.

The truck is a military Mercedes G Wagon with dual rear axles, its roof support bars and canvas top stowed, the front windshield folded down and latched. Pratha lounges against the wall nearby, overseeing the loading of supplies—and ensuring Baphomet and Dimmi stay on their best behavior.

"What's going on?" Zeke asks Fi.

"Hell if I know," Fi replies, exasperated. "They haven't told me much, and they keep speaking in languages I don't understand. But I think we're going to Norway."

"To find Freyja."

"Yeah. They call her The Mother of Cats and Dogs."

"Really?"

"No, I made it up." Fi's condition has made her cranky, but not entirely subdued her sense of humor. "*Yes*, really."

Her snarky reply catches Zeke off guard. He stares, taking in her sparkling green eyes, and it hits him again—she's *alive*. And, disheveled as she is, right now she's the most beautiful thing he's ever seen.

He grins. Fi scowls, then it occurs to her too. A smile emerges, broadens to a grin of her own. They're *both* alive.

Together, they laugh. Foolish, perhaps, absurd even. But they *need* it.

The shared relief subsides and Zeke wipes a tear from her cheek with his thumb. His hand stays on her face.

Fi notices that Zeke is gaunt, pale, with black circles under his eyes, taken by an occasional tremor.

"How about you?" she asks. "You okay? You don't look well."

Zeke breathes deeply to control the shaking. "I'm okay." Flashes of the horrid dreams stab through his mind, but he mentally swats them away. "Just cold, I think. Or maybe I'm getting a cold."

"Great. Just what you need, right?"

The plane bucks again, knocking them off balance, and an odd voice rises.

Mrs. Mirskaya stands near the far wall, face and arms raised, mumbling ancient words.

"What's she doing?" Zeke asks.

Edgar hustles to them carrying two parachute packs by the straps in one hand and Zeke's big blue backpack in the other. The splint on Edgar's arm is gone, the wrist Kleron broke in the tunnels now healed. "She's reinforcing the storm she's summoned," he says. There's a *snap* of lightning and *rumble* of thunder outside. The plane lurches. Fi and Zeke grab hold of each other and squeeze their handholds tighter.

"A storm?" Zeke says. "Is that a good idea?"

"It will hopefully aid in our escape," Edgar answers. He holds up the parachute packs. "Have you skydived, lad?"

"Uh, no?" Zeke says, looking at the chute packs as if they're severed heads of little green aliens.

"I thought not. Put this on, then." Edgar hands the blue pack to Zeke, who grunts and nearly drops it, because it still weighs a ton. Edgar tosses one chute pack on the floor and dons the other.

"What do you mean, *escape?*" Fi asks, her voice a little shaky.

"Escape from *what?*" Zeke adds, his voice a lot shaky.

"Fighter jets, attempting to force us toward shore," Edgar answers, indignant. "And we were over international waters! They're acknowledging none of my clearance protocols—and my privileges are of the highest order, believe you me." He snugs the chute pack's straps in agitation. "Baphomet believes it's Kleron's doing."

A pall falls over Fi at the mention of Kleron. *Lucifer. The Bat.* Attacking the hospital with his minions, killing Billy, setting all those monsters on them at the house—including the buffalo-beast Mahisha and the screaming Tengu-Andrealphus peacock-thing. Tempting her in the tunnel hub chamber beneath Peter's house. Almost biting Edgar's face off, and ordering that horrible Maskim Xul to bite her.

And Max is a *spider...*

"Whose planes are they?" Zeke asks Edgar. "I didn't know Norway had an air force. I mean, did we make it to Norway?"

"No," Edgar grumbles. "We're off the northern coast of Scotland." Now he's really annoyed. "It's the RAF!" He turns in a huff, but Zeke grabs his sleeve.

"Wait," Zeke says. "How long was I asleep?"

"Just a few hours lad. It's still Monday. With the time change, not yet noon. Fiona woke shortly after you nodded off. I hadn't the heart to wake you." He turns to Fi.

"This young man has barely slept or eaten, or left your side, the entire trip. He needs rest and food." He waves his hand in frustration. "Not this bother."

Edgar marches to where Baphomet and Dimmi have finished strapping the load on the truck and are now covering it with a taut safety net. He pushes a large button in a panel on the wall and the aft ramp of the plane drops like the lower jaw of a very large fish, accompanied by the loud whine of servo motors and increased howl of the wind. The water-laden mist of blue-black storm clouds spirals away behind the plane. Flashes of lightning spark the sky pink and green. It's as if they're looking down the eye of a tornado.

"Oh," Zeke says. "I'm not liking the look of this."

"Me neither," says Fi.

Zeke realizes something. "Where's Mol?"

Fi jerks her thumb toward the cockpit. "Up front, with Peter."

"Have you talked to him? Peter, I mean?"

Fi frowns. She's going to have to speak to him at some point. He *is* her long-lost father, after all. She's just not looking forward to it. "Not yet."

Zeke runs his hands through his hair and groans as he watches Edgar fuss with the truck. "Edgar seems pretty worked up. Is he worried?" Because if Edgar's worried, Zeke figures, they *all* should be.

Fi's attention is drawn to something outside the oval window in the fuselage next to them. "Well, there's something else you should see." She points.

Zeke squints through the window. It's all dark rushing clouds. "What?"

"Part of the reason Edgar's upset, I think. They showed up a while ago. Been communicating with Peter and Pratha using some kind of sign language."

"What? Who? I don't see anything—" The mist rips aside and Zeke jumps back. "Holy fuck!"

"That's what *I* thought."

Flying alongside the plane is what looks like a large man with a white bird's head, wings and tail. On his back rides a skinny old man, stringy white beard flapping in the wind and snug knit cap held to his head with a strip of cloth knotted beneath his chin. His clothing, some kind of robe, is similarly lashed to his body to keep it from blowing away. The old man waves, grinning like mad, but loses his balance in his excitement and grabs hold of the bird-man's feathers with both hands.

"Who is *that*?" Zeke asks.

"More Firstborn. They did tell me that. But these are supposed to be on our side. Edgar called the bird-guy Fintán mac Bóchra. Seemed genuinely excited to see him. The little guy on top, not so much."

"Why?"

"That's Myrddin Wyllt, Edgar's grandfather."

Zeke recalls what Edgar told them about his lineage. His father had been Sir Launcelot du Lac, and regardless of what the fables say, Launcelot's real father was... "Merlin. No way."

The mist thickens, obscuring the view. When it clears again, the figures are gone.

Back by the truck, Edgar whistles toward the front of the plane, startling Fi and Zeke.

They hear a familiar bark and turn toward the open cockpit doorway. Molossus,

Fi's uncle's dog, pokes his big sandy head around from where he's perched in the co-pilot's seat. He *ruffs* happily, jumps down and trots to them.

Zeke greets him with a scratch behind the ears. Mol grunts in reply. His bandages are gone and there's little sign of his battles with the terrible wampyr and werewolves, or his run-in with the locust swarm on another world. Instead, he's wearing a makeshift harness of nylon straps and safety belts.

Zeke tugs on the harness. "What's this?"

Fi says, "No idea. Like I said, they haven't told me much. Mostly 'Be still, Fi.' 'You've been through so much, Fiona.' 'You're lucky to be alive, Fi.' 'You should be resting, dear.'" Mol barks and presses his head against her leg. "Ow!" she exclaims. He barks again, wagging his whole body.

Zeke says, "Guess I'm not the only one who's glad you're okay."

She looks at Mol. "Until yesterday I was convinced he couldn't care less about me." She rubs his head. "All this time, I was wrong." Mol barks louder and licks her hand.

"Molossus!" Edgar shouts. "If you please."

Mol trots to the back of the plane and hops into the front seat of the truck. Edgar clips Mol's harness to straps anchored to hooks on the truck floor.

Zeke mutters, "What the...?"

Edgar strides to them. "Not to worry. He can bite through the straps if the raft doesn't deploy."

Zeke and Fi both open their mouths to ask Edgar what the hell he's talking about, but alarms buzz and red lights spin furiously along the ceiling.

Peter's voice roars through the fuselage. "Incoming!"

"For Heaven's sake," cries Edgar. He shoves Zeke down into the seat, causing Zeke to let go of the blue backpack, which he still hasn't put on, because it's really heavy.

"I have Fiona," shouts Mrs. Mirskaya, smashing Fi against the wall with her body, gripping handholds to either side, trapping Fi's face between mountainous boobs.

In the cockpit, the missile approach warning system burps and blinks on the pilot's console. Peter whips off his headset and flips the switches necessary to jettison the tip tanks—oblong storage containers for extra fuel on long flights, attached to the end of each wing.

Back inside the fuselage, there's a loud *pop* and *clunk* as the tanks break free. Not a comforting sound.

Edgar finishes buckling Zeke in, then flips down the seat next to him and sits. With the parachute pack on his back, the best he can do is hang onto the safety belts to secure himself.

Peter flips more switches, deploying the plane's countermeasures, then jams the throttle forward and leans on the yoke.

. . .

Zeke's heart hops to his throat and his testicles feel like they're crawling up into his kidneys as the plane accelerates and dives.

Fi says, "Mmf!"

The plane banks into a sharp turn.

Fi says, "Brmfp!"

Smothered by Mrs. Mirskaya's bulk, Fi can hardly breathe, and she can't see a thing, but Zeke's eyes, wide in terror, catch sight of Baphomet and Dimmi clutching the sides of the truck to keep from flying out the back of the plane. Pratha, on the other hand, holds onto nothing. Her lips move in a silent chant as she somehow remains upright regardless of the plane's pitch and roll.

Behind them, streamers of light and smoke whirl away through the clouds, trailing from flares and chaff Peter has released in hopes of confusing the guidance systems of the approaching missiles. The flares flash bright as fireworks on the Fourth of July.

Still diving, the plane banks the other way, pressing Zeke hard against the back of the seat. Fi voices another muffled complaint, while Mol barks like a puppy, tongue flapping, tail wagging, as if he's on Mr. Toad's wild ride and enjoying the hell out of it.

The plane slams sideways and quakes, the concussion of a near miss louder than thunder. There's another explosion on the opposite side, then two more above.

The fuselage quivers and groans, but the alarms cease blaring and the overhead lights stop flashing. The countermeasures worked. The drone of the engines drops in pitch as the plane levels out.

"The bloody gall." Edgar drops the safety belts and thrusts to his feet.

Zeke never would have thought the incessant noise of the engines and wind could stand in for silence, but it does. He remembers to breathe and liberates himself from the safety harness. Mrs. Mirskaya releases Fi, whose eyes look far too big for her head.

Free of Mrs. Mirskaya's protective mass, Fi says, "Fuck!"

"Fiona," Mrs. Mirskaya scolds, looking her over. "You are all right?"

Fi glares at her. "Are you *kidding*?"

"You are all right," Mrs. Mirskaya replies, satisfied.

Edgar retrieves Zeke's backpack, which has wedged itself between the skid and the front tire of the truck. "Put this on now, lad." Zeke fumbles the straps over his shoulders, too dazed to question. While Edgar tightens them for him, Zeke glances out the window, fully expecting to see the plane on fire and trailing black smoke. And it is.

The end of the wing is aflame where a broken fuel line from the tip tank has ignited.

"The plane's on fire! The plane's on fire!" he cries.

Peter comes striding from the cockpit. "It's all right," he says. "We're not staying." He twists a finger in the air and shouts in his big Peter voice, "Time to go!" He snatches Fi up in his arms and proceeds to the starboard hatch near the base of the ramp. Mrs. Mirskaya follows, protesting in fervent Russian.

On either side of the truck, Baphomet and Dimmi retrieve pneumatic ratchet wrenches attached to the walls by coiled tubing. They look to Edgar, who nods in confirmation. They remove the bolts that secure the truck's skid to the floor. Mol hangs his head over the door to watch.

Edgar reaches into a storage panel on the wall, takes out his scabbard, sword sheathed, and belts it to his waist.

It occurs to Zeke that Edgar is the only one wearing a parachute. "Um... shouldn't—
"

Peter tugs the hatch open, which multiplies the roar in the plane.

Fi gets a blast of cold wind in the face and an eyeful of yawning storm. "Ohh! Peter?!"

Mrs. Mirskaya shouts in English now. "Papa. She is not well!"

Peter peers down through the clouds. "She'll be fine."

"What?" Fi demands. "I'll be fine *what?*"

Mrs. Mirskaya waggles a finger at Peter. "You do not throw sick person from airplane!"

Fi squeaks, "Throw?!"

Edgar raises a hand and whistles sharply. Baphomet and Dimmi train their eyes on him. So does Mol, who barks his readiness.

"I'm not throwing anybody," says Peter. "You ready?"

Fi shakes her head. "No!"

Edgar holds up two fingers, signaling Baphomet to release the small drogue chute from the back of the truck's skid. It flies out the back of the plane, pops open and twists on its cord in the tailwind. Mol barks and wiggles with excitement.

Fi tries reasoning with Peter. "Um, it might be the first time ever, but I think I agree with Mrs. Mirskaya."

Mrs. Mirskaya props her hands on her hips. "You see, Papa? Listen to Mokosh." She turns to Pratha, who has moved closer to the hatch. "You tell him, *Starshaya Sestra.*"

Pratha shrugs. "He's older than I am."

Edgar drops one finger. Dimmi pulls a lever to release the latches that hold the skid in place. Edgar makes a fist and Baphomet looses the larger extraction chute. It snaps out over the ramp and opens behind the plane with a *whump.*

Skid, truck, Mol and all are jerked out with frightening speed. Mol's thrilled yapping fades as the cargo disappears in the mist.

Edgar places his hand over his heart. "God be with you, old boy." He nods to Dimmi and Baphomet, who jog down the ramp and jump.

Peter faces Mrs. Mirskaya. "She'll be fine." He holds Fi out as if in presentation. His voice rises and pride glints in his eyes. "This is *Fiona Megan Patterson!*"

Fi says, "Yeah but—"

"*Finale Omega Paterna. The final and last of The Father!*"

Mrs. Mirskaya stamps her foot. "Papa!"

"She is *Firstborn!*"

Fi says, "I—WAAAHaaaaah...!" Peter has spun, cradling her tight to his chest, and stepped out the hatch. Fi's cry dopplers to nothing as they plummet away.

Mrs. Mirskaya says some very bad words in Russian while Pratha leans out the door to watch Peter and Fi's descent.

Mrs. Mirskaya yells, "Out of my way, Sister!" and launches herself after them.

Zeke is speechless as Edgar drags him to the hatch. "We've no tandem rig," Edgar explains, "nor parachute large enough to accommodate two persons, should we care to rig one." He straightens Zeke's backpack, clasps the waist belt and pulls it tight. "Pratha's plan is the safest." He places a pair of goggles on Zeke's head. "Most likely."

Zeke finds his voice, which is much higher than he'd like it to be. "Most likely?" He looks to Pratha, who winks, and he breaks into a cold sweat. His voice goes even higher. "What plan?"

"It's a sturdy pack," Edgar says in reply, giving the shoulder straps one last check. "The finest craftsmanship." He snaps the goggles down over Zeke's eyes and gives his shoulders a squeeze. "Chin up, cheerio, and all that." He steps to the hatch and crosses himself.

"Wait!" Zeke pleads.

But Edgar is gone.

Zeke clings to the sides of the hatch, watching in terror as Edgar falls through the clouds, dropping fast—much faster than it looks on TV and in the movies—like he's being sucked away by some powerful invisible force. Which he is. It's called gravity.

Zeke's stomach flops, scalp tightens and vision swims. He squeezes his eyes shut to clamp down the vertigo, but the alarms go off again, screeching, buzzing and flashing.

Strong slim hands take him by the shoulders and spin him around. Pratha puts a hand to his cheek. "Relax," she purrs.

Zeke gulps.

Then her mouth is against his, her tongue slithering between his teeth, coiling around his tongue like a snake on a rat and flicking the roof of his mouth. Searing heat of involuntary passion ignites Zeke's lips, spreads downward to melt his icy gut, inflame his loins and curl his toes.

She pulls away, leaving him barely able to stand. The alarms continue to blare as she places an elegant hand upon his chest, glances over his shoulder to the dark sky beyond, and gives him a good hard shove.

ALSO BY DYRK ASHTON

NOVELS

THE PATERNUS TRILOGY

Paternus: Rise of Gods

Paternus: Wrath of Gods

Paternus: War of Gods

SHORT STORIES

"BERSERKER"

A short story framed as a "missing chapter" from *Paternus: Rise of Gods*. It tells of the time when Bödvar Bjarki finally met his father, many centuries ago. Kindle eBook available for .99 through the title link above, or free by subscribing to the Paternus Books Media Newsletter.

LOST LORE

This free fantasy anthology contains "Deluge," a short backstory in the world of *The Paternus Trilogy* concerning the adventures of Myrddin Wyllt and Fintán mac Bóchra in ancient Ireland at the time of the Great Flood.

ART OF WAR: ANTHOLOGY FOR CHARITY

Includes "Valkyrie Rain," a short backstory in the world of *The Paternus Trilogy* that takes place during the great battle of Ragnarok. Forty of your favorite fantasy authors contributed to this anthology. All proceeds go to Doctors without Borders.

HEROES WANTED

A free fantasy anthology that includes "The Death of Osiris," a short story set in ancient Egypt involving Baphomet, Kabir (aka Hem-hor), and Fintán mac Bóchra (aka Horus).

ACKNOWLEDGMENTS

Writing must be one of the most selfish pursuits there is. Only when it's shared do we crazed scribblers really do anything for others. But then our readers give back in return, more than we could ever bestow upon them, and the cycle of selfishness resumes. You have my utmost thanks.

There are more than a few folks to whom I owe a deep debt of gratitude and must be named. I could never have written, promoted or published this book without each and every one of them.

First, my beta readers. Brother Dillon and lifelong buddy John H., who suffered through every draft of every version. Thank you for your masochistic tendencies, the invaluable notes, and your undying encouragement. My parents, Richard and Harriette Ashton, who also read every draft of every version, and loved them all. Each was perfect and needed nothing more or less. Such is the love and perfection of wonderful parents. Thank you for your limitless tolerance and unconditional support. Nina O. and Mr. Christopher H., who were more like editors than readers, hatchet in one hand, scalpel in the other, neither afraid of my wrath nor seeking my approval. Without you *Paternus* wouldn't be what it is, nor I the writer I am (for better or for worse). A. Dale Triplett (yup, I'm using your full name, Dale). A brilliant author himself, he copy-edited and proofed the living shit out of this thing, finding errors and offering insights no one else had. And they were brilliant. My sister Dianna, whom I know was dreading having to read this but now might be my biggest fan. Never stop giving me crap, Nan. Irina A., your help with all things Russian was indispensable! John D., Vince M., Lee F., Zach P., Elizabeth B., Kati A., Tess L., and Michael E. (who told me to just go for it). All of you read it and have a hand in this. You are more than readers, you are dear friends, and in my mind, might as well be family.

Folks who may or may not have read the book, but helped me tremendously along the way whether they know it or not. My brother Drew and sister Daphne, Simon, Sasha, Maggie, Donovan, Wyatt, Weston, Sven S., Dan and Lisby P., Lt. Col. Joe H.,

Steve A., Mark B., Chris L., Ralph C., Jenny L., Edmund L., Risa C., Ben P., Cynthia B., Jonathan C., Don C., all my grad school pals, Donnie B., Joe & Stephanie S., Clay C., John S., Angus B., Jeff D., Ken S., Michael D., Kevin B., Hank T., Josh R., Rafael R., Jorge A., Heidi H. and Jim W.

Everybody at the local coffee shops for letting me squat for years at a time.

All my wonderful friends on Facebook, Twitter and Instagram, a fun and incredibly supportive bunch.

Each and every one of those special people in Maumee who keep me alive and sane. You know who you are. Especially you, yeah you, Tom T.

If I missed anybody, it wasn't on purpose. Let me know. I'll make it up to you in the next book.

Thank you all.

ABOUT THE AUTHOR

Photograph by Lee Fearnside

Dyrk Ashton is a Midwestern boy who spent some time in Hollywood. He teaches film, geeks out on movies and books, and writes about regular folks and their troubles with monsters.

WHAT IS PATERNUS?

Ashton's debut has been called Epic Urban Fantasy, Mythic Fiction and New Weird Fiction, but on one thing readers agree, "*Paternus* **stands out from the crowd**" (*Bookworm Blues*). Josiah Bancroft, acclaimed author of *Senlin Ascends*, says, "There's just something **wondrous and wide-eyed** about Ashton's flouting of convention and genre ... The result is almost giddy." "I think part of its charm," claims fantasy reviewer Tom Owens, "is that it doesn't really care about being pigeon-holed." Author Steven Kelliher says *Paternus* is "one of the most singularly **inventive, creative and exciting** works of fiction I have had the pleasure of reading." According to blogger Phil Charles R, *Paternus* has "some of the brilliance of Gaiman's *American Gods*, detail of Tolkien's *Silmarillion*, and **plenty of identity all its own**."

Join the conversation and see if you agree:

"A wild romp through every religion, myth and culture, uniting them all in some sort of late night Urban Fantasy pan-dimensional smackdown. *Paternus brings it on*." –*Pornokitsch*

"A war of the gods unlike any you've read. Highly recommended!" –**Michael R. Fletcher**

"This is urban fantasy done right. Not a sparkly vampire or shirtless werewolf in sight, and the pace! Don't make plans to do anything else once you start reading this." –**Graham Austin-King**

"Spectacularly entertaining and meticulously-crafted. An exciting tale of myths and monsters in modern-day society." –**Laura M. Hughes**

"One of the most singularly inventive, creative and exciting works of fiction I have had the pleasure of reading." –**Steven Kelliher**

"I was blown away by this book. An adventure that you're going to have to read to believe." –**Maegan Provan**

"Bold contemporary fantasy in the mythic tradition of Neil Gaiman's *American Gods*, with graphic novel pacing and colorful ensemble." –**Vince Moore**

"Grips you in a Gollum-like throttle and doesn't let go." –**Timandra Whitecastle**

"*American Gods* meets *Buffy the Vampire Slayer* in the best possible way!" –**Jonathan French**

"Storytelling at it's best. A must read if you love myths, legends, lore and excitement." –*Fairy Tale Access*

"Cinematic on a grand scale. A surprisingly phenomenal debut." -**David Walters (on *MightyThorsJRS*)**

"So gripping that I couldn't stop reading. Dyrk is the king of action. His fight sequences reminded me of movie frames. I loved it." –*The Bohemian Mind at Work*

"Terrifying characters and true heroes, sacrifice, defeat and victory. And the pace never lets up." –**G. R. Matthews**

"*American Gods* without the whimsy and more psycho scary things." –**Charles Phipps**

"Engaging. Compelling. Evocative. I urge you to read it." –**Peter Tr, *Booknest.eu***

"Exciting and excellently written." –*Fantasy Literature*

"A wonderful book, forged in the deepest recesses of the human imagination." –**Michael Easton**

"A great big mythological smoothie of awesome!" –*Kristen Reads Too Much*

"I love the sheer level of detail that went into crafting the mythos." –*Bibliotropic*

"The action is fluid, visceral, and the suspense is cranked up again and again. I can't recommend this book highly enough." -*House Valerius*

"A fast read, action packed." –*SFBookReview*

"*Paternus* is fantastic. Perfectly timed and very well written." -*Burkhead's Books and Bad Reviews*

"Thrilling to the end. Ashton is an amazing story-teller." *–AudioBookReviewer*

"A story for the ages. I really loved this book." *–Kaladin Stark's SFF Reviews*

"Ashton is one of the best authors out there. If there's one book you must read this month it's *Paternus*." *–DarkMondays*

"Perhaps the craziest story I've ever read, and I mean that in a good way. A wondrously creative and well-realized story that turns the world's mythology on its head. I'm officially a fan." **–Shawn King**

"Myth and legend manifesting itself, for real, in modern day. A smashing debut." **–J. P. Ashman**

"This book became real good, real fast, all the way through to the end. I am eagerly awaiting the next!" **–Travis Peck**

"I had a big smile on my face. The pacing is frenetic with barely a moment's breath from once the action begins till you put the book down at the end." *–Fantasy According to Tom*

"*Paternus* is a rollicking ride of epic proportions." **–T. L. Greylock**

"A fast-paced book with a twisting plot and fantastic suspense! Great for anyone into mythology. An excellent adventure!" **–M. L. Spencer**

"Brilliantly written. I recommend *Paternus* whole-heartedly." **–Daniel Potter**

"Amazing stuff here for those who love fantasy and mythology. Brilliant." **–Sara Dobi-Bauer**

"Truly imaginative... The descriptions are rich, the characters are fun, and the villains are vile. Beautifully done!" **–Joleene Naylor**

"A world-building marvel." **–A. Dale Triplett**

"Ashton weaves together mythology, evolution, geology, and alternate universes, while still writing characters easy to relate to. I was sucked in from the start. Eagerly looking for the next one, and anything else Ashton writes!" **–William C. Tracy**

"A truly epic work." **–David E. Miller**

"I'm staggered that it's Dyrk Ashton's debut novel. Some of the brilliance of Gaiman's *American Gods*, the detail of Tolkien's *Silmarillion*, and plenty of identity all its own." *- Phil Charles R*

"Absolutely thrilling! I could not put this book down." –**Charles McGarry**

"A rip-roaring tour de force." –**T. O. Munro**

"High action, fascinating mythology and world, and surprises on every page. Lots of bloody awesome. The likes of which you haven't read before." –**D. Thourson Palmer**